THE YEA...

Dan sat on, loitering over his breakfast. He was in no hurry. The customers came and went – mostly men, a few in evening dress, heavy-eyed from lack of sleep. Roistering the night away, he suspected . . . And then he saw her, coming along the street with that graceful swaying walk so characteristic of her, and his senses quivered into life. She was smiling as if her thoughts gave her pleasure and he remembered with a mixture of sorrow and despair Ruby's remark about a gentleman friend.

He wanted her to smile at him like that but he knew that even if he knocked on the window and roused her from her walking dream, she wouldn't see him. She might turn and stare with those limpid green eyes that sent him wild and appraise him coolly, but it wouldn't register. He watched as she walked on out of sight, and with a sudden impotent gesture he clenched his fist and smashed it down on the table top.

'I don't care how long it takes but I'll get her,' he vowed. 'I got Thornmere Hall, and I'll get her, too.'

Also by Elizabeth Tettmar

House of Birds

The Years Between

Elizabeth Tettmar

Mandarin

A Mandarin Paperback
THE YEARS BETWEEN

First published in Great Britain 1994
by William Heinemann Ltd
and Mandarin Paperbacks
imprints of Reed Consumer Books Ltd
Michelin House, 81 Fulham Road, London SW3 6RB
and Auckland, Melbourne, Singapore and Toronto

Copyright © Elizabeth Tettmar 1994
The author has asserted her moral rights

A CIP catalogue record for this title
is available from the British Library
ISBN 0 7493 1527 X

Printed and bound in Great Britain
by Cox & Wyman Ltd, Reading, Berkshire

For my grandchildren
who have brought me
so much happiness

PROLOGUE

He was one of twenty boys between the ages of nine and eleven assembled on Thorpe Station, Norwich, one misty day in August 1895, all with their heads cropped like convicts and all labelled like parcels. They waited with the patience born of the discipline and repression of the orphanage.

Daniel, the youngest, just nine years old, was proud of his label. He felt it gave him an identity he was otherwise lacking. His name was the only thing that distinguished him from the other boys. He squinted at it, reading it upside down: Daniel Harker, the first time he had seen his name written out in full.

He waited like the rest, in his rough cloth knickerbocker suit and navy-blue cap with his toes pointed outwards and his hands in line with the seams of his trousers as he had been taught in assembly when the Master of the orphanage read out the collect for the day. His eyes, as blue-black as sloes and rolling from side to side like marbles took in all the strange sights that surrounded him, and finally came to rest on a group of men and women gathered outside the waiting-room. With one of those he might well be staying as a holiday guest for the next two weeks. He looked them over carefully.

The thin ones didn't get a second glance. The plump, well-fed ones looked more promising, though it didn't always follow. The Matron of the orphanage was enormous but the helpings she dished out at meal times were what the other boys called "'alf-'elpings".

'You got yourn 'alf-'elping, Will?'

'Looks more'n a quarter-'elping, this time.'

'Mine looks as if somefink bin dropped on me plate.'

This in undertones in case the Master overheard, which would mean a clip on the ear and supperless to bed.

He also wanted someone with a smiling face, for smiles were strictly rationed at the orphanage. But what was the good of wishing – it wasn't up to him. Their billets had already been allocated way back in the winter by the ladies on the committee of the charitable institution that financed the summer holidays.

And now their names were being called out in alphabetical order. Brown, Carruthers, Deeping, Evans and both Greens had been ticked off the lists and led away by temporary foster parents looking as apprehensive as their charges.

Dan didn't expect much from this holiday. Living at the orphanage since he was five had indoctrinated in him the belief that those who had nothing must expect nothing. Before going to the orphanage, his home had been a workhouse but the memory of those years was hazy. Once, on a tram going along the Mile End Road a grim edifice had been pointed out to him as the place where he had been born. One look at it was enough to convince him that, contrary to the well-known proverb, he had been lucky enough to jump out of the fire back into the frying-pan.

He must, he had been told, consider himself fortunate that he had been selected for a holiday. Not every boy had that good fortune. Under the age of nine they were considered too young to appreciate such a benefit and over the age of eleven too unruly to be trusted.

Some boys returned from their allotted two weeks at seaside or country with tales of wonderful hospitality, plentiful food and warm-hearted goodness. Others of being worked to the bone and treated like lepers. Dan, assessing his luck so far, was quite prepared to finish up in the grasp of some slave-driving miser.

'Daniel Harker!'

'Yes . . . s-sir . . .'

'Pay attention, boy, that's the second time I've called your name. Mr Fraser, this is your charge. He's small for his age but quite wiry. He knows the rules. Any trouble and he's to be sent straight back to us.'

'I doan't think we're going to give each other any trouble, do 'ee, bor,' said a genial, twinkling-eyed giant, pinching his ear. And that was the beginning of the two most wonderful weeks of Dan's life so far.

He was hoisted up into the cab of a baker's delivery van, a green cab with gilt lettering on the side which he spelled out to himself as Albert Fraser, Thornmere Bakery. His mind filled with thoughts of freshly-baked bread, Chelsea buns and apple turnovers, and his mouth filled with saliva. Mr Fraser heaved himself into the driver's seat and took up the reins.

'We've a fair ole ride ahead of us, bor, so I shan't take offence do you fall asleep. I ain't one for making conversation myself – I'd rather save me breath to cool me porridge . . .'

The horse clip-clopped his way through the traffic and

blurred images began to cross Dan's line of vision: streets of houses and shops; trams and buses; leafy suburbs; and when they petered out, wide fields golden with corn. Once in the open countryside the horse slowed down.

'He know his way be now without any help from me,' said Mr Fraser, slackening his hold on the reins. He beamed down on his small passenger. 'Feeling drowsy, eh? Want to have that little snooze now?'

'No fear.' Daniel, now that he had sized up the situation and realised it was very much in his favour didn't intend to waste a moment of it in sleep but, lulled by the steady motion of the van, his head soon began to nod.

He came back to consciousness slowly, awakened by the sudden cessation of movement and then felt himself being lifted down from the cab. He was put into the arms of someone who was warm and soft and cushioning and he opened his eyes and looked straight into a face of welcome. The tempting smell of freshly-baked bread tickled his nostrils and all around him in the garden of the bakery, roses bloomed profusely. Thereafter, the smell of new bread or the scent of sun-warmed roses recalled for him his first visit to Thornmere. That and Mrs Fraser's friendly greeting given in her soft Norfolk accent would, in days to come, be remembered with heart-aching nostalgia. But now, still half asleep and overcome with bashfulness, he listened to the exchange of words between the baker and his wife in a language that was still strange to him.

'You be having your work cut out trying to fatten up this scrawny little ole barrow pig, mawther.'

'Shan't be for the want of trying, Bert.'

'Your arms be empty far too long . . . Thass what you do be wanting, i'n't it. Remember, m'dear, it's not for ever . . . He has to go back in two weeks' time.'

'Two weeks is better than no time at all, Bert.'

Daniel found himself sitting at a table between his host and hostess in a kitchen as big as a dormitory with before him a bowl of soup thick enough to be eaten with a knife and fork. He thought he had landed in paradise.

On the last full day of that memorable holiday he went blackberrying with Mrs Fraser. She knew a lane where the berries grew at their best – plump and juicy and ripe for picking – and this lane led them past Thornmere Hall, the home of the local squire. Daniel came to a halt at the sight of a pair of massive wrought-iron gates and, peering through them, he saw at the end of a long avenue a very large and impressive house.

His bashfulness since living at the bakery had developed into a mild and amusing brashness. ''Oo lives in that whackin' great place, then?' he asked.

'Sir Roger and Lady Massingham.'

'Cor! Any relation to royalty . . .?'

Mrs Fraser laughed, as she did at everything he said. 'No, they ain't related to royalty, but they be very important folks in these parts. Come you on now or I'll be late with Mr Fraser's supper.'

She tried to take his hand but he held fast, staring eagerly through the iron bars at the house beyond his reach. He had long since decided that the meek didn't inherit anything – not even the earth. If you wanted to get anywhere you couldn't afford to be meek, you had to be tough and grab what you wanted when you got the chance. And his chance would come. He made that promise to himself. When he grew up he would be rich and he would also be the master of a house every bit as grand as Thornmere Hall.

ONE | 1922

The roof of the parish church at Thornmere had recently been re-thatched. The war had postponed this most urgent of jobs but now, in 1922, the shining newness of the reeds contrasted sharply with the weather-stained walls of the ancient flint church. Time would put that right, said those old enough to remember the last time the thatch had been renewed – in 1887 to celebrate Queen Victoria's Golden Jubilee.

The church, which held about three hundred people, was full for Sir Roger Massingham's funeral service and the vicar, newly-appointed, very young and very nervous, was praying earnestly in the vestry. This was his first burial service. Dear God, he prayed, give me strength to do that which is right in your sight. And then, as a sort of desperate *post scriptum*, Please don't let me make a fool of myself . . . Don't let me be too verbose.

In the nave the congregation waited in silent reverence for the arrival of the funeral cortège: some with a genuine feeling of loss, others concerned about the changes that were bound to occur as a result of this death. And some, like Helena Roseberry and her mother, from a sense of duty. Sir Roger had been a friend and a neighbour.

Grief can't touch me anymore, thought Helena, hearing stifled sobs from a pew behind. She liked to think she was immune. I don't have to shed tears or express regrets and do and say all the things required of me, her thoughts ran on. I shall, of course, for the sake of good manners, but they won't mean anything. I've been through it all: the longing, the waiting, the grinding sorrow; I'm free of all that. And knowing all the time that she wasn't. She was good at pretending, even to herself.

She recalled the last time she had been to a service in this church. The mood had been quite different then. Sad, yes, but underlying the sadness a deep sense of relief that there would be no more killing, no more dying.

That was the 11 November 1919 and she and her mother, newcomers to the village, had attended the first Armistice Day service to commemorate that first anniversary of the eleventh hour of the eleventh day of the eleventh month. Both Sir Roger and Lady Massingham had been alive then and present at the service: Sir Roger in uniform, wearing the campaign medals of the Boer War, Lady Massingham shrouded in black, still in mourning for her daughter and younger son who had died, both victims of the war in 1918. Helena had never liked Lady Massingham but she had admired her on that occasion, standing proud, her thin lined face showing no trace of emotion, only the trembling of her veil betraying her inner suffering.

Death, death, nothing but death. Helena looked at the memorial plaque on the church wall above the pew in which she sat. Inscribed thereon were the names of all the men from the village who had given their lives for their country. It was headed with that of Sir Roger's younger son, Henry

Massingham, and continued down with names that were duplicated sometimes twice and once three times. Dear God, she thought, is it possible? Brothers, cousins, fathers, sons . . . all from the same small village. How many more times will blood be spilt before the people cry, Enough, enough! No more war.

There was a rustle of skirts, a shifting of feet, as the congregation rose. The funeral cortège was approaching. Helena helped her mother to her feet. The coffin passed them bearing three wreaths: one from the Lord Lieutenant of the county; another from the heir in Africa; and the third from tenants of the Massingham estate. The vicar solemnly began to intone the familiar words of the burial service.

Helena quite liked the Reverend Francis Thomas. He had an easy and pleasant manner and an attractive Welsh lilt to his voice which was now disguised as he assumed the dirge-like tones in keeping with his office. Her mother, however, thought him an upstart.

'Nothing is the same now,' she complained. 'The war has changed everything – even the clergy. One cannot place them anymore.'

'. . . I am the resurrection and the life, saith the Lord: he that believeth in me, though he were dead, yet shall he live: and whosoever liveth and believeth in me shall never die . . .'

Helena closed her mind to the familiar passages. No such words were said over her brother's body. There was nothing left of David to mourn. Her father had been buried at sea. And Rupert . . . but she must not think of Rupert, that way heart-break lay.

Several pews behind her a girl in her early twenties was sobbing quietly into her handkerchief. The tall young man beside her stood uneasily. 'Ruby, do give over,' he whispered. 'Crying always makes your eyes puff up so, and you must look your best for later.'

What Reuben meant by later was the reception at the Hall. After the service she'd have to leave as soon as possible to prepare the drinks and refreshments. The thought of what refreshments to serve had plagued Ruby for the past three days. She had not been present at Lady Massingham's funeral four months ago, for she had been at home then nursing her ailing mother. Sir Roger, for lack of staff, had booked a suite at a Norwich hotel for that occasion. This was different. She had no Sir Roger to advise her, or anyone except Reuben to turn to, though Mrs Crossley, the land agent's wife, was doing all she could to help. If the Honourable Mrs Roseberry had been more approachable she would have gone to her, knowing she was an old friend of Lady Massingham. But Mrs Roseberry wasn't someone who encouraged requests for help.

Ruby had coped on her own for the past few years, running the Hall with the help of a daily woman, not that there was much to do looking after Sir Roger and Lady Massingham. They only occupied one wing of the house and the rest of the place was shrouded in dust covers. But for one brief weekend, she remembered, the Hall had blazed with light as it had in the good old days, before the war had turned everything topsy-turvy. That was in January 1919 on the occasion of the Massinghams' Victory Ball.

Mrs Webster, the Massinghams' old cook, had come out of retirement to help with the preparations and the daily woman had produced daughters and nieces to do the fetching and carrying. Untrained country girls as they were, they had got through the evening without breaking any of the glass or porcelain or scratching the silver.

The war had left Sir Roger impoverished, but for those three short days the hospitality was on a scale as lavish as anything in pre-war times. Lady Massingham had looked magnificent in a black velvet gown and the Massingham diamonds. Over the years skirts had narrowed, split, shortened and dipped and in 1919 were worn a few inches above the ankle, but Lady Massingham was never dictated to by fashion and kept faithful to the styles of her prime: on her they never looked outlandish. It's all to do with presence, thought Ruby, not quite knowing what presence meant. It was a word Mrs Webster was fond of using. 'Her ladyship has such a presence . . . She can carry off anything.'

'. . . O death, where is thy sting? O grave, where is thy victory? The sting of death is sin; and the strength of sin is the law . . .'

Reuben Stoneham, beside Ruby, standing stiffly to attention, wondered what the future held for him. He was nineteen when the war started and was one of the first of the village lads to enlist. This was as much out of expediency as patriotism. When the Massingham horses were requisitioned by the army there was nothing else for it but to follow them to the Front. He enlisted in a cavalry regiment and though in time he got used, though never hardened, to the death of his comrades, he could never get over the sight of a wounded or dying horse thrashing about in the mud of Flanders. It was with some relief, therefore, that he suddenly found himself transferred to a newly-formed Tank Corps. But what after the war, he thought? Would Sir Roger take him back to work in the stables?

Sir Roger did, but not as a coachman. There were no longer horses at Thornmere Hall. Sir Roger could not now afford to hunt but he did require a chauffeur for the Daimler he had bought for her ladyship in 1913. Reuben, who had learned to drive on an army lorry, slipped easily into his new duties but now, he wondered, what would become of the old Daimler – and more to the point, his furnished quarters in the converted coach-house? Would the new squire keep him on? Reuben doubted it and doubted whether he could accept the job if it were offered to him. There was no love lost between him and the heir to the Massingham estate. He had seen the way Joseph Massingham had treated the horses – much the same way as he treated women if village gossip was to be believed. His fists clenched when he remembered the way Lottie Foster, a one-time maid at the Hall, had suffered at the hands of the new owner of the Massingham estate. Work for that man! He'd rather starve.

The stranger sitting at the back of the church, unnoticed in his dark corner, hardly heard a word of the burial service. Not because of the acoustics, which were good, but because he never wasted his time listening to something that held no interest for him. He had at the age of nine decided that there was no life but the present one and, that being so, it was up to him to make the most of it. And he had done that with such success that now, at the age of thirty-seven, he was a wealthy man and could if he wished buy up any or all of those sitting around him. It was a thought that gave him a great deal of satisfaction.

He had not come to pay his last respects to the deceased as he did not know the man, though he had seen him once from a distance many years ago. He had come to see if he could benefit by Sir Roger's death in any way and to revisit the village where he had known, for two short weeks, true happiness for the first and only time in his life.

He had been born, so he understood, in a workhouse and though he couldn't remember any part of that grim Victorian edifice he had visited it on one occasion since. Not out of sentiment – he had no time for sentiment – but to compare it with the orphanage which had been his home for as long as he could remember and he had come away with the opinion that there wasn't much to choose between the two institutions that had been responsible for his welfare for fourteen years.

Still, he was grateful to the orphanage for one thing – it had introduced him to Norfolk. He had come to Thornmere as the guest of the village baker and his wife, Mr and Mrs Fraser – the boulanger and his wife.

'D'you know what boulanger means, bor? Thass French for baker. 'Tis the only French word I know and the only French word I need to know. I can go anywhere in the world and say I be a baker or a boulanger and the people will know my calling. Now you, you're an orphan. What is French for orphan? You don't know and nor do I. We must look it oop.'

Daniel thought that orphan in any other language would sound just as grim.

Mr Fraser was a rare one for reading. His idea of a day's outing was to go to Norwich and browse round the second-hand book shops. He was up at four to make his bread and to bed at nine with a candle in one hand and a book in the other. It was he who introduced Daniel to the world of books.

I owe everything to him, I owe everything to the Frasers, Daniel mused. Mrs Fraser's warm humour and Mr Fraser's dedication to learning had laid the foundation for his own success. The one regret he had was that he had not adopted their generosity of spirit. His years at the orphanage had precluded that.

Lost in the past, he was unaware that the funeral cortège was now returning down the aisle. The congregation had risen. He got to his feet and looked among the chief mourners for the young woman who had taken his eye when he first entered the church. He had spotted her in the first pew, her profile turned his way as she spoke to the elderly lady at her side. He was immediately touched by her beauty as, when staying with the Frasers all those years ago, he had been similarly struck by the sight of a field of ripened corn. He now knew it was an appreciation of nature at its best, as he could now appreciate the pleasing arrangement of the girl's features: the straight nose; the curved eyebrow; the subtle contrast between the pallor of her complexion and the brightness of her hair; and the extraordinary greenness of her eyes which, when she turned to look over her shoulder, returned his admiring stare with a look of marked detachment.

The whole lot of them, he thought, the whole bloody gentry had that same way of looking down their noses at lesser mortals. His resentment boiled. Lesser mortals! He was as good as any of them. The only difference between him and that lot was that they didn't have orphans – they had bastards instead.

What, he thought as, last to leave the church he followed the procession out into the sunshine, what would happen if, by the slightest chance, Thornmere Hall should come on the open market? He'd bid for it of course. That was what he was here for, on the odd chance, knowing all the time that the odds were against him.

He had kept in touch with Mrs Fraser. When Mr Fraser died she sold the bakery and moved to a cottage in the village street and from there from time to time she sent him undistilled news of Thornmere. It was she who informed him that Sir Roger was dead and that the heir, Joseph Massingham, was on his way from Kenya to claim his inheritance.

'. . . Man that is born of woman hath but a short time to live, and is full of misery. He cometh up, and is cut down, like a flower . . .'

Ruby's thoughts were back with the refreshments. Triangular sandwiches; vol-au-vents (Mrs Webster had made the pastry, puff pastry was something Ruby had never mastered); sausage rolls and cheese sticks. Oh dear, so much pastry, so much stodge. She should have settled for more variety. There were the trifles, of course, and the fruit salad and Mrs Webster's chocolate cake. But was it enough? Would there be enough to go round, mindful of the fact that the estate workers and tenants would foregather in what was once the servants' hall? She heaved a deep and troubled sigh, thinking how easy the past two years had been for her: how little trouble she had had looking after Sir Roger and Lady Massingham. They wouldn't have noticed if, every day, she had served them shepherd's pie.

This was the fourth time the Massingham tomb had been opened in four years, she thought, as she stepped back to make way for latecomers. Henry Massingham and Lucy Massingham in the spring and autumn of 1918. Lady Massingham earlier this year and now Sir Roger. Somehow she and Reuben had become parted and now she could cry without him whispering to her to give over. The Massingham burial chamber was surrounded by iron railings and stood well apart from the other graves; even so, now that the mourners had been joined by others from the village, there was quite a bit of jostling and treading on unmarked graves.

Opposite Ruby, on the other side of the tomb, stood Sidney Foster, a signalman, with his son Ted, a level-crossing keeper, both employed by the Eastern and Coastal Railway of which company Sir Roger had been the Chairman. Their appearance had caused some eyebrow-raising among the villagers, for they were a pair who kept themselves to themselves and were rarely seen in church.

Ruby could remember them in the days before the war: happier days when Ted and his brother Alf had worked at the Manor Farm. They had been happy-go-lucky lads then, smart-looking too in their Sunday best with a flower in their buttonhole. But Alf, poor lad, had been killed on the Somme and Ted wounded and their father widowed the same year. 1916 had seen the end of the Foster family as she knew them.

Sid Foster had always been a quiet and thoughtful man, compassionate too so everyone thought until the trouble with Lottie flared up. That soured his nature to begin with and later the war left him invisibly scarred. He hasn't any wounds that show, thought Ruby, seeing his drawn and bitter look, but he suffers just the same.

Ted had scars that showed. Sometimes at night his injured leg ached so much he stuffed the sheet in his mouth to prevent his father in the next room being woken by his groans. He hadn't wanted to come to the funeral. He couldn't stand for long without his leg playing up, but he thought it his duty to pay his respects. In that he was one with his father.

Beside him Sidney Foster was thinking: Oh Lord, how much longer is this charade going on. He shifted his weight from one foot to the other and took refuge in meditation. He pondered afresh on something that had been worrying him for weeks. The Railway Act of 1921 was due to come into force in January of next year and he wondered how that was going to affect the future for himself and Ted. It would certainly mean the extinction of the Eastern and Coastal Railway Company. It would mean the end of many of the main line railways and in their place would come the Big Four as they were already being called: the London, Midland and Scottish; the London and North Eastern; the Great Western; and the Southern. The old Eastern and Coastal would be swallowed up by the newly-formed London and North Eastern Railway – the LNER. What place would rural Norfolk have in that, Sidney morosely asked himself as he again shifted his weight to the other foot.

He could remember as a small lad being carried on his father's shoulders across the fields to watch Irish navvies digging with their picks and shovels the railway cutting that was being excavated out of the chalky soil on Massingham land.

'They're rare ones for work, the Irish,' his father declared. They were rare ones for talking, too, and joking and laughing among themselves. They lived and slept in an old railway coach that followed them along each section of the line as it was laid.

Saturday nights they got as drunk as lords and fought among themselves and anyone else foolhardy enough to interfere with their pleasure, but Sunday mornings they were up at the crack of dawn, freshly-shaved and wearing clean neckerchiefs ready for the three-mile walk to the Catholic church at Beckton Market.

And now all that work and effort was to be taken over by some unknown management in London or Newcastle or Scotland – anywhere but in Norfolk. Old loyalties would be discarded and the sense of belonging to a family firm with local names on the Board would be lost. His job could be on the line, too, thought Sidney. He might be asked to take early retirement and some callow young upstart from Suffolk or Essex put in his place. Loss, he had suffered nothing but losses since 1914.

'. . . I heard a voice from heaven, saying unto me, Write, From henceforth blessed are the dead which die in the Lord . . .'

Where did you die, Rupert? Are you dead? Missing, believed killed . . . Oh God, it's the not knowing that's killing me. Helena blinked to stem her tears. This interminable service, when would it end? All these people – had they come to mourn or gape? What was there to see anyway? Just a coffin being put into a mausoleum – hideous thing, horribly outdated. The Victorians had no taste. Yet mother had taste and she was a Victorian, both in her manners and in her way of thinking.

Poor mother, the war had changed her, she seemed to have shrivelled within her skin, leaving her arms and face a network of fine wrinkles. The loss of her husband and then her son had left her marked. One blow after another and on top of that to lose her home. Some distant cousin was now in possession of the family house at Beckton Market. Helena didn't mind so much for her own sake; Ardleigh House, built like a fortress, was cold and uncomfortable and impossible to run without an army of servants, which was out of the question these days. Very few former kitchenmaids or parlourmaids were willing to give up their better-paid jobs in shops or industry to return to service. Helena considered Rodings, the charming little Queen Anne house in Thornmere where they now resided, a better exchange. But her mother, she knew, felt differently.

Helena's eyes rested on the stranger whom she had seen in the church. He was standing next to the vicar and taking a deep interest in the proceedings. She had taken him for one of the villagers or someone who had once worked for the Massinghams. He was dark and swarthy like a gypsy with bushy overhanging brows that emphasised rather than hid his sharp black eyes. She had thought his manners questionable when he had stared at her in church but had put it down to ignorance. Now she wasn't so sure, for he caught her eye again and gave her a look that was one of blatant familiarity. And she was also wrong about him being a labourer. No labourer could afford a silk shirt and a suit of that cut. Presumably, that gleaming American car parked in the street was also his. Perhaps he was an ex-Massingham employee who had made good. Her lip curled. The only ones who had made good out of the war were profiteers, a breed she despised, and she let that show in the look she gave him in return.

'. . . We give thee hearty thanks, for that it hath pleased thee to deliver this our brother out of the miseries of this sinful world . . .'

She had met Rupert Downs-Barwell soon after her debut into society at one of Lady Massingham's dinner parties. It was love at first sight, as simple as that, and within six weeks they were engaged. War had burst unexpectedly upon them and like thousands of other young men, spurred on by love of country and lust for adventure, Rupert had rushed to enlist.

Both sets of parents suggested the marriage be put off until after the war, which everyone said would be over by Christmas anyway. In Helena's case, as she was under twenty-one, she couldn't marry without her parents' consent, but that didn't stop her making a private vow that if, by the time she came of age the war still wasn't over, she'd marry with or without their permission. But by the time she was twenty-one her father was dead and she wouldn't dream of going against her mother's wishes, no matter how much Rupert pleaded with her. She saw him at infrequent intervals. He split his leave between his parents' home and Ardleigh House. He had been in a strange mood their last weekend together, edgy, impatient, lapsing into long melancholy silences and finally snapping at her when she went on too long about her Red Cross work.

'You make this bloody war sound like one long social event: it's anything but. Coffee mornings, tea parties, dances, whist drives; it's all a game to you, isn't it?'

She was stung by the unfairness of his accusation. 'We're raising money for the war effort. We work untiringly all day long – even mother, as ill as she is, knitting, knitting, knitting. And she hates knitting.' It was their first quarrel. She burst into tears.

He was all contrition. 'Darling, forgive me, it was just that . . . I can't explain. It's so different at home here than it is at the Front. Out there it's filth and mud, and the stench of rotting flesh, constant bombardments – and always death. We share all that, we're all in it together, we're comrades. At home nobody seems to understand – or tries to understand. They have no idea of what the war is really like. I saw a woman yesterday hand a white feather to a lad who couldn't have been more than sixteen and the poor little devil, he went so red. I said to him, "It is she who should blush for shame, not you." But she was too thick-skinned to get my meaning.'

He kissed her in a hungry and greedy fashion. 'I can't wait any longer for you, Helena, I've been patient far too long. Darling, look at me.' He lifted her chin, looking earnestly into her tearful eyes. 'Don't send me back to that hell on earth with only your kisses to remember you by. I want more than that – I want something to live for, something to keep me sane.'

He had deflowered her with tenderness in the garden chalet at Ardleigh House and she had clung to him afterwards, weeping tears of joy. It was not as she had imagined it – it wasn't gritting one's teeth and bearing it – it was a deeper, more wonderful emotion beyond any previous experience and she was sorry she had hung on to her virginity for so long. She had denied Rupert the fulfilment of their love for the sake of a white wedding, for she was old-fashioned enough, being the child of elderly parents, to believe that girls who did not get married in white were, well, kind of suspect and she didn't want that thought of her by their friends and relations.

When the telegram came telling her that Rupert was missing believed killed she had held fast to the belief that he was only missing, not realising then what missing really meant. Perhaps he had been taken prisoner, perhaps he had lost his identity disc and was lying wounded in some foreign hospital. Day followed day and hope began to fade, so she clung to another possibility – that she was carrying Rupert's child. But when her time of the month came round and she was denied even that consolation she felt that God had deserted her.

Then her self-control snapped and all her pent-up grief gave way to a storm of uncontrollable tears. Her mother made no attempt to stop her.

'That's what I've been waiting for,' she said. 'That brave face you've been putting on didn't fool anybody. Cry, Helena, cry. Get it out of your system, then put it behind you and get on with living, as I've had to. It will be easier for you – you have youth on your side.'

'I'll never love anyone else. I'll never marry anyone else. Nobody could ever take Rupert's place . . .' cried Helena passionately.

Her mother sighed. 'We all think that when we are young.'

The service was over. The vicar and the sexton went back to the church; the undertaker and his men left discreetly. Old friends stayed to chat; the villagers slowly drifted away. Reuben had driven Ruby, the agent and his wife, back to the Hall. The mourners followed in the funeral cars. Helena and her mother were among the last to leave, Mrs Roseberry out of interest pausing to read the name cards on the wreaths.

'There!' she exclaimed crossly, seeing the last of the retinue disappearing down the lane. 'They have gone without us.'

'It isn't too far for us to walk, Mother.'

The stranger, who had been lounging by the lych-gate watching the departure of the mourners, straightened up and approached them.

'Can I give you a lift,' he said, an offer which Mrs Roseberry obviously considered an impudence. She looked him up and down, then stared significantly at his car.

'It is quite possible that you *can*,' she said. 'But highly improbable, I would say. I have not yet lost the use of my legs. Helena, your arm, my dear.'

Daniel stood watching them as they crossed the road. Helena, so that was her name. Yes, she looks a Helena: Greek, the bright one. His mind was full of bits of useless information like that, a legacy of a lifetime of voracious and indiscriminate reading. He was not at all put out by the fact that he had been snubbed. He was rather amused.

The two women crossed the road, both erect and swaying gracefully as they walked. They reminded him of characters out of a Jane Austen novel, *Pride and Prejudice*. Yes, that description suited them very well. And, as likely as not, as poor as church mice. He'd rather have money in the bank than blue blood in his veins, for though money couldn't buy blue blood, there were other things in life it could. Thornmere Hall for instance. Just put the chance his way and he'd show them.

TWO | 1922–1923

Two months later, on a murky November day when mist lay in the hollows like water in runnels, the American car was again seen in Thornmere High Street.

Helena, coming from the Post Office, recognised the distinctive shape of the maroon-coloured tourer and wondered idly what it was doing outside Mrs Fraser's cottage. The owner couldn't be paying a call on the baker's widow – or could he? Did he know her? Helena knew her from the days when, their delivery man having been called up, Mrs Fraser took his place, perched up high in the seat of the little tip-tilted van, going the rounds of the houses and cottages in the district, coming out as far as Ardleigh House during the time they were without a cook.

A Chevrolet this year's model, too. She frowned disapprovingly. That her own baby Austin was just one year old was beside the point. What was that man doing back in Thornmere? It was just a passing thought, she had no real interest in him or his whereabouts, could hardly recall him except for his heavy brows and deep-set eyes. Her mind was on more important things.

She had just returned from Norwich where she had lunched with an old school friend. Midge Harding's marriage had not survived the war and her husband was now living with his mistress in France. There was much discussion in Parliament at present about giving women equal rights with their husbands in the matter of divorce. The present system, whereby women could not divorce their husbands for adultery, was considered unfair by some Members and they wanted that put right by law. After all, they argued, men had enjoyed that privilege for centuries so now, in this modern age, why not the wives? Others were outraged at the mere idea. This is the outcome of giving married women the vote, they said. But if it did become law, Midge was determined to take advantage of it.

'Won't there be a lot of talk – newspaper gossip, that kind of thing,' said Helena as they sipped Martinis in the lounge before lunch. 'Will you mind that?'

'Of course I shall mind, but anything is preferable to living in the kind of purdah I do now. Pitied, you know. A wife yet not a wife. A widow yet not a widow. At least divorce means freedom and a chance of marrying again.'

'Anyone in mind?' said Helena artlessly.

They continued their conversation at the table.

'No one in particular ... at present,' said Midge, considering the question carefully.

Poached salmon was placed before them and a bottle of Moselle, opened by the waiter. It was Midge's treat and she was doing Helena proud. She put her elbows on the table and rested her chin in her hands, staring at Helena with her pale, almost opaque grey eyes.

'I have something else in mind,' she said, picking up the conversation where they had left off. 'I'm thinking of setting myself up in business.'

26

Helena smiled. 'I'm not surprised at anything you'd consider doing. I wouldn't turn a hair if you told me you had joined a flying circus. Business, eh? Being you, it's sure to be something in the dress line . . .'

The used dishes were taken away and veal cutlets served.

'Nearly on target,' Midge said. 'But not a dress shop. I thought a milliner's . . .'

Midge, though not beautiful, never went anywhere unnoticed. Today she looked stunning in a lime-green tunic dress and a rope of coloured glass beads that reached down to her waist. Her wisp of a hat was made entirely of peacock feathers. Helena looked at it enviously. 'Is that one of your own creations?'

'Unfortunately not and what I paid for it gave me the idea of going into the hat trade on my own account. I've got a good head for business – I can sniff out trends long before they become trends. Just think, hats are worn on every occasion, they're never likely to fall out of fashion, so I thought I'd be onto a good thing there. More importantly, hats can be made for a few shillings and sold for pounds. If I can find the right premises and the right clientele, I'll be in business. But I shall need a partner. Someone on the design side, someone who could create . . . let us say, something like this thing I'm wearing . . .'

She idled with her fork, giving Helena an obscure look from beneath her long sandy lashes. 'I'm thinking of you. You have such a flair for design. I'll never forget the japes we got up to at school, when you used to trim your panama with a few flowers or a chiffon scarf and then, on half-holidays, sally forth in it.'

'Only because you dared me. I was scared out of my wits half the time in case I got caught.'

'And now I'm daring you again, Helena. You too need

27

something to do. Just being your mother's companion is not enough ... It's talent wasted. Come in with me.'

'But I have no capital.'

'You won't need capital. Dougie will supply the capital. That's the least he can do. My life is so empty. If we had had children ...' Midge shrugged that regret away. 'Fortunately, we didn't. We would have been such rotten parents, Doug and I. Don't say no. Take your time, think it over.'

But there was her mother. She couldn't desert her mother. Cecilia's life was empty, too, and only she, Helena, could fill it. There seemed to be few friends or relatives in the offing, except her husband's nephew at Ardleigh House and he was beyond the pale.

Her mother's past, to Helena, was a closed book. Cecilia had married young to a naval officer many years her senior and had then led the normal life of a sailor's wife. Long partings interspersed with months, perhaps years at some shore base like Malta or Gibraltar or Singapore.

'What were they like, those glamorous places you lived in, Mother?' asked Helena once.

'Glamorous! Phsaw — nothing but smells and dirt and flies, that's all I can remember of them.' Mrs Roseberry didn't like abroad. She didn't care much for the other officers' wives — and she certainly didn't like foreigners. She told Helena once in a rare fit of confidence that she had longed for a pregnancy just to have a legitimate excuse to stay in England. As things turned out she did fall pregnant but perversely it was not until she no longer needed an excuse to stay put, for she was by then already mistress of Ardleigh House.

The previous year her father-in-law had died and Leopold had retired from the navy and now, newly-installed in what they hoped would be their final home, they set about making plans for improvements which did not at first include a nursery suite. Leopold was much annoyed at the pregnancy and Cecilia felt that fate had played her a rotten trick. She was thirty-nine and most of her contemporaries had long since put motherhood behind them.

Eighteen months later, when David was going through what she thought of as the tiresome stage, neither a babe nor yet a child, she found she was pregnant once again. Her indignation was nothing compared to that of her husband. At his time of life, he said, when he was looking forward to the approach of old age as from a visit of a quiet and companionable friend, he was suddenly plunged into a world of nannies and nurseries, perambulators and cots and one in which a wife was never available when wanted. There must be an end to this nonsense he informed her and off he went to his London club, returning to Norfolk for weekends only. As soon as the children were old enough to be packed off to school he again took up residence at Ardleigh House and in the twilight of their marriage the Roseberrys enjoyed a brief but honeyed resurgence of their love. Such a comfortable state of affairs did not last – war came and the Admiral was recalled to the colours. At his age there was no question of active service, but a man of his experience was of great value to the Admiralty.

'Of course you know well enough I won't take no for an answer,' said Midge, dipping her spoon into a bowl of chocolate cream. 'You know me, I'm like a bulldog – once I get my teeth into something I won't let go. I won't let *you* go, Helena.'

'My mother is more of a terrier – she worries at things,' said Helena vaguely.

But Midge had planted a germ of an idea and it lay there

in her fertile mind, teasing her with possibilities. 'I wonder if I could,' she thought. 'I wonder if I dare . . .'

The sight of the stranger's Chevrolet outside Mrs Fraser's cottage had distracted her only momentarily. She walked to where she had left the Austin Seven, parked in a space behind the Post Office. There were very few cars in Thornmere so no provision had been made for parking. Soon, thought Helena, when the powers-that-be realise we are now in the twentieth century, we may, if we are lucky, even have a petrol pump installed. The nearest pump was as Beckton Market which was a great inconvenience if one ran out of petrol, but as Helena had had the tank topped up in Norwich she knew she would be all right for a day or two.

The small Queen Anne house which was now her home, a gem of a place she had grown to love, red brick with white panelling and a tiny front garden completely shaded by a walnut tree, was at the northern end of the long village street.

She had reversed out of the space behind the garage and was driving slowly through the village, when the approach of a much larger car coming at speed forced her to take avoiding action. It was the Massingham Daimler and driven not by Reuben, but by Joseph Massingham himself.

'Beast,' she muttered. 'Road hog.'

Braking suddenly, she had stalled the engine. She hated cranking the starting-handle and usually found someone to do it for her – a brawny roadman if possible. Today there was no one in sight. She fitted the handle into the hole at the base of the radiator and gave it a quick turn. The engine misfired. She had been told that a handle could jump back and break one's arm and she had never had much stomach for cranking after that. Today it took three attempts before the engine sparked into life. It left her hot and dishevelled and with grease on the sleeve of her coat, but feeling well pleased with herself.

She found her mother in the drawing room working at her tapestry fire screen. Helena had washed her hands and changed into a skirt and jumper, a garment which her mother referred to as 'that shapeless thing'.

Mrs Roseberry put away her embroidery and rubbed her eyes with her fingers. 'It has seemed such a long day,' she said.

'I have been gone less than four hours, Mother.'

'It seems longer. Fetch me my smelling salts, will you, dear. My head is bothering me . . .'

Helena fetched, besides the smelling salts, a footstool and a shawl, forestalling other requests her mother might think up for her. Then she sat down herself.

'And what news of that Madge . . . ?' her mother enquired, indifferently.

'Midge, not Madge.'

'*Midge*, such a stupid name. Is she still living apart from her husband?'

'That is no fault of hers.'

'In a case like that, there is usually fault on both sides. I suppose you had tea in Norwich?'

'I didn't even stay for coffee, I knew you would be getting anxious.'

'Then you must be dying for a cup – I know I am. Oh, and ask Mrs Taylor to make me a sandwich. I missed luncheon.'

'Why was that?'

'You know I dislike eating on my own. I must say I felt rather sorry for myself thinking of you lunching at the Maid's Head.'

'Oh, Mother!'

When Helena returned with the tray her mother was going through her writing case. 'Did you remember my stamps?' she asked, without looking up.

'Yes. I popped into Mrs Timms on my way home.'

Her mother turned a face from which all trace of querulousness had vanished. Interest kindled in her eyes. 'Did she have any news – news about Thornmere Hall, I mean?' As the village postmistress, Mrs Timms was the fountain-head of information. 'That dreadful man, that Joseph Massingham, he didn't even have the courtesy to return our call. He's ignoring everybody – spends most of his time in Norwich I hear. The least he could do is put an end to all these rumours. Well? Any news?'

Helena looked amused. 'That's the very question Mrs Timms put to me. She doesn't know any more than we do, but she seems to think that Joseph Massingham may be selling up the estate. She says he'd had several letters from his solicitor. And,' Helena hesitated a moment, a teasing smile playing about her mouth, 'she did happen to overhear a telephone call Sir Joseph made to his bank in Nairobi, but that was about money matters . . .'

'Mrs Timms just happens to overhear every telephone call that is made in the village. It is a pity that the Post Office cannot think of a better system. As for Sir Joseph, he has been troubled about money matters since he was at school, so that isn't news.' Mrs Roseberry was very put out. She, too, suspected that Joseph Massingham was planning to sell the estate, but the last thing she wanted was to have her fears confirmed.

'It will be too bad, just too bad,' she said, 'if he does break the entail. But he never did show any interest in the estate, other than how much money he could squeeze

32

out of it. Even before the war Roger and Lucinda were constantly paying off his debts. I could always tell when there was another financial crisis because Lucinda would start another of her economies. Throwing good money after bad, I warned her. Joseph Massingham was always shiftless. Coffee plantation! Racehorses, gambling, and women more likely. No wonder he hasn't had the nerve to show his face in Thornmere. He can't swagger about here – we know too much about him . . .'

'He happens to be in Thornmere today. I passed him just now, in the Daimler.'

Her mother's interest was immediately rekindled. 'And did he acknowledge you?'

'I don't think he even saw me. He nearly ran me into the ditch. He shouldn't be allowed on the road.'

Cecilia sighed. 'If only he was more like his brother. Then he would have been such a good match for you . . .'

'Mother! You know there will never be anybody but Rupert.'

'So you say, dear.'

Mrs Fraser's front room measured ten feet by nine. What space was not taken up by Daniel Harker, who was a burly man, was filled with oddments from the parlour at the bakery, the largest of which was a horsehair sofa on which Mrs Fraser herself was sitting.

Dan's chair was wedged into a tiny bay window and from there he had a good view, albeit through the leaves of a massive aspidistra, of what was going on in the street – not much on this cold and miserable afternoon, though the Post Office stores kept up a steady trade.

He saw Helena Roseberry enter the Post Office and watched for her to come out again. She emerged about fifteen minutes later and stood for a moment on the step while she drew the collar of her coat up round her face.

Yes, she was just as he remembered her: taller than average and shapeless, like most of the young women these days. She wore her clothes well though he didn't think the tight-fitting hat suited her. In his eyes it looked like an upturned pudding basin. Still, that was the fashion and all the ladies were slaves to fashion. He wanted to see more of the red-gold hair that had shone like a burnished lamp in the dull interior of the church and which had first attracted his attention. He ached with a sudden and unassailable lust for her. And I'll have her, he thought. I don't care how long it takes – but I'll have her.

He saw with amusement the disdainful look she threw at the Chevrolet. Don't be too haughty, my lady, you may be glad of a lift in it one day. She disappeared around the back of the Post Office and reappeared driving a baby Austin. He gave a derisory grunt, partly because he didn't think much of a car that looked like a biscuit tin on wheels and partly because he was scornful of women drivers, though he had to admit, watching how she manoeuvred the narrow turn into the street, that she was a dab hand at the controls.

Mrs Fraser woke up with a start.

'Enjoy your forty winks?' he said, grinning at her.

'I weren't asleep. I was just restin' my eyes. Now, what about that cup of tea?'

'You stay put, I'll make it.'

Over the intervening years Mrs Fraser had put on a lot of weight and her movements were consequently slower. She sank back on the sofa with outward relief. 'You know 'twere everything is. An' du you find anything in the cake tin, bring that in.'

The kitchen was the only other room downstairs. The

earth closet was at the bottom of a rather small garden. On a nail on the fence, which divided Mrs Fraser from her neighbour, hung a zinc tub in which she did her weekly wash and took her weekly bath.

Daniel had often played with the idea of buying a modern house with an indoor lavatory and bathroom complete with geyser and installing her in it, but he knew he would come up against stiff opposition. Mrs Fraser shied like a horse at any hint of charity. Still, if the sale of Thornmere Hall did go through, which now seemed likely, there would be plenty of room for her to come and live with him. That is, if she wanted to.

'Any further gossip for me,' he said, placing the tea-tray on a rickety three-legged table, the only one free of knick-knacks.

'Gossip!' she rolled her eyes ceilingwards. 'That go on and on like a pig in a harvest field. An' the joke is, Daniel, they doan't know the half of it.'

'You haven't told anybody . . . ?'

She pretended to look hurt. 'After you telling me not to? But why you du want to be so secretive, I doan't know.'

The secrecy wasn't of his making, though he thought it advisable until the contracts were signed. Through his dealings with Joseph Massingham he had found him an insensitive man, caring not one whit what others thought of him, so he couldn't understand why the fellow wanted to be out of the country before the news broke.

He had contracted to buy the Hall with the lodge and park and once the transaction had been finalised and Joseph Massingham was safely back to Kenya, the rest of the estate – the farms and cottages and remaining land – would be put up for auction. Only he and Mrs Fraser and the solicitors knew this, though he suspected that the gloomy chauffeur and the mousy little housekeeper up at the Hall knew more than they let on. They went about their duties with unsmiling faces and Ruby's eyes and the tip of her nose were perpetually pink. He very much wanted to assure them that their futures were secure. That they could, if they liked, stay on in his employ.

The bombshell fell on the 25 February. The tenants of the two farms and the fourteen cottages belonging to the Massingham estate were informed by letter of the forthcoming auction. The properties were going under the hammer. The tenants were given the option of buying the freehold of their homes beforehand if they liked; if not they would be requested to vacate by a given date. Later, there would be a further auction of the contents of Thornmere Hall and catalogues were available from Messrs Whitmore and Barley, Auctioneers, of Norwich.

When Daniel Harker saw a copy of this letter he exploded with anger. He was in Mr Whitmore's office at the time.

'Bloody insensitive morons! A bloody printed summons to quit your home – that's what this means to the recipient. Couldn't they have worded it a bit differently, softened the blow a little. This is a straightforward either or. How many of these poor devils can afford to buy their properties! Turned out without a penny – that's what it amounts too. And that bastard not even having the guts to tell them personally. Not even a goodbye and that to people who have known him and served him since his childhood. He's left me right in it, hasn't he? I'll get the blame and it won't do much for my popularity. I'm looked upon as a bloody interloper as it is.'

Mr Whitmore, sitting at his desk, glanced nervously at

the door. His secretary in the next room, a reserved and rather strait-laced young woman, must have heard every word. So could everyone else in the office come to that and anyone passing in the street.

'We are not used to that kind of language in here, Mr Harker,' he said stiffly.

'Then you damn well soon will be. I'm a plain-spoken man and I say what I think.' Then both Dan's expression and tone of voice moderated slightly. 'No, you are quite right and I apologise. You were only carrying out instructions.'

Even more stiffly Mr Whitmore pointed out that they were doing no more than carrying out the usual practices and he took instructions from no one on how to run his business. Seeing that he had ruffled the old chap's feelings, Dan bit back the rejoinder that in that case the practices were in need of reform.

'In any case,' Mr Whitmore went on, 'the farmers and several of the tenants are intending to buy their properties. For Mr Bowyer of Manor Farm this chance is a godsend. Bowyers have farmed that land for generations. His father and grandfather would have given their right arms to be able to buy the freehold. To him it's a dream come true – he told me so in this very office. You are a Londoner and a stranger. You have no idea what land means to a countryman.'

'I don't see any dreams coming true for the poor bloody pensioners,' retorted Dan. 'They won't be able to buy the cottages which they thought they had for life. D'you think any of those poor wretches envisaged being turfed out on their ear one day! And where can they go? The workhouse?' The thought of a workhouse – any workhouse – petrified him.

Mr Whitmore sat back in his chair coolly appraising his

visitor. He didn't much like or approve of what he saw: a man of coarse visage and aggressive manner. Yet, thinking back, he hadn't liked Sir Joseph any better, but at least Sir Joseph was a gentleman. This fella – what was he? A factory owner, a canner of foodstuffs. Made a fortune out of the war by supplying tinned food to the armed forces. Did he really think that kind of money could buy him a place in the county set? He had a lot to learn.

Rolling a fountain pen between his fingers he said, 'What's to stop you putting in a bid for the remaining cottages yourself? There will be no question of poor wretches being turfed out on their ears then.' His voice was heavy with sarcasm.

Smarmy old devil Dan thought, but the idea appealed to him. It wasn't new, it was something he had been toying with since he became the new owner of Thornmere Hall. But it was a question of money. Joseph Massingham had driven a hard bargain sensing, with a gambler's intuition, that Daniel Harker would take any risks to get the Hall, so he had called this Johnny-come-lately's bluff and taken him for every penny he could spare knowing that this was his last chance to raise the capital to prop up his failing coffee plantation.

They had disliked each other on sight, these two men, but they needed each other, for one was in desperate need of ready cash and the other obsessed with the desire to own Thornmere Hall.

'I'd like to be able to say I would,' Dan admitted candidly. 'But I'll have to seek the advice of my accountants first. Give me a few days to think it over. And if I do decide to go ahead and take over the cottages I'll have to do something about them. I don't want my tenants using outside lavatories and relying on the village pump for water. I want them to have decent homes to live in and if that means raising the rent, then I'll have to raise the rent.'

'Not all of the tenants are paying rent – certainly not the Massingham pensioners.'

Dan shrugged his shoulders dismissively. 'I'm a business man, not a philanthropist. You'd better warn them.'

Mr Whitmore scribbled aimlessly on his notepad. 'They won't like it. They'll be quite happy to go on living with earth closets and pump water – they've known nothing else.'

'Well, I'm sorry if they won't like it, but they'll have to lump it if they don't want to get evicted.'

The cottagers under threat of eviction did not, as Dan had predicted, turn on him with their anger, frustration, anxiety and fears. They kept that for the land agent, Arthur Crossley. He was the go-between, the scapegoat. He was the one who had distributed the notices from the auctioneers. He was available and Joseph Massingham wasn't.

Major Crossley, Arthur's father, had managed the estate for Sir Roger for twenty years. When he died Arthur, recently demobilised and glad of an easy and well-paid job, stepped into his shoes. On the strength of this appointment he married the VAD who had nursed him after he contracted malaria at Gallipoli. Never fully recovered from his illness, the coming of Sir Joseph Massingham and the consequences of his visit, undermined his state of health.

''E's beginning to look,' said the villagers, 'like somethin' fit to scare the crows. Du, we see 'im stuck in a field come Rogation Sunday.' All the blame for Sir Joseph's perfidy was laid at his feet.

The sale of the contents of Thornmere Hall made but a ripple in the affairs of the village. The deluge that had gone before had already exhausted their emotions. Everyone who could had crowded into the auctioneer's hall on the Cattle Market to learn the fate of themselves and their homes. It was a time of tension and stomach-churning worry, but it passed off better than many had anticipated.

Most of those under danger of eviction returned home poorer in pocket but, for the first time in their lives, freeholders. Whether they could afford to keep up the mortgages was another matter. They were just relieved to know that for the time being they still had a roof over their heads.

There were four who were not so fortunate, all of them once in the service of the Massinghams. One of these was Mrs Webster, the one-time cook at Thornmere Hall. Her future looked very bleak. Who would employ her at her age? Where was she to go? She sat in the cosy nest of her parlour and gave way to tears. This was her punishment, she thought. All those years ago she could have spoken up for Lottie when Joseph Massingham raped her. She had held her tongue because she knew that when she retired a rent-free cottage was in the offing. Now Joseph had come back into her life and taken the cottage from her. Whatsoever a man soweth, that shall he also reap. Yes, she was learning that the hard way.

Mrs Roseberry was in a state of frustrated disappointment. She had come on both viewing days to Thornmere Hall to pick out the best pieces listed in the auctioneer's catalogue only to find that all were marked with an asterisk. That ursurper, the war-profiteer, that upstart with his foreign car had, prior to the auction, grabbed the lot.

'Not everything,' protested Helena. 'And don't forget, Mother, the Massinghams had been selling off their pictures and the best of their furniture for years. They had no alternative – it was their only income.'

'I know Lucinda wouldn't have sold her jewels, she looked upon them as heirlooms. I wonder what has become of them?'

'According to Mrs Timms the diamonds and other valuable pieces went back to Africa with Joseph Massingham.'

'For one of his whores, I presume,' said Mrs Roseberry tartly. Her eye fell on a rather nice escritoire that she had always coveted and she looked for it in the catalogue. Seeing that it was also marked as sold her nostrils flared. 'That common little man! His greedy mark is on everything!'

'He's hardly what you'd call little, Mother.'

'Don't be tiresome, girl, you know what I mean. What could he want with Lucinda's escritoire?'

'Perhaps he has somebody in mind to give it to.'

'There was something else of Lucinda's I rather liked. A medallion-type brooch with Henry's photograph in it. She treasured it. That's strange – I don't see it listed in the catalogue.'

'I don't see it either,' said Helena, turning the pages. 'Do you think it could be among the items marked miscellaneous?'

'Certainly not – it was made of Limoges enamel with gold filigree. I wonder what became of it?'

'Perhaps Joseph took it with the rest of the jewellery?'

'I doubt it. The brothers were anathema to each other.'

'Then Lady Massingham must have sold it.'

'No, she would not have sold it. Neither would Sir Roger, but after her death he might have given it away. He was an impulsive man.'

Mrs Roseberry, after more than an hour inspecting

those articles which were still for sale, now found herself very weary. She sat down on a very fine example of a Chippendale chair unconcerned that that, too, was marked as sold and fanned herself with the catalogue. For early March the day was warm.

'Do you remember the dances here?' she said, looking around her with a wistful expression. 'No, perhaps you wouldn't, you were too young. They were always such elegant occasions. The fashions were so different in those days, so much more gracious. Silks and taffetas and satins, so full, so flattering, unlike the skimpy dresses of today. It was a different world, Helena, a civilised world.' Like many of her generation, Mrs Roseberry believed that all graciousness and culture had come to an end in 1914.

'This room we are in now, this large drawing room, this is where we danced when the Massinghams gave a ball. Even the music was more melodious in those days. Not like the dreadful noise they make now. This noise they call jazz.' Mrs Roseberry gave an exaggerated shudder followed by a genuine sigh. 'But you are too young to remember all that ... Such a pity, you will never know what you've missed.'

But Helena could remember very plainly the dinner party given by Lady Massingham where she was introduced to a tall fair-haired young man called Rupert, one of Henry Massingham's Cambridge friends. That was during the long hot summer of 1914. After dinner, because the evening was so warm, some of the guests had strolled out onto the terraces.

Rupert had suggested a walk to the mere and for the first part of the way Henry had accompanied them. Always a quiet, rather withdrawn young man, that evening he had seemed more so and suddenly, with some vague excuse, he had left them to go on on their own. Helena, with an amused thought at what her mother would say about her going off with a strange young man without a chaperone, was rather pleased.

She wondered whether her feeling of reckless and blissful joy was due to the wine she had drunk at dinner or was a foretaste of love. No, more than a foretaste, it *was* love. But could one fall in love, just like that, like snapping one's fingers? It was magic. It was more than magic, it was sheer enchantment.

They stood by the clear waters of the mere looking down at the reflection of the dying sun and Rupert broke the silence by saying, 'This may sound like madness, Miss Roseberry, but I think I have fallen in love with you.'

The world was all golden after that: the surface of the lake; the windows of Thornmere Hall like panes of gold in the sun; and Rupert's hair, shining like a golden halo.

Where did those golden days vanish to, that last peace-time summer? Her golden time didn't last but it stayed on in her memory and she thanked God for it now. She pressed her thumbs into her eyes to stem the rising tears and decided on the spur of the moment to revisit the mere. Her mother was asleep, sitting bolt upright as she always did, her hat a little awry. Kinder to leave her where she was, dreaming of her own golden youth.

In the hall she came face to face with the new owner. To her consternation he stopped, not accosting her as such, but bowing very slightly. She wondered if such a gesture from him was a form of mockery.

'Ah, Miss Roseberry, I hoped you'd be here. Is there anything I can do . . . Anything I can show you?'

They had not been introduced, but here he was addressing her as if she were an acquaintance. She drew back.

'I was just about to take a last look at the mere,' she said.

'Not the last, I hope. You will always be welcome to come and go as you please. Would you like me to show you the way?'

'Thank you, but I do know the way.' That sounded very much like a snub and she hadn't meant to snub him. She tried to explain. 'I just want to be on my own . . . to remember old times.'

He stood aside and let her pass him without further comment. She walked through the long wet grass of the park not caring that her new Russian boots were getting soaked. Everywhere there were signs of neglect. The walks were grown over and the trees had not been managed for years. Dead and dying branches hung uselessly from main branches like broken limbs, evidence of lack of care or more significantly, perhaps, lack of money. There was a rookery in a clump of elms, noisy and busy with nest building, and a blackbird sang from a perch in a massive holm oak that had been cleft by lightning. She stopped to listen, remembering.

A blackbird had settled on the ridge of the garden house at Ardleigh that afternoon of lovemaking on Rupert's last leave, trilling out his flutey song like a valediction. For sentimental reasons she had wanted the garden house to go with them to Thornmere, but the timbers were rotten, and the removal men said that if they tried to dismantle it it would fall to pieces. Now, whenever she heard a blackbird sing, she thought of Rupert.

Someone had beaten her to the lakeside, a solitary figure staring down into the dark waters of the mere. Arthur Crossley. He raised his hat, then stood nervously twisting it round and round in his hands as if he didn't quite know what to do with it. The lake was green with algae and choked with weeds – what little water was visible was turgid. Helena wished she hadn't come.

'Sir Roger always planned to do something about the mere but somehow we never got round to it.' Arthur Crossley's expressionless voice cut through her thoughts. He looked, she thought, extremely ill.

'These past few months haven't been easy for you,' she ventured, feeling sorry for him.

He threw her a grateful look. 'For none of us. But it's nearly over, thank God.'

'I hear you are leaving the village?'

'Yes, it's all arranged.' He dropped his gaze. 'Next week Louise is going to stay with her mother in Hampshire while I finish up affairs here.'

'But hasn't Mr Harker asked you to stay on? I understand Reuben and Ruby jumped at the chance.'

'Well, you see, there isn't an estate as such to manage any longer, though Mr Harker was anxious for us to stay until we'd found somewhere else to go. But I couldn't, not as it is. No it wouldn't have done, to stay on, I mean. And Louise doesn't like Norfolk. She couldn't get used to the cold winds up here.' He gave a nervous cough, spluttering into his handkerchief. 'We're thinking of emigrating to Australia. Starting afresh . . .' His eye-lids fluttered nervously. 'I'd better get back – there's still some last minute things to see to.' He put on his hat in order to raise it to her once more, then walked away, his shoulders bowed like a man carrying a heavy burden.

After that Helena didn't linger. She wanted to remember the mere as it used to be, golden and bright with the sunlight reflected on Rupert's hair. Not dank and dark and rather sinister as it looked now. She turned and walked reluctantly back the way she had come.

The upheaval of the past few months slowly subsided. Life went on and even the changes in the village became yesterday's news. Work at once commenced on the modernisation of the Hall and local builders rubbed their hands in anticipation.

'I don't care if he be as rich as the Aga Khan,' said Fred Cartwright of Beckton Market. 'I sharn't go doffing my hat to him. He's nothing but a get-rich-quick Johnny and I'm as good a man as he.' All the same he was one of the first to put in his tender when the agent sent word round.

That was the last time Arthur Crossley appeared in the village. His wife had already left and he was following her as soon as their furniture was put into store. The agent's house, a fine brick and flint building with two acres of land, had been bought by a physician at the Norfolk and Norwich hospital.

Arthur Crossley left finally, like a thief in the night, undetected. It was a nine days' wonder in the village, then the gossip gradually died down. Slowly, sympathy for him, unexpected and long submerged, began to surface.

'Poor chap, 'e's 'ad a rotten ole time of it, havin' to go round givin' out them notices, being spat at in the street. No woonder 'e didn't want to say no goodbyes.'

Suddenly the village had something else to talk about, a royal wedding. The Duke of York, the king's second son, was to be married to Lady Elizabeth Bowes–Lyon on 26 April. This news caused much local speculation. In the old days no royal occasion went by uncelebrated. Even during February of the previous year when Lady Massingham's illness prevented any form of merry-making, Sir Roger wouldn't allow the marriage of the king's only daughter, the Princess Mary, to Viscount Lascelles, to go unmarked. He arranged a tea-party for the village children and every pensioner was presented with a free bag of coal.

'Carn't see this outsider giving out no bag of coals,' grumbled one old villager.

'You might, if you lucky, be getting a tin of bully beef instead,' said another who considered himself something of a wag.

'You du, it sarten t' be army surplus,' countered a second.

THREE | 1925

On 20 November 1925, the morning papers were edged with black to mark the death of Queen Alexandra, the Queen Mother. Cecilia Roseberry, reading this news over her morning cup of tea in bed, silently mourned the passing of what was to her, the epitome of everything that was lovely and gracious.

Downstairs in the breakfast room Helena was opening the morning post. The only personal letter was for her and that was from Midge Harding, written on heavy cream paper and embossed with the one word *Toppers*.

> . . . Now if I had an elegant name like yours, darling, I would call my shop Madame Helena. But Madame Midge – can't you just hear them all laughing!

A letter from Midge brought her a whiff of that world which was closed to her. A world of gossip and fashion and bright young things. Bright young things, she thought as she looked critically at her reflection in the looking-glass over the mantelshelf. Was there ever a time when she was bright and young? She was twenty-nine and felt middle-aged. She returned to her letter.

> . . . My divorce, when it at last came through, has proved very good for business. Prospective buyers came to see the notorious woman who had dragged her husband through the divorce courts and named his mistress as co-respondent. I was damned by the press for not going about it more discreetly. Lovely publicity! They came to gawp and stayed to buy. Any chance, darling, of cutting the umbilical cord? I've been asking you that for the past eighteen months – now I'm begging. I can get five guineas for my top models, but with you to fashion them we could easily make it double that.
>
> I have three women outworkers at present and am aiming to engage more. Ideally I would like my own workshop, but I would need someone to help me run it. Any chance, old friend? We are coming out of the post-war doldrums – business is booming and London is seething with excitement. Darling, you don't know what you're missing . . .

Five guineas for a hat! Helena could remember her mother once saying that the most she had ever paid for a hat was fifteen guineas, but that was for a special occasion, the wedding of one of her grander relations. And that was in the days when hats were heavily decorated with ostrich or aigrette or osprey feathers. Today's hats were little more than unadorned moulds – certainly not worth five guineas! Her dress allowance was only a hundred pounds a year and it took ingenuity and thrift to make it stretch that long.

Helena was never sure if her mother was careful or hard up or just downright mean. Cecilia never discussed money as she considered the subject vulgar, but she usually had one of her bad heads after a larger than usual bill had been presented. Since the Admiral's death she was morbidly fearful of falling into debt. Helena was secretly of the opinion that in some unknown bank or other her mother kept a well-filled stocking.

Midge, characteristically, had added a postscript.

> . . . Have you ever thought of a companion for your mother? Some genteel war-widow in dire need of board and keep? Test the water, sweetie . . .

Oh Midge, don't put such ideas into my head.

Her mother's voice floated down the stairs. 'Helena, are you busy . . . ?'

'No, Mother, I'm just coming . . .' There was a bill from her mother's corsetière and another for the rates. Aspirin time this morning.

But she was wrong. Her mother threw the bills aside as if they were of no consequence. 'Have you seen the newspapers?'

'Just the headlines about the old queen . . .'

'The old queen! Queen Mother if you please. But strange that you should think her old. I always thought of her as ageless . . . Yet I suppose she must be, what, good gracious, eighty – eighty-one? I was presented to her once, when she visited Portsmouth. She always took such a great interest in the navy. She was known as the sea-king's daughter, you know, and now she has gone.' A sigh. 'This is the passing of an era.'

So many eras had passed for Mrs Roseberry. They had

come and gone like the seasons. She leant against her pillows looking cast down and somewhat frail. Helena was filled with a sudden compulsive pity for her. How can I possibly leave her? How could I live with myself if I ever did?

'You get depressed from staying in too much,' she said. 'Let me take you to Norwich. It's a long time since you've visited the city. We could have lunch at Chamberlains, or . . .' In a fit of generosity and willing to mortgage a part of her dress allowance if it would give her mother pleasure, she added, 'I could take you to that new restaurant on Timber Hill.'

'A nice thought on your part, dear, but I don't think I could lunch out today – not happily. There is something you could do for me though, as you are motoring into Norwich. Arrange for some roses to be delivered to Sandringham House. I believe Queen Alexandra was fond of roses.' She took note of Helena's doubtful expression. 'Just a small tribute to times past,' she said wistfully.

'Of course, Mother.'

On her way back to Thornmere Helena broke her journey at Beckton Market in order to buy petrol. The one garage in the town used to be a bicycle shop and still stocked bicycles, though only as a sideline. The proprietor, a self-taught mechanic, was building up a reputation as an expert on motors. It was he who had taught Helena to drive.

'Good morning, Miss Helena,' he said, as she pulled up in front of the petrol pump. 'How's the baby? Past the walking stage yet?' It was a joke that hadn't worn thin throughout the years of their acquaintance.

'I don't get overtaken by bicycles any more, Mr Smithson, but she jibbed a bit at Kett's Hill this morning. She's not old really, is she? Just a toddler in human terms.'

Mr Smithson pursed his lips. 'She won't live to be as old

as the Admiral's old motor car, or wear as well. Beautiful bodywork it had – all made by craftsmen. We won't see the likes of that much longer, more's the pity. The usual, Miss Helena?'

Helena left him working away at the pump, knowing that by the time she returned he would have replaced the oil, cleaned the windows and polished the bodywork. She had had a successful morning's shopping. Midge's letter had left her restless and eager to try something new. She had thought about having her hair shingled, then decided her mother wouldn't be able to stand the shock. She had been prostrate for days when Helena had had it bobbed. Her hair was the bane of Helena's life. It was thick and curly when hair that was sleek and shining and fitted one's head like a cap was all the rage. She was dissatisfied with everything about her appearance lately.

With hats in mind she went to an establishment which sold buckram shapes and after much searching bought two she thought would suit her purpose. And then to Bonds to buy the trimmings – velvet with silk braid for one, velour and moire taffeta for the other. She had bought the materials with the idea of making hats for herself and then had a better idea. Why not make them as samples to send to Midge? She could dispatch them by Carter Patterson or – and at the very thought her heart beat faster – why not deliver them personally? It was ages since she'd been to London, she could get there and back in a day, or perhaps Mrs Taylor would agree to stay overnight. Then she would be spared the worry if her homeward-bound train happened to be delayed. Anticipation of a treat to come lifted her spirits. Her step was lighter, the day much brighter.

But now, as she walked through the narrow streets of Beckton Market, past shops with overhanging upper storeys that told of different uses in days long gone, her thoughts were taken up by plants rather than hats. Gardening, she found, was a great solace. Out there, digging or planting or weeding, she was impervious to her mother's demands and, though a jobbing gardener was employed twice a week, the garden was too large for him to keep in good order unaided. Faced with the choice of paying him for extra time or losing her daughter's company for an hour or two a day, Mrs Roseberry grudgingly gave way to the latter.

There was a neglected corner of the garden Helena had decided needed brightening up. Benson, when dragooned into helping had grumbled about the soil being sour and overshadowed by trees and said that nothing would grow there, but she had turned a deaf ear to his complaints and between them they had dug and mulched and hoed and now it was ready for planting. She envisaged a spring garden. She had already designed it in her mind's eye: wallflowers and tulips and polyanthuses, all in bloom at the same time, a colourful floral carpet against a screen of Portugese laurel. She'd be able to see it from her bedroom window and that thought alone brought her pleasure. Her whole way of life, it seemed to her, survived on anticipation.

A greengrocer's in the square sold bedding-out plants as well as spring-flowering bulbs. She asked the assistant, a boy of fourteen, to pick her out two dozen mixed tulips. He licked his lips and looked nervously over his shoulder to check that Mr Black the greengrocer was out of earshot.

'I'm sorry, miss. I don't know the difference between tulip and daffodil bulbs. P'raps you could give me the wink?'

Helena smiled. 'I'll do more than that. I'll select the bulbs myself and in the meantime you can make yourself useful by parcelling up for me two dozen polyanthus plants and four bundles of wallflowers. And would you please see that plants and bulbs are delivered to Rodings, Thornmere, as soon as possible.' Humming to herself, she picked over the bulbs in an unmarked sack. Tomorrow, if this fine weather held, she'd spend the morning planting out.

She walked out of the dull interior of the shop into the November sunshine. The light dazzled her. She hesitated on the step for a moment, waiting for her vision to clear, and it was then that she saw Rupert across the square. He was standing with his back to her, his left hand tucked into his coat pocket, looking into the window of a tobacconist's. Bareheaded, standing in full sunlight, his fair hair seemed to have acquired a golden halo as it had that day by the mere.

Recognition hit her like a blow in the face. All these years she had clung to the hope that he could still be alive and here he was, standing but a few yards from her: not a vision, not an image conjured up from her loneliness, but Rupert himself. Her heart thudded with painful joy. Running across the road to him, she called his name. He didn't hear her, but that was, she knew, because she hadn't the strength to call aloud. Her cries were coming from her heart.

'Rupert,' she said and touched him lightly on the shoulder. Slowly he turned.

'Oh God,' she moaned. There was a rushing noise in her ears followed by a feeling of weightlessness and she would have fallen, except that Rupert's arm shot out to support her. But no – not Rupert. She had made a mistake. Someone of Rupert's height and build and with Rupert's light-coloured hair, but there all resemblance ended. This man was older, extremely tanned, with lined, lean cheeks. The sleeve tucked into his pocket was empty.

From far away she heard an anxious, 'Are you all right? Don't faint on me, for God's sake.'

She tried to straighten up, but felt too weak. Any moment now her legs could buckle.

'I'm sorry,' she said, speaking with much effort. 'I've never fainted in my life . . . or come near to it. It was the shock . . . I - I took you for someone else . . .'

His mouth twisted into a grim smile. 'Yes, I do seem to have that effect on people.'

'No – it was the shock of disappointment. I took you for my fiancé. He was posted as missing, but I've always hung on to the thought that he was still alive . . . perhaps suffering from amnesia. You do hear of such things . . .' Her voice was an echo of her dying hope.

'Only in fiction,' he said brusquely. He studied her features more closely. 'What you want now is a stiff drink. A brandy?'

She protested. 'I've left my car just along the road. I shall be all right now . . . Really, I can manage.'

'You're not fit enough to walk let alone drive. Come, just a small brandy to put some stiffening back into your legs.'

With his arm around her waist he propelled her towards the King's Head. She saw, as they passed the greengrocers, Mrs Black staring all agog from the window. Mother will hear of this, she thought, the news will be delivered with my order and she suppressed an untimely and somewhat hysterical giggle.

It was colder in the public house than out in the street. But she was grateful to find the saloon empty; she wanted no more witnesses to what they might think was her inebriated state. Voices drifted from the public bar and the landlord appeared and looked meaningfully at the clock. It was nearly closing time. She couldn't stop shivering and though there was a small smoky fire in the Victorian grate, it gave out little heat. A glass of brandy was thrust under her nose.

'Get that inside you . . . it will make you feel better.'

She hated spirits, she hated the smell and normally she would have pushed it away, but now she took it and gulped it down.

Warmth came suddenly and set her tingling all over. It was ridiculous how quickly alcohol – any form of alcohol – affected her. The effect now was a sudden gush of heart-broken tears. The man pretended not to notice. He sat down at the other side of the wrought-iron table, looking at his feet until she recovered. She wondered how she could have mistaken him for Rupert. Rupert, even after years of warfare, had not looked that embittered.

He proffered an open cigarette case and she shook her head.

'You don't smoke?'

'Rarely.' She did occasionally, out in the garden, out of sight of her mother.

'Good for you. Smoking is a filthy habit.' He grinned and with an ease of long practice he extracted a cigarette from the case and lit it. He snapped his lighter shut and squinted at her through the smoke.

'Do you want to talk about your fiancé or would it pain you too much?'

As if talking about Rupert could cause her pain. It was not having the opportunity to talk about him that hurt most. She told him about their first meeting, of their short engagement, of his last leave and then the fatal telegram.

'When was he killed?'

'1918. He went missing early in the morning of the 11 November.' There was no need to enlarge on that. The simple explanation hit him forcibly. Just another example of war's bitter little ironies, he thought. He couldn't look at Helena just then; it would seem too much of an invasion of her private sorrow.

Silence fell. The fire suddenly sparked into life. Helena could feel it scorching her legs but she didn't move. She felt lazily tired. Out of the corner of her eye she saw the landlord look up at the clock again as he polished glasses.

Her companion was suddenly overtaken by a paroxysm of coughing. Even that didn't prevent him lighting another cigarette. He was an incessant smoker.

'Does my smoking worry you?'

'No, of course not, but I feel I ought to go. I have taken up enough of your time as it is.'

'I have plenty of time to kill. I made a mistake and got off the train at Beckton Market and now I have over an hour to wait for the next . . .'

'Where to?'

'Thornmere Halt.'

'Why, that's only the next stop — you could have walked it.'

'So I was told at the station. But I thought I would browse around and see what Beckton Market had to offer in the way of lunch.'

'And what did you find on offer?' she said, taking up the levity of his tone.

'A very welcome plate of meat and Yorkshire pud and

two veg in a poky little café in a side street. All for one shilling. Of course I could have eaten in grander style at the Trust House, but I didn't think I could do it in an hour. I tried the pubs, but all they had on offer were bags of crisps and I'm not much of a crisp man.'

He was more of a champagne and oyster man, or claret and steak, thought Helena. In that he was also like Rupert.

'If it had been market day, any one of the town's three pubs would have had plenty to offer.'

'Then I must remember, the next time I get stranded at Beckton Market, to make sure it's market day.'

They exchanged smiles. 'Last orders,' called the landlord.

'Another?' He nodded towards her glass.

'Oh, no – no thank you.' She hesitated. 'I'm going on to Thornmere, I live there. I could offer you a lift . . .'

'Why do you say it in that apologetic tone? You'd be doing me a favour.'

'And you'd accept it?' She looked surprised. 'In my experience, most men are scornful of women drivers.'

'Only the egotists.' He looked at her with sardonic eyes. 'There are exceptions. I'm a frightful egotist myself, but I never scorn a favour. I've even been known to go out of my way to cadge one. And so, if I am to place my life in your hands, may I know your name?'

'Helena Roseberry.'

'Paul Berkeley.' He held out his hand and she shook it.

'Time gentle*man* please,' said the landlord wearily.

Never had the drive to Thornmere seemed so short. She eked it out by driving as slowly as she dared. Having Paul Berkeley beside her was like having Rupert back again. She found she could talk to him as easily as she had talked to Rupert, fluently and without restraint, and in her enthusiasm not realising that the information she gave so freely was coaxed from her by his judicious line of enquiry.

As they passed Ardleigh House, only its turrets visible above the trees, she broke off to point it out to him. 'There it is, my old home – that ugly grey building. One of my bourgeoisie great-grandfathers with more money than taste was responsible for that monstrosity. It sticks out like a sore thumb, don't you think?'

He screwed around in his seat, watching it as it slowly receded. 'What I can see of it looks all right to me. It blends in well with the landscape.'

'Yes, well, I suppose everything matures with age. But I much prefer the little house we live in now.'

'Tell me more about this interloper in the village.'

'Daniel Harker? I've told you all there is to tell. We don't see a lot of him – he's been too busy modernising the Hall. Thank goodness he's had the sense to leave the exterior alone. I've heard we wouldn't recognise the interior: walls taken down, doors put up, even one cut through a tapestry in his bedroom and the billiard room has been turned into a sort of office.'

'I suppose that's feasible. A business man wouldn't have much time for leisure.' His tone was slightly ironic. 'But I'm surprised you have had to rely on hearsay. You haven't been invited to see for yourself?'

'We were. Soon after the alterations were completed he gave a cocktail party for everybody around he considered of importance. My mother declined. First, because she never goes to cocktail parties and second, because my cousin and his family from Ardleigh House were going. I was disappointed. I don't mind admitting I would have enjoyed a sneaky preview. Afterwards we heard it was a tremendous flop. Guests formed into their own little cliques and didn't mingle and all of them combined to ignore their host. Not out of maliciousness – they just forgot him. Of course, we took all that with a pinch of salt, but I expect there was a grain of truth in it. Anyway, he never repeated the experiment. The only people he invites to the Hall these days are business acquaintances – real war-profiteers – which doesn't go down well in the village.'

Her companion rumbled with quiet laughter. 'What is the difference between a real war-profiteer and a false one?'

'A war-profiteer is always depicted as a bloated personage smoking a fat cigar and speaking with an awful accent. You must have seen caricatures of them in *Punch*.'

'And Mr Harker doesn't look like that?'

'Not quite. But all the money in the world couldn't make him into a gentleman. I suppose he isn't a war-profiteer in the true sense of the word and I have been told that he tried to enlist in 1914, but the work he was doing being essential to the war effort, he was turned down. Of course, that could be a rumour he started himself – I wouldn't put it past him. He's something to do with the canning industry, has a factory in the east London area, I believe.'

They came to a narrow hump-backed bridge which she crossed with care. Down river a flat-bottomed boat containing, besides the ferryman, a bicycle and its owner, was crossing to the other side where a shabby but picturesque inn squatted by the waterside. Further along, Helena pointed out to him a small wooden structure situated, it appeared, in the middle of a field.

'That's Thornmere Halt. It's only another mile to the village now,' she said on a dying note of regret.

And very soon afterwards the red roofs of Thornmere village came into sight. The ploughed fields and high hedges gave way to groups of cottages, then a chapel and a school, the village stores and a church. Paul Berkeley sat up and looked about him with interest and it occurred to Helena that she was doing all the talking. In the few miles they had travelled together she had confided to this stranger a potted history of her life. Yet he had told her nothing about himself or the reason he had come to Thornmere. She was weighing up the pros and cons of asking him outright or introducing the subject in a more roundabout manner when he took her by surprise by saying:

'I suppose you're wondering what I'm doing in this neck of the woods?'

'Actually, at this very moment I'm wondering if there is anything in this talk of telepathy.'

'I see.' He grinned, then out of the corner of her eye she saw his expression turn to one of introspection. 'I'm on a pilgrimage of sorts. I'm on a visit to the level-crossing cottage.'

'A pilgrimage to the gatehouse?' Her voice rose on a note of surprise. 'But nobody ever goes to the gatehouse. Don't tell me Sidney Foster invited you.'

'No. He doesn't know I'm coming and I don't expect he'll let me cross the threshold once I tell him I'm an old friend of his daughter, Lottie.'

Helena took her eyes off the road to stare at him. 'You know Lottie Foster?'

'Very well at one time. Why?' He returned her gaze, registering for the first time the unusual greenness of her eyes. 'You know her?'

'I know of her.' She gave her attention back to her driving. The tone of his voice as he spoke of Lottie left her in no doubt as to the true meaning behind that old friendship.

Lottie Foster, a legend in her own lifetime – a signalman's daughter who, in 1913, had left Thornmere in disgrace – was now the proprietress of a fashionable London restaurant. There were not many in Thornmere who did not know her or know of her. Whenever her name was mentioned old arguments resurfaced. For everyone who cheapened her name, two rushed in to defend her. 'Raped,' cried one woman scornfully, who had been outshone both at school and in service by Lottie. 'Six of one and 'alf a dozen of the other if you arst me.'

'You'd 'ave to wear a mask 'fore anyone take a liberty with you, Gert Cooper,' came the quick retort.

It was common knowledge at the time that one of the Massingham boys was responsible for Lottie's condition. The finger of suspicion fell on Master Joseph whom everyone knew was a thoroughly bad lot, whereas Master Henry, though something of a weakling in the eyes of many, had never been known to be anything but honourable. All three had left the scene shortly after the scandal broke and the talk died down. Then news filtered back to Thornmere that Lottie was doing very well for herself in London. Another example of the wicked flourishing like the green bay tree, said the likes of Gert Cooper.

What was it about that girl, Helena wondered, that had brought this stranger to a remote corner of Norfolk to seek out the cottage where she had once lived? A sudden and irrational envy of the unknown Lottie swept over her. She assumed what she hoped was an air of indifference.

'I'll take you as far as the gatehouse,' she offered. 'I'm in no hurry.'

'It's kind of you to offer, but no.' He was very decided.

'If you could just drop me at the top of the lane, I can walk the rest . . . yes, here will do nicely.' He got out of the car and, leaning through the window, shook hands with her. He thanked her warmly for the lift, raised his hand in a farewell salute, then turned and walked off with a loping stride, his one arm swinging briskly.

She watched his receding figure, sick at heart that he had made no suggestion of seeing or getting in touch with her again. But why should he? She was just a transient stranger who had done him a small favour. Tomorrow he would have forgotten what she looked like, but she would remember him for days, weeks, perhaps for ever, living the dream that for one short interlude taken out of time Rupert had come back to her.

It took her just over a week to complete the hats to her satisfaction and nearly as long to get her mother to agree to her visit to London. She had to go about it circumspectly, slowly injecting the idea drop by drop. It was no good asking outright. That never worked with Mrs Roseberry. The drop that finally put the stamp on her mother's approval was the suggestion that she call in at Harrods to renew Cecilia's stock of winter combinations.

It was the evening before her departure, a day when the first few flurries of winter snow powdered the lawns and evergreens like icing sugar. It soon melted. The sun came out, fitfully at first, then shone quite brightly during the afternoon. But the threat of frost lingered and Helena decided on the morrow to wear her woollen coat dress, the latest and most fashionable garment in her wardrobe with its waistless, bustless and hipless look. And over that her old tweed cape made by the village dressmaker.

She wished she had some stylish evening wear, for

Midge was making up a party to visit a nightclub. Helena only possessed two evening dresses, neither of them new. Her green crêpe-de-chine was the prettier, though dated by its length and she hadn't time to shorten it. It would have to be the beige georgette which was smarter, except that the colour made her skin look sallow. Faintly, from downstairs, she heard the telephone ringing. Oh no, not Midge telephoning at the last minute to cancel or postpone her visit. She'd never forgive her if it was.

She made no haste to answer it, deliberately stopping to replace the dresses in her wardrobe. If it was bad news she wanted to delay it as long as possible. She knew her mother would not answer the call. Mrs Roseberry never used the telephone and had not wanted such a nuisance installed in the house in the first place. By her orders it was placed well out of sight in an alcove under the stairs.

It wasn't Midge. It was somebody whose voice she did not at first recognise.

'I thought you must be out and was just about to hang up. Remember me?' That agreeable baritone voice punctuated by an ear-splitting cough? Of course she remembered him.

'How did you get my number?' She felt both flustered and flattered and hoped she didn't sound it.

'Through the operator. The ladies of the GPO are most obliging in that respect. Well, how are you, Miss Roseberry?'

'Where are you? Beckton Market?'

'Good gracious, no. I'm back home. Home being a studio flat in Pimlico.'

'London, you're speaking from London?' He was chatting as if it were a local call. The pips would go any minute.

'Is this call urgent?' She was horrified at the thought of what it must be costing him.

'Depends on what you mean by urgent. I urgently desired to talk to you.'

'You did! Why?' She groped for a chair and sat down. If he didn't mind the cost, then why should she?

'I suddenly thought of you and wondered how you were and on an impulse called you up to find out.'

She giggled. 'Do you often do things on an impulse?'

'Always. That's how I happened to be in Beckton Market in the first place. Don't you ever do anything on an impulse?'

'I'm afraid never . . . I always have to plan well ahead.'

'I wanted to apologise for the abrupt way I left you. I thought afterwards how discourteous it was of me after you had been so helpful. At the time I only had one thought in mind.'

She waited for another bout of coughing to cease. She could visualise him so vividly, a cigarette held loosely between his long thin fingers, one lock of fair hair obscuring his eyes, his eyes a vivid blue against his tan.

'How did your visit to the gatehouse go off?'

'Not all that successfully. Old man Foster was still on duty. I'd forgotten about him being a signalman. It's his son who looks after the level-crossing, but he was out. A battleaxe of a woman was left in charge. She was civil enough but extremely suspicious of me. I didn't leave a message. No matter. I accomplished what I set out for — to see Lottie's home.'

'Yes . . . I see.'

'And now I would like to see you again, very much. Could we meet one day, in Beckton Market?'

'I can do better than that. I could meet you tomorrow in London.'

'I thought you never did anything on an impulse.'

'This visit to London isn't on an impulse. It is the result of many hours of careful planning.'

'Have you got to get back to Norfolk tomorrow evening? You haven't – fine. Then may I take you out to dine?'

'My friends want to take me to a nightclub.'

'Ah.' He sounded disappointed. 'A nightclub is fine if you don't mind noise. I was thinking of somewhere where we could talk.'

She gave him Midge's business number. 'You can reach me there anytime from midday onwards.'

Her mother appeared as a shadowy figure in the dimly-lit hall. 'What are you doing, sitting in the dark, talking to that instrument?' she asked.

'Just making last minute arrangements for tomorrow, Mother. I think I'll catch an earlier train. I would like to get something to wear myself while I'm in Harrods.'

'All this unnecessary gadding about,' said Mrs Roseberry crossly.

FOUR

Helena was vastly pleased with her morning's purchases. She stood in the dress department at Harrods trying on one model after another, bemused at first by the variety of choice, but when the assistant appeared with a little number in green her mind was made up before she'd even tried it on.

It was a slinky, clinging, chiffon sheath lined with shantung silk and from the hips down, layered by row upon row of heavy fringe. To enhance the straight-down look she was advised to wear one of the new style brassières, a straight firm band of material guaranteed to withstand any attempt at projection. It was only after she had committed herself that she noticed the price tag on the dress, then she blanched.

The assistant caught her eye. 'Modom won't regret it. It's the exact shade of Modom's eyes.'

Encumbered by two hat boxes, her weekend case and now several Harrods bags, she fumbled in her purse for the half-crown tip for the commissionaire who helped her into a taxi.

'Toppers, somewhere near Bond Street,' she told the driver and wasn't surprised after all Midge had told her that he knew just where to drop her.

The amount of motor traffic now on the streets of the capital surprised her. It was her first visit to London since 1920. Her parents had never thought it necessary to have a town house. Whenever the Admiral wanted to visit London he stayed at his club. Cecilia saw no reason to visit London, let alone stay there. Norwich, she considered, had everything to offer that London had including a good bridge club and for anything else she had accounts with both Harrods and the Army and Navy Stores.

Five years, Helena mused, five years since she was last here. That was the occasion of the Remembrance Day service at Westminster Abbey for the interment of the Unknown Warrior. An unknown soldier had been brought home from the battlefield to be given a hero's funeral. A hopeful fancy that the body could be that of Rupert had drawn her to the service. A misplaced hope she knew but that didn't matter, the unknown warrior represented all who had no quiet graves in which to lie at rest. He was Rupert, he was David, he was the husband or son or lover of all those other women she saw around her, women whose eyes were also sad and wistful.

She came away from the Abbey, her face stained from weeping, but it was the first time since Rupert's loss that she had been able to cry without bitterness. The first time too that she began to notice with more awareness the life that was going on around her and it had seemed to her, then crossing Parliament Square, that horse-drawn vehicles were still holding their own against motor traffic. Now that was no longer the case.

There were still horse-drawn tradesmen's vans of course,

plenty of those, and always the odd coster's barrow, pulled in most cases by a donkey, but the hansom cabs she could remember from her schooldays seemed to have gone for ever, superceded by modern taxi-cabs. Taxi-cabs had played a big part in the recent war, she recalled, ferrying soldiers to the front.

She had previously arranged with Midge to go straight to the shop rather than to her private apartment near Cumberland Gardens. Midge was disappointed that she could only stay the one night; she never relinquished the hope that one day Helena would come and stay with her for good.

The drive took longer than she had allowed for. Piccadilly was chaos, the traffic disgorging in all directions, watched dispassionately by the flowersellers in their customary places on the plinth supporting Eros. There must, she thought, be some code of practice soon or London will grind to a halt. The combustion engine had a lot to answer for, but oh, how convenient it was. And for another thing, it didn't leave steaming dung all over the road, just spots of oil occasionally. Yet she hated to see the changes in London. She resented the vulgar hoardings that were lit up at night like fireworks, advertising different brands of drink or cigarettes or coming attractions at cinemas and theatres. In some ways, she suspected, mildly mocking herself, she was very much her mother's daughter.

Toppers, when they reached it, turned out to be on the ground floor of a narrow but tall building squeezed between two imposing-looking premises which looked like private residences but which, Midge had previously told her, belonged to well-known couturiers. It was a street famous in the fashion world and Midge, with unerring instinct, knew

71

that having the right address was halfway to success. She greeted Helena effusively.

'Darling! You have brought the hats? Oh yes, I see you have. And Harrods bags! You've been shopping at Harrods? Why couldn't you have waited for me? I would have taken the time off this afternoon and gone with you and we could have had tea there. I love tea at Harrods – all those dainty little sandwiches. What have you been buying? No, don't tell me, let me guess. A hat? You've bought a hat, of course,' and she roared with laughter. She was in one of her teasing moods and was delighted to have someone she knew to tease.

'I needed something to wear tonight. Midge, I'm meeting someone . . .'

'I know, darling, it's all arranged. We're going to the Blue Moon . . .'

'No. I mean . . . There is someone I have personally arranged to see.'

But Midge wasn't listening. She was diving into the hat boxes, emitting breathless oohs and ahs. 'Why, these are utterly utterly divine . . . so frightfully bliss-making . . . absolutely super-duper . . .'

She caught Helena's puzzled frown and let forth another honk of laughter. 'No, I haven't gone barmy – not quite – but that's a sample of the way most of my exclusive clientele speak to one another and all at top C. I sometimes think their voices carry because their heads are empty, like echoing chambers. But what does it matter so long as they do have heads, and go on paying fantastic prices for hats to hide them in.'

'Midge, you are becoming frightfully cynical.'

'No, darling, just practical. And in business one has to be practical to be successful. You will discover that when you come to me as my millinery designer.'

'Oh, Midge. Not when . . . If.'

'We'll talk about that later.'

Helena looked around for somewhere to sit. The shop was fitted out like a drawing room with thick pile carpets, mirrors lining every wall and handsome ornate cabinets, presumably where Midge's stock was stored because there wasn't a hat in sight. The only chairs were gilt-painted spindly affairs, too flimsy to sit upon, thought Helena, who was dying to rest her feet. They were there for decoration presumably.

'They will take your weight and more,' Midge said, seeing the cautious way Helena eyed them. 'Not all my customers are sylph-like young things, some are quite fat old trouts. But nice old trouts for all that, and they never buy just one hat at a time, but always two or three, so I hope when you go back to dreaded Norfolk you'll think up some styles suitable for them.'

'Dreaded Norfolk to you, Midge, but not to me. But I must admit it is heavenly to get away from it once in a while.' Helena kicked off her shoes which were pinching her and massaged her toes.

Midge knew Helena was using Norfolk as a euphemism for her mother. She could see she had a hard task ahead of her, breaking through the barrier of Helena's old-fashioned notions of duty and family loyalties. She earnestly wanted Helena to come and work with her and not entirely for selfish reasons. She hated seeing a life wasted or a talent lying buried, and being Norfolk-born herself she knew how insular life in Norfolk could be. Remembering Helena in her salad days, full of gaiety and always ready for a bit of fun, and knowing the boredom Helena would endure if she spent the rest of her life as the spinster daughter of a demanding mother, she was determined not to allow that to happen.

What Helena needed was a man in her life. Not just any man, but someone who would provide her with stimulating companionship. To that end she had arranged for James Trevase and Donald Conway, her present *inamoratos*, to make up a foursome that evening. James was a man of the world. Some would call him a ne'er-do-well, but for all that charming and extremely likeable. She had had a brief affair with him after Douglas left her and he had been the perfect antidote for her wounded feelings. The only danger was that Helena might fall in love with him and that could spell disaster: James was not the marrying kind and Helena, she knew, equated sex with marriage. All she wanted was James to entice Helena away from Norfolk, not into his bed, but machiavellian strategems, she knew, did not always run true to plan. Being naturally optimistic, she hoped for the best.

Helena was thinking that what she wanted more than anything at the present moment was something to eat for she had skipped breakfast that morning and had not stopped for coffee while shopping. Then a hot bath and a rest, in that order. She was just about to ask Midge if there was any chance of one or all three when the telephone rang.

Midge disappeared into an inner sanctum to answer it. She returned looking curious.

'It's for you. And such a deep and mellow voice, I was really charmed. Now, who would know you are here? Helena — are you by any chance keeping anything back from me?'

'Where's the phone?'

'Behind the curtain, mind my chair . . .' But it was too late, the chair went flying as Helena dashed off to answer the call.

'Mr Berkeley?'

'No, Paul. I refuse to answer to the name Berkeley.

You made it then, I'm so pleased. I hope I haven't called too early? No? Good. You sound very bright. Had a good journey? Your train was on time? I don't believe it. Not the Late and Never Early Railway.' They laughed together. 'Now what about this evening, Helena? Do I pick you up at Toppers? Yes, I know the address, I looked it up. Yes, I'll hang on . . .'

Helena poked her head round the curtain. Midge was in front of a mirror trying on one of the hats. She saw Helena's reflection and looked over her shoulder. 'Who is it,' she mouthed.

Helena held the mouthpiece to her chest. 'I have someone calling to take me out tonight,' she said. 'Shall I tell him to pick me up here or at your flat?'

'Tell him the flat,' said Midge, much put out. This wasn't at all what she had planned.

'I thought you'd come to London to see me,' she said when Helena re-emerged. 'Not to meet some admirer. Very underhand of you. I should be offended considering the trouble I've gone to to arrange a partner for you this evening.'

'Oh, Midge, don't scold. I haven't felt as excited as this for years. I did try to tell you but you wouldn't listen. You were too engrossed with the hats. I had given him your telephone number – I knew you wouldn't mind. He's calling for me at seven.'

'So that explains your shopping spree in Harrods.' Midge removed the hat and laid it carefully to rest among the tissue in the hat box. 'In that case you'd better come along to the flat straight away. You'll need to rest if you're going out on the town later. Do I know your caller? Is he a Norfolk man?'

'No, on both counts. His name is Paul Berkeley.'

'Paul Berkeley,' repeated Midge thoughtfully. 'I once knew a Paul Berkeley. He was wounded . . . at the Somme, I believe. He lost an arm.'

'But what a coincidence. It has to be the same Paul.' Helena's eyes glinted excitedly. 'How well do you know him?'

'Not at all well really, and I haven't seen him in years. But I do see his wife occasionally when she comes up to Town.' Midge paused and gave Helena a speculative look. 'I do hope you know what you are doing.'

She lay on the divan in Midge's slip of a spare bedroom drifting in and out of sleep. Sheer physical exhaustion had at last overcome the turmoil in her mind.

The timely arrival of Candida, Midge's assistant, back from lunch, put a stop to any interrogation in the shop and on the short taxi ride to the block of service flats near Cumberland Gardens, Midge held her tongue, perhaps because of lack of privacy. Helena followed her into the scented warmth of Hanover Mansions like someone walking in her sleep.

Paul, married! She had arranged to go out with a married man! Strangely enough, the thought that overcame all others was, what would her mother say? Not that that danger would arise. There was no question of her seeing Paul now.

A uniformed hall porter came forward to give Midge a message about some flowers she had ordered, addressing her in that mixture of respect and friendliness that Midge generated in others. He would have engaged her longer, for Midge was always ready for a laugh, but today she did not encourage him, sensing Helena wilting beside her. The lift took them up to the second floor where Helena was ushered into an apartment of such comfort and luxury that she was jerked into uttering the same little oohs and ahs with which Midge had greeted her hats.

Midge said, 'Have you eaten yet? No, I thought not. Neither have I. I'll phone down to the restaurant and ask them to send us up a sandwich. Here's your room. It isn't very large but it contains everything you'll need. The bathroom is opposite. You look all in, Helena. Get to bed. I'll bring my lunch in here and have it with you.'

Helena obeyed without question, slipping off her outer garments and getting in between soft, fluffy, satin-edged, peach-coloured blankets which, even in spite of the lethargy which had taken hold of her, aroused a passing interest. What would her mother have made of those, she wondered. The last word in decadence, no doubt.

When Midge brought in the tray she found Helena lying on her back, staring at the ceiling. She placed the lunch tray on the bedside table and drew up a gilt and white chair similar to those in the shop, for herself.

'Isn't it time we had that talk?'

'I thought I was supposed to be resting.'

'And I suppose that's just what you are doing. Talking won't tax you. It never has yet.'

Silence fell. Midge ate her smoked salmon sandwich without enjoyment. Helena didn't even start on hers. The thought of a possible scene robbed them of their appetites. Midge took up the plates, returned them to the kitchen, and switched on the coffee percolator. A cup of coffee would revive them both, she hoped. It helped a little.

'Now, what about that talk.'

'Midge, there is nothing I wish to talk about.'

'You can't bottle it up. You've had a shock — I saw that as soon as I let slip that Paul was married. You looked stunned. That meant only one thing to me and that was that Paul had deceived you. I must say I was surprised, I wouldn't have expected it of him. Whatever his faults, he always seemed a very open and frank kind of person – too much so, in some ways. It got him into trouble during the war, saying what he thought, I mean. Or in this case, printing it. It caused quite a hoo-ha at the time, and I think there was some kind of court martial. When the war was over, he just disappeared from the scene – went off travelling, I believe. If it's any consolation to you I don't think he's living with his wife anymore.'

'What makes you think I need consoling?' Helena's voice just then sounded dangerously like Mrs Roseberry's, Midge thought. 'After all, I hardly know the man. I only bumped into him by chance.' Suddenly her voice cracked. 'Oh, Midge, who am I trying to kid. He reminded me so much of Rupert – I tried to pretend he was Rupert. And now, knowing he belongs to someone else, it's . . . it's like losing Rupert all over again.' Tears began to well and Helena searched fruitlessly for her handkerchief.

Midge was by her side and her arms were around her. 'Don't you think it's time you let Rupert go,' she said softly. 'Even the dead need peace.'

'But I don't want him dead.' Helena's tears were flowing freely now, coursing down her cheeks unheeded. 'I don't know what I've done with my hankie,' she said helplessly. 'I must have left it in my bag.' She wiped her eyes with her hands.

Midge produced a handkerchief. 'Helena, my pet, you are such a child. You must learn to grow up. You must face up to the fact that Rupert *is* dead and not go looking for him in every man you meet. Now, what are you going to do about Paul? Do you want me to telephone him and make your excuses?'

Helena thought about that. Finally she said, 'I don't know his telephone number or his address. Only that he lives in a rooming-house in Pimlico.' With the handkerchief obscuring all but her eyes she gave Midge a beseeching look. 'How would you feel about me going out with a married man?'

Midge suppressed a howl of laughter. She rose from the bed and straightened out her crumpled skirt. 'You know I'm not one to make moral judgements, and the very fact that you asked such a question shows that you already know the answer.'

'Well . . . it's just that I feel that I should hear what he has to say.'

'Right. That's settled then. But for goodness' sake, get this coffee down you, and then try and get some sleep or you won't be fit to be seen.'

Sleep was what she did not get, just this dreaming wakefulness, and in her dreams she saw Rupert again as she first knew him: young, boyish-looking, full of ideals. He wasn't the type to go around masquerading as a single man if he wasn't. But had Paul masqueraded as a single man or had she just assumed he was? If I'm going to have these stupid arguments with myself, she thought, I may as well get up and take a bath.

Midge had left her a note written in her over-large sprawling handwriting. 'Popped back to the shop for a couple of hours to give Candida a hand but will be back before you leave. Don't hesitate to help yourself to anything you need. There's tea and coffee or booze, whichever you prefer. Or easier still, just ring for room service. That's what a service flat means. Toodle pip.' Toodle pip? So who hadn't grown up!

The kitchen was much the size of a galley in a Broads yacht, which meant it was very small. It was obvious that Midge didn't do much cooking for the pint-size cooker looked untouched. Helena found the tea-caddy and milk in the refrigerator, her first introduction to this latest example of what was to her modern domestic technology. It was twice the size of the cooker, but then it needed to be, for besides a half-pint bottle of milk and a packet of butter, it contained two bottles of white wine, a bottle of ginger ale and three bottles of ready-mixed cocktails with names like Sidecar, White Lady and Green Goddess. She was glad to see that Midge had got her priorities right.

Midge couldn't believe the change in her. It wasn't only the dress, which certainly made her look wonderful and did inexplicable things for her eyes, but her whole demeanour had altered. She sparkled.

'You're so right, Midge,' Helena said. 'And I've been such a fool, making a fuss about nothing. For goodness' sake, I've only met the poor man once and spoken to him twice on the phone, and yet I carried on as if he owed me something. So what if he is married – we are not contemplating an affair. It's nothing more than dining out together, nothing of consequence.'

'That's rather an expensive dress for something of no consequence,' Midge said drily. 'But I get your drift. You look lovely, Helena, clever girl to pick a dress to match your eyes, but your cheeks are a little too pale. Have you any rouge?'

'Rouge! Midge, you know my mother Do you really think I could get away with rouge? She sulked for weeks after I took to lipstick.'

'What your mother doesn't see won't harm her. Come with me.'

80

Helena had already peeped into Midge's bedroom. Like the hat shop it was all white and gilt with mirrors multiplying every reflection several times, giving the effect of the room going on and on into infinity. Everywhere she looked she was faced with a woman in a vivid green dress and a bush of red hair. She sighed over the hair.

'I wish I'd had time to visit a hairdresser. My hair looks awful,' she wailed.

'It only needs taming. I'll see what I can do.'

What Midge did do was to spray it lightly with brilliantine which flattened it a little and made it gleam a lot, then she dressed it with a narrow band of silver. She brushed Helena's cheeks with rouge and applied the merest film of mascara to her lashes. 'Now, what do you think?'

Helena looked at herself and gasped. 'My mother would say I look like a trollop . . . But I like it.'

'Did you bring any jewellery with you?'

'Only Rupert's ring.' It was an antique ring of pearls and emeralds which had belonged to his grandmother.

'Just right with that dress,' said the ever practical Midge. 'But you need something on your arms, they look so bare.' She opened a drawer in the chest and took out two identical silver slave bangles. 'You wear them above your elbows – like so.' Midge put her head on one side and viewed the result. 'I can't see any room for improvement. You'll do.'

'Why are you doing all this for me, Midge?'

'Because I love you. Because in my crafty and devious way I'm hoping to woo you to stay on with me. But mainly because if anyone deserves a night out on the tiles, you do.'

'I think you could have put that a little more delicately.'

The house phone trilled. It was the hall porter to say that

a Mr Berkeley had called for Miss Roseberry and should he come up?

'I think it would be better if you met him downstairs,' said Midge. 'He might not remember me, but just in case . . .' She watched in horror as Helena hid her finery beneath her old check cape.

'What on earth have you put that awful old thing on for?'

'Because it's all I have.'

'Oh, no it isn't.' There was a coats' cupboard in Midge's narrow hall and from this she took out a three-quarter-length chinchilla coat. 'Try this on for size.'

'Midge, no. I can't possibly borrow anything else of yours, and certainly not this coat. I might lose it, or spill something on it, or . . .'

'Stop clucking like a fussy old hen. If I'm not worried why should you be?' Midge forcibly pushed Helena's arms into the sleeves, then pulled the collar up around her cheeks and kissed her.

'Go forth and multiply your joys,' she said. 'But remember the old saying – if you can't be good, be careful.'

It was, thought Helena, a strange place to have brought her. No soft lights, no palm court orchestra, and very few women. The place was dominated by men, all gourmets she decided, seeing the way they tucked into their food.

They were sitting, Paul opposite her, on high-backed settles which enclosed them as if they were in a narrow, very private cubicle. There was no hint of ostentation anywhere: no fancy table linen; no highly polished cutlery; no attempt to woo customers with presentation. The place could have come straight out of Dickens, except that the linen was startlingly white.

'How did you know about this restaurant?' she asked.

'A chap on the same paper I work for comes here often. He writes a column entitled "Eating about Town", and he rates this as the second-best restaurant in London.'

There was only one thing to say to that and Helena said it. 'And which does he consider the best?'

'A little place tucked away in a corner of Soho called Fosters . . .'

'Fosters?'

'Yes. Lottie's place, the girl from the Thornmere gate-house.'

Silence fell. Helena stared fixedly at her hands. She had tried so hard to be scintillating, to capture those moments of exhilaration which had buoyed her up at the thought of seeing Paul again, but the moment she stepped out of the lift and went to meet him only one thought was uppermost in her mind: he was a married man. She was going out with a married man, and suddenly the evening was cheapened.

Paul's welcoming smile had faded. They exchanged polite greetings: they kept up a civilised conversation but only as strangers and insidiously the constraint between them deepened. And now the spectre of Lottie. What had Lottie meant to him? Had he a mistress as well as a wife?

'It was a mistake to bring you here,' he said. 'The Savoy would have done more justice to that lovely dress. You had other plans. You were going to a nightclub with friends, you were going to have fun. I've spoilt all that. I can see I've made you miserable.'

She made no attempt to answer. She didn't know what to say without sounding insincere. A waiter hovered and Paul said, 'Perhaps we could have this out after we've eaten.'

Afterwards, she hoped, it would be too late for explanations – or the wish for them on the wane. Then she could slip away, no worse for the encounter, marking it up as just another experience that went wrong.

But all through the meal she was conscious of his physical presence, so near that she had only to move her foot to touch his. She was hungry and ate whatever was put before her. But it all tasted the same and forever after she could never recall what she actually consumed. She did notice, however, that Paul's dishes came ready cut into small pieces so either the manager had been previously warned, or else Paul was a regular customer.

He was right, the dress didn't belong here, and she felt self-conscious about the fancy headband and the slave bangles. The other women were older than she and wore matronly outfits in beige or grey. She boosted her flagging spirits by drinking several glasses of dry white wine.

When coffee was served, she excused herself and walked unsteadily to the Ladies' Room. Focusing on her reflection in the looking-glass, she was horrified to see that the heat combined with the wine had given her a very high colour. That supplemented by the rouge made her look like a circus clown. Furiously she plunged her face again and again into a bowl of cold water and came up spluttering, but sober. There was little improvement, her face was now blotched with mascara. She filled her hands with soap and washed away all traces of make-up, then she scrubbed herself dry with a freshly-starched huckaback towel. She felt fresher, but now her face was so shiny it looked as if it had been wax polished. She toned it down with her powder puff, took off the headband and then the bangles and stuffed them into her handbag. Her hair in the front was wet, and when it dried it would frizz. She was past caring.

'You look less like a tart, more like your mother's daughter,' she told her reflection. She couldn't get away from the fact that she *was* her mother's daughter. She froze like her mother, becoming silent and unreasonable when anything upset her. She returned to the dining room resolved to make amends.

Coffee had been served in a heavy-plated silver coffee-pot. She poured a cup for Paul and then one for herself which she took black.

'Would you like a liqueur to go with that?' Paul asked, helping himself to sugar. He made no comment on the change in her appearance, and she wasn't certain if it was her imagination or if there was indeed a glimmer of amusement lurking in the depths of his deep blue eyes.

'No, thank you. I feel I've consumed too much alcohol already.'

He smiled, altogether more relaxed as if the very tone of her voice had reassured him. 'Not too much, just enough to make you feel mildly intoxicated. A good palliative taken at the right time.' He leaned forward, earnest now. 'Where did I go wrong, Helena? Tell me. Why did you freeze up on me?'

She swallowed, finding difficulty with the right words. 'You should have told me you were married.'

'Ah.' He took his cigarette case from his pocket, extracted one, lit it, inhaled, then blew the smoke away from her. 'So, someone told you. You think it wrong to have a date with a married man?'

'The way I was brought up, decidedly yes.'

'Even if, in the past fifteen years, it has been what is commonly called a marriage in name only?'

She hesitated. 'I think . . . . well . . . yes.'

He nodded. 'That is what I expected you to say, and that is why I didn't tell you. I so wanted to be certain of seeing you again that I dispensed with the niceties. I thought an intimate little meal like this, a glass of wine, both of us in a mellow mood – then I would have told you.'

'That's an honest admission anyway.'

'I see I shall have to be extremely honest if I want to retain your friendship. And I do want your friendship, Helena. I want even more than your friendship . . .'

Their eyes met across the table and what she saw was just the reassurance she needed. This man was not dallying with her. It was a case of instant attraction on both sides.

'And Lottie,' she said. 'Did she know about your wife?'

'She did, and that's partly why I lost her.'

'But I don't see . . . I mean, if your marriage has broken down so completely, why don't you –' She broke off, her under lip caught between her teeth. 'Forget I said that. It's no business of mine.'

'You're thinking why didn't we get a divorce? Yes, that's the simple answer, but things are never as simple as they seem.' He stubbed out his cigarette. Then he reached across the table and took hold of her hand. 'I wanted to talk about us. I wanted this evening to belong to us, but I see I must get the past out of the way first. Can you bear with me?'

This isn't a story of marrying in haste and repenting at leisure, she thought as she listened. It was the story of two old Catholic families with roots going back before the Reformation. Of two young people known to each other since childhood, and Paul having the misfortune of being the last of the Berkeleys.

'This must sound to you like something out of a novel,' he said, 'but it is not so uncommon as you think. My father, and Sylvia's father too, wanted an heir. What they were both frightened of was that either one of us might marry out of our faith. I was quite happy about the arrangements. Sylvia

86

was a good-looking girl, rather reserved with me, but I put that down to modesty. Not known for modesty myself I found it rather refreshing.' He let go of her hand in order to reach for another cigarette but thought better of it.

'And it didn't work out,' said Helena when he fell silent.

'It didn't take me long to discover that the physical side of our marriage was abhorrent to Sylvia. She had to brace herself even to let me touch her. Does my speaking as openly as this embarrass you?'

To her surprise it didn't. His easy-going manner left no room for embarrassment. 'It must have been very difficult for you,' she said quietly.

'Much more difficult for Sylvia. She was deeply in love with another man, but he was a Protestant, and as a good Catholic and a devoted daughter she wouldn't do anything to harm her church or her family. She tried to be a dutiful wife, but she was too honest to pretend. I used to hear her crying and in the end I got the truth out of her.'

'What did you do?'

'Initially, you mean? I went out and got very drunk. Then I picked up a prostitute, and the next morning I went to confession. I may as well admit now that that was the last time I went to confession – the last time that I went to church. God, Sylvia's God, the church's God, never meant a lot to me and later, in the trenches, I lost him altogether. Do you want me to go on, or do you find this all very boring?'

It was anything but boring. She could listen to him for hours. Gradually, she was building up quite a different image to the one he presented to the world. An image of a deeply sensitive and unhappy man hiding beneath a cloak of easy cynicism.

'So you and your wife separated?'

'No, we did not . . . not at first. We kept the charade going. I would have liked a divorce, but I knew that was out of the question. Sylvia filled her life with good works – on committees of different charities, that sort of thing. Then the war came. I was delighted. It was the answer to my problems. Now I had a purpose in life, something worthwhile to do. A call to the colours.' He broke off and gave her a quizzical smile. 'Do you ever read the *Daily Encounter*?'

'No, but I have heard of it. Known for its radical views, isn't it? My mother thinks it isn't fit to light the fire with.'

He laughed, his eyes glinting mischievously. 'A lot of people would agree with her. Actually, I'm rather fond of the old rag but then I have a vested interest. It supplies my bread and butter.'

'So, you're a journalist.' She had wondered about his profession. A journalist! Hm, another reason to keep this meeting from her mother. Journalists to Cecilia Roseberry were little better than confidence tricksters.

'In the spring of 1916 I wrote an article for the *Encounter* setting out my reasons for ending the war. By that time I had discovered there was very little glory in modern warfare. Gore, yes, plenty of that, but precious little glory. I was disillusioned and sickened by the killing. I saw young men, boys some of them, straight out from school and going into action and being mown down like sitting ducks. I said in my article that the brass hats likened the war to a game of chess. Safe in their quarters behind the lines, moving us around like pawns, their object being checkmate. How many pawns they lost to achieve that end was immaterial. I said it wasn't a game they were playing, it wasn't even war – it was slaughter of the innocents.'

He had, he told her, when on leave, defaced a poster of

Lord Kitchener. Under the words 'Your country needs you' he had added in black crayon, 'Enlist today – you won't live long enough to regret it.'

She remembered Midge saying something about a court martial. 'And you were found out?' she said.

'Not exactly. I reported myself to the police.' He sat back and waited for her reaction, dreading seeing those remarkable clear eyes cloud over with shame for him, but instead he saw that he had lost her. She wasn't even listening.

His voice had faded from Helena's hearing. She was back with Rupert on his last leave. She could not recall the sound of Rupert's voice any longer but she still remembered most of his words: 'You make this bloody war sound like one long social event: it's anything but . . . It's filth and mud and the stench of rotting flesh, constant bombardments – and always death . . .'

Paul's voice broke through her reverie. 'I *am* boring you, you're miles away. You didn't even hear what I was saying . . .'

'I did, oh, I did.'

'And it didn't shock you?'

'I was thinking of Rupert. He wouldn't have gone as far as you did, but he certainly thought like you, towards the end, anyway. It takes a certain kind of bravery to rebel against a public conscience, and Rupert didn't have that kind of bravery. His bravery took him back to the battlefield, and he was killed.'

Paul regarded her steadily for a moment or two, then his expression broke up into a remorseful grin. 'Actually, there were quite a few in my battalion who wished the same end for me. It would have been an easy way out of a difficult situation. Strangely enough, defacing Kitchener's poster enraged them more than my article did. The brass hats took that personally. The article got more publicity. Headlines such as, INFANTRY CAPTAIN SAYS, "PUT A STOP TO THIS STUPID BUTCHERY". And others not quite so mild. TRAITOR, COWARD. They are an example of epithets hurled at me. White feathers came by every post. My poor mother, I hadn't anticipated the consequences for her.' His eyes saddened and Helena wanted very much to return his gesture, to touch his hand, but an inbred reserve prevented her.

'I was put through a form of court martial,' he said. 'Though the verdict was a bygone conclusion – dishonourable discharge. Oddly enough, the General overruled the decision of the court. Not out of consideration for me, I hasten to add. He said the best thing would be to send me straight back into battle and with any luck I might get killed. Disappointingly for him and the others who shared his sentiments, I didn't lose my life, only my arm.'

She winced at the bitterness in his voice. After all this time, she thought, it still gets him, the disgrace, the rejection . . .

'And your family? How did they react to all this?'

'They forgave me, which angered me more than if they had disowned me, which would have been more honest. In their hearts they never forgave me, but they would have overlooked my sins if I had returned to Sylvia. That was impossible, but I couldn't tell them why.' He gave a sudden bark of laughter. 'The irony of it all was that I was recommended for a Military Cross, but nothing came of it. I think the General put his oar in there. When I was discharged from hospital the *Encounter* offered me a job and I've been with them ever since, until recently as a foreign correspondent or roving reporter in modern jargon. Wherever there was trouble, there I was. Earthquakes, riots, war or revolution, it was all grist to the mill of the intrepid

Encounter. I was good at writing about trouble. I was even accused of stirring it up in the first place in order to get copy. That wasn't necessary. Trouble was always there waiting for me.'

'Is that why you have that tanned and leathery look? Living in hot countries?'

'Leathery?' He laughed. 'So you think I look like a piece of old cowhide?'

'No, no, I didn't mean that.' She was embarrassed. She had been brought up never to make a personal remark and felt she had let herself down.

'But you are right. I'm just back from a stint in South America. There's always plenty of action in South America.'

'And you didn't go back to your wife?'

'No, I respected her too much to inflict that on her. She's in the West Country now, running a home for war orphans. Poor Sylvia, she would have made an ideal mother,but even that was denied her. Goodness knows, she's got enough of the wretched little devils to mother now.'

A bout of coughing caught him unawares, racking him until he gasped for breath. 'I've been talking too much,' he said. 'A fault with me when I get a good listener. Do you mind if we get out of here? I can't breathe in this close atmosphere.'

They walked out into a crisp and starlit night where in the light of the street lamps the untrod pavements glimmered faintly under a fine veneer of frost.

'It is customary for the gentleman to walk on the lady's right,' said Paul. 'But then I wouldn't be able to offer you my arm. Do you mind if you take my place on the outside?'

'I never know when to take you seriously.'

'I have some difficulty with that problem myself.'

They walked mostly in silence, though sometimes Paul would fill her in with another section of his background. He told her about Lottie Foster and their brief affair.

'It all started on New Year's Eve, 1918, the first New Year in peacetime and I was living in digs at the time. I couldn't face my own company that night. I had heard of Fosters in Boot Lane and so I went there to celebrate, and suddenly, sitting there, I looked around at those animated, well-heeled diners at the other tables, and I thought of the wretched ex-servicemen I'd seen begging in the streets: some limbless, some blind; tattered scarecrows for the most part, selling matches or bootlaces for a few coppers. A few months previously they had been in the trenches and fêted as heroes. Now they were down and outs. Suddenly, I saw red. I jumped to my feet and shouted insults at the other diners. I called them parasites. I asked them what sacrifices they had made for the war effort. I demanded to know if any of them had gone hungry or known homelessness. It was the drink talking, of course. They ignored me for the most part, but some of them laughed, and that's what undid me. I began to weep. It was the most shameful moment of my life, until Lottie appeared and led me away. She took me to her private rooms and made me coffee and she listened while I ranted on about the rotten world and the rotten people in it.

'She was good for me, she had a calming influence. She could see that my wounds weren't only physical. I clung to her when it was time to leave. I told her I couldn't face the thought of going back to my lonely room and she understood. She knew it wasn't just sex I needed as much as company and she took me into her bed out of compassion. From that a very deep relationship developed between us.' He hesitated. 'Not love exactly – at least, not the romantic concept of love – a trust, a need of each other, for I had this feeling that she needed me as much as I needed her. She came into my life when I was at my lowest ebb and she uplifted me. I was better for knowing her.'

Now she could understand why Lottie still had such a hold on him. 'How do you mean, better?' she said, for she couldn't imagine him other than he was.

'I became calmer in spirit, more ready to listen to reason, more able to see other people's points of view. For a time, anyway,' he added wryly. 'Those other diners I had insulted might have been scarred by the war, too, Lottie told me. It wasn't just my private fight, she said. Others had gone through the trauma of losing loved ones. She herself had lost the man she loved. She had lost a brother, and her mother and younger sister had died as a result of the war.' His voice grew tender. 'We had a few idyllic months together, then my paper decided to send me to Shanghai on a special assignment. It was a good opening for me and I couldn't afford to turn it down. I pleaded with Lottie to come with me, but she wouldn't – or rather couldn't. She had a small daughter and was trying to build up a secure future for her, and she felt that leaving her behind or uprooting her from her familiar surroundings could equally disrupt her life.

'If I could have offered Lottie marriage, if I could have made a home for her in this country, I think she might have given in to me, but she chose what was best for her little girl. I was bitter at first, but I realised afterwards that she had done the right thing. I was no good to any woman. My way of life was nomadic, I couldn't settle. I hated the war and yet I missed that sense of excitement it gave me. Travelling amid the trouble spots of the world made up for that.' He broke off to tap his chest. 'But my travelling days are over now. From now on it's a sedentary life for me, and all because of this bally cough.'

'And you have never been tempted to get in touch with her again?' Helena feared but needed to know.

'I've been tempted, yes, but thank God had the sense not to give in to temptation. Lottie has made a successful life for herself and I with my selfishness – yes,' as she made to protest, 'I am selfish. I latch on to people I think can ease my loneliness, so beware.' He smiled at her, then began to cough, and she heard him curse under his breath as he took out his handkerchief.

Talking so much had tired him out. She could faintly hear his laboured breathing as, with her arm tucked into his, they walked the near-deserted streets of London. Occasionally a taxi-cab overtook them and in the distance they sometimes heard the clattering hooves of some coster's pony. The chimes of Big Ben struck midnight, and Helena saw the gleam of the Thames, black and oily in the lamplight. She had no idea where they were heading, and wondered if Paul had any plan. She was content to go on walking in this magical night-time London that was all new to her.

They walked slowly along the Embankment, spinning out their time together. The ornamental lamps, brilliant in the frosty night air, cast shimmering images in the sluggish waters below. To Helena it was all vastly romantic, like being in a foreign country. Even the outline of the buildings on the opposite bank took on the allure of a mysterious and Oriental skyline. The whining of a tram broke her train of thought. During the day, trams ran every few minutes, but at this time of night they were non too frequent. This was a single-decker, designed to fit into the tramway subway that ran underground from the Embankment to Kingsway. They stood to watch as it clanged past, sparks flying off its iron wheels, then it disappeared into the black maw of the tunnel like some prehistoric creature going to earth.

Big Ben struck the half-hour. They had been walking without any objective in sight, putting off the moment when Paul would have to return her to Hanover Mansions.

'What time is Midge expecting you?' he asked.

'I didn't specify any time. She gave me a spare key.'

His eyes glittered keenly in the lamplight. 'Do you know what I would like more than anything?'

'What?'

'For you to come back to my place.'

She didn't hesitate. 'I would like that, too,' she said.

It had been a dismal evening, a wash-out, a disaster. Two's company, Midge thought, and three's none. Whoever thought that one up knew a thing or two. They'd obviously experienced the sort of evening she'd only just survived. James had thrown a fit of sulks, quite out of character with his image, but then it was a new experience for him, being ditched for another man. And Donald, twitching like a dog who sees another contender for his bone, had snapped and snarled all evening. She was glad to see the back of them both, ducking them as they left the nightclub and taking a cab back to Hanover Mansions alone.

Midge looked at the clock. Nearly one o'clock and Helena not back yet. Being a few years the elder and her hostess she felt responsible for the girl, then reminded herself that Helena was not a girl, she was a woman approaching thirty and well able to look after herself. All the same, in some ways she was very naive. No, naive wasn't the word, inexperienced rather. She had only ever had that schoolgirl crush on Rupert. Midge poured herself a small brandy and switched on the electric fire. She appreciated central heating, it was a great improvement on the open fires that scorched one's front and left the back to freeze, but she had to admit that with central heating, towards the evening, her feet and legs always got cold.

The telephone shrilled. Now if that was James to complain one more time or Donald to apologise, she'd hang up on them. She'd had enough. It was Helena.

'Midge, I just phoned to tell you not to stay up for me. I don't know what time I'll be home.'

'Where are you?'

A pause. 'I'm at Paul's place . . . he's just making coffee. Midge, hullo, Midge . . . Are you still there?'

'I'm speechless for the want of anything to say. You're the last person I'd have thought . . .'

'I don't need a lecture, especially not now.'

'I have no intention of lecturing. Are congratulations in order?'

'Midge, please don't make fun of me. I'm so very happy.'

'Bless you, darling, I wouldn't dream of making fun of you. Just as long as you're happy, that's all that matters.'

Midge replaced the receiver with a smile of satisfaction. Fate had played nicely into her hands. Perhaps Paul could accomplish that which she had been unable to do, though she had been trying for years: lure Helena to London.

FIVE

Christmas was approaching. It was not a thought that gave Dan Harker the slightest pleasure. He considered it a waste of two good working days and an unnecessary interruption to the winter. More than anything it was a con, a device to part the gullible from their money. He much preferred the New Year. New Year was another matter altogether. For one thing, it wasn't a public holiday – except for up North and in Scotland. New Year meant a new beginning and, if one were lucky, renewed hope.

Hope had died for him one Christmas and did not surface again until that holiday at the Thornmere bakery. There he had recovered hope, but he had never recovered his faith in Christmas.

Until he was six he believed fervently in Father Christmas. Father Christmas and Our Father in Heaven were one and the same to him. A benign deity to whom all things were possible. And it was to this deity that he prayed most fervently for a kaleidoscope that particular Christmas.

One of these tantalising and delightful objects had appeared at the Home a few weeks previously in the possession of a small boy who had recently lost his parents. When an attempt was made to prise it away from him to add to the common pool of toys, his screams were so heart-rending that the house mother finally relented. From then on the friendship of this new boy was much sought after, for he would loan out his magic property on a barter system. The only thing Dan had to offer in exchange for the privilege of temporary ownership was his morning slice of bread and margarine. He considered it worth going hungry for the pleasure of watching tiny pieces of coloured glass form into amazing and varied patterns.

Then, just before Christmas, an unknown aunt of the new boy arrived and spirited him away and, much to the distress of the other inmates, the kaleidoscope went with him. With its going went all the colour and magic from Dan's life, but he didn't despair. Father Christmas in Heaven would hear his earnest pleas and bring it back.

On Christmas morning he found, together with the usual orange and handful of nuts, not a kaleidoscope but a pair of new boots. He was in need of boots. His present pair were now so small that they rubbed blisters on his heels, but he could put up with pain. He found it harder to put up with disappointment. And as for Father Christmas or Our Father in Heaven, whoever he was, he decided in future to have no more truck with him.

Thinking of that Christmas now Dan took the well-trodden path down to the mere, one of his favourite walks over spongy turf and through a copse of silver birch where a robin sang his winter song. Bass trotted ahead of him. All country gents owned dogs, he knew that from looking through quality periodicals. They were never photographed in their country tweeds without a dog or two in attendance, usually some breed of gun dog. He didn't go in for pedigrees himself, a mongrel was good enough for him, and as for tweeds! He rumbled silently at the thought of himself in a Norfolk jacket.

He had found just the dog he was looking for in a home for strays. The scruffiest one on offer, his ribs showing through his coat and one ear torn. He was mostly terrier but he could have had a pug ancestor somewhere along the line for his tail was hairless and coiled like a pig's. The lonely look in the dog's toffee-coloured eyes had struck a chord in Dan's heart.

When Dan put his hand through the bars of the cage and scratched behind the undamaged ear the dog drooled.

'You took a risk doing that,' remarked the attendant. 'He could have given you a nasty bite.'

'Bite! He hasn't got the strength to take a bite out of a dish of butter, let alone out of my hand. What is his name?'

'We don't know. He's a stray. We call him Gyp.'

Dan nodded. 'I'm not surprised. Just lately every other mongrel I've come across answers to the name of Gyp. This poor little blighter deserves something more original. I'll call him Bassett.'

'That's rather grand for a dog like that, isn't it? There isn't a trace of hound in him.'

'No, but there's plenty of all-sorts,' Dan retorted with a chuckle. He reached for his wallet. 'How much do I owe you?'

'We don't make a charge. We're only too pleased to find homes for our strays. But, of course, if you would like to make a small donation . . .'

Dan produced a five-pound note. The man goggled. 'But you could buy a pedigree dog for that.'

'I don't happen to want a pedigree. I haven't got a pedigree myself and I don't want any dog feeling superior to me. Come along, Bass, ole chap. You and I were made for each other.'

Whatever his name in his former life it didn't take Bass long to learn his new one. He put on weight, his coat acquired a gloss, his ear healed, he regained his youth. He would never be handsome but he was completely lovable, and as a guard dog as useless as a clockwork toy. He was also untrainable. Every command Dan gave was treated as a game, and Bass made the rules. Dan thought of those gentlemen in *Tatler* posing with guns under their arms and dogs like statues at their feet, and congratulated himself on his good fortune.

Bass was now tugging at the turn-up of his right trouser leg, urging him to get a move on. 'Stop that, you little tyke,' he said affectionately. 'That suit cost me ten nicker.'

Tyke said like that in fun reminded Dan how far he had come since he himself was called a tyke. He had cringed at the word, but Bass took it as a term of endearment, rolling on his back and offering up his pink spotted belly to be tickled. Dan obliged. All these wooded acres, he thought, as he straightened up: a ten-guinea suit; a house built for a country squire; and grounds designed by Capability Brown. All this now belonged to him. He whistled a command. 'Come on, Bass, come along you mutt. Let's finish our walk.'

Bass was the first to reach the lake and at once started to nose among the reeds. Once he had put up a water vole and had never given up hope of repeating such an achievement.

Dan beside him, stared reflectively at the expanse of rank water. The sight depressed him. When he first took possession of the Hall he had planned to have the mere drained and refilled, then restocked and replanted. There were once fish in the mere he had been told, and water-lilies like waxen goblets floating on the surface, and golden king-cups that lit up one stretch of water like a sheet of sunlight. Now only the blackened, slimy stems remained, and an oily skin dulled the surface. Coots no longer nested in the reeds and mallards and moorhens had deserted their old breeding grounds. Yet the expense of returning the mere to its former glory appalled him. He turned and walked away, and the smell of decay followed.

Ever since becoming owner of the Massingham estate he had spent freely. Too freely, according to his accountants, beavering away over their ledgers back at the works. Rebuilding the house and bringing it up to modern standards had made a large hole in his capital. And it hadn't stopped there. He had gone on spending money, trying to buy himself popularity, according to public opinion.

Thornmere now possessed a cricket field complete with pavilion, sight screens and changing rooms. Even the non-cricketers among the villagers approved of this as did the wives who were coerced into helping with the teas.

'It do make a bit of a treat,' they said. 'To walk in the park without being had up for trespass.' It was a better treat for the poachers who could now mingle with the spectators on summer evenings, disappearing into the shadows as soon as dusk fell. But the spice had gone out of poaching since old Todd the gamekeeper retired and hadn't been replaced. This new chap up at the Hall, they grumbled, had no respect for game at all.

The cricket field had been a great success. Not so Dan's next venture, the Memorial Hall. Seeing that the village lacked a communal meeting-place Dan decided to do something about it. There was a piece of land not far from the church known locally as the pightle, and to approach it one went by way of Pightle's Loke. It was another example to Dan of a language that was constantly baffling him. Pightle meant what it was, a piece of waste land, and loke was a lane with a dead end. This was explained to him by one of the village elders in a manner suggestive of talking to a backward five-year-old.

That the pightle was never used except as a depository for odd bits of rubbish and unwanted bedsteads and mattresses did not stop the villagers being up in arms when the builders moved in and began to clear it. The grumbles started.

'Oo wants a 'All – we've managed without one so far. Memorial 'All. What's a Memorial 'All when it cooms home to roost? Where we goin' to dump our rubbish in future?'

'He sez it's a tribute to the lads of the village what got killed in the war.'

'What's wrong with a proper war memorial then, in the churchyard where it ought to be. We're the only village in these parts wiv'out one.'

'I can't understand these ruddy people,' Dan complained to Reuben when the first murmurings of dissent reached his ears. 'I thought I was doing them a favour. The way they're carrying on you'd think I was asking them to pay for it. Every village has a hall. I'm surprised Thornmere has gone all this time without one. Can't they see how useful it will be? They can use it for concerts and meetings and socials. They can have bazaars and whist-drives – that is if they know what a whist-drive is.'

'They know about whist-drives,' said Reuben drily. 'They know about bazaars and jumble sales, too. They use the school for that sort of thing.'

'Well, now they'll be able to use a proper meeting-place, and a darn sight more convenient they'll find it. For one thing there's electricity, and a kitchen. And something else the school hasn't got – flush toilets.'

'Oo-ah.' Reuben allowed a small flicker of a smile to cross

his face. 'You've put one over 'em there, but as most of 'em in the village haven't got flush toilets in their homes, I don't think it counts for much. What they would have preferred is a war memorial.'

Dan let out a groan of extreme irritation. 'It *is* a war memorial. Can't they get that into their thick heads?'

Reuben had not forgiven Dan his remark about 'these ruddy people'. Now came thick heads. They were his people and he wasn't taking that from a mere outsider.

'If you understood these ruddy people better,' he said, 'you would have known the kind of memorial they wanted is the kind they're putting up in churchyards all over the country. Tha' would really have meant something to them. They could've gone there on Armistice Day and paid their respects. They could've gone there for the two minutes' silence. You can bring people together in a hall, but you won't get no silence.'

There was silence now, aggrieved on both sides, but Reuben wasn't one to hold a grudge. Besides, he felt he had more than evened the score and could now afford to be magnanimous.

'They du say the parson is mighty pleased about the new hall. They say he sez that now they got somewhere more convenient for church meetings. They used to meet in the Vicarage drawing room, but it's a festy ole room — don't warm up even in summer. They say they be looking forward to having somewhere cosy to meet for a change.'

'It's gratifying to know the parson is pleased about it. I was beginning to think my effort had been a waste of time and money.' But Dan's heavy sarcasm was wasted on Reuben who took every spoken word at its face value. 'And what about the chapel-goers? Have they expressed any opinion? Have I managed to please them, too?'

'Oh ah, you won't find any of the chapel lot agoing to the hall. They're already calling it the Devil's meeting-place.'

'Thank you very much. It's nice to know I'm held in some esteem.'

'It's not you they're getting at, Mr Harker. They're a funny ole lot. They're against any form of gambling.'

'So they consider playing whist gambling?'

'Any game of chance is the work of the devil. So's a raffle and a lucky dip. Any innocent pastime that gives pleasure is a sin to them.'

'Reuben, let me tell you something. You don't have to be a chapel-goer to think like that. I was brought up in a place where even laughter was strictly limited. So was everything else except hard work,' Dan added reflectively. He whistled to Bass who was nosing around in the empty stables, sniffing out lingering odours from long ago. 'Here boy . . . here. Come along, walkies.'

'They'll accept it in time, Mr Harker,' Reuben called after him. 'Thass takes time for something new to be accepted in these parts, but when it du nobody can fathom out how they managed without it.'

If there was meant to be comfort in that remark Dan missed it. His only answer was a grunt. He ambled off with Bass skittering about his ankles, threatening any minute to trip him over. Reuben watched until both were out of sight, then went across the yard to fill his bucket at the pump. He gave the Daimler a wash over every day whether it needed it or not, and as he worked he hissed through his teeth like an ostler grooming a horse.

He was rather chuffed about the new hall himself, though he wouldn't give the guv'nor the satisfaction of knowing it. It wouldn't be long, he knew, before the villagers were boasting about its merits, comparing it to the squitty old wooden affairs erected in less fortunate villages. But they would never call it the Memorial Hall. It would either become the New 'All or the Village 'All or more than likely the Dan'el 'arker 'All. Norfolk folk had their own way with names.

That exchange with Reuben had taken place two months ago when the trees in the park were newly turned to the tawny colours of an autumn canvas. The autumn beauty of the country never ceased to amaze Dan. He had hardly noticed autumn in London except for the mess the leaves made on the pavements. The sight of a wooded valley turning into shades of gold and russet, red and amber, satisfied some hunger in his soul. He thought of it as a kaleidoscope, and whenever that word came to mind his eyes grew tender remembering the disappointment of that small boy he used to be.

You blithering idiot, he was fond of saying, talking to himself, which he did quite often as he had no one else to talk to, you never give up feeling sorry for yourself, do you! But his sympathy was for the six-year-old, not for a man of thirty-nine. He could not afford such self-indulgence now.

Christmas – to blazes with Christmas. He wished he could hibernate until it was over. Christmas was the last thing he wanted to think about this morning. Yesterday he had passed Helena Roseberry in the village street. She was walking for a change, not driving. She acknowledged him as she always did, nodding slightly, never stopping to talk, walking on in that stately, unhurried manner that made him wonder if she had been brought up to believe that it was common to hurry.

She had changed. Even in the short while it took for their paths to cross, his eyes had drunk in everything about her. She was not wearing the Burberry or the black and white check cloak, the only outer garments he had ever seen on her. This coat was new and expensive, for he had some knowledge of the cut of a garment, and with a fur collar that reached up to the tips of her ears. Her tight-fitting hat was made of matching fur and revealed just a glimpse of the brightly-coloured hair that so wildly excited him, rousing in him erotic images of a slender white body and a seductive mound of reddish hair.

But the change wasn't only in the style of her clothes, it was also in her expression. What had happened to her in the few weeks since he last saw her, this woman he lusted after, who entered unbidden into his dreams, waking him with the force of his hunger and sending him from his bed to the bathroom, staggering with sleep and swearing at the weakness he could only dowse with cold water?

There was a warmth in her eyes now and a hint of a smile on a mouth that before had seemed tight-lipped. His immediate thought was that she had found herself a lover. He had seen that look before on faces of women who had surrendered themselves uncommittedly to love. No woman had ever looked like that for him, hang it. He dragged his thoughts reluctantly back to Christmas. Thinking of Helena Roseberry excited him, but thinking of Christmas only made him wilt.

Yet there had been one Christmas that had altered the whole course of his life. He had been going on seventeen at the time, and had been living rough for the past two years. At fourteen, the guardians of the orphanage had apprenticed him to a tailor's and cutter's in the City Road. He stuck it for six months, then punning outrageously, told his boss that he wasn't cut out to be a tailor.

'You don't have to tell me that.' The boss, a shrivelled little man, bent with arthritis and in constant pain, hardly capable now of holding a needle, completely incapable of feeling pity or compassion or even liking for another human being, peered over the top of his spectacles. 'I'll tell you what you're cut out for, a criminal. A good-for-nothing, thieving little tyke, and you'll finish up in clink, where you should 'ave gone when I caught you selling orf me off-cuts.'

The guardians had paid a premium for Dan to be apprenticed to the tailor which included, as well as learning a trade, his bed and board until such time as he was useful enough to earn his keep. His bed, he discovered, was a palliasse in the corner of the cutting-room floor and his board was such that made him recall, with a somewhat ironic wistfulness, the meals at the orphanage.

He didn't mind it at first. He saw in his situation a tenuous link with Oliver Twist – his favourite fictional character. He dreamed constantly of meeting a genial benefactor – but soon the gnawing hunger pains became so unbearable that he could think of nothing else but food. It was this that drove him one day to gather up the bits of cloth from the floor of the cutting room and sell them to a rag and bone merchant. With the threepence he received in exchange he bought himself a substantial helping of fish and chips. His belly full, he took with equanimity the thrashing he got when his crime was discovered, knowing that he would never get a second chance to err.

He left the tailoring business without regret and without any prospect of future employment. If the worst came to the worst, he'd beg. He was only one of many living on the streets, and he had no need to hide, like some, when a copper came in sight. And as for Mr Lane reporting him to the authorities, he had no fear of that, for that would mean the old skinflint having to return the premium. What a hope!

He earned a few pence holding horses' heads. He became quite adept with horses, and was not above pinching a handful of their oats if he was hungry. He learnt to hang around bakers' shops at closing time, for they would often give away left-over stale bread and cakes. And there was always rotten fruit to be had at street markets.

The cold was the worst to bear. He rarely had a hot meal. He had no coat and his jacket was wearing thin, but he was hardy and tough and he let his hair grow to protect his neck from the worst of the draughts when sleeping in shop doorways.

The eve of that memorable Christmas was a miserable night; raining hard, and a wind blowing from the north-west. He was hoping to get a bed at a Salvation Army hostel, but he would have to get there early for the vagrants started queueing before it got dark. He had not eaten since the evening before and was on the look-out to earn a penny or two so that he could buy himself a helping of pease pudding before the pork butchers closed.

Some shops kept open until midnight on Christmas Eve, especially the poulterers and fruiterers, selling off their products at knock-down prices rather than have them left on their hands over Christmas. It was always bad luck for the shopkeepers when Christmas Day fell on a Friday, especially if the winter was mild. Any stock left over when the shops reopened three days later was likely to be high. For weeks now, it seemed to Dan, turkeys and pheasants, chickens and hares had been hanging outside the premises of poulterers and butchers, tormenting him with images of hot Christmas dinners. He believed that the day would dawn when he would sit himself down to a hot roast dinner at his own table in his own home. The streets of London were paved with gold. Though as yet he hadn't found as much as a half-sovereign, it didn't stop him looking. He was naturally optimistic; he wouldn't have survived this long if he wasn't.

He was full of optimism now. Being Christmas he expected to be tipped a sixpence instead of the customary penny – the going rate for minding a horse. It had happened once before, and then he had eaten his Christmas dinner at Lockharts where the knives and forks were chained to the bare wooden tables. It could happen again and his hopes rose as an old-fashioned but smart little gig drawn by a handsome bay stopped outside the Traveller's Rest where he had taken up his pitch.

'Mind your horse, guv,' he said, tipping his cap to the man who was climbing ponderously down from the driving seat. When straightened up he wasn't much taller than Dan himself. A man in his sixties, Dan thought, a barrel of a man, in a tight-fitting coat and wearing an ancient beaver hat. He had small, bright, quizzical eyes in a large cherubic face.

'D'you know anything about horses, son?'

'Yessir, I do.'

'Can you drive one?'

Once, under Mr Fraser's tutelage, he had been allowed to take the reins of the baker's van. 'Yessir, I can.'

'Then if you'll wait for me and drive me home afterwards, I'll give you a half-crown.'

Half-crown! Dan went weak at the thought. He could get a bed in a doss house for sixpence. He could get supper and breakfast and still have enough over for a Christmas dinner. What's more, he wouldn't have to walk five miles back to the hostel.

'Yessir!' he said enthusiastically.

It was nearly Christmas. The town hall clock had just struck the quarter to midnight. He had watched the devout, heads bent, holding umbrellas aloft as they made their way through the driving rain to midnight communion at the parish church. The last tram had passed some minutes since, the flanks of the horses steaming in the rain. There were still a few buses on the homeward route with passengers both inside and out clutching last minute shopping. Those on top, exposed to the elements, looked as miserable as he was feeling.

'I will have earned this half-crown by the time I get it,' he grumbled as he stood shivering by the horse. He wondered how far he would have to drive to get the stout old gentleman home. They were on the outskirts of Stratford. If it was only as far as Leytonstone he might still have time to find a bed in a doss house, but if it was any further north he didn't fancy his chances.

Just then the portly gentleman came staggering out, down the steps of the public house, his legs bowed with the effort of keeping his broad squat body upright and his top hat in place. With a masterly effort, and some help from Dan, he heaved himself up into the passenger seat where he immediately settled down to sleep, his lower chin fitting comfortably into his collar.

Dan climbed up beside him, already beginning to regret his over-confidence. The horse knew at once that there was an inexperienced hand on the reins. He whinnied fretfully, pawed the ground, then started off at a spanking trot – there was nothing for it but to let him have his head. Dan put his faith in his memory of Mr Fraser's horse who, given charge of the bakery van, had led them safely through the lanes on the last lap of the journey to Thornmere, that memorable first day of his Norfolk holiday.

This horse he thought seemed just as reliable as Mr Fraser's old nag, but was a darn sight more lively. Fortunately there wasn't much traffic and very few pedestrians. Pub-leavers mostly, stopping to relieve themselves in the gutter before reeling off to wherever they lived. Dan looked at them with disgust. Not because they used the gutters as latrines – he often did so himself if there was no one about – but because they had used good money, and money they could ill afford he suspected, filling themselves up with liquid and almost immediately letting it out again. What a waste of cash, and he hadn't had a decent meal for days.

The horse led them into territory new to Daniel. The shops and public houses petered out, giving place to private residences and open spaces with many trees. The rain had turned to sleet and particles of ice stung his eyes and cheeks. There was a waterproof apron attached to the dashboard: he unrolled this and tucked it over himself and his passenger. Then old man's hat had fallen forward and was now resting on his nose. Dan rammed it back into place.

The horse who had shown signs of lagging, suddenly perked up and broke into a trot. Dan took that as a sign that they were on the home stretch. They had left the main road behind them and the iron-rimmed wheels of the gig rattled noisily over the cobbles of a narrow side street.

The street lamps were few and far between and he found it difficult to make out his whereabouts. He picked out the outline of what he took to be a factory rearing up on their left, then came a foundry chimney and a cluster of roofs belonging to some smaller buildings, sheds of some kind. Finally he saw illuminated by the light attached to a pair of gates, an enamelled hoarding which informed him that this was Thurgood's Tinplate Works – est. 1830.

The gates were open, with intent he suspected, as the horse smartly wheeled and cantered through them ignoring Dan's frantic sawing on the reins. The bay was in control:

he knew just what he was doing and where he was going. He followed the curve of a high brick wall topped with broken bottles and, crossing a wide cobbled yard, came to a halt, breathing noisily, at the entrance of what appeared to be a private residence, dimly lit and covered completely, except for its windows, in ivy.

Now what, Dan wondered, looking at the inert bulk of flesh beside him. His half-crown seemed as far away as ever. Short of going through the man's pockets and helping himself, he would have to wake him up, help him down from the gig, up the steps to the front door and then, by some miracle, get him into the house. It couldn't be done. He stared helplessly at the light that shone faintly through the tinted fanlight over the door, and wondered if there was anybody about to give him a hand. Stiffly he clambered down from the gig and went round to the horse's head.

It was nervous. It reared its head and gave a high-pitched whinny, and immediately there came an answering whickering from nearby stables. Stables where the factory's delivery horses were bedded, Dan decided. That meant there must be help at hand. He was glad of that for the bay needed attention. A good rub down, then stabled and fed. It had been out in the cold for several hours, it must be as tired as he was himself. With relief he saw a light appear and move in his direction. It was a lamp, and as it drew nearer he saw it was carried by a tall rail of a man wearing a leather apron.

'Thank the Lord for you,' said Dan. 'I didn't know how I was going to manage with the horse and the old gent all by myself. It's Mr Thurgood, isn't it? I saw the name Thurgood on the board. Look at him, he's been like that ever since we left Stratford. Sleeping like a baby.'

The newcomer didn't answer but looked Dan up and

down and grinned, then made signs to show how best to go about the problem of getting Mr Thurgood out of the gig. Thin, pinched-looking, and with a slack mouth that revealed a few broken and discoloured teeth, he was nevertheless a man possessed of enormous strength. Or was it just a knack born of long practice, Dan wondered?

Once on his feet, and revived by the stinging rain, Mr Thurgood began to come round.

He blinked at Dan, supporting himself with one arm round the boy's shoulders. 'Well done, lad,' he said, breathing whisky into his face. 'You got me home. Now just get me indoors and I'll pay you what I owe you.'

He turned unsteadily and peered closely into the face of the thin man who hovered near. 'That you, George? Happy Christmas, old chap. Put Darby up for me will you? I'll see you right in the morning.'

It was morning already. A church clock on the main road struck one. By now, Dan had cottoned on to the fact that George was deaf and dumb. He used the same signs and made the same grunting noises as Sam, the deaf mute who had been a gardener and odd-job man at the orphanage. Dan wondered then, and had wondered several times since, why such people were called dumb when the loud and harsh noises they made in lieu of speech proved anything but.

The boys at the orphanage had mocked old Sam unmercifully, calling him loony and mimicking his grimaces, knowing they could easily outrun him when he gave chase, which he always did. Dan was not one of the mockers, remembering what it was like to be mocked himself. When younger he had been called names like Titch and Weedy and Sparrer until he grew big and aggressive enough to stand up for himself. He had followed deaf Sam about, too, but not in order to mock. Just to study him. He was fascinated by the way Sam's fingers rapidly spelled out the deaf and dumb language, accompanied always by grunts and grimaces. Dan monitored every move he made. Soon, in his inept and clumsy way, he was able to hold a conversation with the old gardener.

A touch on his arm brought him back to another time and another deaf mute, motioning him to pull his weight – or rather, Mr Thurgood's weight. They struggled with the helpless man and got him safely up to the door of the house. He was fully awake now, though not fully sober. It took him a long time to find his key. Dan stayed glued to his side, determined not to be done out of his half-crown. He heard behind him the jingle of harness, the ring of horses' hooves on cobbles. George, his help no longer needed, was taking the horse and gig round to the stables.

The door opened onto a cavernous hall where the glowing embers of a dying fire gave out more heat than light. The gas was turned down low. Mr Thurgood stood on tiptoe to reach the bracket and turned it up. Dan blinked in the sudden light. He looked at his whereabouts, looked down at himself, and thought he knew how Tom, the chimney-sweep, must have felt when he found himself in Effie's bedroom.

Mr Thurgood, full of liquid bonhomie, rocked backwards and forwards on his heels. 'Well, young fella me lad, I mustn't keep you any longer. Your folks'll be wondering where you've gone. I reckon you've earned more than that half-crown I promised you. Let's see now, what have we here?' He took a handful of loose change out of his pocket. 'It's Christmas, ain't it. We mustn't forget the spirit of Christmas. Hm . . . how does a half-sovereign look to you, me lad?'

It looked to Dan like the first chip of gold off the legendary streets of London. He felt his life had taken a definite turn for the better. He was too overwhelmed to speak.

'Got far to go, son?'

'Just to the nearest doss house, sir.'

Mr Thurgood rocked back on his heels again, jingling the coins in his pocket. He thrust out his bottom lip, his brow furrowed. 'Homeless, eh?' Slowly his brow cleared and a smile spread over his puckish features. 'Can you play backgammon, boy?'

Experience had taught Dan that it was usually more advantageous to answer yes than to answer no. He risked it now, 'Yessir,' he said.

'Good. That takes care of tomorrow then. You stay here tonight and tomorrow we'll play backgammon. It'll be a change to have a young 'un about the place. Usually, it's just me and my housekeeper. I don't know about Mrs Prescott but I'd welcome a bit of young company.'

For a large man he had a very light voice, a genteel voice larded with cockneyisms. He paused with one foot on the bottom stair. 'There'll be some refreshment left out for me in my bedroom. You'd better scout around for something for yourself. Through there.' He indicated a door at the rear of the hall. 'That'll take you to the kitchen quarters, and then if you take the first door on your left you'll find the pantry. Left mind you – not right. Right is the door to Mrs Prescott's bedroom. If you walk in on her and wake her up she'll have a fit. We want her well for tomorrow, lad, or we'll go without our Christmas dinner. There should be some bread and cheese in the pantry and the remains of the pork brawn I had for supper. Take what you want, but for goodness' sake lay off the Christmas cake. I'll never hear the end of it if you touch that blessed cake. She's been on about it for weeks. She *feeds* it with my best brandy. I thought cakes were supposed to feed us, not the other way round.'

He went up two more stairs, then paused again. 'And you can kip down on the hearth-rug in front of that fire. Or there's an old couch in the kitchen, if you'd rather. Personally, I'd settle for the hearth-rug. Mrs Prescott snores fit to raise the dead.' He managed to make the rest of the stairs without another interruption.

Dan stirred himself, staring down at the murky waters of the lake, slowly bringing himself back from where wayward thoughts had taken him. He stared up at the leafless trees and then down at Bass, sitting patiently at his feet. The past had been like a warm and familiar coat. He shivered, feeling the cold, and went back for it.

'You took an almighty risk that night, taking in a ragamuffin like me. You didn't know anything about me. I could have robbed you while you slept, I could have set the place on fire, I could have murdered you in your bed. What made you trust me?'

They were sitting over their port and nuts in the oak-panelled dining room of Ivy House. Mrs Prescott had taken away the remains of the turkey and brought Christmas pudding and brandy sauce, then in turn, mince pies and fruit. Coffee awaited them in the drawing room, but they were too comfortable to move. Another Christmas, thought Dan, his twelfth with Timothy Thurgood and getting better every year. Maturing like good malt whisky.

'You said you could play backgammon. That was good enough for me,' said Timothy, cracking a walnut between the palms of his hands.

'But I couldn't play backgammon.'

'I guessed as much, but you soon learnt, didn't you? It wasn't long before you were tanning the hide off me. Dan, my boy, you were the best thing that ever happened to me. I knew it when I saw you standing in my hall, a street arab if ever I saw one. But there was something else besides . . .' Timothy broke off, studying Daniel with quizzical eyes that, as he grew older, grew even smaller, swallowed up by puffy upper lids and the pouches underneath.

'I know I've asked you this umpteen times before, but are you sure you don't know who your parents were?'

'No, and I've given up caring. What do I want with a father and mother when I have you and Mrs Prescott?'

Timothy chuckled. He didn't miss the irony regarding Mrs Prescott, who at best treated Dan as a necessary evil. 'I only wonder,' he said. 'Because I could tell at once you were a cut above the other street urchins I had come across.' He tapped his forehead. 'You had it up here. You'd taught yourself to speak intelligibly and you'd read a dickens of a lot . . . you could outmatch me in every book I mentioned.'

'That's because public libraries are free and keep open late. I went there for shelter and stayed to read.'

'Yes, you're a self-taught man like my father was, and there's nothing wrong in that. Anything you put your mind to, you can do. Look how you've got on at the works. First tea-boy, then office-boy; under-manager; partner; and since my retirement, boss. It's in the blood, Dan. You're an uncommon sort of chap, which means you must have had uncommon parents.'

'There's nothing uncommon about ships that pass in the night.'

'Depends on the ships, I s'pose. Does it worry you, Dan, being born in a workhouse? It's never worried me. I pride myself on my judge of character and I judged you aright as soon as I clapped eyes on you, otherwise I wouldn't have taken you on trust. Best thing I ever did was to drive out to Stratford that Christmas Eve to have a drink at the old Traveller's Rest. Your coming meant a new lease of life to me. More important, a new lease of life for the works. God, what a worker, what ideas, what innovations. Got rid of all the dead wood, instilled new life into the place. My father wouldn't recognise it if he were to see the old place now. I told you how he started with a workforce of five and just a few ramshackle sheds.'

'Many a time, Tim.'

'It won't hurt you to hear it again. It'll do you good to be reminded what determination and grit and faith in yourself can do, though that's a bit like preaching to the converted.

'When my father started up here, this was a little bit of no man's land surrounded by the ragged bits of Epping Forest. That was long before 1878 when Epping Forest was given over to the people. Before that it was always having bits lopped off it, taken for pasturing or building. There's not much left of Epping Forest in these parts now. No, it's all shops and houses and tramlines. Not that I mind, it brings in more business. My father prospered and built this house so as to be within sight of the works. He liked the idea of walking out of his front door and straight into the factory yard. He thought to raise a family of sons to carry on after him, but all he raised was me, and a great disappointment I turned out to be. I didn't marry, I didn't produce a son to carry on the family name. Mind you, I thought about marriage from time to time, but I kept putting it off. Then when I found I could've done with a wife, it was too late to change my ways. Don't you go making the same mistake, Dan. You should start thinking of settling down now.'

'I haven't met the right one yet, Tim. Perhaps I never will – perhaps, like you, I'll remain a bachelor.'

Timothy didn't answer. His thoughts had wandered. 'All this talk of war – we've only just got over the Boer War. 1901 doesn't seem all that long ago, does it? That was a momentous year for me, Dan, it was the year you happened. Momentous year for the nation, too, the death of the old Queen. Seemed funny having a king again after all those years.' He reverted to his former fears. 'It couldn't happen again – war, I mean?' Like a child, Timothy needed reassurance. Like a child he was now, in many ways, looking to Dan for guidance. 'What about this balance of power, they talk about? I thought that was supposed to prevent another war.'

Dan had mixed feelings regarding the prospect of war. 'Have you considered that war would increase the demand for tinplate? War could make us very wealthy.'

'But at what cost, Dan? Think of the cost.'

Indeed at what cost. A year later, in 1914, the casualty lists following the Battle of Mons brought it home to them. The first wave of fervour that had greeted the commencement of war four months before began to wane, and Dan's conscience began to trouble him. The war indeed was making them rich. He thought it time to redress the balance.

He was twenty-nine and extremely fit, nobody seeing him now would recognise in him the little sparrow from the orphanage. His country needed men like him. Every hoarding carried a poster of Kitchener telling him so. He went along to the nearest recruiting office to enlist.

Yes, it was true that they needed men to fight, he was told by the recruiting sergeant, but he was of more use to his country producing tin for the war effort. The work he did was on the list of reserved occupations. He was reminded that the tin-box industry was in constant demand. Tins were needed for mess-tins, water bottles, tobacco, ammunition boxes.

'It's a pity,' said the sergeant, 'that we can't can our own food like they do in America. That's where a lot of our tinned food comes from, and too much of it ends up on the ocean floor. Bloody U-boats.'

A germ of an idea was planted in Dan's mind, but it didn't come to fruition until over a year later. By then the shortage of food was beginning to have effect. He thought of the cultivated fields of Norfolk, the acres of peas and beans and potatoes and carrots. He remembered the farms he visited with Mr Fraser, the well-stocked piggeries and poultry yards. There was a market to be tapped there, if one knew how to go about it. Why shouldn't the Thurgood Tinplate Works go over to canning home-grown food instead of canning the food already processed and mostly sent over from America?

Full of enthusiasm he put the idea to Timothy who, by now an obese old man, rarely moved from his fireside chair.

Tim, like many old men, mistrusted change. He shook his elephantine head. 'It's a risk, Dan,' he said. 'It will mean new machinery and new methods. What'll happen if we sink all our capital into this new scheme of yours and the whole caboodle goes down the drain?'

'It won't. Have any of my ideas cost you money? You know they haven't.'

'But what little we could produce compared with the big canneries would be just a drop in the ocean. It wouldn't make an 'appence of difference. We can't compete with those big American firms.'

'We wouldn't be competing, Tim, we'd be supplementing. I wouldn't attempt to compete with established canneries, not for the time being, anyway. But I don't see what's to stop us processing our own home-grown food, and doing our own canning. It will mean learning new methods and investing in new machinery as you say, but think what it could lead to. Any little extra towards the food supplies will be helping the war effort. It will be a gamble but a patriotic gamble – think of it in that light, Tim.'

In the depths of Tim's faded eyes a spark of sardonic humour flickered. He knew that with his protégé the margin between patriotism and profit was extremely narrow. But what Dan said made sense. Queues for food were on the increase; women were queueing for hours for a bit of marge or some extra milk. Rationing as yet was not official. There were still many foodstuffs available for those with money or influence, but for others it was a soul destroying trek from shop to shop.

'Don't you see,' said Dan persuasively, sensing a chink in Tim's armour. 'Even if we only produce enough to supply local shops, it's something towards helping the shortage. I'll write to the Frasers and ask them to put feelers out among the local farmers. My idea is to form a sort of co-operative, a partnership between us and the Norfolk farmers. Lincolnshire growers, too, are renowned for their kitchen gardens. We'll share the profits. If we make the carrot tempting enough they'll be sure to nibble.'

Timothy lived long enough to see their new venture flourish. The cans with their brand name Country Fare appeared in the shops throughout East Anglia. Dan was wise enough to keep distribution on a limited scale. When the war was over would be time enough to expand, he said. In the meantime the demand for tinplate went on unabated. It seemed there could never be enough tin to supply the needs of the armed forces.

He remembered his loneliness when the war was over, spending Armistice Day on his own. Timothy hadn't lived to celebrate the peace. Dan kept himself busy during the day, but the evenings seemed endless. The backgammon board remained in place now, never used. He missed old Timothy Thurgood, not as the benefactor he had dreamed of but as the father he had never had. Oddly enough he missed Mrs Prescott too, when her time came in spite of the fact that in all the years they had shared the same roof the only time she had ever smiled at him was on her deathbed. Even then he wasn't sure if it was a smile of valediction or relief at seeing the last of him.

He had rattled around in that gloomy old ivy-clad house. He brought deaf-and-dumb George Gilbert in to share it with him, turning the top floor into a self-contained apartment for George and Mollie, the childhood sweetheart George had married during the war. They had met at the Royal School for the Deaf at Margate, and now they had a son, a lively three-year-old who was not affected by their inability to hear or speak. He prattled away all day long in baby language, at the same time watching with fascinated eyes the way his parents used their hands to communicate. It wouldn't be long, thought Dan, before he'd be just as adept at speaking on his fingers.

He drew the collar of his coat up about his ears. He'd come out without a hat, and though his hair was thick it wasn't thick enough to keep out the cold. With Bass leading the way, he retraced his steps back towards the Hall.

What about inviting George and Mollie and little Joey to Thornmere Hall for Christmas? He'd done very little entertaining this past year. His part of the old house in the factory grounds had now been turned into offices, with a room reserved for him when he stayed overnight. He entertained his business associates at his club.

He could give George and Mollie a real old-fashioned Christmas. The sort of Christmas he used to dream about when at the orphanage. But it was an idea he knew was impractical. Apart from the fact that the Gilberts had relatives who always had them to stay for Christmas, he knew they wouldn't feel comfortable as guests at the Hall. They would think of it as stepping out of their class — they were great ones for keeping the social order. And to be honest with himself, he wouldn't feel comfortable with them either. He had never mastered their language sufficiently to sustain a conversation for long, and their stay could prove an embarrassment for them all.

The one he really wanted, of course, was little Joey. That bright-eyed child with his ready laugh and winning ways had wormed his way into Dan's heart. God, how he wished he had a son, his own flesh and blood. A son with burnished hair and the clear green eyes of his mother, an incredible idea that gave rise to a self-mocking laugh. But thoughts of Joey had served their purpose. A plausible idea began to germinate in his mind.

It was a day that would make even a saint feel gloomy, thought Ruby, feeling so cast down she was near to tears. The sky was pewter coloured, a depressing grey that played havoc with her nerves. Moisture from the trees dripped on her hat and her shoulders and watery slush filled her shoes. She pulled her woollen scarf more tightly around her neck, stopping up the gaps from which the warmth of her body was escaping. It had been madness to leave the warmth of her kitchen for what could be a fruitless journey, but she had promised Mr Harker. She was on her way to the gatehouse to call on Mrs Webster.

Her way of life had been transformed since the coming of Daniel Harker. She had more money, more time to herself, and better living conditions. The only thing that hadn't changed was Reuben's indifference.

She couldn't claim that he ignored her. He would often come to her kitchen for his morning cup of tea, sitting by the newly-installed vitreous enamelled stove, with Bass, if not out with his master, lying contentedly across his feet.

He didn't come to talk – talking wasn't much in Reuben's line, she accepted that. In any case, his company was sufficient. She feasted her eyes on him when he wasn't looking, not that it mattered if he was. She knew that even when he was looking at her, he didn't see her. But even that had ceased to hurt. The mere fact that he was still around gave her hope. He had got used to her, and perhaps in time he would get so used to her that he would suddenly find he couldn't do without her. A hope that he had innocently but cruelly shattered only yesterday.

She thought back to that moment when, quite casually, he had announced that he was thinking of emigrating to Australia. Judging by his tone of voice he could have been saying he was just popping down to the village.

She had stood perfectly still, clutching the sink, willing herself not to do anything foolish like show the rawness of her feelings. She went cold all over.

'Australia?' she repeated stupidly. 'Why Australia?'

Out of the corner of her eye she saw him shrug. He often shrugged when nonplussed. She waited. 'There's a better future for the likes of me out there – better opportunities,' he said slowly.

'But how could you leave – leave all this?' She turned, her face rigid with the effort of preventing it from quivering. 'You can't seriously be thinking of leaving Norfolk. You be Norfolk born and bred.' She swallowed her despair, and her voice relaxed a little. 'What put it in your head to go to Australia?'

She suddenly thought of Arthur Crossley, the land agent

in Sir Roger's time. He had gone to Australia and what had happened to him? Lost and forgotten; swallowed up by that vast and unfamiliar continent. Helpless tears filled her eyes.

'Do you go, you be sorry,' she persisted. 'No job to go to, nowhere to live. What'll become of you?'

'A lot better I hope than if I stay here,' said Reuben morosely. 'I'm sick to death of not having a real job o' work to do. Chauffeuring? What chauffeuring? You know the guv'nor prefers to drives hisself in his own car. I only get the Daimler out once a week, and thass when I take you to Beckton Market for the shopping.'

'I'm sorry if you think tha's beneath you,' said Ruby, colouring up.

'Don't be so touchy, girl, you know I didn't mean that. It's just . . . well, it's just that I've got no pride in me work anymore. I'm nothing but an odd-job man. I spend most of my time looking after that ole boiler what works this so-called central-heating. Central heating! Central swindle, I call it. A tilley lamp would give out more heat that that du.'

It was the longest sentence Ruby had ever heard Reuben utter and he had immediately lapsed back into silence. Central heating! He was glad enough to have the boiler to see to when the days were cold and wet. Yet she understood what really grieved him and sympathised. He had been so proud of his horses in the old days, exercising them, doctoring them when they were ill, and polishing up their harness before taking Lady Massingham out for an airing in the carriage. And for a short time after the war, in his new status as chauffeur, driving Sir Roger and Lady Massingham in the Daimler to Norwich or to visit friends in the district, and even once, to a shoot at Sandringham. It was true. He was nothing but a handyman now.

She could understand his frustration. He wasn't the only one to feel unsettled, he wasn't the only one to get bored. She missed the old times, too. There had been no time for boredom in those days. Always at someone's beck and call – up and down the stairs all day carrying interminable buckets of coal or cans of hot water.

But then there was the other side of the coin. The parties and Christmas festivities. The entertainments in the large drawing room, and the servants' ball. Some of the senior members of staff could remember when the Massinghams had kept a town house in Kensington, and even greater jamborees had been the lot of those who had accompanied the family to London for the season. But the London house had had to be sold to pay off mounting debts long before she joined the staff. She felt herself lucky just to have seen the tail-end of the Massinghams' prosperity.

And now all that was left from the splendour of those pre-war days was just the two of them – she and Reuben – looking after a man who spent most of the week at his factory in London and his weekends shut in his office, answering business letters. What sort of life was that for a man in the prime of life? What was the point of buying a great place like Thornmere Hall if he didn't intend to take a wife? Perhaps he did, perhaps he had someone in mind, or perhaps, like her, the one he wanted was unattainable. Even the rich and successful, she thought, couldn't always get what they wanted.

When Reuben got up to leave he said, 'Thank you for the tea,' and added, as he always did, 'very welcome.'

'You let it get cold.'

'Oo ah, I did. But I drunk it.'

She took a deep breath, she took the plunge. 'Reuben, what colour are my eyes?'

He had really looked at her then, he looked at her as if she had taken leave of her senses. She turned away.

'Well . . . I . . . er . . . um . . . Blue?'

She turned to face him again, hiding her hurt behind a smile. 'No, Reuben, tha's hazel. But then, I don't s'pose you remember the colour of Mrs Webster's eyes, either?'

He looked bewildered. 'What the matter Rube, I've never known you be like this before?'

'Tha's the trouble; you've never known me, not really.' She waited until he had reached the door then called after him. 'What colour was Lottie's eyes?'

'Brown,' he said without hesitation. 'I thought you'd remember that, you two being as thick as thieves.' Then he had left, shutting the door behind him, leaving her in tears.

She hadn't seen him to speak to since. He hadn't come in for his tea that morning. She passed him when she crossed the yard to take the short cut through the park, but he didn't see her, he was too busy cleaning the Daimler at the time. She wondered what he was thinking as he worked the wax into the bodywork, polishing it until it gleamed like glass. Australia no doubt, or happier days before the war? She sighed, and hastened her step.

The familiar smell of herbs and apples and bacon simmering on the hob greeted her as she pushed open the back door into the gatehouse. The rush of warm air made her cheeks tingle.

'That be rafty ole weather today,' she said as she loosened her coat. 'Phew – it's like a furnace in here.'

Mrs Webster sat with knees spread, warming her legs by the fire. It bothered Ruby to see the change in her since she moved to the gatehouse. She always remembered Mrs Webster sailing majestically around her kitchen at

Thornmere Hall encased in corsets as rigid as armour plating. Now, slumped in a chair, she looked as shapeless as one of the gargoyles on the roof of Thornmere Church. Either the corsets had long since worn out or been discarded as being unsuitable for heavy work. She turned on Ruby a pair of faded and weary eyes.

'Like a furnace is it! So it should be considering the amount of coal we use. We burn coal like other people burn paper.'

It was a sore point with Mrs Webster, the free coal allowance to railway workers, thinking of the days in her tied cottage when she was paying out a half-crown a hundred-weight. A half-crown was a lot out of her meagre pension. Now she had all the coal she needed, but a fire kept alight by charity she found gave out little warmth.

'What brings you up here on a day like this?' She made it sound as if her visitor was unwelcome which was not the case. As much as Mrs Webster yearned for company, Ruby was a painful reminder of the days when it was she who ruled the kitchens of Thornmere Hall. Now here she was, little more than an unpaid drudge, looking after two uncommunicative and unsociable men whose only contribution to the meal table was the sound of slurping and chewing as they made inroads into the meals she put before them.

It wasn't that she was ungrateful. If Sidney Foster hadn't made his offer when she was evicted from her cottage it would have meant the workhouse for her or, nearly as bad, falling back on the charity of her relations. That meant going back to London after a gap of forty-odd years. No, she couldn't face it. The gatehouse seemed the only alternative.

When she first arrived at the gatehouse she was appalled at its condition. A slur, she thought, on the memory of Mrs Foster, a houseproud woman. But what else would you expect, she asked herself, from two men who lived more or less like recluses: working, eating, sleeping, and an occasional half-pint at the Ferry Inn? That was their life. And hers now was . . . what? Free board and lodging to be sure, but she was working harder now than in the days when she first went into service.

It was the loneliness that got her down more than anything else. The loneliness and the seclusion and the everlasting wind howling around the chimneys. There was no getting away from the wind. In winter it blew from the north-east, freezing the blood in her veins every time she went down to the privy. In summer it came from the south-west lifting the dust from the fields and depositing it all over her clean washing. Then the trains – she just couldn't get used to the trains. Evil-smelling things, constantly belching out soot and sparks. She'd stand by the window and watch them go by, staring at the passengers and wondering where they were going, and often wishing she could go with them. She was a prisoner in the gatehouse, trapped by poverty.

I can just about bear to live here, she told herself, but I don't want to die here. Dear God, please don't let me die here. For one thing, they'd never get her coffin through that narrow door, it would have to go through the bedroom window. The thought of the ignominy of such a departure kept her going on days when she felt she had nothing left to live for.

Ruby hung her coat on the peg behind the back door. 'How you been then,' she said as she took a seat not too near the kitchen stove. 'You looking kind of poorly.' Actually, Ruby thought Mrs Webster was looking awful. She had lost weight and her cheeks were beginning to hang down like dewlaps.

'I'm only looking my age, gel,' said Mrs Webster

apathetically. She roused herself. 'And now that you're here, you can make yourself useful. Put the kettle on. I'm just about ready for a cup of tea.'

Ruby filled the kettle from the pitcher of drinking water on the dresser. Mrs Webster's tone of voice took her back to her first day at the Hall, just thirteen and away from home for the first time in her life. Intimidated by her grand surroundings and by the vastness of the kitchen, but intimidated more so by the upper servants with their superior airs.

Mrs Webster, though brusque in voice and manner, had sat her at the table and put a plate of cold meat and pickles before her. 'Get that inside you,' she said. 'You're nothing but skin and bones. We'll have to build you up before we get our money's worth out of you.' She was generous with her helpings, she was thoughtful not to work her too hard at first, and when bedtime came she put her in the charge of a dark-eyed girl called Lottie Foster who helped her through those first agonising days of homesickness. She sighed. Hard to believe that now she was sometimes homesick for the past.

Mrs Webster heard the sigh and put her own interpretation on it. 'Things not too good up at the Hall, eh? The gilt beginning to wear off the gingerbread?'

'I wouldn't say that. I certainly won't die of overwork. And the master – he be really nice when you get to know him. But it's different, Cook.' The old familiar term slipped out. 'I keep comparing it with the old days. Tha's not the same. There's something missing, an' I don't know what.'

'Breeding,' said Mrs Webster emphatically. 'Mr Harker is a factory-owner not a gentleman, and he should be back in London running his business, not up here aping his betters.'

'His betters, Mrs Webster? D'you think Sir Joseph any better? He behaved a lot worse than Mr Harker, in my opinion.'

That was an opinion with which Mrs Webster agreed though wild horses wouldn't drag such an admission from her. She didn't know whom she despised the most; Sir Joseph for selling off the estate or Daniel Harker for taking on the mantle of squire but not the responsibilities. With his money he could have afforded to buy the tenants' cottages instead of letting most of them go under the hammer. That's what Ruby meant by differences at the Hall. Money talked, but with an uncaring accent.

They drank their tea in silence. Some coals shifted in the grate shooting sparks out onto the hearth-rug, the hooked rug that Ruby recognised as one that Lottie's mother had made from bits of cloth cut out from discarded suits and overcoats. Nothing was wasted in that thrifty household.

Mrs Webster eased herself into a more comfortable position. 'What's this rumour going around about Reuben going off to Australia? Has he said anything to you about it?'

Ruby merely nodded. Every time she thought of Australia she curdled inwardly. Mrs Webster gave a snort of exasperation. 'What's the matter with the fellow? He's got a cushy job and good money too by all accounts, and he must know how you feel about him after all this time. You're not playing your cards right, Ruby. For one thing you could smarten yourself up a bit. Get your hair cut and buy yourself some new clothes. That old coat doesn't owe you anything. You've had it so long it could find its way up the lane without you inside it.'

'I could paint my face and have my hair marcel waved and wear high heels and Reuben still wouldn't notice,' answered Ruby bleakly.

Mrs Webster gave her a sharp look. 'Don't tell me he's still hankering after Lottie. I thought that fire died down years ago.'

'I wouldn't know. He never tells me anything. Do he like to talk about her though. The only time there's any talkin' done is when we mardle about the old days, and tha's Lottie we always seem to talk about.'

Lottie. Strange how even the sound of her name could still rouse long-dead emotions. Mrs Webster's thoughts went back to the recent past soon after she moved to the gatehouse. It was a gloomy Saturday morning, something like today but not so cold, and both the men were staying indoors because of heavy colds. They sat either side of the fireplace, hacking and coughing and spitting phlegm into the fire. Mrs Webster at the table was rolling out the suet crust for the beefsteak pudding she was making for dinner.

The post was delivered, an unusual event in that friendless house, and the men, roused from their lethargy, looked round to see who the letter was for. For neither of them. They resumed their contemplation of the fire.

It was a letter from her niece, Agnes Sharp, who worked with Lottie in a restaurant in Soho. Why had Aggie decided to write all of a sudden? With difficulty Mrs Webster made out the ill-spelt and spidery writing. It was an offer of a job. The restaurant was expanding and Lottie was engaging extra staff. It would mean working under a chef, but he was an easy man to get on with and there was an opening for a good all-round cook like herself. She'd have plenty of help, and her own bed-sitting room, and hours to please herself.

For one fleeting moment Martha Webster was tempted. Then she remembered what the restaurant had been before the war. Nothing more or less than a knocking shop. It was a fashionable restaurant now, but its reputation lingered on, and not all its modern trappings of respectability could banish the memory of that.

No, it was out of the question, she couldn't bring herself to work in a place tainted by its past. In any case, how could she go back to London at her age; she wouldn't fit in. She had lived in Norfolk for so long that her roots had gone down deep, and like they said, you can't transplant old trees. All the same, it wouldn't hurt those two miseries by the fire to know about this offer, to know that there was an alternative to living at the gatehouse.

'That was a letter from my niece, Aggie Sharp,' she said, throwing the remark casually over her shoulder. 'Perhaps you remember her, Mr Foster? She came and stayed up at the Hall a couple of times before the war. She got very pally with your daughter, Lottie. By all accounts they've done very well for themselves. The restaurant is a success and now Lottie is branching out . . .'

She became aware of a sudden cessation of noise, a stillness that seemed to hang suspended like a chilly cloud. It was broken when Sidney Foster pushed back his chair with a sound that jarred on her nerves. She watched as he went to the door and flung it wide, letting in a gust of wind that whipped up the loose flour from the table-top, and sucked a fall of soot from the chimney.

'Out you get,' he said. She stared at him in disbelief. His eyes, she thought, looked mad. Ted sat tight-lipped and white-faced, avoiding her gaze. Her face turned a mottled red.

'Am I being turned out?' Her cheeks shook with anger.

Mr Foster cleared his throat and spat in the direction of the garden. 'Anyone who mentions that harlot's name in my house is shown the door. You're not the first and I don't suppose you'll be the last.'

'Pa,' cried Ted, panicking. 'Isn't it about time we forgot all that . . .'

'You shut up. And you,' Sid Foster gestured at her again, 'out.'

Mrs Webster drew herself up. She hadn't worked for Lady Massingham for all those years without some of that lady's imperious manner rubbing off on her.

'Right, I'll go this minute, and I'll take this pudding with me, and the fruit cake I made for tea tomorrow, and the jars of chutney I made last week. There's some ironing I haven't finished in the cupboard under the stairs, and socks waiting to be darned in the sewing-basket. There's also your dirty bed-linen soaking in the zinc bath in your bedroom. That needs rinsing out and hanging out to dry. There's a nice drying wind, shouldn't take more'n an hour or two. It'll be ready for mangling by tea time.'

'Father,' came Ted's frantic bellow. 'Think of the beefsteak pudden. When did we last have a homemade beefsteak pudden? Don't go an' spoil things for us now!'

Another spark flew out on to the hearth-rug, jerking Mrs Webster back to the present. Automatically she put her foot on it, extinguishing the faint smell of burning dust. 'Is there another cup of tea in the pot, Ruby? All this talking has made me thirsty.'

There hadn't been much talking for the past few minutes, thought Ruby, wondering whether Mrs Webster had dozed off with her eyes open, or was just sitting thinking. The poor woman looked so tired. It was all wrong that she had to work so hard at her age. It seemed so unfair – but then life was unfair. She thought of Reuben going off to Australia. Dear God, it isn't much to ask for. Just for him to notice me, I won't mind if he never loves me. Just don't let him go to Australia, please.

'Mind what you're doing, gel,' said Mrs Webster. 'You're slopping tea in the saucer.'

Ruby fidgeted, taking surreptitious glances at the clock. It was nearly time for her to go and she still hadn't got round to the purpose of her visit. And while she hesitated, wondering how to introduce the subject, Mrs Webster made it easy for her.

'And has his lordship made any plans for Christmas? A servants' ball perhaps, just for you and Reuben?'

Ruby, like Reuben, was immune to sarcasm. Her face brightened. 'Funny you should mention Christmas 'cos tha's what I really come to yours about. To ask if you would like to come and give me a hand on Boxing Day.'

Mrs Webster's face registered mild interest. 'What's fixed up for Boxing Day that you need my help? One of his lordship's dinner parties?'

'No. He wants to give a party for the village children. He's going to dress up as Father Christmas an' give out presents from the tree. An' there's going to be a magic lantern show, an' a cold table . . .'

'For the *children*?'

'No, for their mums and dads when they come to fetch them.'

Mrs Webster snorted. 'I'm sure you can cope with that standing on your head. You don't have to make any fancy dishes for the villagers, just give them what you enjoy eating yourself. Half of them'll be there out of curiosity anyway, and the other half for the booze. Tell him to get in several kegs of ale, that'll make him popular. That's what it's all about, isn't it? Buying popularity.'

'To be fair to Mr Harker I think he's doin' it to please the children. He's fond of children. Don't scoff, Mrs Webster, he is. And it isn't only to help me on Boxing Day either.

He said to tell you your old job is awaitin' for you anytime you'd like to come back to work for him.' Up till then Ruby had kept to the formalities, ignoring Mrs Webster's unkind digs, now she was prepared to plead for herself.

'Oh please, Mrs Webster, don't say no without thinking it over. You don't know what a difference it'll make to me, having you back at the Hall. Tha'uld be like old times.'

'You can't put back the clock, Ruby, and I can't take ten years off my age. And I certainly can't start cooking for house parties again at my time of life.'

'There b'aint any house parties anymore. He did have one or two to begin with, but they kinda fizzled out. Perhaps it was my cooking – perhaps it wasn't worth their while coming all this way for.' Ruby hesitated, feeling that she had got onto the wrong tack. She saw suspicion dawning on Mrs Webster's sagging face.

'Are you thinking of leaving? Have you any foolish notion in your head about following Reuben to Australia?'

Ruby reddened and tossed her head. 'And let Reuben think I was chasin' after him! I got me pride.' She was tired of this cat and mouse game of question and answer. She came to the point. 'If you must know, the master is really concerned about you – he thinks you're having it too hard living here. It's on his conscience, too, being the cause of you losing your cottage, and he feels he ought to make amends.' She saw by Mrs Webster's expression that this was the wrong approach, but she blundered on, hoping to find the right way. 'An' he seen some of your old menus and tha's made him realise what he's bin missin' all this time. He would really appreciate it if you came and cooked for him.'

But that didn't work either. Mrs Webster glowered.

'So, he wants to ease his conscience, does he? He thinks he can buy me the way he's been buying everybody else in the village. A cricket field, a village hall, and now a party for the children. And I'm to have my old job back and bygones will be bygones. Well, miss, you can go back and tell your master that he won't find any price tag on me, and you can also tell him that I wouldn't demean myself by working for some jumped-up, get-rich-quick, war-profiteer. Not after working for the *real* gentry.'

Despondently Ruby got to her feet. 'You're an obstinate an' ungrateful ole woman and I don't know why I bother with you,' she said.

'Neither do I,' said Mrs Webster drily.

Ruby's face puckered; she struggled against tears. 'I bother because I care,' she said. 'Oh, Mrs Webster, I didn't mean what I said, you know that. It's only that I'm so disappointed. I did bank on you comin' back to the Hall.'

'You're a good girl, Ruby, and I'm sorry to disappoint you, but it's out of the question.' Mrs Webster stared moodily into the fire. 'I can't desert Sid Foster. He was the only one in the village to offer me a home when I was turned out of my cottage.'

'Only 'cos he wanted a housekeeper on the cheap. Please, please, Mrs Webster don't set your mind agen it.'

'It's no good, Ruby.'

Yet after Ruby had gone, Mrs Webster moved restlessly about the kitchen, tidying drawers that were already tidy, clearing cupboards that didn't need clearing. The thought of her old job being hers for the asking plagued her with its possibilities. That large and comfortable old room overlooking the kitchen garden. And that kitchen – that enormous kitchen, modernised out of all recognition if she could believe all Ruby said about it. She'd love to see it just one more time. She couldn't put back the clock, but perhaps she could slow it down a little . . . it was worth thinking over.

Ted came in blue with cold and made straight for the fire. He had been out all afternoon helping in the beet fields, making a little bit of cash on the side. If the old girl minded being left in charge of the gates for an hour or two, she never said. She didn't have much to say for herself, anyway. But could she cook! They lived like lords, these days.

He sat down by the table and began to massage his bad leg. On a day like this when the cold got at his old war wound, he remembered how he had pleaded with the doctors not to amputate. He didn't want to go around for the rest of his life with a wooden stump like the old tramp who used to pass through the village when he was a lad. He and the other village boys would follow in his wake, mocking, 'Poor ole Peggy Wooden-leg. He can't work so he has to beg. Poor ole Peggy Wooden-leg . . .'

He felt that his sins had found him out when he saw his shin bone sticking out through his flesh, out there in no-man's-land, and he had cried like a child at the thought of becoming another Peggy Wooden-leg. Now he sometimes wished he had, for at times like this the pain was unbearable. But it was also at times like this that he blessed the day his father asked the Webster woman to come and live with them. Now it was a pleasure, after a cold day working in the fields, to come home to a warm and tidy kitchen, with something savoury simmering on the hob.

'Smells good,' he said, jerking his head in the direction of the stove.

'Boiled ham and pease pudding.' Mrs Webster could be just as economical with her words.

To her surprise a smile spread across Ted's unshaven face, for a smile in that house was something of a rarity. And more than that, a look of relish in his eyes that went straight to her heart.

'I haven't had pease pudden since my mother died,' he said.

Could she leave him to go back to those scratch meals of cold boiled bacon and mashed swedes, fish and chips, or shop pies? Of course she couldn't ... it wouldn't be human.

The Christmas post was arriving later every day, being delivered in a basket on wheels pushed by two temporary postmen. Among the bundle of letters left at Rodings that morning was one addressed to Helena from Paul. She slipped it out before her mother noticed and took it away to savour in private.

Paul wrote:

Dearest Helena,

It is six weeks now since we were together, six days since you last phoned me, six minutes since I received your last letter. When am I going to see you again? I'm tired of asking you. I will come to Thornmere and take you by force if you don't agree to see me soon.

I am not joking, Helena, I sicken for you. My work has gone to pot and I lie all day on my back in bed – in the bed where we made love – cherishing every moment of the memory. I smoke cigarette after cigarette wallowing in self-pity, and if I didn't know better I could make myself believe that you wanted nothing more to do with me. But those three wanton days we spent together assure me otherwise. We are infected you and I . . . infected with each other. Sentimentalists would call it love, but I call it need. Don't think you can ever escape me now – you're in my blood. And I beg of you, don't make me have to come to Thornmere to fetch you for I fear that that will alienate you from your mother, and I have enough on my conscience without adding another family alienation to it. You mentioned something about getting your mother a companion to take your place. Have you thought any more about it? I keep asking, but you never answer. Darling, have a heart, I need you so.

Then written as an afterthought, dashed off in haste, and barely legible:

To hell with need it's love I'm talking about – naked love. Naked literally, I mean. I want the feel of your warm, sweet flesh against mine, and if you don't do something about it soon, I'll do away with myself.

She smiled. His exaggerated and impassioned words brought him sharply into focus. She could hear his voice – pleading – begging – demanding, but this was the first time he had threatened. She didn't fear him doing away with himself but she did dread him appearing suddenly and giving her an ultimatum.

The night in November when she had returned with him to his studio flat in Pimlico had stretched to two more, leaving poor Midge to deal with her mother's frantic telegrams. At the time she had not worried. Thornmere was a long way away her mother could not get at her, didn't know where she was even. She had made her covenant with Paul and nothing could ever part them.

'You are flesh of my flesh,' he said, 'and what God has put together no man can put asunder . . . particularly not your mother. What did Midge tell her?'

'That I had caught a chill and the doctor advised that I stay in bed.'

'Sensible chap, and I shall see that you carry out his orders.'

And how willingly she had concurred, she thought, looking back on those three stolen days. There had been no embarrassment and no restraint, that first occasion they made love—just a fear on her part that her inexperience would mar his enjoyment. Paul had been gentle and patient with her, until her sensuality aroused, he coaxed her into ready compliance. When the climax came, leaving her breathless, amazed, and delighted, she cried out spontaneously. 'I wasn't expecting that — nobody ever told me about that', which brought such an explosion of laughter from him that she hurriedly put her hand over his mouth. 'Shush, the other tenants will hear.'

'Lucky them.' He drew her close, bent over to place a kiss on her breast, then her lips. 'Lucky me, too, so what about giving them an encore?'

'That's not very romantic.'

'When you get to know me better, my love, you'll learn that nobody can ever accuse me of being romantic.'

Later, passion giving way to a deep and satisfying peace, Helena lay cossetted in the crook of his arm. I shall remember this day for the rest of my life, she thought. If all else is taken from me I shall have the memory of this hour. Her hand resting on Paul's chest felt the steady beating of his heart. She stretched out her arm to embrace the whole of his body and, unexpectedly, her hand came into contact with the stump where his left arm should have been. There was a momentary recoil which she quickly mastered, then she leant over and tenderly pressed her lips against the scarred tissue, for how could she now, after such commitment, reject any part of his body?

She paid dearly for her days and nights of pleasure when she returned to the Queen Anne house at Thornmere. Her mother did not believe Midge's story of a sudden feverish cold or the doctor's advice to stay in bed. She herself had taken to her bed, *her* doctor summoned, and Helena found herself once more in the role of dutiful daughter and prisoner of her conscience.

Thank God for Christmas, she thought. Her mother's childlike delight in Christmas brought her release from bondage. She was detailed to help with the Christmas preparations and sent off to do the Christmas shopping. It was during her trips to Norwich that she made her long and life-saving calls to Paul.

She knew she couldn't keep him waiting much longer, neither did she wish to. She must invent a reason for going up to London again soon. Hats for Midge was no longer a valid excuse because now they were dispatched by carrier. Perhaps she could drop a hint about something for her mother she had seen in a London store. Her mother would balance her self-gratification against suspicion of Helena's deviousness, and Helena was pretty sure that self-gratification would win.

Just one day with Paul. One day in the studio flat in Pimlico, a lifeline to look forward to, but would it be enough for him? In his way, Paul could be just as demanding as her mother. She knew he would only be appeased when she did something definite about engaging a companion. After Christmas, she thought, putting off something she dreaded and longed for with equal passion. I can't do anything about it now, but after Christmas.

Her mother's voice came fluting up the staircase. 'Helena, de-ah. Can you come here a moment?' Something in the post had obviously pleased her. Her voice was as silky as the purring of a cat.

It was, Helena discovered, an invitation to Christmas luncheon from General and Mrs Alastair Carter-Howard.

'You must remember the General, Helena. Your father was always speaking of him, they were at Marlborough together. We dined with the Carter-Howards just after you came out. I was so proud of you on that occasion.'

'You were, Mother?' Helena racked her brains. She dimly remembered the dinner party as exceedingly boring, the other guests being the same generation as her parents. She had been lectured on the evils of women's suffrage by her partner on the right and completely ignored on her left. So what had she done, or more likely said, that could have given such pleasure to her mother?

With an expression of self-satisfaction Mrs Roseberry held out the engraved invitation card for Helena's inspection. 'Yes, I remember how anxious I felt when you helped yourself to a banana, but I worried needlessly. You did know the correct way to eat it. I was so very proud of you.'

Helena stared at her mother in disbelief. The merit cards for good work at school; the time she won the accolade for the most popular girl of the year; her prize for needlework. All met with benign approval when presented to her mother. But pride! No, that had been reserved for the Carter-Howards' dinner party.

'You were proud of me because I knew how to eat a banana correctly!'

'Of course, my dear, it was such a relief. I knew I could take you anywhere. Helena, where are you going?'

'I won't be a moment, Mother. I have an important phone call to make.'

She got through to *The Lady* without any trouble. 'Is that the classified ads. department?'

'It is.'

'I want to insert an advertisement for a lady's companion

. . . immediately if possible. Am I in time for next week's issue?'

'That's the Christmas number, madam. Might it not be wiser to wait until after Christmas? The advertisement could be overlooked during the festivities.'

'I'll risk it, it's very urgent.'

'Very well. Name please . . .'

SIX | 1926

That part of the journey from Stratford to Liverpool Street, Helena always found depressing. The houses were tall and grim with narrow sooty gardens that backed on to the railway embankment, and it smote her conscience to think that some people were obliged to live out their lives in such inhuman rookeries. She wondered where the children played. Not in the barren yards, depositories for bits of broken machinery, bikes, or old bedsteads, for she rarely saw children there. Where then? In local parks or in the streets? There was poverty in the country, too, even in Thornmere, but at least clean air was plentiful, and even if most of the countryside was privately owned, the quiet lanes and leafy roads were anybody's property.

Today, though, nothing could repress her spirits for long. She was free. She had fought her last battle with her mother and had retreated, not without wounds, to pack her bag and leave Rodings if not for ever – though she could not convince her mother otherwise – at least for the time being. The hardest part had been to confess that she was going to live with a married man, a very effective way of stopping further discussion. Her mother had turned her back and ignored any further entreaties.

She had shocked her mother, she had expected that. What she had not foreseen was that she would also shock herself. Hearing the words spoken out loud brought home to her as nothing else had done exactly what she was contemplating. Would it be possible to flaunt convention, to disregard the mores of her upbringing? Could she take such a step? Yes, she could. Her love for Paul was stronger than her sense of duty to her mother; stronger than the fear of being ostracised. Her doubts about the morality of her decision were short-lived, but her sense of guilt took longer to come to terms with.

'You just go, dear, and stop worrying about your mother,' Mrs Taylor urged. 'If you give in to her now you'll never leave home and finish up like a lot of other unmarried daughters, with no life of your own, and always at your mother's beck and call. Forgive my straight speaking, Miss Helena, but I feel strongly on the subject.'

'If you can just stay overnight, Mrs Taylor, I'm hoping the new companion will start tomorrow.'

'I'll stay as long as necessary. And don't go worrying about your mother. She may look frail but she's very tough. Nothing is going to happen to her. Take no notice of what she said, that if you left her it would kill her. Selfish people don't die young.'

'She's not young, Mrs Taylor. She's in her seventies.'

'She'll live to be a hundred. Mark my words.'

The call from Amy Cousins had come earlier that day. Helena was coming down the stairs when the phone shrilled, a sound that usually made her heart leap. But not today, because she knew it was unlikely to be Paul.

After seven years, the occupation of the Rhineland was

over. British troops were pulling out at the end of January. 'I was in at the beginning – now I want to be in at the end,' Paul wrote her. 'I'm planning to go over to Germany on Christmas Eve. If there was any chance of seeing you during the Christmas holiday I wouldn't give it a second thought. But as it is, I'd rather spend Christmas in Cologne with strangers than in London on my own.'

She lifted the receiver, announced her number and heard a girlish, rather breathless voice. 'Is that Thornmere 38?'

'Yes. Who's that speaking?' The voice gave Helena the impression of someone with fluffy fair hair and huge doll-like blue eyes. She racked her memory for someone of that description among her acquaintances.

'It's about the advertisement in the Christmas edition of *The Lady* – the one about a companion for an elderly lady. I have got the right number, haven't I? There was no name or address. I would have phoned before this, but I have only just seen the advertisement. Is the job, situation, still available?'

The speaker made no effort to hide her eagerness and Helena's heart did now indeed skip a beat. That copy of *The Lady* was three weeks old and in all that time she had not received a single enquiry. She had given up hope.

'Where are you speaking from?' she asked.

'A place called Raneleigh in Essex . . . from the station.'

'Oh dear, that is rather a long way from Norfolk and I would rather like to discuss this with you personally. Is there any chance of you coming up here?'

The voice was muted. 'I'm afraid not.'

'Well, let's see what we can do over the phone. Have you had any experience as a companion?'

'No, but I've had some experience in nursing.'

Helena felt a tremendous sense of relief. This girl was

young judging by her voice and she would have preferred someone more mature, but then she said she was a nurse and that made all the difference. From the small room at the front of the house where her mother liked to sit she could hear the sound of movement. Her mother coming to investigate as she normally did if she heard someone on the phone.

'Are you free to start straight away?' she asked hurriedly.

'I'm free – absolutely free.' Free – absolutely free, echoed Helena enviously, the words evoking an image of a soaring lark. The operator's voice intruded. 'I'm sorry, caller, but your time is up. Do you wish to extend this call? If so, please will you insert . . .'

Helena said, 'Could you reverse the charges, operator? Thornmere 38, thank you.' The line was cleared. 'Hullo, hullo – I thought we had got cut off and you have yet to tell me your name.'

'Amy Cousins.'

'And I'm Helena Roseberry.' The door to her mother's sitting room was opening slowly. Helena lowered her voice. 'I'm looking for a companion for my mother. By the way, how old are you? You sound very young?'

Pause. 'I'm twenty-four.'

'Oh dear, that is rather young for a companion, but then you have had nursing experience. Not that my mother will need nursing,' she added, quickly. 'She's quite active, really. Well, it all seems very satisfactory but for my mother's sake I must see you personally before making a decision. I've just had a thought. I could get to London by this afternoon. I have a friend who lives near Cumberland Gardens, we could meet there. Are you familiar with the West End?'

'I'm afraid I don't know London at all. I've lived all my life in Kent – before I came to Raneleigh I mean.' There was another pause, then a sudden rush of words. 'Miss Roseberry, I feel ever so embarrassed having to admit this, but . . . but I've only got enough money to get me to Fenchurch Street. Is there any chance of you meeting me there? There's a nice refreshment-room where we could talk. I'm sure once you saw me, I've had a lot of experience of looking after old ladies – well, one old lady in particular. Please, please, Miss Roseberry, give me a chance. You won't regret it.'

But by saying that she immediately raised doubts in Helena's mind. There was an urgency, a trace of desperation in the girl's voice that put her on her guard. A lack of restraint was a sign of an unstable personality, her mother was fond of saying. Yet . . . the girl's eagerness to satisfy was only surpassed by her own eagerness to be satisfied. Give me a chance, the girl had pleaded. This was her chance, too. If she passed it up, would there be another?

'I still think my idea of meeting at my friend's place is a better option,' she said. 'But I'll telephone her and ask her to meet you off the train if that's what you want. Fenchurch Street station, you said? Tell me, Miss Cousins, how shall I describe you?'

'I'm just ordinary-looking really. I'm about five feet four and I've got brown hair and brown eyes, and I'm wearing a navy coat and a fluffy red hat.'

The blue-eyed doll vanished. In her place stood a trim-looking young woman in a nanny's uniform, though the fluffy red hat seemed somewhat out of place. 'What time does your train get to Fenchurch Street?'

'There's one due to leave here in five minutes and the journey takes about an hour.'

'Well, goodbye for now. I'm looking forward to making your acquaintance.'

Helena replaced the receiver wondering what sort of

image her voice had suggested to Miss Cousins. Someone prim, precise, and in complete control of her feelings, no doubt. Oh, if it were only so. She sighed and turned to see her mother's questioning gaze upon her.

'Mother,' she said. 'There is much to be discussed between us. Shall we return to your sitting room?'

They were running into Liverpool Street station, crossing over a network of railway lines, entering a dark and smoky tunnel. The train pulled in at a platform with a rattle of wheels, a hiss of steam, and a juddering of carriages. Almost immediately she felt a sense of being released from her ties. That the interview with the unknown Amy Cousins might not prove fruitful was something she did not even consider.

Still feeling as if she was walking in someone else's shoes, someone without responsibilities or family ties, someone with a mind of her own, she light-heartedly followed the elderly porter carrying her case, and as he helped her into a waiting taxi, tipped him generously as if she wanted him too to share in her good fortune.

Her state of euphoria lasted until she reached Hanover Mansions, until she walked into the hushed and warmly-scented foyer and there found Midge waiting for her. From the stormy expression on Midge's face, she knew that something had gone disastrously wrong.

'A word with you before we go upstairs,' Midge said. She took Helena's arm and guided her towards the hall porter's lodge. 'We can talk in private here. I bribed Briggs for the use of his room for ten minutes, and the last I saw of him he was making a beeline for the nearest bookie's runner. Helena, have you any idea what you have let yourself in for? Let *me* in for, come to that. Upstairs, in sole occupancy of my apartment, is the most incredibly neurotic and hysterical female I've ever come across. Helena, have you taken leave of your senses?'

Helena rallied her sinking spirits. 'You didn't take this tone with me on the phone,' she said. 'You were only too ready to collude with me then. Anything to do the Hon. Mrs one in the eye was, if I remember rightly, the expression you used. What has happened to make you change your mind?'

'Miss Amy Cousins has happened that's what. I arrived at Fenchurch Street station in good time. I asked the taxi driver to wait for me.' Here, as she quite often did, Midge went off on a tangent. 'You and your Norland nanny,' she snorted. 'If it hadn't been for the ghastly headgear, I wouldn't have given her a second glance. Yes, she was certainly wearing a navy-blue coat, a shabby velour miles too big for her. She stared at me like a hypnotised rabbit when I approached her.'

Glancing at Midge's wrap-round coat of purple tweed with its flamboyant collar of white fox fur, Helena didn't doubt it. Such a symbol of affluence was enough to transfix any lesser mortal.

'What did you say to her?'

'Very little except to ask if she were indeed Amy Cousins. Then I bundled her into the taxi and brought her here. And she's waiting for you in the sitting room. Hardly daring to breathe I shouldn't wonder.'

'You could have said something to put her at her ease.'

'My dear Helena, it was I who needed putting at my ease. What was I going to do with this twitchy, nervous female until you came? She looked any minute as if she were going to erupt into tears. Never indulging in tears myself, I don't know how to cope with women who do. I cursed you in my heart, Helena Roseberry. I cursed you to kingdom come.'

'She sounded quite confident over the phone. And she can't be all that unsuitable. After all, she's had nursing experience.'

'Stop right there. Yes, she's had nursing experience, all of three weeks. She ran away from her aunt and went to work at a sanatorium for consumptives near Southend, and hated every minute of it. The first opportunity she got she bolted – and your advertisement was the opportunity she was looking for.'

'Midge, you're joking!'

'Ask her yourself.'

The first thing Helena noticed about the girl was the slenderness of her wrists and ankles. She had narrow feet with high insteps which could not be quite disguised by her cheap shoes. That was a point in her favour, thought Helena vaguely. Her mother put great store on neat feet. It was a sign of good breeding, Mrs Roseberry was fond of saying, not unaware that her own feet were exceedingly neat.

'I'm Helena Roseberry,' she said, walking forward with hand extended.

The girl rose immediately. She had been sitting on one of Midge's rose-coloured damask chairs, crouching over the red hot wires of an electric fire. She was still wearing the navy velour which she clutched to her thin form as if she were cold. Her hair was the colour that Cecilia Roseberry referred to as housemaid's brown, and her deep-set light brown eyes were almost hidden beneath swollen lids.

How deceptive is the human voice, thought Helena wryly, remembering the doll-like figure and smart Norland nanny she had envisaged in quick succession. Then, to be fair, she had coerced with her own self-deception.

'Sit down,' she said kindly, for she saw that the other was trembling like a nervous kitten. Helena felt highly nervous herself. In spite of Midge's warning, in spite of the feeling that she had been deceived, her heart went out to this unhappy-looking girl. Surely, she thought, something could be rescued from their joint disappointment. She recalled the girl's eager, breathless voice on the telephone. Her own sense of freedom when she had stepped out of the train at Liverpool Street station. They had a common purpose, she and this unknown Amy Cousins. Would it be impossible to work out something between them? Anything was better than giving up without a fight. Forget the girl's history, dismiss Midge's biased opinion, the interview starts now.

A sudden rattle on the window panes made them both start. It was hail drumming noisily on the glass. The overcast skies had ended the afternoon before its time. Helena crossed the room, drew the curtains and switched on the lights, an act which immediately dispelled the gloom and bathed the room in a rosy pink glow. Amy Cousins, in this flattering light, looked less insubstantial.

'Mrs Harding has already told me something about you – what you told her that is.' Helena seated herself on another of Midge's pink damask chairs. 'I gather that you telephoned me on a sudden impulse. I also acted impulsively when I inserted that advertisement. What I am trying to say,' she added with an encouraging smile, 'is that if you have second thoughts, please say so. I shall quite understand.'

The girl gave her a wary, sideways look. 'Have *you* had second thoughts, now that you've met me?' she said.

Helena hesitated. 'No. But I would like to know more about you. For instance, could I rely on you? You see, my mother isn't happy about this arrangement at all. I shall have to sell you to her, if you get my meaning. And I couldn't do that with any confidence if I thought that you might take it in your head to leave again rather suddenly.'

'Running away, you mean. You're thinking of me running away from the sanatorium?'

'And running away from your aunt, too, I understand.'

'No. It wasn't quite like that.' The girl turned her head and Helena saw in the diffused light the glint of tears on her cheeks. 'I could have given your friend the wrong impression,' she said. 'I rather lost control of myself. It – it was the whisky, I think. I've never touched alcohol before, but I was so cold Mrs Harding suggested I had some to warm me up. Aunt Flora was a strict teetotaller, and she made me join the White Ribboners when I was six.'

'White Ribboners?' said Helena, mystified.

'A children's temperance league. In order to join I had to sign the pledge.'

Midge, in the kitchen, drawing anxiously on her cigarette, heard an unexpected peal of laughter. This calls for a celebration, she thought, reaching for the whisky bottle.

'I didn't know I was illegitimate until I was about ten.' To Helena's relief Amy had discarded the heavy velour and was now sitting more at ease in her chair. 'I knew my mother died having me and that grandfather died shortly afterwards. Aunt Flora and my mother had looked after him since their mother died. They lived in Gravesend then, but after grandfather died, Aunt Flora sold the house and moved to Sunsfield, that's a little town in the Medway valley. As soon as I was old enough I began to ask questions, but I soon learnt not to mention my father, and when I kept pestering her about my mother, all Aunt Flora would say was that I had been the death of her. I grew up thinking I was a kind of murderer. I was laden with guilt thinking I had killed my mother until Dr Hamilton talked some sense into me.'

'Dr Hamilton?'

'Our doctor, he's the best friend I've got.'

She could have said her only friend, because Aunt Flora did not encourage friendships. They lived a lonely and frugal life in the small Victorian villa in Chancel Terrace. The two of them and a succession of lodgers. Dr Hamilton came breezing in like a breath of fresh air, and he breezed in often, for until she was in her early teens Amy suffered from periodic attacks of asthma. It wasn't until Dr Hamilton convinced her that she wasn't responsible for her mother's death that the attacks stopped.

She discovered, too, that being illegitimate would leave its mark on her for the rest of her life, or until she got married which was her ultimate goal. For on the birth certificates of illegitimate offspring the space where the father's signature should have been was left blank. She had discovered that disturbing fact from a book she had borrowed from a circulating library. Ever since she was able to read she had taken refuge in a world of fantasy, living the life of the heroines in the books she devoured so avidly. She lived in perpetual hope of finding someone to love and to love her in return. At school she had crushes on older girls and then on mistresses, and since leaving school on a series of silver screen heroes. But they were all, she knew, just rehearsals for the real thing. One day she would meet her one true love and live happily ever after.

Helena, watching expressions of despair, hope and wistfulness flicker like shadows across the other's face, knew she had lost the girl's attention. Amy's gaze was fixed vacantly into space, her eyes glazed over with the faraway look of someone seeing inward images. Having something of a wandering mind herself, especially when her mother was speaking, Helena felt some empathy with the girl. She gave a discreet cough and instantly Amy was all attention.

'I was saying, was she unkind to you, your aunt?'

Amy coloured. 'Oh no, not unkind. Strict, though. She wouldn't let me out of her sight, especially when I got older. In case I went the same way as my mother, she said. She treated me like a child, even after I left school. I wanted to go on to a commercial college and take a secretarial course but she didn't want me to go out to work. She wanted me to stay at home and help in the house. It was just to keep an eye on me, really, but she was fair. She paid me a small allowance.'

It was while she was dusting her aunt's bedroom one day that she discovered the photo of her mother. Not a studio photograph, but one taken out of doors with a box camera. She had dusted it for many years unknowingly, for it was hidden in a frame behind another photograph, that of her grandparents, Emily and William Cousins. Her grandmother was an angular seated figure encased in a stiff black gown, relieved from complete unadornment by a cameo brooch pinned at the throat. Her husband, a big man, stood upright by her side, his top hat held in the crook of one arm. They looked a fearsome pair and Amy was relieved to think they had both died before she was born, for it could have proved more difficult to live with them than with Aunt Flora.

For the first time she noticed that the photograph was not lying flat in its frame. It bulged a little, and the clips that held the glass to the backing were under strain. It could be that something was hidden under the photograph or been placed there to keep it safe. Curiosity got the better of her and she nearly split her fingernail prising the frame apart.

She had imagined a letter from her mother, perhaps written on her death bed; or a diary; but what Amy uncovered was another photograph. She slipped it out of its hiding-place and held it to the light, and as she looked long and fervently at it, tears thickened in her throat. It didn't take a passing resemblance to Aunt Flora to tell her that this handsome, smiling woman was her mother. She knew it instinctively.

She was seated posed on a low bough of a spreading tree, her feet a few inches off the ground. She was wearing a frilly blouse that tapered into a tiny waist of that period, and a dark voluminous skirt lifted a little at one side, purposely Amy felt, to reveal a few inches of slender ankle. What caught Amy's eye more than the winning smile, the loving look with which the sitter faced the photographer, was the large cameo brooch pinned to the frill at her neck. Proof, if proof were needed, that this indeed was her mother.

She turned the photo over and on the back, written in a bold and masculine hand, she read, 'Flossie. Greenwich Park. 1904.' Flossie? Short perhaps for Florence. Flora and Flossie – twins, but not identical. One pretty and one plain. One sour and one sweet. She turned the photograph face-side up again, and because her mother looked squarely into the camera, it now appeared as if her loving smile was directed straight at her daughter. Amy held the photo to her lips and kissed it and it was then that it was snatched away from her.

Amy had no idea that Aunt Flora had come into the room. She willed herself to turn and face her. 'Why did you hide my mother's photograph from me?' she said.

'Don't flatter yourself. If I wanted to hide anything from you I know of a much safer place. I had my reasons for not wanting it on show.'

'You're ashamed of my mother.'

'I'm ashamed of the way she behaved.'

Tears pricked Amy's eyelids. Indignation on her mother's behalf made her bold. 'At least she knew what it was to be loved,' she said recklessly. 'You've never been loved in your life . . . you're just jealous of her.'

Amy thought she was about to be struck. Her aunt raised her hand, but it was only to get a firmer grip on the photo, and before Amy could stop her she had ripped it into tiny pieces.

Amy tried to get a hold on the pieces of pasteboard but without success. 'I hate you,' she said sobbing. 'I hate you . . . I hope you rot in hell.'

Aunt Flora grinned back at her out of the ghastly mask that was her face. 'So, you know how it feels to hate,' she said. 'Now you know how I felt about your father.'

Helena tapped her on the knee. 'Miss Cousins, don't you think Mrs Harding has been a captive in her kitchen long enough? If you keep losing yourself in your thoughts like this, we'll never bring this interview to an end. My mother, you know, needs a great deal of attention. Undivided attention.'

Amy's embarrassment was almost too painful to witness. Tears were very close. 'I'm sorry . . . Oh, I'm so sorry, I didn't realise. It was the things you asked me . . . They triggered off memories, events . . . Some things I would rather forget.' 'Then let's get down to the nitty-gritty. You said you had had experience of looking after an elderly lady. You weren't referring to your aunt, were you?'

'Oh no, Aunt Flora is not that old. No, it was a Miss Self, my aunt's lodger, her last lodger. She stopped taking in lodgers after Miss Self died. She was a retired school-teacher and her sight was fading and she liked me to read the newspaper to her, and write her letters and run little errands. Towards the end, when she became too weak to look after herself, I helped my aunt to nurse her. We would have looked after her until . . .' But Amy couldn't go on.

'Dr Hamilton thought it best for her to go into hospital,' she added lamely.

Did this experience influence the girl's decision to take up nursing, Helena wondered. But why a sanatorium and not a general hospital? No qualifications? According to Midge, the sanatorium had been a refuge, a place of shelter, somewhere to escape to. It was obvious the girl wanted a home as well as a job. Dare I take a chance on her, she wondered. It was a gamble and if it didn't succeed it could backfire on her mother.

An image of Paul rose before her. Paul with his quirky smile and fierce blue eyes and confident voice saying, 'Grab her while you've got the chance, you might not get another. If your mother takes to her, all to the good. If she doesn't, she'll soon send her packing.' A possibility that was more than likely in any case, thought Helena ruefully.

Midge, unable to get to her house phone had been down to the porter's lodge to use the one there. She rang through to the restaurant and ordered an evening meal for three, and had just returned to the apartment when Helena came out of the sitting room closing the door carefully behind her. She looked tired.

'Well, I hope you've done the sensible thing,' said Midge, but in a tone of voice that belied such hope. 'Offered her a bed for the night, a meal, and a loan to tied her over until she finds herself a job.'

'I suggested she came on a month's trial.'

Midge shrugged. 'I should have saved my breath.' She led the way into her bedroom where she seated herself before the dressing-table and started on repairs to her make-up. She carefully outlined her generous mouth with pink lipstick before she spoke again.

'You'd made up your mind before you even saw the wretched girl, hadn't you? Well, you know the old saying, "Decide in haste and repent at leisure".'

'I know no such thing. You could be a little more helpful, Midge. You could be a little more supportive. It wasn't easy, interviewing Amy Cousins. I had to drag every bit of information out of her, and now I feel drained. I was looking to you for encouragement, but all you do is carp.'

Midge was up like a flash and, coming over to the bed, put her hands on Helena's shoulders and looked contritely into her clouded green eyes. 'Darling, I'm sorry, truly sorry. You mustn't take notice of me. You should know me well enough by now to know that I don't mean half I say. You're like a sister to me, Helena, a very dear sister, and I wouldn't do anything to hurt you. I was only thinking of you and what you might be letting yourself in for. But, tell me, did you really have to drag everything out of her? I couldn't stop her talking.'

'Perhaps that's why she seemed frightened of letting herself go a second time. Perhaps another glass of whisky might have helped. Anyway, she was more forthcoming towards the end. She admitted she had lied about her age.'

Midge dismissed that as irrelevant. 'Who hasn't lied about their age at sometime? It's just one of those female vagaries. What did she do, drop a few years?'

'No. Added them on. She thought if she gave her correct age I wouldn't even consider her. She's only twenty-one.'

'Great Scott, she looks much older. Twenty-five at least!'

'Twenty-one.' Helena gave a ghost of a sigh. 'Can you remember what you were doing when you were twenty-one, Midge?'

'Getting married, more fool me. What about you?'

'Worrying endlessly about Rupert. Waiting anxiously

for news of my brother. I wouldn't want to be twenty-one again for anything.'

Midge squeezed her hand. 'No morbid thoughts, duckie, not today. A whole new life is starting up for you.' Then she too sighed. 'That is if everything works out as far as your Miss Cousins is concerned. It would be a good idea to ask for a reference.'

One thought alone had filled Helena's mind after Amy's phone call – the chance of an escape from Thornmere. Practicalities such as a reference had passed her by.

'What about this Dr Hamilton?' Midge suggested. 'He seems to have played a large part in her life. A respectable family doctor, who better? Write to him first thing in the morning. In the meantime, what are going to do with her?'

The room sparkled with reflected colours. The many mirrors, acting like prisms, fractured the lights into a thousand rainbows. The two of them, sitting close together on the bed, were mirrored *ad infinitum*.

'What is it like, sleeping in this miniature hall of mirrors? Seeing yourself everywhere you look? Isn't it a bit off-putting?' said Helena.

'You'll find out for yourself tonight, chum. You'll be sleeping here with your old school pal, because Miss Weepy will be in the small room. Unless you think she'd be better sleeping with me in case she attempted to do another bunk. Mind you, that would be one answer to your problem, wouldn't it?'

'Midge, please be serious . . .'

'I am serious. I am seriously wondering what the devil we are going to do with her while we are waiting for a reference to materialise. Have you thought of that?'

No, she had not thought of that, or even planned how

she would get the girl to Norwich if everything worked out satisfactorily. She had had some hazy idea of putting Amy Cousins onto the train at Liverpool Street and asking Mrs Taylor to meet her at the other end. She now saw how impossible that was, and heartless, too. She could not push her responsibilities on to someone else's shoulders and leave it at that. Neither could she go back to Rodings herself, for she knew she would never escape her mother a second time. She appealed to Midge whom she knew she could rely on for a solution, for in the old days back at school Midge's quick wits had got them out of many a scrape, forgetting for the moment that it was Midge and her zany ideas that had got them into a scrape in the first place.

Midge came up with an idea at once. 'She can sleep here, of course, and during the day she can come to Toppers with me. I can find plenty of jobs there to keep her occupied, and at the same time it will give me a chance to assess what she's capable of. It will mean you having to share my bed for the time being. You won't have any scruples about that, I hope?'

'Scruples?'

'The possibility that our friends will think we're lesbians.'

'Lesbians?'

'Do you have to keep on repeating everything I say? You surely know what a lesbian is.'

'I've never heard the word before.'

'You and Queen Victoria too – I don't believe it! Lesbians, Lesbos . . . Sappho . . . savvy?'

'If you mean, do I know what you're talking about, yes, I do,' said Helena, affronted by Midge's tone. 'I just didn't know there was a word for it, that's all.'

'Then it's certainly time you came to the big bad city and learnt the facts of life. But joking apart, Helena, it's good to have you here. Not only for yourself, but for all those lovely hats you're going to design for me.'

'Not all the time, Midge. I shall be flat-hunting, I hope. Paul's bed-sit is too small for the two of us. He says he fancies somewhere in Bloomsbury. I could start looking tomorrow.'

Midge let out a little squeal of protest. 'Bloomsbury! Among all those long-haired intellectuals! To say nothing of museums and hospitals and publishers. Miles away from shops and theatres. Oh Helena, you can't.' Her expression changed, became hopeful. 'Why not here? One of these apartments happens to be vacant. I could make enquiries for you.'

Helena smilingly shook her head. 'Considering our unorthodox relationship I think we could live without comment in a place like Bloomsbury. And that's not all. Can you really imagine Paul amid all this perfumed lushness?'

'No, you're right, I can't. But darling, anywhere rather than Bloomsbury!'

Amy, lying between peach-coloured sheets, though physically tired was too overwrought to sleep. The whole day had been like some nightmare she had travelled through in painful stages. She should be able to relax now but she couldn't. For the first time in weeks, it seemed, she was really warm. For the first time in her life she was lying in a bed as soft as a cloud. She had eaten, not food to her liking for it was too rich and left her feeling rather queasy, though there could be another reason for that, she suspected.

So now it was a question of Dr Hamilton's reference. She had no qualms about that. The qualms were for all the plans being made on her behalf. She had sat silent all evening only half-attentive to the remarks and suggestions lobbed back and forth above her head. Names that had no significance for her were bandied about freely: Paul, Mrs Taylor, and a Mr Smithson of Beckton Market, and something about teaching her to drive. She had come to on one occasion to find both Miss Roseberry and Mrs Harding looking at her questioningly.

'I was saying that if you do decide to stay at Rodings, it might be useful for you to know how to drive. I know a very good instructor, a Mr Smithson. He taught me to drive my Baby Austin. Would you like to learn to drive a car? You'll find it a very useful attribute.'

She felt like a child being offered an unwanted treat. The thought of driving terrified her. She had only been in a car once and then she was sick. She didn't know what an attribute was, but knowing her luck it was sure to turn out to be something she couldn't master. She thought it unfair of Miss Roseberry to say, 'If you do decide to stay at Rodings,' knowing full well that the decision didn't rest with her. But nevertheless, she quite liked Miss Roseberry whom she thought looked beautiful with her creamy complexion and brilliant eyes and red-gold hair.

Mrs Harding was a different matter. The thought of living and working with her brought her out in gooseflesh. She listened while they mapped out plans for her, feeling invisible, for at times they seemed oblivious to her presence. It was then that she took refuge in her inner world, going over in her mind the start of it all, the events of the past few weeks which had led finally to bitter disillusionment.

It began the day she sat facing Dr Hamilton in his surgery and asked him for a character reference required by the sanatorium. He had not been at all pleased by her decision. His heavy black brows, like two furry caterpillars, had met together in a frown.

'D'you know what you're letting yourself in for,' he

growled. 'A sanatorium isn't like a hospital. A hospital is a place where people go, hopefully, to be cured. The same can't be said of a sanatorium. There is not yet a cure for tuberculosis. Only palliative treatment which is bed rest and fresh air. If your ambition is to become a nurse, for God's sake do the thing properly. Apply to a training hospital and work for your S.R.N.'

Her ambition was not so much to be a nurse as to get away from Chancel Terrace. The sanatorium would keep her and pay her while she trained. Not many jobs offered those prospects.

'A general hospital wouldn't take me without some qualifications,' she said. 'You know I missed a lot of schooling because of my asthma. I never caught up. Dr Hamilton, this is my one chance to get away from home, and you know what it's like at home.'

Indeed he did. Miss Cousins, whose chronic discontent was writ large on her face, had reared her niece out of an ingrained sense of duty. She had caused a small stir in the community when she had arrived there in the summer of 1906, taking up residence in a small terrace of Victorian villas, and bringing with her a year-old baby girl. She was outwardly respectable and attended chapel regularly, but tongues wagged until it was established that the child was the daughter of a deceased and unfortunate sister; then speculation about the newcomer died a natural death. To eke out a small private income she took in a lodger, but that caused no eyebrows to rise. Many widows in the same position as herself were obliged to do the same.

'You realise,' Dr Hamilton said, 'that they want you to start a week before Christmas. Does it worry you, the thought of spending Christmas away from home?'

'There's never been much in the way of Christmas

'jollification at Chancel Terrace,' she replied, and he wrote out his recommendation without further argument.

From the next room Amy could hear the sound of whispering, faint and sibilant like the twittering of birds, and an occasional eruption of smothered laughter. Miss Roseberry and Mrs Harding, lying in bed, talking about her, laughing at her, she suspected, and tears of mortification filled her eyes.

She prayed earnestly that Dr Hamilton would soon put her out of her misery but after that, what? The grains of information she had picked up from remarks dropped about the Honourable Mrs Roseberry did nothing to dispel her foreboding.

But what were the alternatives? To return to Chancel Terrace and eat humble pie? Or even worse, to return to the sanatorium like a dog with its tail between its legs and beg to be reinstated? Mrs Roseberry couldn't possibly be worse than Matron who read her the list of rules, known to the staff as the Probationer's Creed, the day she arrived and put the fear of God in her.

The afternoon's hail had turned into heavy rain that drummed continuously against the window. Raining the way it had rained on Christmas Eve, she remembered, when the local choir visited the ward.

The wards of the sanatorium were long, timber, hut-like structures, linked by concrete paths amid extensive grounds. Perhaps in summer when the flower-beds around the buildings were bright with colour, they might not have appeared so forbidding, but at first sight, in the bleakness of midwinter, with nothing to protect them from the mists rolling up from the marshes, they looked to her as bare and cheerless as army barracks.

Wasn't this taking the fresh air treatment a bit too

far, she thought, staring in disbelief at the open-fronted cubicles. In a warmer climate or even in Switzerland, where the air was crystal clear, she could see some sense in such an arrangement, but here in this cheerless Essex flatland, it seemed incredible.

The wards were heated by radiators that never really got hot, and to supplement this background heating the patients were supplied with stone hot water bottles that cooled down within a matter of minutes and were constantly having to be renewed. This was one of the first tasks allotted to her.

The patients on Ward Three for the terminally-ill aroused in her a feeling of inadequacy. Most of them were too weak to do anything but lie motionless in their beds. Some were racked by harsh and painful coughing attacks which left them breathless. The nurses were under instruction not to touch the metal sputum dishes kept in lockers by the bedsides. These were collected in the night by special orderlies and taken away to be cleaned and sterilised.

She recalled now, as she lay warm and wakeful in Mrs Harding's guest room, how she had huddled under the bedclothes on her first night at the sanatorium, unable to sleep because of the cold. Her modest bedroom at Chancel Terrace, in retrospect, seemed like paradise. So did Kent compared to that bleak south-eastern corner of Essex.

She tormented herself with thoughts of the cherry orchards at home in spring, acre upon acre of foaming white blossom; the hop fields in summer, humming with the sound and laughter of Cockney voices; the muted colours of the Kentish Weald in autumn: places she had known since childhood and were now as far away as if they belonged to another planet. She wept, she knew, not so much from homesickness, but the growing conviction that she hadn't got what it takes to be a nurse.

She could get hardened in time to the recurring shock of being noisily awakened at six a.m. She might even get used to the bedpans, though that would take longer. She'd probably get used to the rules and restrictions which to her seemed devised for the sole purpose of making the life of a probationer that much harder. But she would never, she knew, no matter how long she battled on, get hardened to the sight of the sick and dying.

It had rained on Christmas Eve, pouring down relentlessly all afternoon. It was getting dark, and shortly she would be going off duty. She was in no hurry. The ward felt warm for once and looked festive too with its paper chains and tinsel and balloons; the work of those indefatigable nurses who gave up their leisure time to make the wards look as Christmassy as possible. She was reading aloud a letter with a Kowloon postmark which had been delivered that afternoon to a Mrs Drury, a one-time missionary – Amy's favourite patient because she reminded her so much of Miss Self: gentle, long-suffering, uncomplaining.

The sound of singing came from the direction of the men's ward in the adjoining wing of the hut. All the patients, including Mrs Drury, looked expectantly towards the folding doors that led onto the verandah. The choir appeared, wearing black mackintosh capes that glistened with rain, and misled Amy into thinking that they were a group from the police force.

They were, Miss Drury told her, members of the choir belonging to the local Working Men's Club, and they paid a visit to the sanatorium every Christmas.

Now they grouped themselves in the doorway, removed their caps, and said, 'Good evening, ladies.' Then, at a sign from their leader, they began to sing. Their voices were deep and melodious and filled the ward with a volume of sound.

They sang several of the old familiar carols, and finished, as was usual, with 'O come all ye faithful'.

Amy, listening intently, conscious of the heart-catching poignancy of the occasion, became aware of a tiny sound close at hand, like the snuffling of a kitten. Mrs Drury, huddled under the bedclothes, was sobbing quietly.

Never having seen the little missionary other than cheerful, such obvious distress shook Amy to the core. Why was she crying? She had seemed so pleased when the carol singers first appeared. Had one of the carols, or just the occasion itself, triggered off some memory of happier Christmases in some far-off mission school?

Amy eased her weight onto her other foot. She hadn't the foggiest notion how to administer comfort. She had never been any good at expressing her feelings, keeping them bottled up inside her instead. She wanted to put her arms around the little missionary, to tell her she understood, but all she could do was stand there feeling completely useless until finally, Mrs Drury cried herself to sleep, then she tiptoed away unnoticed.

Christmas morning; sausages for breakfast. The sun was shining. A pale wintry sun to be sure, but enough to raise the spirits. She had a present for Mrs Drury. A bunch of snowdrops she had bought from the flower vendor at the gates and kept fresh in the toothmug in her room. She had wrapped the flowers in white crêpe paper and tied it with a piece of red satin ribbon. She would like to have bought something a little more expensive, but she had very little money left from the small amount she had brought with her and her salary was not due until the end of January.

Outside the whole world seemed brighter and cleaner. Last night's rain had dispelled the fog that had been drifting about the grounds since her arrival. The leaves on the Portuguese laurel sparkled with raindrops. A robin sang. For the first time since coming to Raneleigh she felt lighter in heart.

There was a subdued atmosphere in the ward. The patients were quiet and many had left their breakfasts untouched. Mrs Drury's bed was empty. It had been stripped and remade with clean linen. Shock turned Amy numb with cold and she felt an insane desire to laugh. The staff nurse gave her a warning look, then marched her smartly off in the direction of the kitchen.

'Don't you dare break down in front of the patients,' she hissed. 'Don't you dare give way.' Her own eyes were wet.

Amy tried to speak but her mouth was quivering so much it was difficult to form words. Finally; 'When . . . How?'

'In the early hours of the morning. She had been slowly deteriorating for days. Hadn't you noticed? No, perhaps not, you haven't been here long enough to read the signs. They hang on to life, some of them, by the merest thread, and it only takes a little thing to make it snap.'

'The choir,' said Amy in a whisper. 'The choir upset her.'

'I don't know anything about that. It's just a pity it should happen today. A death on the ward affects everyone. A death at Christmas is so much worse.'

'Oh, I don't know,' said Amy, morbidly. 'I think if you do have to die, when better than at Christmas? I wouldn't mind dying at Christmas.'

The nurse gave her a sharp look, then a push. 'Get along to the kitchen and make yourself a hot drink, and if I hear any more talk about dying I'll report you to sister. Hi, what's this?' For Amy had thrust a tiny posy of snowdrops into her hand.

'A Christmas present for you,' Amy said.

New Year came and went. Nothing had changed except

her deepening despair. She had come to the sanatorium as to a safe haven, instead it had brought her close to death and she was frightened. Not because she was frightened of death as such, but because death was so final and could creep up unawares when you least expected it. She could never go back to the ward now without looking round for another empty bed. She sent up a sudden, desperate prayer. Oh God, dear God, get me out of this place. Show me a way to escape.

Her prayer was answered she thought when during her next off-duty period she picked up a back number of *The Lady* from the table in the nurses' common room. She turned the pages listlessly, not taking in what she was reading until one advertisement jumped out of the page at her: 'Wanted. Companion for elderly lady living in Norfolk. Comfortable home and good renumeration for the right person. Experience not necessary. Duties light. Must be good listener. Ability to drive useful but not essential. Phone Thornmere 38.'

And here she was as a result of it, and all that remained now was the important letter from Dr Hamilton. She pictured him in her mind, beetle-browed, jutting chin, piercing eyes that could turn gentle at a blink. She hoped that when she met Mr Right he would be a younger edition of Dr Hamilton, but she couldn't see it happening. Nothing ever worked out right for her. She finally went to sleep to the sound of the early morning road cleaners shouting cheerful and ribald remarks to one another across the square.

The Pimlico flat was as cold as charity. Helena had looked for and found the key where Paul said he kept it, under the mat outside the door, of course. Inside were some shillings on the mantelpiece. She took one and inserted it in the meter then lit the ancient gas fire in the hearth. The previous evening she had phoned Paul's hotel from Midge's place and by great good fortune had found him in. It was the first time she had made an international call and was amazed that in spite of the interference and distortion, she could hear Paul quite easily.

He couldn't believe at first that it was really she at the end of the line. He wasted precious seconds firing questions at her. More than anything he was hoping she had telephoned to tell him she was joining him in Germany.

'Better than that. I am joining you at Pimlico,' she quipped. 'You will find me installed in your flat when you return.'

'I'm returning tomorrow, I'll terminate my contract.'

'Don't be foolish, darling, what will we live on? I shan't be making much for some time yet.'

The call went on and on. She tried not to think of the bill she was running up for Midge. They had so much to say to each other and so little time to say it in.

'I thought I would call in at your flat tomorrow, to give it an airing. If there's any post for you, shall I send it on?'

'No. Bring it in person.'

She rang off at last to see Midge contemplating her through a drift of cigarette smoke.

'That sounded a worthwhile little chat,' she said.

'Midge, don't think I'm going to bilk on that call, because I'm not. I'll call the exchange right now, and check the amount . . .'

'Oh shut up, you idiot. The only payment I want from you is some more designs. I only wanted to ask about Paul, but I don't have to. I can tell by the sparkle in your eyes that he is in good form. Helena, what about coming to the shop tomorrow? I could show you the plans I have made for the new workrooms on the top floor.'

'The day after tomorrow. Tomorrow I am going to Paul's flat.'

So here she was in a very unlikely-looking love-nest. Paul had obviously left in a hurry, or did he always live like this? Clothes and books and papers were strewn about everywhere, dirty dishes left in a bowl that was used in lieu of a sink. Water came from a tap on the landing. She set to clearing away and tidying up and washing the dirty plates in water she heated on a gas ring. At first sight in November, it had seemed to her very Bohemian, very romantic. Even now, reliving memories, it was romantic.

On that bed, that narrow bed, one side jammed against the wall, she and Paul had made love. She stretched herself out now, pretending his body was warm beside her. With her arms clasped behind her head, she stared up at the cracked and yellowing ceiling. Three nights of love, she thought, wondering if she had heard that phrase before because it came so readily to mind. Three nights of love – she relived every moment. Would they take up where they had left off, she wondered? Would things change and the first flush of passion die out when they settled down together, faced with the minutiae of day-to-day living like any newly-married couple? For her part no; she was so sure of the depth of her feelings. But Paul? She smiled confidently to herself. She couldn't believe that he would disappoint her. Three nights and days together, that was the sum total of their acquaintance, yet already she felt she knew him better perhaps than he knew himself.

And the days, they had been good too, cementing their relationship in a way that lovemaking alone had not. Not less or more, but different. He made her walk He was a great walker himself, or had once been. When the exertion got too much and a bout of coughing shook him up, they would search out somewhere for refreshments. That was how Helena was introduced to Lyons and the ABC. There seemed to be somewhere for breakfast, lunch, afternoon tea and supper at every street corner. And it didn't surprise her that most of their perambulations were in the vicinity of Fleet Street. Paul was a journalist and Fleet Street was his stalking ground.

'I remember,' he said, 'just after I left school and before I went up to university, I made visits to London just to walk along this street. I vowed to myself then that one day I would work here, on one of these papers. I went so far as asking – no begging – my father not to send me to college but to allow me to try and get a job in journalism. He couldn't have been more put out if I had said I wanted to go on the stage.

' "A scribbler!" he said. "No son of mine will ever demean himself in that manner. A term at varsity will soon knock that nonsensical idea out of your head!" '

'But you got there in the end?'

He smiled. 'By a very devious route, I did. And the satisfaction, Helena, the satisfaction.' He lifted his head and sniffed. 'Get that smell? The smell of Fleet Street, I call it. Printer's ink. You can smell the ink, can't you?'

She said yes to please him but all she could smell were exhaust fumes.

His enthusiasm grew. 'I could take you into any one of these newspaper buildings and down in the basement you would hear the presses pounding away like a giant heartbeat. Fleet Street's heartbeat. Switch those presses off and this particular Grub Street would die.'

He spoke a language she didn't understand, but that

didn't matter. She just loved to listen. 'I don't see the *Daily Encounter* building,' she said.

'You won't find the *Encounter* in Fleet Street, or *The Times*, but they're both within sniffing distance. There's something else I would like to show you though . . .'

He led her into a little court not far from where they were standing.

'There you are, see that neat little period house over there. That was where Dr Johnson – that most famous hack – once lived. God bless you master, I salute you.' And he gave a mock bow.

'Hack? Dr Johnson!'

'At the beginning. Even great writers have to start somewhere.'

In the narrow passage that separated the court from Fleet Street he pointed out a post whose rounded top was polished to a state of shining perfection.

'Dr Johnson's work, so the story goes. He couldn't go past without giving that post a rub. What surprises me is that he ever got through the gap at all considering his girth. Rub it for luck, Helena. Make a wish.'

'I wouldn't have taken you for a superstitious man,' she said. Nevertheless she gave the top of the post a good rub, then laughed. 'I think there was enough friction there for two wishes. One for each of us. Where now, back to the flat?' He missed the wistful note in her voice.

He led her out of the court and across the road. 'There's an eighteenth-century coffee-house higher up which now provides a very good lunch. We might find a settle where the great man himself used to sit. Want to give it a try? Then I'll think up something else for this afternoon.'

She stopped dead. 'Paul! I've traipsed with you through the city of London to see such places as Little Italy and St

Bartholomew's Church and Clothfair and Saffron Hill – shades of *Oliver Twist* you called that. I've been marched through High Holborn to look at Brownlow Street, and what was there to look at when we got there? A name plate. Another connection with Dickens I discover. And then to Doughty Street to see the Dickens' House. Paul, are you trying to educate me? Are you trying to tell me something?'

She said all this with a laugh, but he saw it for what it was, a *cri de coeur*. 'I'm a mindless, selfish, insensitive oaf,' he said. 'And I've worn you out. I was only trying to repay you for that wonderful day when I saw Thornmere through your eyes. I wanted to show you my part of London, but typical of me, I overdid it. And I wanted you to be fresh for tonight. I have planned something special for us this evening. No more walking, I promise. Just eating, and eating in a very special place. Now, we will go home and practise some gentle horizontal relaxation.'

A crowded bus trundled past on its way towards the Strand. Two of those on the open top deck glancing down saw a couple on the pavement standing in close embrace. 'That's one way of keeping warm,' said a long-faced, red-nosed passenger.

'They should be horse-whipped behaving like that in public,' snorted his wife.

Later that afternoon, Helena surfaced from a deep and refreshing sleep. Relaxing in the way Paul practised it was very soporific. The room was in shadow. It could be anything from four o'clock in the afternoon to midnight. The short afternoon had turned to night while she slept, and now seen through the uncurtained windows, the sky was black. Slowly, as her senses sharpened, she became aware of a caressing hand gently massaging her back.

'Oh darling,' she murmured drowsily. 'I find that so very soothing.'

'My intention was to arouse you, not to send you off to sleep again.'

'I am aroused,' she said, turning to face him.

The only dress she had with her was the Harrod's model she had lived in for the past three days. And it looked it, she thought regretfully, as she examined it closely.

'This place you are taking me to,' she said. 'Is it one of those places one dresses up to eat in?'

'For dinner, yes. What you've been wearing will do very nicely.'

'Not looking like this, it won't.'

Helena had been rubbing out her underwear every night, leaving it to dry on a piece of string slung from end to end of the mantelshelf. But a silk dress with a fringed skirt required more professional attention. She could, she knew, have gone back to Hanover Mansions for a change of clothes, but that would have meant facing Midge, and she wasn't quite ready for Midge yet. Besides she liked the green dress, there was nothing among her other things to compare with it.

Paul solved the problem for her. While she bathed in the ancient and freezing bathroom on the floor below he took the dress along to the steam pressers in the next street and returned with it looking as fresh as new. Helena felt she had lived a lifetime in that dress, and so, in a way, she had.

'Can't I know where you are taking me?' she asked when he returned from getting a taxi. He threw away his half-smoked cigarette and grinned at her. 'No. It's a surprise.'

'Is it the Ritz?'

He grimaced. 'Do I look the kind to frequent such large and fashionable places?'

'That little place near Piccadilly where we went our first night?'

'You're not even warm. Come along, my sweet, the meter's ticking over.'

She loved being driven through London at night. She tried to pinpoint landmarks. Westminster Abbey and the Houses of Parliament passed in quick succession. Twisting around as she was doing made Paul laugh.

'You're like a child trying to take in everything at once.'

'London looks much cleaner at night. And brighter – the soot doesn't show.' She gave a deep and contented sigh. 'Thank you for giving me these three precious days, Paul.'

He took her hand and kissed it. 'Thank you for making it possible.'

'Isn't this Soho?' she said, as they drove along Dean Street. Still she didn't suspect. The taxi turned into a dark and narrow, partly cobbled, thoroughfare and stopped. Just ahead she could see the light from a tall and narrow building. It appeared to be a restaurant. A chilling sensation settled in the pit of her stomach.

'Paul, you are not taking me to Lottie's place?'

Paul was paying off the taxi. He turned on her that teasing lopsided smile that was so characteristic of him. 'You can't be shy of Lottie. Nobody could be shy of Lottie. Come along.'

She still hung back. 'I think it so unfair of you,' she said. 'To let me in for this. I'm not yet ready to face your other conquests.'

It was a cruel thing to say. Even before she saw the way his face changed she regretted it. 'I'm sorry,' she cried. 'I'm sorry. Heavens, how I hate myself at times.'

'If it weren't for Lottie,' he reminded her – as if she needed reminding – 'we wouldn't have met. I went searching for reminders of her and found you instead. That was fate.

That was the way it was intended. I just want you to meet Lottie, because in so many ways you two are similar. Listen, Helena, in this life there are just two lots of people – those who give and those who take. Both you and Lottie are givers, and in your different ways have given me so much. Please come and say hullo to her, for my sake.'

It was very quiet in this little corner of Soho. So quiet that she felt sure her heartbeats were audible. There was a bay tree standing either side of the entrance to the restaurant, sheltered, like the step, under a striped French blind. Only when they were up close did she see the name Fosters painted in gold lettering on the fanlight.

It was more like stepping into someone's home than into a restaurant she thought as they crossed the threshold. It was small and cosy and compact. They were ushered up to the first-floor dining room where their feet sank into thick pile carpet; from somewhere unseen came the muted sound of an orchestra. The predominant colour was pink: pink tablecloths and table napkins and rosy light from pink satin lampshades.

Helena said, 'Midge would like this, she's fond of pink.'

'It's a warm colour. A feminine colour.'

'And I can't wear it because of my hair.'

'Rubbish. You could wear any colour.'

They sat at their table sipping aperitifs and listening to the quiet buzz of conversation. Paul was studying the menu and Helena taking discreet stock of their fellow diners, when Lottie appeared.

Helena, knowing only of Lottie's humble background, did not at once equate this stylish and elegant figure in black with the proprietress of Fosters. She took her at first for a regular customer for many of the other diners waved to her and beckoned her over, but her eyes roved around the room as if seeking someone she knew and then they alighted on Paul. Helena, seeing the way her face lit up, experienced just the slightest twinge of disquietude, but when she saw them greet each other like long-lost friends, her mind eased. She had nothing to fear from this woman any more than Paul had to fear from her memories of Rupert. The past was a brief interlude, no more than nostalgia, in which they all indulged.

'I was on the lookout for you,' said Lottie, taking the spare chair at their table. 'When Jacques said you had phoned to make a reservation I knew there couldn't be two Paul Berkeleys. I've been keeping track of you, you know, by your writings. I'm proud of you, Paul.'

They shared reminiscences and Helena was not made to feel the odd one out because they drew her into the conversation at every opportunity. 'Where's that pretty little toddler who was always with you?' Paul asked.

'She's away at school and nearly as tall as I am, now.'

He laughed. 'Gosh, that makes me feel old.' He reached across the table and took Helena's hand in a proprietary fashion. 'When I introduced you two I forgot to tell you that Miss Roseberry also comes from Thornmere.'

'Ardleigh House, originally,' said Helena.

Lottie stared. 'Helena Roseberry, of course, I should have known. I remember you as a child riding on your little fat pony. You rode sidesaddle and wore such a natty little habit. But you wouldn't remember me. I was the girl your age who opened the level-crossing gates to you and your groom. I would watch you go cantering down the lane, and how I envied you.'

Helena could vaguely remember a tall spindly-legged child with a heavy plait of hair and enormous dark eyes. What she could not accept so readily was that this elegant and sophisticated woman in the tailored suit and smart coiffeur was that same young child now grown.

Lottie's eyes had a far-away and somewhat saddened look. 'Any news from Norfolk?' she said.

Helena racked her brains. In Norfolk they had moved in different circles. 'I can't think of any. I lived a very quiet life there.'

Lottie hesitated. 'Any news of the gatehouse? Any news of my father or brother?'

Helena would have given anything to be able to answer differently. The suppressed longing in the other's voice was painfully manifest. 'I rarely go down that way,' she said. 'But I do know that your old friend Mrs Webster is looking after them now.'

Lottie nodded, not looking up. 'Yes, I heard that. They couldn't be in better hands. So,' she rose, very much her professional self again. 'You must excuse me, but I have to go and speak to my other guests. I hope you will come again. I'm always delighted to see old friends.' She was about to add something else, but was interrupted when Paul was suddenly taken by a violent paroxysm of coughing. Over his head her eyes met Helena's questioningly.

'He smokes too much,' said Helena.

'He always did. He had no idea how to look after himself. But now he has you.' Trite words, but not trite in the way she expressed them. She smiled and left them, blowing them both a little kiss.

At the end of the evening which lingered on until nearly midnight they took a taxi as far as Victoria Station and then walked back to the flat along Buckingham Palace Road.

'So what did you think of Lottie?' asked Paul.

'I liked her. I liked her tremendously, but . . .'

'But what?'

Helena paused, having difficulty finding the right words. 'I think it was rather insensitive of us springing a surprise on her like that. It would have been better if you had gone on your own. I shouldn't have gone.'

'But I wanted her to meet you. I wanted you to meet her.'

'Yes, and if I had come from anywhere but Thornmere it would have worked.'

'I thought she would enjoy talking about the old days.'

'She did up to a point. But there were other memories, too, not such happy ones. Oh, Paul, she was near tears once.'

They were walking close with his arm around her, now he bent and planted a kiss on her hair. 'You're a tender-hearted creature,' he said. 'And I love you for it.'

'Well, was there any post?' asked Midge on her return to Hanover Mansions.

'Nothing that can't wait.'

'What have you been doing all this time? You look frozen.'

'Tidying up. Measuring up for curtains.'

'That couldn't have taken you long. What else?'

'Just remembering,' said Helena, happily.

Midge snorted. 'I shall be glad when we hear from this Dr Hamilton. Then perhaps we can get on with our lives again.'

The letter arrived two days later. Helena read it through and handed it to Midge.

He wrote:

> Thank God. I was wondering where the devil the girl had got to. I had a terse and brief phone call from someone at the sanatorium asking who would pay for the return of her suitcase and contents. The aunt

didn't bat an eyelid when I passed on the message. Said she expected as much. You ask for a reference. Of course I'll give a reference, not only to satisfy you, but because I believe in Amy. But is a reference from me worth the paper it's written on? I vouched for her to the sanatorium, remember. I believe in that girl. There's good in her and she's loyal to those she likes. She had a rotten start in life, unwanted and unloved. Once she finds herself secure and needed she'll prove her worth. She's a good little worker. Give her a chance . . .

'Well,' said Midge, handing the letter back. 'I don't know what to make of that as a reference. I think it tells us more about Dr Hamilton than it does about Miss Amy Cousins. I notice he thanks God rather than you for letting him know her whereabouts.'

'All the same, his letter has put my mind at rest. I feel easier about Miss Cousins now. Does your offer to take her up to Norfolk still stand?'

'D'you know,' said Midge. 'I shall miss her. She's made herself very useful about the shop. And Dr Hamilton is right about one thing. She's not afraid of work.'

SEVEN

The last part of January was extremely wet. February was even wetter. It had rained incessantly for more than two weeks. Helena, looking out of the windows of the studio flat in Pimlico, and seeing the rivers of rainwater flowing into the gutters recalled the lines of verse Nanny had taught her many years ago in the nursery of Ardleigh House:

> January brings the snow,
> Makes our feet and fingers glow
> February brings the rain,
> Thaws the frozen lake again . . .

and so on, throughout the year. February and the rain stayed in her mind. The cruel monotonous rain that interrupted her search for alternative accommodation and, so she believed, was the reason Paul could not throw off the chest infection he had brought back with him from Germany.

She had not gone to the station to meet him the day of his return. She had prepared a meal and was keeping it hot on a plate over a saucepan of boiling water on the gas-ring.

Later, they could go out and celebrate, she thought. She had filled a pudding bowl with white chrysanthemums — there was not a vase in the flat — and was keeping a bottle of wine cool in a bucket of water.

When she heard his step on the stairs her heart had flipped over. She had dreaded that encounter in case the magic had gone and she saw only uncertainty in his eyes. Uncertainty! There was gladness there and something else that sent a tremor through her and filled her with an unexpected bashfulness. No bashfulness on Paul's part, however. He hugged her until she could scarcely breathe, gripping her as if fearful she might vanish. He admitted as much. 'I've dreamed about you so often that I can't believe you are really here and not just a figment of my imagination. Did they happen, those three wonderful days, or did I imagine them, too?'

She felt the colour rush to her cheeks. Shy with Paul! Impossible. 'They happened,' she said and laughed, but her laughter subsided when she saw how tired he looked and that his tan had been replaced by pallor.

'You look as if you could do with a good night's sleep.'

He grinned lopsidedly. 'I have plans for tonight, and sleep doesn't come into them.'

Even the wet and miserable days that followed couldn't dampen her spirits. She and Paul were together in a home of their own and that's all that mattered. Well, it did until she began to feel that the rain was never going to stop. In the paper that morning she had read that after eighteen days of continuous rain some suburbs of London were seriously flooded. Suburbia was an uncharted country as far as she was concerned. She had lived in the country; she had lived in London, but the suburbs were an unknown quantity. Everywhere would look equally dreary, she speculated, after eighteen days of continuous rain.

Paul's piece on the evacuation of the British Troops from the Rhineland had, on the whole, received a good reception. Because it dwelt on the particular rather than the general, and cited many cases of personal relationships which had flowered between the Allies and their former enemy, his reporting was described as heart-warming. But because the article appeared in the *Daily Encounter*, that most radical of newspapers, it was castigated by the Establishment and eschewed by the Brass Hats who still, ten years later, considered hanging, drawing and quartering too good for the ex-infantry officer.

Paul promised her that there would be no more partings, but when the foreign editor dangled a carrot before him in the form of an assignment to Berlin to report on Germany's bid to join the League of Nations, he was eager to take the bait. He was a staunch pacifist and saw in the newly-founded League the only hope of preventing another World War.

Helena was alarmed. 'You're mad even to consider it,' she said. 'Paul, darling, you know very well you're not up to it. By rights you should be in bed. Remember what the doctor said.'

'I'm never one to pass up an opportunity to stay in bed as long as a gorgeous strawberry blonde keeps me company,' he quipped.

His studio was furnished with a three-foot bed, an ottoman, a gate-legged table – the only piece of furniture of any value – a few ill-assorted chairs, a kneehole desk bought second-hand along the Portobello Road and badly infected with woodworm, a deal table supporting a double-ringed gas hob and, as a nod to the current trend towards Art Deco, a hideous green and orange vase used as an umbrella stand. Their clothes, along with his files and notebooks and other impedimenta of a writer's craft, were stored in a closet under the eaves; a convenient glory hole that ran the length of the room and was a repository for anything that hadn't got a permanent home. The two wide window sills acted as bookshelves.

'This studio,' exclaimed Midge when she first set eyes on it, 'is nothing more or less than a slum.'

'More rather than less,' agreed Paul, in the genial manner he used for baiting Midge. It was a source of ongoing irritation to Helena that the two people she loved most in the world didn't get on. She tried to comfort herself with the thought that their mutual dislike was prompted by jealousy, but she knew it went deeper than that. They were just not compatible. What Midge admired most in a man was success and wealth and a determination to be top dog, all traits that Paul despised. What Paul most disliked about Midge was her good sound business sense.

When he told Helena that she was speechless. 'Great Scott! If it weren't for her good sound business sense the shop wouldn't be where it is today, and I wouldn't be here with you. What have you got against good sound business sense anyway?'

'In a woman? It robs her of her femininity.'

Helena laughed. 'That's rich, I've never seen anyone more feminine-looking than Midge.'

'You're mixing femininity with sensuality, my love, and there's a world of difference between the two. You have more femininity in your little finger than Midge has in the whole of her lush body, so just you come over here and give me a demonstration.'

Helena pretended umbrage. 'At least Midge has more

backbone than I have. She wouldn't allow herself to be treated as a doormat.'

'A most elegant and expensive doormat, I must say. Genuine Aubusson, no doubt. A mat any man would be proud to wipe his feet on.'

'Oh, Paul, you idiot.'

'*Come here!*'

'Not now, Paul, we can't. The doctor will be here any minute.'

'Plenty of time for a quickie,' he said firmly.

Though Paul had turned it into a joke, truth underlined Helena's remark about being a doormat. Once, in an edgy mood, Midge had compared her to a Virginia creeper: 'Because you cling. Because you allow Paul to twist you round his little finger.'

Helena had laughed but only to hide her true feelings. Midge's remark was too near the bone for peace of mind. 'Or rather are you inferring I'm a creep?' she said in a jokey tone.

Midge looked shocked. 'Darling, that wasn't what I meant at all.'

'But I am a creep where Paul is concerned. I thought I loved Rupert. I thought I would die of love for him, but I didn't know then what love was all about. I was too young . . . too inexperienced. It's different with Paul. I *would* die for him. I've only known him a few months but I couldn't live without him and I never stop telling him so, either. Oh yes, Midge, I am indeed a creep.'

And yet sleeping with him in a three-foot bed had its problems. Sometimes she would wake to find herself wet with his perspiration for he generated a lot of heat. Often, unable to sleep because of his restlessness she would slip out of bed onto the chilly bareness of the studio floor, grope for her dressing-gown and, taking a shilling from the mantelshelf, would feed it to the gas meter. At such times the ottoman came in useful, but at five feet long it was several inches too short for comfort and she would lie, wrapped in blankets, with her legs curled up, listening to the popping of the gas-fire until lulled into sleep.

So few of the flats she had viewed so far had proved suitable. Those with possibilities were beyond their pocket. Those they could afford she knew Paul wouldn't have as a gift. The studio flat at Pimlico had its drawbacks, but it had its attractions also. She was within walking distance of the Tate Gallery and in the other direction Chelsea Embankment. Even the Mall was not beyond her, or Trafalgar Square. She was a great walker and as she walked she absorbed the sights and sounds of London to such an extent that she sometimes felt she was in danger of losing her country roots.

One day, when Paul was resting and the rain had eased a little, she had taken a bus to Victoria Station and then another to Bloomsbury. She was unfamiliar with Bloomsbury, she had only been there twice before and both times to visit the British Museum: the first time when she was eight years old and accompanied by her governess, Miss McGowan, an inveterate sightseer. Helena was staying with her cousins at Lancaster Gate at the time, the London home of her mother's sister.

Her first sight of the British Museum had completely overawed her. She decided that such a vast and splendid building could only be a royal palace, but when she saw, as they walked through the colonnaded entrance, that Miss McGowan had assumed her pious expression, she changed her mind and decided it must be a place of worship, for Miss McGowan only wore her holy face when visiting cathedrals.

She was quite startled, therefore, when upon reaching one of the galleries, her governess bent towards her and whispered urgently in her ear, 'Don't look up, whatever you do, don't look up! *Keep your eyes on your feet!*'

Miss McGowan's tone of voice was enough to command instant obedience. Helena tried not to imagine what unknown horror threatened her. Something akin to the Gorgon's head, perhaps, suspended from the ceiling and ready to turn her into stone if she so much as blinked in its direction. She wished Miss McGowan had given her the same warning before they entered the Egyptian room, for then she would have been more than willing to keep her eyes on her feet. But this time Miss McGowan was quite enthusiastic, urging Helena to look at an Egyptian Mummy which turned out not to be the sort of mummy she had imagined but a dry and shrivelled body tightly wrapped in brownish-white rags and lying exposed beneath the open lid of its painted casket.

'It is thousands of years old and was once a great Pharoah. You remember, Helena, as in the Bible . . . A king of Egypt. Oh, how amazing! His hair must have gone on growing after he was dead, perhaps even after he was embalmed. I can see a tuft of it poking out between the bandages. Do look, child!'

Helena looked and promptly vomited. Fortunately, Miss McGowan had her capacious handbag handy. More fortunately still, a ladies' cloakroom was within easy distance. Helena was mopped down and cleaned up, and the contents of the handbag disposed of. Looking down her nose, Miss McGowan decided, much to Helena's relief, that they had had enough culture for one day. There was still, however, the ordeal of the Gorgon's Gallery to overcome before they reached the safety of the streets, and again the renewed and urgent instructions: 'Don't look up . . . Keep your eyes on your feet whatever you do. Don't look up!'

Ten years later, in London for her first season and again staying with Aunt Agatha at Lancaster Gate, Helena made her second visit to the British Museum, this time in company with Midge, who didn't take lightly to visiting a museum on a fine summer's afternoon until Helena explained the reason why, then nothing would keep her away.

When they saw what had caused Miss McGowan's nervousness they were so overcome with laughter that they had to stuff their handkerchiefs into their mouths. On both sides they were beset by statues, mostly male, and many not wearing fig leaves.

Helena wiped her eyes. 'Poor old Mac, she was so easily shocked. She tried to get me to say lady dog instead of bitch. She didn't last long after Father heard about it. She did me a favour really, because the governess idea was quashed once and for all and I was sent to school instead. I wonder why she thought the sight of a naked male statue would corrupt me? After all, I had a brother, and when we were small Nanny bathed us together. If I had told her that, I might have prevented her having such qualms.'

'You may be sure that the qualms were all on your behalf. I bet while you had your eyes glued to your feet, hers were glued somewhere else.'

'Which reminds me, Midge, you have no brothers. I hope you've got your eyes firmly glued to your feet.'

Midge grinned. 'What makes you think it's only brothers that come so endowed?'

Helena's next and subsequent visits to Bloomsbury were on home-hunting expeditions, though she did once take shelter in the museum when overtaken by a heavier than usual downfall of rain. She was an expert on the geography of Bloomsbury by then. She knew where to find the best coffee shops, or the obscure little restaurants where the food was good as well as cheap. She was impatient for Paul to get well so that he could share these forays with her, for flat hunting on one's own was a thankless task. She knew what she liked and what they could afford, but she hadn't lived long enough with Paul to know all his likes and dislikes. Of only one thing was she absolutely sure. Neither of them wanted to exchange one cramped attic bed-sitter for another.

But now, standing at the window of the studio, watching the rain drops spurt off the pavements like miniature geysers, she began to feel depression stealing over her. It was the incessant rain, she told herself. It was enough to try the patience of a saint, and she was no saint. She knew her mother would fully endorse that sentiment, for as well as being an undutiful daughter, was she not now also living in sin?

Was the way she and Paul were living sinful? She didn't feel sinful. She had not made her vows before an altar or promises in a registry office but she felt as committed to him as any lawful wife to her husband. How did the other tenants in this rooming house regard their misalliance? With a lack of inquisitiveness that bordered on indifference, she suspected. They were all living their lives in their own way and letting others get on with theirs. The live and let livers, Paul called them.

She knew they wouldn't be able to live together openly in Thornmere without causing gossip but once that died down they would have been accepted. 'It stands to reason you can't 'spect city dwellers to behave like simple country folk. They got different standards to go by, see. They 'aint doing nobody any 'arm, so wha's the 'arm in what they're adoing,' would be the strongest condemnation. Puritanism was not spawned in the country. It was a by-product of urban life, and these days of suburban life in particular. It amused Helena, trying to visualise Paul living in a leafy, respectable, middle-class suburb. He would be as much of a fish out of water there as in Hanover Mansions.

Thornmere and the little red and white Queen Anne house impinged on Helena's thoughts regularly these days. More and more she was being nagged by her conscience. Though she had written several times to her mother, her letters had gone unanswered. The only communication she had had from Thornmere was a letter from Mrs Taylor assuring her of Amy's safe arrival. Since then, nothing, and only one thing prevented her from writing back: she would rather not know if Amy had done another bunk. But as day passed day without such dreaded news she guessed that in spite of Midge's misgivings, Amy was still *in situ*. All the same, she would feel easier in her mind to know for sure how things were at Thornmere.

Downstairs in the hall there was a pay-phone attached to a large black metal box that swallowed an assortment of coins as greedily as the gas meter swallowed shillings. Every time she passed it she suffered a severe attack of uneasy conscience. It was no good telling herself that her mother would let the telephone go on ringing until Doomsday before answering it. There were others in the house who would.

She looked at the rain slicing across the window. She looked across at the bed where Paul was sleeping off one of his wakeful nights, and then she looked at the portfolio of half-finished hat designs on the gate-legged table. Midge was waiting for those designs and she had promised them for tomorrow, but she felt she would scream if she tried to think up a different way of presenting a swathe of silk or velvet or crinoline straw. What she wanted was a change of scene or the sight of green fields, or the feel of country air on her face. She wished, just for a fleeting moment, that she was back in Norfolk, then was ashamed of what she felt was a betrayal of her commitment to Paul. She fell on her knees beside the bed and gently kissed his hand. He did not move.

In repose he looked relaxed. The exhausted, impatient look he wore when awake was non-existent, yet it wrung her heart to see him so thin and pale-faced. When they first met he had been tanned and fit and his eyes had laughter lines at the corners. The tan had gone and his eyes – those fearless blue eyes – had sunk deep in their aureoles of darkened skin. She wished it were possible to gather him up in her arms as one does a child and take him off to some life-preserving resort – or some place in the world where it never rained. Even, as it was more feasible, to Norfolk where the air was bracing.

Possibilities bounced in and out of her mind. But neither she nor Paul were free to think only of themselves. She was committed to Toppers. And Paul? Paul had no commitments at present except to get himself well, and she knew that in any case she could never get him to leave London. He was always quoting Samuel Johnson to her: 'The man who is tired of London is tired of life.' Paul was not tired of life, he was just tired of the life he was living at present.

She rose to her feet. He would sleep for another hour or two so she could take the opportunity to grab a breath of fresh air. Rain or no rain, a walk round the block or down as far as the river would give her the boost she needed. Ideas would then come more freely.

The house was silent as it always was at this time of day when the other roomers had dispersed to their different places of employment. As usual, the same guilty pangs assailed her as she passed the phone, but this time instead of suppressing them she returned to it and lifting the receiver asked the operator to put her through to Thornmere 38.

She could hear it ringing. She could picture the hallway of Rodings with the phone on the sofa-table in the alcove under the stairs and the monk's chair beside it. A feeling akin to homesickness caused her eyes to water. The ringing continued. It would be a touch of irony she thought, if now she had taken the plunge, her call went unanswered. She realised how much she wanted to know how her mother was – wanted even more to speak to her. She tapped with impatient fingers on the wall and, just when she was giving up hope, the ringing stopped, and a breathless, girlish, 'Hullo – Hullo,' came over the wire.

Helena inserted the first of her coins, pressed button A, and then learnt the reason for Amy's breathlessness. She had been upstairs cleaning the windows of Mrs Roseberry's bedroom.

'Cleaning the windows!' Helena wondered if she had heard aright.

'Yes. The cleaning woman hasn't been in this week and Mrs Taylor was called away suddenly as her husband was taken ill, and it's all rather sixes and sevens here this morning.'

'But, Miss Cousins, you shouldn't be cleaning windows.' Helena felt outraged on Amy's behalf, and indignant on her own. It wasn't that she considered cleaning windows a demeaning task, but she had engaged Amy as a companion for her mother, not as someone to clean her mother's windows. 'I hope my mother didn't bully you into doing it?'

'Oh no, not at all, and please call me Amy, everyone here does, even Mrs Roseberry. And she didn't bully me, really she didn't. She just said it was such a pity the windows were so dirty as she wasn't able to see the sunrise properly.'

And when did mother ever watch a sunrise, thought Helena, her mind going blank. Was her mother trying to make a point? Showing that she was still the mistress of the house even if someone else was paying her companion's salary? 'Well, as long as you don't make a habit of it,' she conceded. 'But you mustn't allow my mother to take advantage of you, otherwise . . .' She was about to say she will treat you like another servant but changed it to, 'Keep you on the trot all the time. Tell me, how is she keeping?'

'Oh, ever so well, really. She had one of her bad heads last week, but she was all right again the next day.'

Helena guessed some bill or other must have arrived, or an overdue account from one of the London stores. 'Would you tell her how much I would like to speak to her? Try and coax her to come to the telephone.'

There was just the slightest hesitation. 'Yes, of course I'll ask her, Miss Roseberry. But you know how she is about the phone.'

Helena waited, conscious of the painful throbbing of her heart. In no time at all, Amy was back.

'Well?'

'She's doing a difficult piece of tapestry work at the moment, Miss Roseberry. She said she'll speak to you another time.'

'Tell me exactly what she said. I can take it.'

'She said that as you've taken so long to enquire after her it won't hurt you to wait a little longer for the answer. I'm sorry, Miss Roseberry.'

Helena took a deep breath. It was a while before she could trust herself to speak, then she inserted another shilling in the coin-box. 'Tell me, Amy, how are you getting on yourself?

Has my mother asked you to read to her yet? She likes being read to.'

'Not by me, she doesn't. She says I gabble, which I know I do. She is teaching me to play bridge, though.'

'Is there such a thing as two-handed bridge?' said Helena faintly. This girl was full of surprises.

'We only play a mock-up game, just so that I get to know the rules. Then, Mrs Roseberry says, when I'm good enough to play properly I'll be able to partner her at bridge drives.'

Helena had a sudden and devastating feeling that as a daughter she had been surpassed. Her mother had once tried to teach her the rules of bridge but given her up as a lost cause. This perfectly ordinary, timid and uneducated girl had succeeded where she had failed, and not only in mastering cards. In her quiet and unassuming way she was building a bridge between herself and Mrs Roseberry. Helena didn't know whether to feel pleased or not. What she actually felt was a slight dismay. It was obvious that her mother felt that a willing little companion was a good exchange for an unsatisfactory daughter.

Thoughtfully, Helena replaced the receiver. There was one thing in Amy's favour. She was not emotionally involved. Emotional ties, Helena knew by now, were easier to bear at a distance.

A change had taken place while she was speaking on the telephone, for now the hallway seemed much brighter. She looked up and saw that a pencil-thin shaft of sunshine had pierced the fanlight over the door and planted a spectrum of coloured patterns on the wall. She stared at it as if at some long forgotten wonder, and her heart lifted.

Going out into the porch she saw that the rift in the clouds had widened. To the east, where the sky was black, it was still raining but here the sun was shining. She turned her face up to it imagining she could feel its warmth, and as she did so, she experienced a sudden and illogical rush of affection for her mother. I won't phone, I'll go and see her, she thought. I'll bribe her if I have to. I'll make her a hat, a hat in pale blue grosgrain, her favourite colour. To be fair to her mother, she wasn't all bad. Over the years she had given her as much cause for laughter as for tears. Perhaps she thought the old adage, 'Absence makes the heart grow fonder,' might work as well for daughters and mothers as for lovers. All the same she was determined to lessen the distance as soon as possible.

April was her first opportunity. Paul was now well enough to be left on his own, and working all hours she had finished the spring collection for the shop. If she was going she'd better go while the trains were still running, advised Paul; fears were growing of the possibility of a general strike.

She carried with her, apart from her overnight case, a red and white hat box containing the pale blue grosgrain peace offering modelled on the toque, a shape much favoured by Queen Mary. When she took it from its nest of tissue paper and held it up for her mother's approval she thought she saw her mother's eyes light up with pleasure, but decided as there was no other reaction she must have imagined it. She sighed.

'It is a very splendid hat,' her mother conceded. 'Your latest model?'

'Yes. And for you, Mother. Entirely exclusive.'

Mrs Roseberry's expression did not change. 'I shall keep it for church,' she said.

'But Mother, you never go to church except to attend a funeral, and then you always wear black.'

'Quite so,' her mother said.

Helena took her anger and disappointment out into the garden. Her purging place where an hour's hard labour left her feeling clean and refreshed. She took a Dutch hoe from the potting shed and went to work on the herbaceous border until she had worked herself into a lather and a calmer frame of mind. She paused to take breath and slowly the peace and tranquillity of her surroundings seeped into her senses like a healing balm.

It was too early yet for the full promise of the spring garden that she had planned the day she first met Paul, but most of the polyanthuses were in flower, and the tulips and wallflowers were keeping pace. Unfortunately, it was too early for the cuckoo and this spring she would miss it altogether unless, later on, she took another trip into the country somewhere. A thrust was singing. She pinpointed him on the topmost branch of a fir tree, the sun reflected off his speckled breast. A good second best to the cuckoo, she thought, for she had a soft spot for the cuckoo.

The leave-taking with her mother went off much better than her homecoming, for in the meantime the atmosphere had thawed.

'Mother, I'm ready to leave now,' she said, experiencing to her surprise a marked echo of the past when on the first day of a new term she left to go back to school with mixed feelings of relief and pain.

Her mother looked at her with an arch expression. 'You may leave the hat box.'

Helena's eyes widened. 'You intended to keep the hat all the time, didn't you?'

'You don't think I would let a hat like that slip through my fingers, do you? I shall wear it at Daphne Lorimer's granddaughter's wedding, and have the satisfaction of seeing Daphne go green with envy.' Mrs Roseberry bent once more over her embroidery. 'You don't have to bring a hat with you everytime you come,' she said graciously. 'I shall be quite pleased to see you for yourself.'

'Oh, Mother!'

Theirs was not a demonstrative family. Kissing was a mere brushing of cheeks. Helena felt very much like hugging her mother just then, but a lifetime of restraint held her in check. In time, she thought, in time.

She cleared her throat. 'Mother, may I try to explain about Paul?'

Her mother stiffened. 'I have no wish to hear about your paramour,' she said. 'How you live is your own affair, but please don't expect me to discuss it with you.' Her voice was devoid of censure, only her heightened colour betrayed the extent of her feelings. Yet when Helena turned, dispirited, in the direction of the door, she called after her and said in a more equitable tone of voice, 'Thank you for finding Amy for me. I think with training she will become a very satisfactory little companion. Quite a good idea on my part, don't you think?'

For a moment Helena was bereft of speech, thinking of all the things she could have said if she dared. In the end it was a very lame, 'Well, I'd better go or I shall miss my train. Goodbye, Mother. I shall be up again as soon as I can.' Then, with greater spirit, 'Perhaps one day, you will allow me to bring Paul along, too.'

But there was no answer.

It was the first of May, and even here in the heart of London, permeated by the smells of hot petrol engines and fresh horse dung, there was a touch of spring in the air; a welcome mildness in the weather. On a placard outside Piccadilly Underground station Helena saw printed the words, BREAKDOWN IN TALKS WITH MINE-OWNERS. MINERS LOCKED OUT, and her heart plummeted. Everyone she had spoken to had hoped that at the last moment a general strike would be averted. Now it seemed inevitable.

She walked with the freedom her short skirt and loose jacket afforded. Underneath all she had on was a pair of silk camiknicks over a narrow lace suspender belt, and it amused her to remember that when she was fifteen her mother had taken her to a corsetière to be measured for her first pair of corsets. To protect her figure, she had been told at the time. Rather to torture it, she thought, recalling the utter relief of shedding the corsets at the end of day. She hadn't worn any support now for years, and her figure didn't seem any the worse for it. She walked with an easy swing of her hips that drew admiring glances in her direction. Her hat, green and white to match her jacket, fitted her like a helmet and completely hid her unruly hair except for a curl on each cheek. She was still in two minds about whether to have her hair shingled or not.

She had been on an errand for Paul. To get him cigarettes at his tobacconists in Burlington Arcade, which she purchased regularly for him, a hundred at a time. She was in no hurry to get back to Pimlico, Paul was busy writing a series of articles on the working conditions of the men employed in heavy industries. The first one on the steelworkers had gone down well with the features editor and now, in view of a crisis in the coal industry, he had commissioned Paul to write a topical article about working conditions in the mines. This was a challenge that Paul relished, and Helena knew what the outcome would be. A tirade against the colliery owners.

Paul, she knew, was a joke among their friends, who laughingly referred to him as 'the red under the bed'. But he was no communist. He had a healthy contempt for ideology of any colour and was too much of an individualist to hitch his star to any particular political party, but she feared for him nevertheless. His sense of injustice, his burning desire to help those he considered the underdogs had become more than a crusade – it was an obsession that was slowly undermining his health.

He was a rapid writer, though every few seconds he would put down his pen in order to pick up the cigarette left smouldering in the ashtray. 'Why don't you use a typewriter?' Helena asked him once, and then could have bitten off her tongue because even as she spoke she knew the answer.

'Because it's easier for a one-armed man to use a pen,' he said cordially.

Looking over his shoulder she read, 'Have you, my serious readers, ever wondered how those human tunnellers down in the belly of the mines answer the call of nature? There is no plumbing at the coalface. There are no baths at the pit-heads. Those men, when their shifts are up, go off to their homes wearing an extra skin of coal-dust, the dust they have been breathing in throughout their shift, and swallowing down with their sandwiches. And these are the men who are being asked to sweat extra blood for less pay.'

'Oh, Paul.'

'Why do you say "Oh, Paul" in that tone of voice?' he said, not pausing in his writing.

'That, about sweating blood. Oh, darling, you too. That's what you are doing, constantly fighting other people's battles. Please, can't you ease up a little?'

He put down his pen and reaching up behind him, took her hand and brought it down to his lips, kissing each finger in turn. 'Don't worry, pet, if the compositors come out in sympathy with the miners, this piece won't be printed anyway.'

She couldn't believe this. 'But surely the printers who work for the *Encounter* wouldn't go on strike, would they? Your paper has always made plain whose side it's on.'

'That won't stop the printers from obeying their union.'

'I don't understand,' she lamented. 'All your effort for nothing.'

'It gets something out of my system.'

And now she was standing in Piccadilly Circus reading from the placards that the talks between the miners and colliery owners had broken down. That could only have one outcome and Paul wouldn't know unless he went out to buy the midday editions of the newspapers, which she doubted, for once he had started on a piece of work he didn't let up until it was finished.

He was the last person to dream of going on strike himself, yet he would give his whole-hearted support to those who did if he thought the cause warranted it. Thass a funny ole world as they say in Norfolk, she thought dismally.

On the plinth beneath the statue of Eros she caught sight, in one of the flower-sellers' baskets, of a glowing mass of yellow mimosa, and her spirits revived. She loved mimosa. She loved its colour and its fragrance, and the soft, fluffy touch of its flowers. It brought back to mind her one holiday in the south of France, before the war. All she could remember of that holiday now was an impression of gleaming white villas, empty golden beaches, the sparkle of the Mediterranean, and terraced gardens sunlit with mimosa. The whole of life had seemed clean and bright and sparkling that last peacetime summer before the war erupted and split her world wide open, revealing for the first time the extent of the poverty and malnutrition among the underprivileged.

Why can't I see a bunch of mimosa without my conscience nagging me, she wondered. She hadn't even known what a social conscience was until Paul had schooled her. Now it cast a shadow over her sunniest days until, to ease her guilt, she gave more than she could afford to the homeless and unemployed. It wasn't the answer she knew to a social problem, but it bought her peace of mind until she came upon another limbless or blind ex-serviceman selling tape and cotton and buttons or boxes of matches.

But now one of her florins went to buying a bunch of mimosa and she was holding this to her nose breathing in its fragrance when, mounting the last flight of stairs to the studio, she heard the easily-recognisable voice of Dr Percy, who had called regularly on Paul since his bronchial attack in late winter.

Helena, knowing his views on Paul's smoking, put the incriminating packet of cigarettes into her handbag where, to her mind, it bulged suspiciously.

'May I compliment you on your appearance?' the doctor smilingly said, as he rose to shake hands. 'You breeze in here like a breath of spring.'

'Did you get my cigarettes?' said Paul.

Dr Percy looked at her with disappointment. 'So you encourage your husband to smoke, Miss Roseberry.'

The ambiguity of Dr Percy's turn of phrase always made Helena smile, though not today. She was annoyed to think that he should have such a poor opinion of her for she had always backed him in urging Paul to cut down on smoking. Dr Percy didn't expect Paul to give up smoking entirely, that was asking too much of anybody, and he himself enjoyed an occasional cigar, just to ease up a little.

'I do not encourage him,' she said with spirit. 'I just can't bring myself to refuse him.'

The doctor looked contrite. 'I know you don't encourage him, I expressed myself badly. And I do know just how demanding our patient can be. I was just telling him that some in the medical profession now think that cancer of the tongue is linked with smoking. Even that thought doesn't worry him.'

'I avoid thoughts that worry me,' said Paul, taking the packet of cigarettes from Helena's bag, opening it, extracting one, lighting it, inhaling, then letting the smoke trickle slowly through his nostrils. He included them both in a capricious grin. 'I couldn't get through the day without my regular dose of nicotine,' he said.

'Could I make you a cup of coffee, doctor?'

'Thank you no, Miss Roseberry. I only dropped by to have a word with my favourite Red.' He looked quizzically at Paul. 'So you avoid thoughts that worry you, do you? Well, here's a bit of free advice. Stop thinking about the miners. Stop tormenting yourself by worrying about things that you can't put right, and you might find yourself able to get through the day without your regular dose of nicotine.'

'I'd find it a lot easier to get through the day without a visit from a pedantic old quack.'

Helena followed the doctor onto the landing metaphorically wringing her hands. 'Please make allowances for him,' she begged. 'He's not well yet. Better, but far from well, otherwise he wouldn't be acting so outrageously. But I don't have to tell you that, do I?'

The doctor patted her arm. 'Actually, I'm glad to see him with such spirit, it's a sure sign he's turned the corner. Convalescence is a trying time for anyone, but more so for someone of your husband's disposition. Never mind, my dear, he's making very good progress – more to your credit than to mine, as I would be the first to admit. What you both need now is a holiday. A change of scene.'

'I've been looking for a change of scene for the past three months, and had nothing but disappointment. I sometimes feel like giving up.'

'No, don't do that. The property market is sure to buck up soon. Do you want to buy or rent?'

'We prefer to buy, but we don't mind either. Just so long as it's self-contained. It would be heavenly to have our own kitchen and bathroom.'

'I'll ask around. Sometimes one hears things on the grapevine.' He regarded her in such a kindly and thoughtful manner it made her wonder what was in his mind. Actually, he was lamenting the fact that the attractive bloom he had so admired in her had faded. Though she had never had a lot of colour she had glowed with the good health he associated with country air, and that was now lacking. And her beautiful green sparkling eyes, sparkled less. Anxiety over Paul had more to do with it, he suspected, than London smoke. He often wondered why they weren't married for it was obvious that they were deeply in love. But it wasn't his business and he wasn't one to question another's way of life.

Such thoughts, if she had known them, would have had a chastening effect on Helena, for she had always looked upon Dr Percy as a pompous little man and a bit of a dandy. To her he cut a comic figure in his Marlborough suit and buff-coloured spats over well-polished shoes, and always with a carnation in his buttonhole. As he took his leave of her, pausing at the bend in the stairs to raise his hat, she had no inkling what a valuable friend he would one day prove to be.

But, after all, it was not Dr Percy who solved their housing problem. It was an old school friend of Paul's, and not just a bit of a dandy, but someone who made a full-time profession of it. He was one of the first in their set to wear soft collars; one of the first to go in for plus-fours though he never played golf; one of the first to wear sleeveless pullovers; and one of the first to be seen in the absurd so-called Oxford bags. His acquaintance with Oxford was very brief. He was sent down during his first year for reasons undivulged.

His name was Hugo Frame and he owned the lease of a charming house in Doughty Street, and though he and Paul were as different as chalk and cheese they were drawn together like opposite poles in a magnetic field. He would disappear from their lives for weeks on end and then reappear, bringing with him a bottle of claret, a Stilton cheese, and a loaf of French bread, and while away the night with tales of his latest trip to Florence or Bruges or anywhere it was that had suddenly taken his fancy. Curled on the ottoman, propped up by cushions, Helena would be lulled, against her will, into a state of drowsiness by the rise and fall of their voices. Paul's andante to Hugo's allegro. They were nights she loved because she knew that next day Paul would be all the better for Hugo's visit, for that was the sort of tonic he thrived on.

But late one sunny morning, sitting in the gardens of Bedford Square, Hugo was the last person she had in mind. The general strike had started five days previously. The transport workers, printers, builders, heavy industrial workers, and engineers had come out on strike, not to gain anything for themselves but to show solidarity with the miners.

Paul spent most of his time, now that there was no outlet for his writing, with his head clamped into a pair of black bakelite ear-phones. One of the other tenants in the

Pimlico house, a science student in his final year at London University, had lent them a crystal set, and had himself rigged up wires that connected the set to the aerial in the garden.

'Why is it called a wire*less*, when without wires, it wouldn't work?' Helena asked Paul.

'Don't ask me,' he said. Science and technology belonged to another world as far as Paul was concerned. All he knew was that the wireless set brought a new dimension to his life; he didn't question the manner of it. Without newspapers, he had been starved of news. Now he had the BBC.

There was one paper still being printed, the *British Gazette*, a government newssheet, which Paul said he wouldn't touch with a barge pole because of its biased viewpoint. 'D'you know what Churchill is demanding now,' he asked her. 'Unconditional surrender! To hear him talk you'd think it was a bloody war going on out there.'

It was a war of sorts she thought, and the British public were responding to it with the sort of phlegm and good-humour that always emerged in times of crisis. She never ceased to admire the Londoners' ingenuity in finding ways of getting to work. A lot walked, as she did herself when going backwards and forwards to Bond Street, a walk that had seemed unending at first, but now, with familiarity, was getting shorter by the day. Others went by bicycle and those lucky enough to own cars suddenly discovered a lot of new friends. Some commuters cadged lifts in tradesmen's vans or lorries. A skeleton fleet of trams and buses were still running, manned by volunteers drawn from the middle classes.

Their friendly science student was working as a bus conductor. He told them of trouble in the East End where many buses were being wrecked by angry strikers, and where the older boys from council schools, eager to join in the fray, were throwing bricks at the windscreens of any passing vehicle. To the student it was a kind of game, a tremendous lark. Rupert, and her brother David, would have felt the same Helena knew, eager to enlist once more, helping their country in time of trouble. That was something she couldn't discuss with Paul.

So now, sitting on a shaded seat in Bedford Square with sunlight dappling the plane trees and sparrows hopping about her feet in a hopeful quest for crumbs, she fought against a rising tide of depression.

It had been another disappointing morning. Dr Percy had tipped her off about an available flat near the museum.

'Self-contained,' he said. 'Just the thing you're after. I'll make an appointment for you to view.' And she had gone along there this morning with her hopes running high, only to have them dashed when she was shown over.

It had all the things they wanted. A separate bedroom and sitting room, a bathroom with a geyser for hot water, and a slip of a kitchen with a full-size cooker. The only trouble was that the combined floor space was less than that of their studio flat. They wanted more room, not less.

The gardens were filling up. Young men and women from nearby offices, singly and in pairs, coming to eat their lunchtime sandwiches in this little oasis of leafy quiet. One figure alone, a man, made a bee-line for her seat and she reluctantly moved up to make room. When he got closer she saw with pleasure that it was Hugo.

This morning, for him, he was soberly dressed. No multicoloured pullover, no wide-bottomed trousers that flapped around his ankles like an Edwardian woman's skirt, no jaunty soft hat on the side of his head. But he was wearing co-respondent shoes, which she deplored, and more for effect than as an aid to walking he carried a silver-topped cane. She welcomed him with a delighted smile.

'The sight of you is just what I need to cheer me up,' she told him, as he sat down beside her. 'But how did you know where to find me?'

'I called in to see Paul and he told me your likely whereabouts. I didn't stay, he is such a bore about that new plaything of his. Such a dreadful-looking contraption – so unflattering. And those antennae, I told Paul it made him look like some outsized insect. He made me listen in, as he called it, and all I could hear were the sounds of insects too – buzz buzz buzz. Very boring. How can the poor dear stand it?'

'He listens to the news. He lives for the news bulletin.'

'News! What news? I dread the day.' He sighed. 'So I left him to it and whistled up a cab. And one appeared like magic, lucky me. And here I am – very tired. I've walked miles tracking you down.'

He was not exaggerating, he did look tired. Even more he looked downhearted, something she found hard to associate with him, for part of his charm lay in his unwavering good humour. Now, he was both listless and restless.

'You said you needed cheering up?' he reminded her, as he traced a pattern on the ground with the ferrule of his cane.

His face was partially turned from her, his brown eyes completely obscured by his extraordinary long lashes, lashes which many women would envy. He had everything: money, looks, and a brain which Paul said was in danger of becoming atrophied for lack of use. Helena loved him because he made Paul laugh, but for some reason which she could never understand, she often felt desperately sorry for him. He seemed lost somehow, and rudderless as if he had no purpose in life other than that of enjoying himself.

'This morning I was sure I was after the very accommodation we've been looking for,' she said. 'But I drew another blank. Not that it wasn't a nice little place, but too poky for us. That's why I need cheering up.'

'Why has old Paul set his heart on Bloomsbury? I could give you some addresses further west.'

'To be within easy reach of the British Museum reading room. As soon as we are settled he is going to make a start on that book he has always wanted to write. If we are ever lucky enough to find a place somewhere in this area, I can see him spending all day in the museum, so I wouldn't be doing myself a favour by moving to Bloomsbury. But that is what I want because it is what he wants.'

'Would he consider Doughty Street near enough to the museum?'

She turned to him with an eager look. 'Do you know of a place in Doughty Street?'

'Indeed I do. Highly suitable. A flat with access to a pleasant little garden. Largish, airy rooms. Plenty of space. The interior decoration is a bit outré for your pedestrian tastes, but you could change that if you wanted to. Need I go on?'

Her heart sank. 'I'm not in the mood for that sort of teasing right now, Hugo. I thought you were serious.'

'I am serious.'

He returned her look with one that was completely guileless. But underlying that look was an expression she couldn't quite fathom. She still thought he was having a game with her.

'How long has your flat been available?' she asked sceptically.

'From this very moment. I'm sick of London. I'm sick

of the public putting a brave face on their difficulties. It makes me feel uncomfortable, and I object to being made to feel uncomfortable. And there's another reason.' He looked away. 'I don't like the strike one little bit, it is very inconvenient, but I like even less the way the government is handling it. When I see the stunted and undernourished miners on the newsreels and compare them with the sleek and well-fed MPs and the assured and self-righteous colliery owners, it makes me cross. I don't want to be here when the bullies get the better of the little men.'

She stared wide-eyed at him. 'Why, Hugo, I didn't dream that you of all people had a social conscience. Has Paul's been rubbing off on you?'

He pouted. 'Don't laugh at me, Helena, please, not when I am baring my soul to you. I haven't got a social conscience – I don't even know what a social conscience is.' He gave an ashamed little laugh. 'I'm not being entirely honest with you. Actually, it would be expedient for me to leave the country as soon as possible. If I stayed, I might be in serious trouble. More to the point, it could affect someone who means a lot to me.' And she saw, with a shock of surprise, a flicker of panic in his eyes.

'Is she married?' she said gently.

He smiled in a half-hearted manner. 'That's the nub of the problem, it isn't a she.'

Helena rose briskly to her feet. 'Come along, Hugo,' she said. 'No more morbid introspection. You can buy me lunch, and then we'll go along and inspect your flat. It sounds too good to be true.'

Hugo had made some structural changes when, at the close of the war, he converted the four-storey house into four separate apartments, retaining the ground floor for his own use when in London. The other floors were let to tenants. One important addition was the balcony that overlooked the garden. They sat there now drinking coffee and listening to the intermittent hum of a bus or car not far away.

He was all for handing over the keys and moving out straight away, yesterday couldn't be soon enough, he said. He wanted to go to Berlin where one was at liberty to express one's own personality without danger of being arrested, where all was gaiety and fun and there was a freedom not to be found in strait-laced old England. He loved the German people, he said. He loved their music and their literature, and he was particularly impressed by the films they were making there at present. 'They make ours look like magic-lantern shows for Sunday-school parties,' he said.

Helena looked thoughtful. 'I don't think Paul would agree with you – about the freedom and the fun, I mean. He fears the consequences if that Adolf Hitler ever gets a whiff of power.'

Hugo scoffed. 'Him! That frightful little man! He wouldn't take the risk of being clapped in prison again. There is nothing to fear from him.' He changed the subject. 'So you really like my flat?'

She loved it. Like Hugo himself, it was pretentious and colourful, but that was only on the surface. The rooms themselves were well proportioned and full of light. The kitchen which, though small was well-equipped delighted her. All the rooms, the bedroom, the sitting room, even the bathroom, were meticulously tidy.

'I'll never live up to your standards, Hugo,' she said. 'Both Paul and I are notoriously untidy.'

'Busy people usually are, but that doesn't matter now. From this moment on, it is *your* home – I am giving it to you. You must do as you please with it.'

'Don't be so ridiculous. Paul wouldn't agree to that. You will have to come to some arrangement with him. And what about the furniture? It is so individual to you. Will you put it in store?'

The furniture was a mixture of Art Deco and Oriental. Some Helena quite liked, but some she knew she couldn't live with, especially not the animal skins or the brass and marble table. It wouldn't bother Paul. A chair was a chair, a table was a table. As long as one was comfortable and the other functional, that was all that mattered.

'If you would rather have your own things around you, just get in touch with my trustees. What you don't want they will arrange to have put in store.'

She thought of the worm-eaten desk, the three-foot bed, the other second-hand bits and pieces in the Pimlico studio and smiled to herself. She felt more relaxed and contented than she had for weeks. Most of the garden was in shadow, shaded by an enormous mulberry tree, but one corner caught the sun. A wisteria growing over the wall was breaking into flower. She was pleased to see that steps from the balcony gave access to the garden. She would enjoy pottering about in it.

'It is all so perfect,' she said, unaware that she spoke aloud. 'Compared to Pimlico this seems like Paradise.'

'Even Paradise had its serpent,' Hugo reminded her. 'Not that you will find serpents here, far from it. There are three other tenants, but I don't think they'll bother you, they keep very much to themselves – and there's Jacob Church in the basement. You've heard me speak of him. Very useful chap, sees to the cleaning and that sort of thing. I'll continue to pay his wages, so you won't have that worry.'

'Hugo, I have a feeling that you are doing this to help Paul and me out of a tight spot.'

'Definitely not. I'm catching the boat-train the day after tomorrow, whether you and Paul take this place on or not.'

'Definitely on, Hugo. Nothing could stop me coming here now, and I know Paul will feel the same.' She regarded Hugo with affection and he looked back at her with the limpid eyes of a forlorn spaniel. It struck her for the first time what a wrench it must be for him to leave this old house where both he and his father were born.

His father had been an unsuccessful publisher who had married a wealthy American beauty whose money, coupled with her enthusiasm, had injected new life into the business. And it had flourished. In 1912 she had sailed on the ill-fated Titanic on a visit to her family in New York, and thus ended a chapter in their lives. The business began to falter again, this time from lack of interest on Hugo's father's part, and the war finished it off. The war finished off old man Frame too.

In 1919, when Hugo was demobilised, all he possessed in the world was the lease of the Doughty Street house plus some rather rusty presses. Then his maternal grandfather died and left him a considerable fortune, and he had lived the life of a hedonist ever since. All this Paul had told her one evening after Hugo's first visit to the Pimlico studio.

She reached over and placed her hand on his. 'We will take care of your house,' she promised. 'We will cherish it and love it. And whenever you get tired of the gay life in Berlin, just come back and claim it.'

It didn't surprise her that his eyes misted over. 'I'll never come back,' he said on a falling note of regret. 'I feel it in my bones. But thank you, darling, all the same.'

EIGHT

The general strike of 1926, that lasted from the fourth to the twelfth of May sent repercussions throughout the country. Not a village, town, or city was unaffected. Thornmere was no exception for there, indirectly, the strike was the cause of a death, a marriage, and an unrequited love that was to lead to far-reaching consequences.

Daniel Harker, seeing the likelihood of an all-out strike had made his plans accordingly. He summoned Reuben to the room that had once been Sir Roger's billiard room and now in part looked more like a lady's sitting room than the office it was meant to be. Some of the furniture was much too dainty and delicate for a man of Mr Harker's build in Reuben's opinion. The only thing that suited his bulk was a heavy and cumbersome roll-top desk he had brought from Ivy House. It was strong and workmanlike but not very handsome. Come to think of it, reflected Reuben, not unlike the master.

'Have you got over that tomfool idea about emigrating to Australia?' Daniel said. Reuben took a long time to make up his mind about anything, but this was becoming ridiculous.

Reuben cleared his throat. 'I'm still considering it.'

'Then you can put your considerations aside for a week or two while I go down to London. I'd like to leave you in charge here.'

'Keep an eye on things, you mean?'

'Yes, that too. But I mean in charge, really in charge. See to any emergencies that might crop up. For instance, should the trains stop running, there could be difficulty getting supplies into the village. I want you to use the Daimler to help out. And if anybody urgently needs to get to Norwich, take them. There's no sense having a car standing idle in the yard when people need transport. I'm taking the Chev, just to get me to London, I won't use it while I'm there. No sense in risking the tyres getting slashed. Another thing you can do while I'm gone is to get the cricket field prepared for the season. Get a couple of men up from the village to give you a hand. If you need to get in touch with me I'll be at Ivy House. The telephone number is on the pad. I'm not anticipating any reason for you to do so but you never know. Look upon yourself as my factotum.'

Reuben wasn't quite sure what a factotum was but it sounded like someone with responsibility and he wasn't happy with responsibility. He shifted his feet. Bass, who had been asleep under the desk, crawled out, put his chin on Reuben's boot and looked up at him with adoring eyes. 'As long as thass don't mean handlin' money,' Reuben said.

'You can't pay out wages without handling money, can you? Look at it this way, if I can trust you to handle money, surely you can trust yourself. Unless, of course, your reluctance is due to principles?'

First responsibilities and now principles. Reuben felt that he was being plunged, much against his will, into deep waters. 'I don't follow.'

'I mean would it go against the grain with you to help, even in a very small way, to break the strike?'

'I ain't thought about it one way or other. I wouldn't go on strike meself, but thass not to say I'm against the unions. Pity they can't do more for the farmworkers, wha' with the miserable pittance they be living on. And I tell you what, I wouldn't go down the mines, not even for ten poun' a week!'

Daniel grinned. 'Ten pounds a week, for a working man! The Sahara will freeze over before that happens. I assume then that it's all settled? Right. I'll make an early start first thing tomorrow.'

'What did Mr Harker want? Anything partic'lar?' asked Ruby later when Reuben joined her in the kitchen for supper.

Reuben gave her a baleful look from beneath his brows. 'Only if you think buying popularity is something in partic'lar, because tha's what he's still trying on.'

Ruby paused with vegetable spoon in hand. 'What d'you mean?'

'If there should be a general strike he expects me to use the Daimler as a public service vehicle – give lifts to all and sundry, help out with deliveries, that sort of thing. You know there's some around 'ere who's never been out of Thornmere in all their lives, but if they was to hear there's free rides on tap they'd suddenly be having dying relations all over the place. Beckton Market, Norwich, even as far out as Yarmouth.'

'Reuben Stoneham, you should be ashamed o' yoursel', having such a low opinion of them you've known all your life.' But he had put an idea into her head. 'I wouldn't mind having a ride over to Burston,' she said reflectively. 'I 'aven't seen my poor ole dad since Mother died.'

Reuben grunted. 'Thass just what I mean.'

Though Daniel was up early Reuben was up before him and was giving the Chevrolet a final polish over when its owner came walking across the stableyard with Bass snapping excitedly at his heels.

'There was no need for you to see me off,' Daniel said, but inwardly he was pleased. He had a deep and warm regard for Reuben, and saw in him a trusted friend. It wasn't only for convenience sake he wanted him to stay on at Thornmere Hall and not go hiving off to Australia. He would greatly miss the man.

Reuben placed a large suitcase on the back seat of the car. Also a packet of sandwiches and a Thermos flask of tea. Ruby's contribution, as for her a journey by road to London had all the dangers of exploration into darkest Africa, and she wouldn't dream of letting the master set off without provisions.

'I was planning to have breakfast at the Bell at Thetford,' Daniel said. 'But thank Ruby for the sandwiches, tell her they won't be wasted. Thoughtful girl, that,' he added. He paused as he was about to step into the car. 'Have you ever considered marrying her?'

Reuben's cheeks turned a mottled red. Daniel's question came like a sudden blow in his solar plexus. 'I ha'n't ever thought o' marrying anybody,' he said huffily, which he knew wasn't true. There was a time in his life when he had thought of nothing else but marrying Lottie Foster. Anger kindled in his eyes. What right had the master to make him feel such a fool?

'It occurred to me that you could do a lot worse. At your age, a man needs a proper home, not just a room in a coachhouse. You marry Ruby and I'll let you have the lodge rent-free as a wedding present. No, don't say anything now, just think on it. Something like that can't be decided upon on the spur of the moment.'

'Likely you thought it up on the spur of the moment.'

'Not really, it's been in the back of my mind for some months. Thought it was time I mentioned it, that's all.'

'What I can't understand,' said Reuben, bringing out his words slowly, 'is why are you doing this for me? You could sell that lodge if you've got no use fer it.'

'I hoped it might help you to forget Australia. And also I like to see my staff happy.'

Reuben snorted. 'Can't say my mates wha' are married look that happy.'

'Actually, I was thinking of Ruby.' Smiling to himself, Daniel took his place behind the steering wheel, started the engine, revved, and was out of the yard and into the lane before Reuben fathomed out what he meant.

Sidney Foster, unlike the majority of the villagers who traditionally supported the Tories, had always voted Liberal until, in the election of 1910, he switched his allegiance to the Labour Party. However, this did not prevent him from disagreeing with some of their policies and he was decidedly against the decision of the TUC to bring their members out in support of the miners.

It didn't bother him all that much to think that industry might grind to a halt, or that trams and buses might stop running. What really hit him in the core of his conviction was that there would be no more trains. The thought that *his* railway, Sir Roger Massingham's railway, the railway that he had watched being built, for which he had worked since he was a lad of thirteen, had at a stroke of a pen been put out of action, filled him with silent fury. For four days now not a single train had run past the gatehouse, and the silence and emptiness of the rails was breaking his heart.

The sight of Ted, raking over the vegetable patch with quiet satisfaction goaded him beyond endurance. Ted was all in favour of the stand being made by the railway workers. He had shut the gates against the track and padlocked them in that position in case any strike-breaker sneaked out behind his back and opened them again. His cocky manner sent his father's blood pressure soaring. He pondered ways and means of getting even.

As if by mutual consent neither of them mentioned the dispute, not because they respected each other's views, but because each feared an open confrontation. The silent hostility mounted; tension hung in the air like poison. Mrs Webster, with her nerves on edge, finally lost her temper.

'Two grown men behaving in this childish manner!' she stormed one day. 'You can't put things right by sitting there glowering at each other. If you're fed up with having nothing to do I can find you plenty of jobs. There's the washing-up for a start, and the windows could do with a polish and the door to the cupboard under the stairs is hanging loose. What – no offers,' she mocked, as without a glance at her they got up and made towards the door. She shouted after them. 'Good job I haven't gone on strike, else there'd be no dinner cooked today. What about the housewives then? Isn't it about time they had a union? What do you say to that, young Ted?'

But Ted had limped off in the direction of the gates to make sure his padlocks were still intact, then with a grunt of satisfaction, he skirted the woodshed where his father had taken refuge, intending to hoe the vegetable plot but when he saw the butcher's boy cycling down the lane he retraced his steps. Charlie Nott might have some news.

He did. The stewing-steak he had come to deliver lay

forgotten in his basket; he was red-faced and out of breath; he had cycled as if Old Nick himself were after him and he couldn't get his words out quickly enough.

'There's a train coming! I sor it, just leaving the 'Alt. Ole Mr Golightly driving it, an' a soldier on the footplate with him. Sent along to guard 'im, I 'spect. Hee, hee.' The thought of anyone trying to guard Mr Golightly struck him as funny.

Mr Golightly was a retired locomotive driver. He had retired when Ted was still in the army and since that time had been living in a railway cottage in Beckton Market. Ted's face flooded with angry colour.

'The old fule,' he said furiously. 'Driving a train at his age! It's against the safety rules. Wha's he hauling, coaches?'

'Nah. Trucks full o' coal.'

'Cocking a snook at the strikers, eh, I'll show him, I'll call his bluff.' Ted limped over to the middle of the crossing and took up a stand. The train would have to crash the barriers before he gave an inch, though not for a moment did he imagine such a contingency would arise. Mr Golightly would apply his brakes long before that. The old engine driver had too much respect for railway property to do it harm.

His father, in the woodshed, sucking morosely on his pipe, became aware that the ground was humming beneath his feet. His ear, attuned by years of listening, could pick up the sound of an approaching train a mile or two away. He knew every bend in the track, every gradient of the rails by the variation in the sound of the wheels. Like many solitary men, living on their memories, he was inclined to fantasise, and in his fancies he imagined that the trains sang to him. One was singing to him now, telling him it was slowing up as it approached the gradient at Thornmere Park. Within a minute or two it would come at full steam towards the gatehouse emitting a triumphant blast on its whistle as it rattled past.

A broad grin spread over Sidney's face. There was only one man he knew who would defy the unions like that. Only one man who could get away with it. Old Samuel Golightly, a pensioner of the Eastern and Coastal Railway Company. Sir Roger Massingham himself had pinned a long-service medal on Samuel's uniform the day he retired in 1918. Whistling tunelessly between his teeth, Sidney knocked the cold ashes from his pipe, then put the pipe away in his pocket. It wasn't until then that he remembered the padlocks on the gates.

Scraping carrots in the kitchen Mrs Webster thought she was hearing things. A train? It couldn't be. She had never liked the trains – messy, dirty, noisy things – yet she had to admit that in the past few days life had been very dull without them. They added a spark of excitement to an otherwise very dull life.

The kitchen floor was vibrating and the crockery on the dresser jingled. She put her head on one side and listened. Sure enough a train was approaching, and at speed. Angry shouting was now added to the noise of locomotion. The door flew open and a frightened errand boy burst in upon her.

'Come you quick,' Charlie gasped. 'Mr Foster's got an axe an' is trying to smash the padlocks, an' Ted is trying to stop 'im, an' there's a fine ole ding-dong battle goin' on out there, an' the train be still acomin'.'

Though she was past the age for running and carried more weight than was good for her, Mrs Webster could move fast when the occasion called for it. Her cheeks shook like unfirm jellies as she hurried after the butcher's boy, but when she reached the gates all she could do was cling to them until she got her breath back. The two men ignored her. Each was too intent in getting possession of the axe. Only young Charlie's scream of 'It's 'ere . . . it's 'ere . . ' brought them to their senses.

'Get them gates open quick or there'll be murder done,' Sidney Foster shouted.

'I'm no blackleg,' Ted shouted back.

'You're no son of mine,' his father retorted. His face was purple with rage and exertion.

Samuel Golightly saw the gatehouse approaching and braced himself for trouble. This wasn't the first level-crossing he had tackled that morning and wouldn't be his last. The young squaddie on the footplate beside him was sweating. It could have been because he had been shovelling coal, but Samuel recognised fear when he smelled it. Poor lad. He'd been trained to fight the enemy, not his own people. Not that it would come to that, he thought complacently. Sidney Foster knew how to control that son of his, the gates would be open for him. Then, rounding the curve, he saw that wasn't the case – they were closed. Bugger this, he thought.

The scream of skidding wheels and the noisy rush of escaping steam as the brakes were engaged galvanised the frozen figures on the track into action. Sid and Ted jumped to one side of the rails and Mrs Webster and Charlie to the other. They stood and watched with blank faces and slack mouths as the train, moving in slow motion, went through the gates like a knife through butter and finally came to a halt just past the end of the gatehouse. Waves of silence followed.

It was Mr Golightly who broke it. 'Someone will have to pay for them there gates,' he said. 'An' it won't be me.'

Ted was the first to recover from the shock. He hobbled furiously up the line until he stood level with the driver's cab. 'You stupid old fule, why didn't you stop,' he bellowed. 'Couldn't you see that the gates were closed? If you had kept out of this and minded your own business, this wouldna' have happened.'

Mr Golightly gave him a withering look. 'This is my business – railway business. The coke works at Staveley 'ave run out of coal and if I don't get this load down to 'em, they'll soon be running out of gas. And I'm not 'aving any little whipper-snapper still wet behind his ears telling me how to do my job. I did stop in time. It were the locomotive that went on.'

'Gas! What's so important about gas?' Ted was beside himself. 'If we kin make do without gas in Thornmere so can other places. The men there shouldn't be working anyway, they should be on strike. Blacklegs, the whole bloody lot of them. And that goes for you, too, you ole fule.'

Mrs Webster was incapable of keeping quiet. She raised her voice. 'Your mother would turn in her grave to hear you speaking to Mr Golightly in that fashion. She was an upright, God-fearing woman, and she taught her children to have respect for their elders. You're a disgrace to her memory.'

Ted turned his fury on her. 'Nobody asked you to put your spoke in, you meddlesome ole mawther. This is none o' your business, so hold yer tongue.'

Mrs Webster went white and then red. Young Ted to turn on her like that, after all she had done for him. Her cheeks shook. And what was Sid Foster thinking of not having his say at a time like this? Even if he wouldn't stand up for her, she couldn't understand why he wasn't standing up for Mr Golightly considering how highly he thought of him. But there he was leaning against the fence as if all the stuffing had gone out of him. A poor thing he was in an emergency, she thought. A poor thing he looked, too, and she stiffened as she suddenly realised there was something odd about the way he was clutching at his chest. She hurried across to him just in time to catch him as he fell.

Ted turned his wrath back on Mr Golightly. 'They put you out to grass years ago. Why couldn't you have stayed put, you ole fule, instead of comin' pokin' yer nose in 'ere not knowing what you doin'?'

Mr Golightly made a noise like that of a turkey cock, a familiar sound in Norfolk. 'I'm not too old or too stupid to give you a lamming,' he said, making to climb down from the footplate. 'I ken remember you in petticoats, an' you were a cheeky little bugger even in them days. I'll show you if I know what I'm doing or not.'

Ted's temper went down like a punctured tyre. It wasn't that he feared a bout of fisticuffs, but not with someone old enough to be his father, especially if he pulled his punches, which he knew instinctively he would, and then get the worst of it. That wouldn't go down well at the Ferry Inn. He'd never hear the last of it, being beaten by an old man.

'Du you intend to deliver that coal, don't take all bloody day about it,' was his parting shot as he lurched away. 'An' get this blasted train off my stretch so I can start clearing up this mess.'

'Tell them to send the bill for the gates to Ted Foster, late of the LNER,' chortled Mr Golightly, good-humoured once more. He winked at the soldier who all this time had kept an uncomfortable silence, wishing he were safely back in barracks on Mousehold Heath. The train steam ballooned out noisy white clouds as it gathered momentum, and then the soothing rhythm of wheels rattling over metals echoed across the quiet fields. Peace.

Ted, making his way clumsily back to the crossing,

collided with Charlie's bicycle propped against the wall of the gatehouse and gave it a vicious kick with his good leg. It fell on its side and spilled the contents of its basket.

'Hi!' protested Charlie. 'I'm the one 'oo'll get a thick ear if tha' bike gets damaged.'

It was only then that it dawned on Ted that neither his father nor Mrs Webster were present. 'Where be they?' he barked.

Charlie had righted the bicycle and was looking over it anxiously. 'Yer father was took poorly, but you was too busy shouting at Mr Golightly to notice, an' Mrs Webster took 'im back indoors.' Hardly had Charlie uttered these words before Mrs Webster was back again.

'Quick boy,' she said, ignoring Ted. 'Go for the doctor as fast as you can. Tell him it's urgent.'

Ted felt as if his collar had tightened. 'Is there anything I can do?'

She narrowed her eyes and looked through him. 'Haven't you done enough already?' she said.

Twilight settled over the silent fields. The day was ending. The agony and despair, the accusations and denials, the comings and goings, the doctor and undertaker, the district nurse, sympathisers and those offering help, for Charlie Nott's story had run round the village like wildfire – all that was at an end. It was all over. His father was dead.

Ted tramped on up the lane, his hands deep in his pockets, the collar of his jacket turned up against the coolness of an evening breeze. He walked aimlessly, not heeding where he was going, churning over in his mind the events of the past few hours, trying with desperation to recall something said or not said as proof that he was not the cause of his father's death.

Mrs Webster thought he was and had said as much. It was she who had witnessed his father's collapse when he himself was too busy exchanging insults with Mr Golightly to notice. She who had helped his father back into the cottage, had got him into a chair and loosened his collar and sent for the doctor. By the time the doctor arrived Sidney Foster had slipped into unconsciousness. He died two hours later in hospital of a coronary thrombosis which, spelt out to Ted in simple terms, meant a sudden heart attack. Brought on, said the doctor, by sudden exertion or an emotional outburst or even a heavy meal. Brought on, according to Mrs Webster, by his son's unnatural behaviour. Enough to break a father's heart being spoken to like that, she said.

Ted walked blindly along the lane that led nowhere except to a church the size of a cathedral, all that remained of a once-thriving medieval community. There were other such villages in Norfolk, his father had said, decimated in the Middle Ages by the Black Death – the plague that swept throughout the country and reduced the population by a third.

'That was the only time in our history,' his father told him, 'when the labouring man had it all his own way. There was such a shortage of labour then that the labourer could call the tune. A lot different to what it is now, eh bor?'

He was very young at the time, still young enough to call his father dada, and had been singled out to accompany him on his Sunday afternoon walk. He was so proud of walking beside such a fine-looking man and one who could read books and talk about interesting things. They had walked the dusty lane until they had reached the deserted village, which was now only a name carved on the milestone at the crossroads. And there his father had told him the story of the plague.

He had not walked that lane again until now. He stood where he had once stood with his father, gazing up at the church that reared like a fortress against a darkening sky. He remembered his father's line about the labourers calling the tune, and thought to himself that in a round about way the labourers were calling the same tune again, but who was listening? Certainly not his father who had put his loyalty to the railway before that of his fellow men.

Loyalty was a funny thing, he thought, as he turned his back on the past and headed home towards the gatehouse, for one man's loyalty was another man's treason. Had he been disloyal to his father? His father had thought so – 'You're no son of mine,' were the last words he uttered. I can live with that, Ted told himself.

'I don't bloody care,' he shouted against the wind, shivering in his thin jacket. 'The buggers can think what they like. Thass don't worry me.'

Across the fields he could just make out the shape of the gatehouse, a lone dark bulk outlined against the starless sky but not as dark as the trees that crowded against it. Just one light showed in an upper window, twinkling like a distant star – the candle in Mrs Webster's bedroom. Packing, no doubt, for she was leaving first thing in the morning. There was no question of her staying after the bitter things they had said to each other. Yet later she had relented.

'I can't leave you like this,' she said. 'Not all on your own. How will you get on for your meals and your washing and cleaning? That's not a man's work. You've got to have someone to take care of you.'

'How d'you think I got on afore you come?' he answered with bravado, not wanting her to guess how desperately he wished her to stay. The thought of living alone in that house with its accusing ghosts curdled his blood. 'I don't need you or anyone else to take care of me,' he said. 'I'll be better off on me own.'

Of course he'd be better off on his own, coming and going when he pleased. But where would he go? To the village? To the inn? Imagining every look in his direction and every whisper behind his back was a confirmation of the belief that he had killed his father? No – he'd show the lot of them. He didn't need them.

The railway lines, polished by the constant passage of iron wheels, gleamed like silver in the half-light. Would the strike last long enough for them to turn rusty, he wondered as he picked his way over the scattered and broken remains of the gates. He trod on something that wasn't wood – something that squashed underfoot – and when he picked it up he found it was the remains of the steak that was to make their dinner. With a howl of pain he flung it into the adjoining field then stumbled on to the house, and leaning against the wall he buried his face in his arm. 'If you can hear me, Dad,' he sobbed. 'I didn't mean it . . . Oh God, I didn't mean it.'

Of all the consequences of the strike, the one that affected Ruby and Reuben the most was the unexpected reappearance of Mrs Webster. 'I can't stay up at the gatehouse with him no longer,' she said, flopping down onto the nearest chair. 'If Mr Harker's offer is still open, Ruby, you can tell him I'm willing to take him up on it.'

It was the morning following the sudden death of Sidney Foster. Mrs Webster, taking off her hat and skewering it with a hat-pin, turned her attention to Reuben. 'If you're not doing anything else just now, would you mind going along to the gatehouse and collecting my suitcase. It was too heavy for me to carry and I wouldn't demean myself asking Ted Foster to carry it for me.'

Reuben going off to do what he was bidden had an uneasy feeling that there would be no more opportunities for tête-à-têtes over the cocoa cups with Ruby. He felt that the kitchen was about to lose all its charm for him, and looking down at the faithful Bass who had pattered after him into the lane, said aloud, 'And you'll notice the difference, too,' in which surmise events proved him right, for Mrs Webster, slipping effortlessly into her old role, forbade animals in her kitchen.

On the ninth day of the strike, with time hanging on his hands, Reuben suddenly made up his mind to do something about the trees in the park. There was a coppice on the far side of the lake which was in dire need of attention. It had been neglected for years and the trees were beginning to look like witches' brooms. It was not the best time of year to coppice trees, but a little thinning out would do no harm. His father had been one of the estate gardeners and had taught him many tricks of his trade, and it was a toss up when Reuben left school whether he would follow in his father's footsteps or train as a coachman. The horses had won.

And now there wasn't a horse on the place, he reflected moodily as he pushed his wheelbarrow across the park, and the stables were used to garage cars. The Daimler hadn't left its stall for the past two days. After the initial rush for free rides the demand had slackened off, chiefly because — though this was only repeated behind Reuben's back — ''E's too bloody mean with the petrol, or else 'e's got orders from above. Wha's the use of only takin' as fer as Beckton? We know tha' road so well, we kin walk it backus.'

By lunchtime the trees were trimmed to Reuben's satisfaction, and he had collected a pile of kindling which would keep him in firewood for the winter. His room over the coach-house, draughty all the year round, was like an ice-house in cold weather. The lodge would be a sight more comfortable, came a wayward thought.

He was sitting with his back against a tree rolling a cigarette when he spied Ruby coming towards him carrying a basket. Bass, spotting her at the same time, raced off to meet her. Ruby, to Bass, was a constant source of nourishment.

Reuben got lazily to his feet. He hadn't really noticed before how much Ruby had blossomed out over the years. He remembered her as a scraggy little thing with a peaky face when she first came as a housemaid to the Hall. All eyes and bones. Nobody could call her scraggy now. She had a fine healthy colour and, though her figure was unfashionable compared to these modern girls all as narrow as planks, that's the way he preferred it. She hadn't cut her hair either which showed she was a woman of sense. The girls in the village with their shaven necks looked downright indecent in his opinion. Ruby couldn't be described as pretty or even handsome, but she was sonsy – a word from his mother's vocabulary. He repeated it to himself, sonsy. He liked the sound of it. Then he scowled, remembering the way she had stuck up for Ted Foster when everybody else was accusing him of being an unnatural son, and wondered if there was anything between them.

'He was always a nice, polite lad,' she said on one occasion during a heated argument. 'And thought the world of his mother. I don't believe all the things they say about him. And if he did turn on his father it's no more than Sid Foster asked for. I don't like to speak ill of the dead but these past few years he turned into a right ole killjoy an' made poor Ted's life a misery.'

Reuben had eyed her thoughtfully. 'You taking Ted's part for any partic'lar reason?' he asked.

'I'm not taking his part. I just don't like wha's being said about him, tha's all.'

'You ain't sweet on him by any chance?'

Ruby sniggered. 'The things you do say, Reuben Stoneham. Sweet on 'im, fancy you thinkin' that.' And she had blushed quite rosily and swept out of the room looking so pleased with herself that Reuben was left with the uncomfortable thought that he was not far off the mark.

On the day of the funeral he had watched her closely, but she hadn't once spoken to Ted or smiled in his direction. But that was no proof she wasn't thinking about him. Throughout the service Ted had sat by himself at the back of the church, fending off those who tried to draw him into conversation. And after the committal he had walked away, shunning the other mourners, making his way back alone to the gatehouse. Reuben had not missed the look Ruby sent after him, or the way she surreptitiously wiped her eyes – nor indeed the way she coloured up when she turned and saw Reuben watching her. It all added up to a worrying total, and he cursed the strike for muddying the waters of their quiet and uneventful lives.

'I've brought you something for your lunch,' she said. 'Mrs Webster has spent the morning baking enough to feed an army. You'd think she'd want a rest, wouldn't you? Anyway, she's sent you along a slice of sausage and onion pie, and here's a bottle of tea to wash it down. I put plenty of sugar in, the way you like it.'

'You got summat to eat, too?'

'I had mine with Mrs Webster, but I'll stay an' keep you company if you like.'

He didn't answer. He could rarely think of two things at the same time and now his mind was concentrated on eating. He did that methodically and slowly as he did all things, chewing each mouthful several times. Ruby took an apple from her basket and nibbled on it, a Golden Russet stored over winter in the cellar, a little wrinkled now, but still crisp and sweet. She gazed out over the parkland with a countrywoman's eye noting the lushness of the spring pasture. They could keep a herd of sheep here, she thought, remembering stories when Norfolk had been a sheep county, and wool produced a part of the Norfolk inheritance. But sheep had long since given place to crops, and it seemed a shame to her that all this rich meadowland wasn't put to better use.

Reuben scattered pastry crumbs for the birds, then wiped his mouth on the back of his hand. 'I expect you're glad to have Mrs Webster back?' he said as a feeler, wondering how he would feel if she enthused about what a change it was having congenial company.

But Ruby was rather slow in answering. 'I don't know how it is, but it's not what I expected,' she admitted. 'Either she's changed, or I've changed, or things 'ave changed an' I don't know where I am half the time.'

What she was finding it hard to explain was equally hard for her to accept – her sudden change in status. She had been in charge of the housekeeping of Thornmere Hall for so long that she was not now best pleased to find the reins of office taken from her. This was not what she had had in mind when she first pleaded with Mrs Webster to take up Mr Harker's offer of a job. She had looked forward to having her back at the Hall, a fellow worker and companion. But now she found she was relegated to the role she had occupied before Mrs Webster's retirement, a sort of general servant, and she didn't like it one little bit.

'So you're not so pleased about Mrs Webster's home-coming?' said Reuben, rewording his question.

'Like I said, it isn't working out the way I thought it would, but nothin' ever does, does it?' Ruby, repacking her basket, avoided Reuben's eye. 'As a matter of fact, I've been thinking of moving on. I've been here more'n thirteen years and about time I had a change.'

'It don't do to make up your mind all of a sudden. Mrs Webster's been here less than a week. Once she's got over the novelty of having her old job back, she'll be more'n pleased to hand it back to you. She liked retirement, but she didn't get enough of it. She told me so.'

'It isn't only Mrs Webster. It's me, too. I feel I got in a rut – I'd like a change.'

Reuben didn't like change of any kind. It took a long time for him to get used to things being different. He was only just getting used to thinking of Mr Harker as the guv'nor. He couldn't imagine the Hall without Ruby. He watched with troubled eyes as she rose to her feet and brushed the grass from her skirt.

'Where you be thinking of going, then?'

She flashed him an obscure look. 'I could always go and keep house for Ted Foster 'til somethin' better comes up.'

'I don't call that much of a change, half a mile down the road, and besides, people 'ud talk. You wouldn't like that.'

'I'd be too far away to hear 'em, wouldn't I?'

He had never known Ruby behave this way before, like you'd expect a skittish horse to behave. He knew how to deal with a horse, but he was lost when it came to a woman. You couldn't soothe a woman with a soft voice or a gentle touch. You couldn't coax or lure a woman like you could an unbridled mare. You couldn't tempt a woman into a harness with a handful of oats – or could you?

'Ruby,' he said. 'Hang on a mo' 'til I've cleared up here,

then I'll walk you back to the house. There's something I'd like to talk over with you.'

'So you've managed it at last,' Mrs Webster said, when Ruby told her the news. It was early afternoon and Mrs Webster, rosy from sleep, had just wakened from her afternoon nap. Ruby had laid a corner of the kitchen table with a freshly-laundered cloth and set out three cups and saucers. 'Couldn't you find anything stronger than tea to drink your health in?' she said.

Ruby smirked. 'I be quite satisfied with tea.'

'You're too easily satisfied, in my opinion. Some girls wouldn't have been satisfied with that sort of hugger-mugger way of proposing. More of a proposition than a proposal, I'd say. Seems to me Reuben only popped the question so that he could make sure of getting the lodge.'

Mrs Webster was put out on two counts. Firstly, she had always cherished the hope that one day she might be offered the tenancy of the lodge, and secondly, while she had advocated Ruby's marriage to Reuben as long as it didn't affect her personally, now that it meant losing a very useful helpmate it was a different matter.

But she couldn't hold out against Ruby's state of bliss for long. Only a heart of stone would be unable to melt under the light of such happiness. 'When are you naming the day, then?'

'Not yet awhile, there's a mint of things to prepare first. I want to make a start on me bottom drawer, and Reuben is planning to redecorate the lodge. He's going to drive me into Norwich to choose wallpaper as soon as Mr Harker gets back. We don't like to do anything without the master's permission, and he won't be home until the strike be over.'

'It is over,' said Mrs Webster. 'I forgot to tell you. The postman brought the news along with the second post. The miners are still holding out, but the general strike is over.' Her face darkened. 'This strike has a lot to answer for,' she said.

Daniel knew there was no danger of any of his men going on strike. For one thing none of them were union members, and for another he had a largely contented workforce.

It had always seemed unreasonable to him that any slip of a girl just fourteen years old and straight from school, if working in an office, was entitled to an annual holiday with pay, whereas those who worked on the factory floor, which might include members of her own family, received no paid leave apart from those days on the Christian calendar and public holidays.

Daniel would have none of that. He saw to it that everyone on his pay roll, no matter what their job, was given a week's annual leave without forfeiting their wages. He also instituted a form of sick club to which the staff could contribute if they wished. Most of them did, for though they were all on the panel and thereby entitled to free medical treatment under the terms of their weekly national insurance contributions, this did not cover their wives and children. Daniel's scheme did. So, though he had no fears that his workers would desert him and join the strikers, he thought it wiser to be on hand in case some young hothead tried to make trouble. He lay low, not tempting fate by making himself obtrusive and spent most of his time going through the accounts in the offices at Ivy House.

1925 had been a good year. The post-war tide of unemployment was slowly receding, so hopefully 1926 would prove even more successful. He played with the idea of branching out. What had been a good site for Thurgood Tinplate Works in 1830 was wholly inadequate in 1926.

Much to his regret the last of the trees and open spaces round the works had gone, built over in a higgledy-piggledy fashion without forethought or planning, and the tramlines had been extended to run past the factory gates. The subsequent noise did not affect George and Mollie Gilbert, still living on the top floor of Ivy House, and it seemed to have little detrimental effect on young Joey, a bright lad who had just won a scholarship to the local grammar school. Dan got used to the invasion of urban noises after a night or two, though he was surprised to find how much he missed the peace and quiet of Thornmere. Even so, he was in no hurry to go back there. The general strike was not his only reason for staying in London.

It had dawned on him some weeks ago that Helena Roseberry was no longer living in the village. Once he could hardly drive or walk along the street without catching some tantalising glimpse of her. Days went by without seeing her, then weeks. When next he had occasion to go into the kitchen he casually mentioned this fact to Ruby.

'Oh no, you won't see her about anymore, she's left Thornmere for good. She's working in London now.'

'Working?' he queried.

'Yes, she and a friend, partners in a hat shop. Tha's what I heard. A shop called Hatters.' Ruby frowned. 'No, that don't sound right, somehow. Let me think . . . I got it, Toppers — yes, Toppers. Somewhere in the West End, so Mrs Timms say.'

Daniel knew that the postmistress rarely got her facts wrong, and his heart sank.

'And I presume she is living with this friend?'

Ruby looked coy. 'I don't know nothing about that.

There's talk tha's she got a gentleman friend. Some do say she's gone up to London to get married, but . . .'

'Thank you, Ruby.' Daniel suddenly found the conversation not to his liking. 'When Reuben gets back from Beckton, tell him to come to the office. There's a little job I want him to do on the Chev.'

Within days of arriving at the works and installing himself temporarily in Ivy House, he went on the trail of Toppers. It didn't take him long to pinpoint it – a few discreet enquiries and he discovered its whereabouts and, more to the point some information about its two young proprietors. He learnt quite a lot about a Mrs Harding, but very little about Miss Roseberry, whom the customers rarely saw. Mrs Harding was the lynchpin of the business, but it was Miss Roseberry's designs which added to its reputation as an establishment of flair and fashion.

All this he learnt from Chloe Butler, an acquaintance of many years' standing who lived in Shepherd's Market, and whom for old times' sake he called upon whenever he was in London. She always greeted him with a bright smile and her usual quip. 'Business as usual, dearie, or is this just a social call?'

No, she told him, she wasn't one of Toppers' customers. 'They go in for a classy clientele,' she said. 'They're particular who they sell their goods to, same as me.' She came close to him and he got the full impact of her wide baby-blue eyes. She had a face like a flower, well past its first bloom, but still beautiful. 'You know,' she said, 'where you're concerned, it's not the money that matters – it's you for yourself. Why did you have to move up to that God-forsaken hole in Norfolk?'

'Because I came under its spell when I was ten years old.'

'And now you're under another spell. You can't fool me

– I know you too well. Who is it, the other half of Toppers? The one who designs the hats? I knew it. You wouldn't be asking me all these questions if it was for the other one, the divorcée. She's not your type.'

With a wistful smile she cupped his face in her hands and kissed him full on the mouth, something she refused her other customers. 'You and me both, a couple of fools eating our hearts out for something we'll never have. She's got a fella – lives with him over Pimlico way.' She looked up at him from beneath her gold-tipped lashes. 'You're like me in other ways, too. You wouldn't settle for secondbest, would you?'

He stayed the night with her and left the next morning before she awoke. He left the customary amount on the mantelshelf, then changed his mind and returned it to his wallet. He felt he had no right to go on using her as a prostitute knowing now how she felt about him. He wrote her a note instead – just four words – 'Thank you for everything'. She would accept it as his farewell to her. When the shops opened he would find a florist's and send her flowers, a dozen and a half pink roses – one for every year he had known her. She would understand the subtlety in that gesture and appreciate it.

He stepped out into the freshness of early morning. The air, after Chloe's torrid little room, tasted like wine, and he swallowed it in great gulps. This corner of London was still asleep, the street cleaners still busy. He walked through Half Moon Street into Piccadilly and then along Regent Street. It was strange to see this usually busy thoroughfare void of traffic. A solitary wagon overtook him and the driver reined in his horse. 'Need a lift, guv?'

'Thank you, but no, I'm enjoying the walk.'

'Please yourself.' The man sounded disappointed.

Dan felt in his pocket for a half-crown. 'Here, take this, buy yourself a drink.'

'Well, thank you, guv. Very civil of you.' The man touched the brim of his hat with his whip, then urged his horse into a trot. A telegraph boy cycled past whistling 'Alexander's Ragtime Band'. Fifteen years on and still going strong, Dan thought, remembering a time in 1911 when he and old Timothy had gone to their local music hall and heard the tune for the first time.

'What sort of noise do you call that!' Timothy had grumbled. 'Ragtime! Pshaw! You mark my words, it won't catch on.'

The music hall was still standing, though greatly changed and now calling itself a variety theatre. Daniel had taken young Joey there to see a minstrel show on the boy's last birthday. They had had a wonderful evening together, sitting up in the gods and eating oranges and joining in the choruses. Joey had an ear for music. The next day he was picking out the songs from the show on the old battered piano that had once belonged to his father's parents. Playing the melody with his right hand and harmonising with his left.

Daniel marvelled that such a natural gift should be bestowed on the child of totally deaf parents. Joey could play by ear anything that was whistled or sung to him, and he rarely struck a false note. Daniel despaired to think that George and Mollie could not hear the music young Joey was making, but it was a despair that was largely wasted, for he knew by their expressions that they were happy just watching him play. He often turned over in his mind the idea that he would send young Joey to an academy of music. With the right training he might become a brilliant pianist. Dan possessed no knowledge of music himself, but he had a gut feeling that Joey's talents were being wasted.

Mulling over these plans now, walking aimlessly, he realised he was approaching Bond Street, and immediately thought of Toppers.

It was still early and there were still few people about. He located the milliners without difficulty though he walked past it twice thinking it was a house. Its windows were shuttered. London could have been a city of the dead, he thought. It was only seven o'clock. A solitary policeman came in sight and Daniel asked him if there were any restaurants open at this hour. A small French restaurant was pointed out to him and he found to his surprise that he wasn't the only customer. He took a seat in the window and coffee and hot croissants were placed before him with a dish of yellow butter and another of black cherry jam. The smell of the coffee made him salivate. The brisk walk and the freshness of the morning had sharpened his appetite.

He sat on, loitering over his breakfast. He was in no hurry. The customers came and went – mostly men, a few in evening dress, heavy-eyed from lack of sleep. Roistering the night away, he suspected, dismissing them patronisingly. He had little time for those who didn't work for a living. And then he saw her, coming along the street with that graceful swaying walk so characteristic of her, and his senses quivered into life. She was wearing something in green, he hardly noticed what, but he did see the little knot of mimosa pinned to her jacket. She was smiling as if her thoughts gave her pleasure and he remembered with a mixture of sorrow and despair Ruby's remark about a gentleman friend.

He wanted her to smile at him like that but he knew that even if he knocked on the window and roused her from her walking dream, she wouldn't see him. She might turn and stare with those limpid green eyes that sent him wild and appraise him coolly, but it wouldn't register. He watched her as she walked on out of sight, and with a sudden impotent gesture he clenched his fist and smashed it down on the table top.

'I don't care how long it takes but I'll get her,' he vowed. 'I got Thornmere Hall, and I'll get her, too.'

One dread had hung over Amy Cousins since she first arrived at Rodings, and that was that she would be asked to learn to drive. Every time she stood at the outer door of the kitchen and looked across the yard at the coach-house, her tummy turned over. It menaced her, that little car, squatting there in company with mice, spiders, cobwebs, the remains of a horse-drawn lawn mower, two barn cats and a lady's bicycle, reminding her that the threat of learning to drive had not gone away though nothing had been said since the day of her arrival.

But now that the trains had stopped running and she was unable to get to Beckton Market to renew Mrs Roseberry's embroidery silks and wools, the threat hung over her like a poised axe.

She missed her once-weekly trips to Beckton Market. She usually caught the ten-thirty train from Thornmere Halt and arrived at the market town ten minutes later. There were always little errands for Mrs Roseberry and sometimes for Mrs Taylor, too. She went unhurriedly from shop to shop saving her visit to the haberdashery until last, as a child might save a favourite sweet as a kind of treat. Her treat was the circulating library at the back of the shop, where for twopence a time she could buy enough romance to last her until her next visit.

Always she finished her morning with a cup of coffee and a toasted Sally Lunn at the Belle Vue Tea Rooms before catching the twelve-fifteen back to Thornmere. She had, after a struggle with her conscience, tried to patch up her differences with her aunt. Hanging on to old grievances, she discovered, was more damaging to herself than to others.

In this new-found spirit of reconciliation she wrote a long letter to Aunt Flora, telling her about her new life, giving details of her employment and a description of the Queen Anne house and its occupants. She painted such a rosy picture of her present circumstances, hinting at social events that were purely a figment of her imagination, that she knew in spite of her good intentions the letter was less an honest desire to patch things up than a verbal form of poking out her tongue. She grinned as she posted it. She didn't expect an answer and she didn't get one.

On the fourth day of the strike Amy remembered the bicycle in the coach-house that had once belonged to Miss Roseberry, and according to Mrs Taylor, had hardly been used. It was still in good condition, had been well looked after, the gardener checking it over once in a while. Amy had not ridden a bicycle since she left school, but cycling was something one didn't forget, so it was said. She tried it up and down the yard until she felt confident enough to take it on the road. It was a newer model than her old one which was second-hand when Aunt Flora bought it, had a shopping basket fixed to the handlebars and a guard over the back wheel to prevent her skirts from getting caught in the spokes.

And now she was on her way to Beckton Market again, and her mind on the pleasures to come – books to choose from the library and coffee and a bun at the tea rooms. She had the road to herself and from her vantage point on the saddle she could see over the hedgerows to the fields beyond, greening over with young corn. A skylark was singing overhead and in the distance came the faint call of a cuckoo. She felt on top of the world.

She nearly came to earth quite literally when she reached her destination, for her legs, out of condition for cycling, turned to jelly as she stood down. She would have fallen but for the nearness of a drinking fountain which she grabbed in time. A quick glance round assured her that the only witness to her mortification was a large and mangy cat sunning himself on the cobbles of the square, who blinked at her with indifferent eyes. She propped the bicycle against a convenient post and made her way on unreliable legs towards the shops, trying not to dwell too much on the return journey, which was just as well, for an even more embarrassing mishap awaited her.

Her mind on the forthcoming attraction at the Beckton Regal — a return visit of *Blood and Sand* which she had seen three times already and would happily have gone on watching for ever and starring every woman's secret lover, Rudolf Valentino — she failed to notice until the last minute a large boulder in her path. She swerved, the bicycle skidded and came to a sudden stop but she did not, and sailed on to land, unhurt but shaken, on the grass verge. Almost immediately a car drew up behind her and out stepped the vicar of Thornmere, the Reverend Francis Thomas.

She knew him by sight only, as doubtless he did her, for everybody knew everybody else in Thornmere. He hurried over to give assistance. 'I was just behind you and could see what was going to happen. I shouted, but of course you couldn't hear. Are you hurt? No bones broken?'

She wasn't hurt, but felt extremely foolish and conscious that one stocking had laddered, that her hat was awry, her gloves soiled, her shopping strewn over the road, and that the vicar, close up, had eyes just as dark and heart-stopping as Rudolf Valentino. She went rather weak at the knees when he smiled at her, but put that down to the effects of her fall.

He helped her collect her belongings and paused when he came to the library books, looking at each one in turn. His eyes glinted laughingly as he returned them to her. '*Son of the Sheikh* and *Desert Love*? That sounds like an awful lot of sand.'

She blushed, squirmed, and wished she had chosen something more edifying, something that would have impressed him. Glibly, she said, 'I got those for Mrs Roseberry. She likes me to read something light to her while she does her embroidery.'

Together they examined the bicycle and found the front wheel was badly buckled. 'We'll have to leave it here and send somebody along to collect it,' said Mr Thomas. 'The wheel can be straightened easily enough, so don't worry about that. It's just a question of getting you home now.'

'I – I can walk,' she said, but without enthusiasm. Once upon a time she would have walked any distance rather than go by car, but now the thought of riding as a passenger with this stunning man overcame any fear of car-sickness.

'Good gracious, I wouldn't think of allowing you to walk.' He opened the car door and helped her in. 'You sit there and nurse your bruises while I go and deal with that lump of flint. I expect it fell off a loaded wagon.'

Though he was slightly built and not much taller than she, he was incredibly strong, and she watched with a flutter of excitement as he rolled the boulder off the road and on to the greensward and placed the bicycle beside it.

He was out of breath when he took his place behind the wheel.

'I'm out of training,' he said with a smile. 'I don't get a lot of exercise in my line of calling.'

He smiled a lot for a Welshman she thought, for she was under the impression that the Welsh, like the Scots, were a dour lot. She wondered if he was only half Welsh as Francis wasn't a Welsh name, but when he spoke he was wholly Welsh. The lilt in his voice was music to her ears.

He drove carefully as if afraid of jolting her more than necessary. The hedgerows slipped past. The hood of the car was down and she had to keep hold of her hat to prevent it blowing off.

'Not too draughty for you?'

'No, I love it.'

'How do you like living in Thornmere?'

'I love that, too.'

She meant what she said. She loved everything in sight at that moment: the fields, the wide open spaces, the winding road which, alas, would come to an end all too soon.

'And you don't find the Honourable Mrs Roseberry too intimidating?'

'I did at first, but now I have got to know her better – no, not at all.'

'Well, good for you. I find her extremely intimidating.' She glowed in the light of his praise.

Silence fell between them, an easy and comfortable pause which gave her the opportunity to study him covertly. For such a slight man he had large, powerful-looking hands with well-tended nails. She always noticed people's fingernails. Her own were ugly and misshapen, the consequence of biting them as a child. She took off her hat, put it on her lap and hid her hands beneath the brim before stealing another look in his direction. He had a handsome profile with a straight nose and a sensitive mouth. His dark springy hair grew back from a high forehead, which she knew was a sign of intelligence. She knew he was unmarried, which caused much speculation in the village. The Reverend Mr Thomas would be a marvellous catch for any girl. She suppressed a sigh.

'We never see you in church,' he said. It wasn't a reproach, more a statement of fact, but she coloured up and began to make excuses.

'It's not because I don't,' she groped for the right words. 'It's not that I don't believe, but I am not Church of England. I was brought up chapel.'

He smiled again. 'In our father's house there are many mansions,' he said softly.

She had never fully understood those words before — now he made them sound like music. 'I would very much like to come to your church.'

'I will keep you to that, but let's get one thing clear first. It is not my church. The church belongs to the congregation, to the people who come to worship in it. It will be your church, too, if you want it.'

That night when she went to bed she didn't take either of her library books with her, she took a Bible instead, one she had found among Mrs Roseberry's books. She was not at all conversant with the Bible. At Sunday school and at chapel chosen bits, mostly from the Old Testament, had been read out to the congregation, but she had rarely listened, escaping into her dream world instead. But now she wanted more than anything to be able to converse with Francis Thomas in his own language, and reading the Bible from cover to cover she thought would be a good start.

She turned the pages to Genesis, chapter one, verse one: 'In the beginning God created the heaven and the earth . . .' She settled herself more comfortably against her pillows. 'And the earth was without form, and void; and the darkness was upon the face of the deep. And the Spirit of God moved upon the waters . . .'

Dear God, he is so beautiful and I am without form, and void, and the darkness is often upon my face when I'm in a black mood. I am not pleasing to look upon, Oh Lord, but I might look better if I had a nicer nature. Help me please to do that which is right in your sight and if you could just nudge the Reverend Francis Thomas in my direction a little, I'd be ever so grateful.

She fell asleep while trying to work out in her head how long it would take to read the Bible from cover to cover taking a chapter a night, including the Psalms and Proverbs.

She went to Matins at Thornmere Church the following Sunday. The general strike was at its height, and that was the subject of the sermon. Amy had thought Francis Thomas a gentle man — strong but gentle — but in the pulpit he became transformed into a man of wrath. He struck the open Bible before him with his clenched fist and his eyes flashed like black fire. He leant forward to give weight to his words and thundered at them with a voice that sent icy thrills up and down Amy's spine and made the rest of the congregation sit up.

'I am the son of a miner,' he roared. 'My brothers are miners. They are not withholding their labour because they are shirkers, they are doing it as a matter of principle. They will not give in. Only starvation will force them back to the pits. But they will conquer . . .' His voice rose like a cry to Heaven, and a swallow nesting in the rafters took fright and swooped towards the light where it came to rest on the sill of a jewel-coloured window. 'They will conquer, I say, as all good men who wrestle with the forces of evil will overcome those who oppose them.'

Amy felt at home. This was the sort of preaching she had been brought up on, and it was all she could do to stop herself from applauding when, with a last rousing command for them to pray for victory for the just over the unjust, he brought the sermon to a close. But when he came to announce the number of the last hymn it was in his quiet and lilting voice.

She stood with a hymn book in her hands, opening and closing her mouth in the right places, but without any idea of what she was singing. She was miles away, floating up there in the clouds, nearer my God to thee. Francis Thomas, noticing her for the first time, felt touched by her expression. He was a simple man, dedicated to his calling, and he thought that the ecstatic glow he saw in her face was the visible proof of her deep religious conviction. Lucky girl, he thought. Very few had such a blessing bestowed upon them.

NINE

In Bedford Square the signs of the approach of autumn were showing in the yellow and saffron tints of the foliage; the fruits of the plane trees dangling like wooden decorations between the broad leaves. It was the kind of September day Helena relished, and she could not help thinking of Norfolk when on such an Indian summery day the sky would be a misty blue and the air so still that not a leaf or a blade of grass would tremble.

She had spent the morning at Toppers overseeing in the workroom. Midge employed eight out-workers who did the basic work of moulding shapes and stitching the distinctive green and white labels onto the lining. The trimming and finishing-off was done on the premises, on the top floor, where several small store-rooms had been converted into a large and airy workshop. This was Helena's department, watching over the half-dozen or so part-time skilled milliners, scrutinising each hat as it was nearing completion for sometimes, hats being made to measure, would at the last minute require a small adjustment.

Even those made for the peg – just one of each to ensure

their exclusive tag – could at this point be improved by a slight alteration or a different form of trimming. Such last-minute touches made all the difference between being just smart and being chic, and to Midge's pleasure, more expensive. Just at present they were working on rush orders for hats to go with country tweeds or something dressy for winter town wear. Though Helena had a slip of a room partitioned off from the rest of the workroom where she could shut herself away to sketch out her ideas on paper, she preferred taking this kind of work home. For one thing it was quieter, for the noise of machines and women's voices in the workroom distracted her, and for another there was Paul. Lately she begrudged every minute she was away from him.

Midge was in her element in the shop. She was a born saleswoman, and though she now employed a very capable manageress so that she could be free to attend fashion shows when and where they occurred, nothing pleased her more than selling a hat to a difficult customer who had only come in in the first place, she was assured, not to buy – just to look round. Challenging words to Midge. Her victims rarely escaped and, what was more, came back again and again.

'Thanks to you,' said Midge generously.

'If it was left to me the hats would never leave the workroom,' Helena responded, which she knew was true. She quaked at the thought of trying to sell a hat.

She was humming to herself now as she walked through the gardens, humming a tune that had been the rage for many months, 'Always': 'I'll be loving you, always . . . With a love that's true, always . . .' She hummed it again, aloud this time, getting carried away with the sheer joy of being alive on a day like this and knowing that Paul was waiting for her at the garden flat.

She was feeling particularly pleased with herself for she had solved the problem of Paul's birthday which was only a month away. She had bought him what she considered the perfect present – an electric typewriter: easier for a one-armed man to use than an ordinary typewriter. The electric typewriter had been around for some time, but not in general use, for not every home, or every office come to that, had mains electricity. That wouldn't be a problem where they were concerned. When Hugo had the Doughty Street house converted into separate flats he had had electric sockets installed in every room.

Midge had first put the idea of an electric typewriter into her head as she had considered getting one for her secretary, but when she discovered it meant having the shop rewired she had changed her mind. It was just a question then of knowing where to obtain one. As yet, there were few stockists of electric typewriters in London.

'Try Harrods,' said Midge. 'They guarantee to supply anything from a pin to an elephant. Compared to an elephant I should think an electric typewriter is a walk-over.'

So now an electric typewriter was available, and was being delivered on Paul's thirty-eighth birthday, the 21 October.

On her way home that afternoon she had stopped at Fuller's to buy Paul a walnut cake. Since he had cut down on his smoking he had developed a sweet tooth, but no matter how much sugar he consumed, he still did not put on weight. Paul's thinness was the only cloud on her horizon but she tried not to worry about it, for otherwise he seemed well enough. He had improved a lot since the move to Doughty Street and on fine days when not doing research at the British Museum he liked to take his work out to the balcony. He was writing a semi-autobiographical account of his travels and had made a good start though the miners' enforced capitulation in August had cast him into a silent and melancholy rage from which he emerged eager to get back to his writing, as if the world he was creating within himself was easier to live with than the real world outside.

But sometimes when Helena looked out at him she saw him leaning back in his chair with his eyes closed, as if exhausted. It was then that it seemed to her that he was withering before her eyes and her heart ached with pain and fear for him. Then another time he could be in such good spirits that she kidded herself that the bad times were all in her imagination. She put the blame for his swings of mood on the weather for if it rained and he couldn't get out he became moody. On sunny days she would sometimes hear him whistling, usually something from Gilbert and Sullivan.

She had got so used to the walk to and from Toppers during the time of the General Strike that she now did it as a matter of routine unless the day was too wet for comfort, then she joined the scramble for a taxi-cab. She thought up new ideas as she walked, creating designs for headwear in her mind, often inspired by the sight of a pretty face or the colour and pattern of a swathe of material spotted in a shop window.

She had grown to love London and Bloomsbury in particular. The air-raids had left scars where shrapnel had pierced stone or brickwork on the façade of some of the fine old buildings, but these were honourable wounds and already part of their country's history. She was glad that London would never grow to look like New York with great tower blocks or concrete and glass skyscrapers. She could never understand those of her friends who raved about the New York skyline for she saw nothing attractive in concrete scenery. London was saved from becoming like that – so she believed – because the clay soil on which the city was founded could not support anything above a certain height or weight. She hoped those who assured her were right. The thought of a concrete tower block overshadowing St Paul's appalled her.

She sometimes went home in a roundabout way so that she approached Doughty Street from the other end. This way she passed the Dickens' House and it always gave her a little thrill as she went by to think that Charles Dickens once lived at number forty-eight.

'I've just been past our illustrious neighbour's place,' she said once to Paul. 'I can't understand how you came to miss that out when you took me on that tremendous walkabout that time.'

'I was about to suggest it when you said I had walked your feet down to the ankles, so I wined you and dined you at Lottie's place instead. Remember?'

As she approached their less renowned abode she saw Jake's grey head just visible above the basement steps, obviously on the lookout for her. He often waylaid her if he had a message or some important news to impart.

Jacob caused both Paul and herself much speculation. He wasn't married, seemed to be without family or ties, and in their opinion was wasted in his present job of caretaker-cum-handyman, though that was nothing to go by in these days of high unemployment.

His loss was their gain for he could turn his hand to any task, and did so willingly, often outside his line of duty, like filling their coal-scuttles or moving furniture. He was, according to Paul, a useful source of useless information, and he was one of the 'experts' who had assured Helena that skyscrapers would never rear their ugly heads in London.

In spite of the difference in their ages, for Jake was rising sixty, he and Paul were regular drinking companions, re-living their wartime experiences over a pint in a local hostelry, or on the balcony of the garden flat. Jake was carefully abstemious when in their company, but on his own and at frequent intervals, he let himself go.

Drink was his weakness he told them. Drink had got him into the army when he was well above the age for call-up. One night at a music hall, where a bespangled singer with ogling eyes was seducing the audience with patriotic songs, he had waveringly gone up onto the stage and signed his name on the dotted line. He remembered nothing of the incident until the next morning when his landlady gleefully shook him awake.

'Look sharpish, you prize fool,' she chortled. 'You've got to report to the local war office. You took the king's shilling last night when you were too drunk to know what you were doing, though what good you'll be in the army at your time of life I can't imagine.'

He spent the latter part of his service with the Black and Tans in Ireland, though over that episode in his life he drew a veil. He had an upright carriage and looked younger than his age, and Helena could not understand how he had never married, especially these days when women outnumbered men at about four to one. Habitually he wore a cheery expression but now he looked grave.

'It's Paul, isn't it? It's bad news?' Her words caught in her throat.

He moistened his lips. 'He's been taken to hospital. Please, Miss Roseberry, just a minute,' as she made a dart towards the front door. 'Wait, I have something to tell you.'

'He's dead!'

'No, no, far from dead. It's just that . . . We can't talk here, come down to my place.'

She sat in Jake's kitchen with a steaming cup of hot sweet tea before her and listened, as if to a faraway echo, Jake recounting the events of the morning. Sometimes, during the telling of it, she looked up and saw a pair of feet go past the window and irrationally, with a part of her mind that was not yet numb from shock, tried to envisage the kind of hat to go with certain shoes. She found to her surprise that she was still clutching the Fuller's cake-box, squashed in at the top where she had grasped it during her descent down the basement stairs, not from fear of falling but as something to hang on to in her collapsing world. She placed it on the table. 'It was a treat for Paul, but I don't suppose he'll want it now. Perhaps you could make use of it.' It struck her as odd that her voice sounded so normal when she felt anything but normal.

Jake had taken the usual scuttle of coal up to their sitting room that morning and was laying the fire ready for lighting later when Mr Berkeley, who was writing at his desk, suddenly gave a little choke and out gushed all this blood. It spurted everywhere – all down his shirt, over his writing pad, over the desk, on the floor.

'He didn't say a word. He looked more surprised than shocked. I was the one in shock – I didn't know what to do. It was Mr Berkeley who pulled himself together first and started to rap out instructions to me. I cleaned him up as best I could – he made me do that before I phoned the doctor. By that time he wasn't looking too good. Dr Percy, as soon as he arrived, got things moving. The ambulance was here in no time . . .'

'Where did they take him, Jake?'

'The chest hospital. Dr Percy knows one of the consultant physicians there. Says he's a good man – the best. He said to tell you Mr Berkeley is in good hands and not to worry.'

'Why tell me not to worry when by the very nature of things, how can I not?' said Helena. She brushed her hands across her eyes; not that they were wet. They felt hot and ached.

'I tried to reach you at the hat shop but they said you'd left.'

'I walked. I took my time . . . I was window-shopping.' Oh why, oh why had she today of all days, dawdled on the way home – thinking of Paul, singing to him instead of being with him? She took a sip of her tea but it was cold and she replaced the cup on its saucer.

'Did Dr Percy say what had caused the haemorrhage?'

'He wouldn't commit himself.' Jake sought her glance with compassion. 'But did he have to say anything, Miss Roseberry? Don't you know in your heart what the matter is? Haven't you suspected?'

Yes, of course she suspected, but because she didn't want to know she had put the suspicion out of her mind. Paul's continuous loss of weight, the waxiness of his skin, the feverish brightness of his eyes: consumption, a dreaded word. Not so common these days, but common enough. But it wasn't a death sentence, was it? Her question unasked was in her eyes and went unanswered. Jake, with old-fashioned courtesy, helped her to her feet.

'Why don't you go up to your own room and rest? There's nothing you can do and it could be ages before Dr Percy gets back, and you'll want to feel up to it if he suggests you visit Mr Berkeley later.'

She lay on the bed she shared with Paul and listened to the Parliament clock on the wall ticking away what was left of the long afternoon. The clock looked incongruous in such a luxurious setting but Paul, who still liked to poke around in second-hand furniture shops, had bought it as his contribution to their new abode. 'To counteract all this Art Deco,' he said at the time.

There was a green marble clock on the mantelshelf to which he had taken a strong dislike, but because it was one of Hugo's favourite pieces he let it remain. The Parliament clock was no work of art but it kept good time. Now in the quiet of the empty house it kept time to the beat of her heart. Only when a taxi pulled up outside did it sound to her as if it had put on a sudden spurt. She heard Dr Percy paying off the driver and jumped from the bed, and had the front door open before he could lift his finger to the bell.

He followed her through to the balcony, his hat held close to his chest. It was warm there in the last glow of the dying sun and the basketwork chairs with their deep cushions looked inviting. Dr Percy sank into the nearest one with an audible sigh of relief. He looked and sounded weary, but she had no compassion for him. How dare he sit there making himself comfortable when Paul was lying in some hard, unfriendly hospital bed?

'Can I go to him?' she said.

He leant forward and took her hand. 'Sit down, my dear. You'll see Paul, but not today.' He ignored her tiny moan of protest. 'There are certain tests to be carried out: a sputum test and chest X-rays. The results of these won't come through before tomorrow, if then. A haemoptysis has to be thoroughly investigated, there's no leverage for taking chances.'

'A haemoptysis? Is that a medical term for haemorrhage?'

'When vomited blood is caused by pulmonary tuberculosis, the medical term is a haemoptysis.'

'Pulmonary tuberculosis,' she said leadenly. 'Is that a medical term for consumption?'

'It is the correct term.'

She gave an imperceptible sigh. 'Will you please take me to the hospital now. I want to see Paul.'

'Tomorrow, if it is permissable, I will take you to the hospital. Today you must allow Paul to rest. For both your sakes, my dear, for seeing you will only excite him. Probably you will also have to undergo some tests.'

'TB isn't contagious, is it?'

'Normally, no, but they will want to play safe.'

'And Paul?'

'They will keep him under observation until he is fit enough to be moved. Then I think a transfer to a sanatorium for the right treatment.'

Amy's graphic description of Raneleigh came to her mind. Never would she allow Paul near such a place. 'No! No sanatorium,' she said decidedly. 'I will care for Paul myself.'

He saw that in her present mood there was no point in arguing. 'Do you think I could have a drink?'

'Tea or coffee?'

'I was hoping for something stronger.'

She gave a wisp of a smile. 'I'm sorry, my mind doesn't run along those lines. Let's see what Paul keeps in his booze cupboard.'

Looking back, when Paul was home again, she wondered how she survived the ensuing weeks. Dr Percy was her pillar of strength and sometimes her whipping-boy, suffering her tears and accusations with unswerving kindness and support. If she was determined to go through with this idea of nursing Paul herself, he said, he meant to see that she did it properly. Paul would need a room to himself so it was back to the ottoman in the sitting room for her. On Dr Percy's advice she had the balcony glassed in with windows paned with vita glass so as not to exclude the sun's essential violet rays and furnished it with, among other things, a long cane chair and a cantilever table strong enough to hold the typewriter. All this was made ready for Paul's homecoming which Helena insisted must be by the 21 October.

'Why that date in particular? He is doing so well where he is, why hurry things?'

'Because that is his birthday, and we want to celebrate it here.'

Dr Percy gave her a searching look. 'It you don't take better care of yourself the hospital will only be exchanging one patient for another.'

Having a morbid fear of hospitals, she had gone to a private clinic for her investigation. Her sputum was clear and the chest X-rays had shown no sign of tubercle. When she was finally allowed to visit Paul she had approached his bed with caution, dreading the worst. Her fears proved not unfounded but though he looked, and undoubtedly was, weaker than when she had last seen him, his eyes were cheerful, not feverishly bright and his grin irresistible.

'You beloved fraud,' she said, then fell upon him in a paroxysm of tears.

Sister shooed her out of the room. 'That is no way for a responsible person to behave.'

Helena blew her nose. 'At the moment I feel anything but responsible.'

Sister tched tched. 'Try to think of my patient and not of yourself. I'm the one who has to pick up the pieces after the visitors have gone, so please show a little more consideration.'

'They have taken away my cigarettes,' Paul complained when she returned.

'Good for them. Their stock is rising in my estimation. It was very low when Sister Ferris took me out and scolded me. Oh Paul.' Her enforced cheerfulness began to crack. 'I wish to God I could take you home with me.'

'They're talking about sending me to a sanatorium. They have mentioned Bournemouth. Do you know anything about Bournemouth? I always thought it was populated with old ladies and Pekingese.'

'Darling, you're beginning to sound breathless. We mustn't talk.'

'No, we mustn't waste time talking,' he agreed. He gave her one of his outrageous looks. 'Nip into bed with me instead.'

'Paul!'

'Quick, before the she-dragon returns. We've got ten minutes.'

When Dr Percy was told of this he chuckled. 'Our laddie has got remarkable powers of recuperation. Was he serious, do you think?'

'I never know with Paul. What do you think?'

'I think the wish was father to the thought.'

She pondered on this. 'Would it be safe for me to have a child by Paul?'

'Safe, how? Physically? You yourself are young and fit enough, but Paul . . . Morally, it is not for me to say.'

'I mean, this TB thing. Is it passed on from parent to child? Could our baby be born with tuberculosis, or catch it from Paul afterwards?' She had not yet dared ask if Paul could be cured. She knew that the treatment, even if successful, could take years – and she hadn't got years. She would be thirty next birthday and she desperately wanted a child. Now, more than anything, she wanted something to remember Paul by if – but she closed her mind to that possibility.

'I think that is something you must discuss with Paul,' said Dr Percy gravely. 'I have my own opinion but the decision must be yours alone. And if you do decide to go ahead . . . no, it won't be born with tuberculosis, and provided care is taken there is no reason to believe it would ever contract it.'

'I do hate to hear a baby being referred to as an "it".'

'What then would you prefer?'

'A son. I yearn to bear Paul a son.'

Paul was allowed home for his birthday on the understanding he returned to the hospital for further treatment. One possibility being mooted was artificial pneumothorax, introducing air into the pleural cavity, a form of treatment now gaining favour. Dr Percy was a bit dubious of this. He was more in favour of a spell in a sanatorium, but by mutual consent none of this was to be discussed during Paul's spell at home.

Helena filled the balcony with gold and bronze chrysanthemums. She bought another Fuller's walnut cake and had a brace of pheasants sent up from Norfolk which she cooked from one of Mrs Taylor's recipes. She had no knowledge of wines but a wine merchant in High Holborn said she could do no wrong with a good burgundy, so she took two bottles on his recommendation expecting Dr Percy to join them for dinner.

But he wouldn't stay; a real sacrifice on his part

for he loved good food and the smells from the kitchen were appetising. He helped Paul to the balcony and onto the chair, then took his leave. Helena escorted him to the door trying to persuade him to change his mind, but was not undismayed when he declined.

'You lovebirds will want to be on your own this evening, and Paul must be sick of the sight of me. I think this short sojourn with you will do him good.'

'He looks much improved.'

'He's excited about being home again. Don't let him overdo it and not too much of that rich food I can smell cooking. He has, for the past four weeks, existed mainly on pap, don't forget.'

'It's pheasant. I promised him pheasant and I have broiled it and made mushroom sauce to go with it. I hope it tastes as good as it smells.'

'It smells extremely succulent,' said Dr Percy with a regretful sigh. His digestive organs, cheated of sustenance, rumbled in protest. 'I'll call in tomorrow. And don't forget – any anxiety, any doubt about Paul, just telephone me at once no matter what time it is.'

Paul only picked at his meal but relished what little he ate. He enjoyed the burgundy more and had nearly a bottle to himself. 'Now all I want to finish off that superb repast is a whiff of nicotine. Just one little puff, my beloved gaoler.'

'It's as much as my life is worth.'

'What about *my* life?'

'You'll survive.'

He looked askance at the typewriter, not recognising it at first for what it was. 'It is a very remarkable piece of machinery. What am I supposed to do with it?'

'You type on it, of course.'

'With one hand!'

'It's automatic, it works by electricity, like this.' She demonstrated.

'Very ingenious,' he said with gentle irony. 'I can see you're an expert already, and such expertise will come in useful. You'll be able to do my typing for me in future. I won't have to send out to the agency where no one can read my writing and who overcharge outrageously.'

'You don't like it,' she said, biting back her disappointment. 'I might have known. You don't like anything you haven't chosen for yourself.'

'I can see it becoming absolutely indispensable. Darling, forgive me for not being more enthusiastic. I love you so much and I'm so delighted to be back with you that I can't put my mind to anything else.'

She thought he was teasing until she saw tears in his eyes. She could not remember seeing Paul in tears before which proved to her how weak he was in spite of the good show he was putting on. She had expected too much and too soon. He might never use the typewriter but he would value it because she gave it to him. She went over to him, put her arms around him and rested her cheek against the top of his head and he stroked the back of her thighs. 'Let's go to bed,' he said huskily.

The rat-tat-tat of the postman startled them both. It was nine-thirty and the last delivery of the day.

Helena moved. 'I expect it's another birthday card.' The balcony sill was dotted with them. From the staff of the *Daily Encounter*, from Midge and the girls at Toppers, from Hugo and even from Sister Ferris. This last given the place of honour.

But it was not another card for Paul. It was a letter addressed to her with a Thornmere postmark and written in an unknown hand. As she tore it open, two photographs fluttered to the ground. She stooped and picked them up.

'Well, I never!'

Paul laughed. 'You sound just like my old nanny.'

'My nanny, too. She said that whenever she was flummoxed. Now I know what being flummoxed means, it's how I'm feeling now. I've had a letter from that dreadful man.'

'Which one of your friends is that?'

'No friend I can assure you. The war-profiteer from Thornmere Hall. He never does anything without a motive, and now he has sent me two wedding photographs of people I don't even know. I wonder why?'

'Read his letter and find out.'

'Good gracious! It's Ruby Pearson and Reuben Stoneham! I didn't recognise Ruby behind that huge bouquet. She and Reuben married, what a lovely surprise. They were made for each other those two. Look at the number of guests! Let's see if I recognise anybody. Goodness, there's Amy Cousins, whatever was she doing at their wedding! And Mrs Taylor, too, in the back row, looking very smart. Everybody in the village seems to be there – except my mother, of course. I must take back what I said about Mr Harker. It was very kind of him to send me these photographs, but I still wonder why. Do you think he thinks I'm homesick?'

'I expect he's got a yen for you, and this is his way of keeping in touch.'

'Paul! What rubbish. He hardly knows me. I expect it's all part of his Lord of the Manor act, keeping the tenants happy sort of thing, except that I'm no tenant of his. Oh, that's a bitchy thing to say. Perhaps he just thought I would be pleased to know about the wedding, and I am, of course. I must send a present. I don't suppose Mother would have thought of it.' She breathed a tiny sigh. 'Bother, I shall have to write and thank him, I suppose.'

'Not tonight you won't. Have a heart, darling. Come to bed. I've been on the wagon long enough as it is.'

They both purchased a navy-blue suit for the occasion, and Ruby a navy straw trimmed with white satin. She wore a row of pearl beads with a white crêpe-de-chine blouse, and carried an enormous bouquet of white chrysanthemums. They were spending a week at Yarmouth afterwards and a few days before the wedding Ruby asked Reuben whether Mr Harker had offered him the use of the Daimler for their honeymoon.

'He han't said nothin' about it yet.'

'How're we going to get there if he doesn't?'

'Like anyone else. By train to Norwich, then change.'

It was a beautiful day for the wedding. One of those late mellow September days when the air tastes like vintage wine. The church was nearly as full as it had been on the occasion of Sir Roger's funeral and as then, the interested, the well-wishers, and the curious mingled freely.

Daniel Harker offered to give the bride away as her father was too ill to perform this duty. Her youngest sister Elsie, aged fourteen and the only one of that once-large family still living at home, was her bridesmaid. She reminded Ruby of herself at that age, peaky of face and shy of manner, but today she shimmered in her satin dress, and her narrow face beneath her Dutch-style lace cap was wreathed in smiles. Smiles as much for the joy of wearing flesh-coloured silk stockings as for the importance of her role.

Like Elsie, the bride was also wearing silk stockings, but hers were giving her little joy. One of her suspenders had come undone and every step she took towards the altar was one nearer, she thought, to her final doom. For should the other suspender come undone as well, her stocking would slide down her leg and concertina around her ankle, and it would give the village the biggest laugh it had had in years. She would never, she knew, be able to hold up her head again.

She was out of favour in the village; not for anything she had done, but because fortune had smiled once too often upon her. She had risen too fast and too far. First housekeeper to Sir Roger and Lady Massingham. Then housekeeper to the new owner of Thornmere Hall. Now wife to Reuben Stoneham, a catch for any girl with his good looks and war record. Then to cap it all, Thornmere Lodge for her new home. What had Ruby Pearson, daughter of a farm labourer and not even Thornmere born, done to deserve that? 'Du she just be in the righ' place at the righ' time,' uttered one malcontent.

The familiar words of the marriage service soothed her fears. How many times had she stood and listened, sometimes as bridesmaid, more often as spectator, while other brides were asked to love, honour and obey? She stole a sideways glance at Reuben. Love? Honour? Oh, yes indeed, that would be easy. But obey? She'd need notice of that. A surge of happiness washed over her. The stocking was forgotten.

The reception in the main drawing room at Thornmere Hall, like the ceremony itself, went off without a hitch. Ruby, pink and animated, partly from excitement but mostly from the wine, was quite transformed. The moment of departure came too soon, she hadn't enjoyed herself so much in years. Daniel Harker raised his glass for the last time and wished them future happiness.

'And if you think that I've forgotten the small matter of a wedding present,' he said, 'you've got another think coming. Follow me, I've got a surprise waiting for you.'

Ruby stared. 'But the lodge . . . all this,' she waved her hand at the drawing room at large. 'I thought this – the reception – *was* our wedding present.'

Reuben hushed her. He had already guessed what the surprise might be. He had been sent to give it an extra spit and polish that morning which he thought was a bit thick on his wedding day. Now, like Ruby, he coloured up. He also trembled a little. He took Ruby's hand and together they followed Daniel Harker out through the hall and the double doors, and down the stone steps to the curve of the drive with the assembled guests crowding behind them.

There she stood, the Daimler, gleaming in the bright September sunshine, festooned with white ribbons and with an old boot tied to the luggage carrier at the back.

Reuben's colour deepened and he was trembling visibly now. When he tried to voice his thanks no sound came forth. It was Ruby who spoke up for both of them.

'You don't mean it's ours for keeps – you mean only for a lend, surely?'

'It's yours for keeps,' said Daniel smiling. 'You've cared for it, Reuben. You've cosseted it and cherished it – how long is it, now? Long before I came on the scene. I reckon you've earned it. And may it give you both many more years of good service.'

'An' garridge bills,' came a yell from the back. 'It's all your responsibility now, bor.'

Another voice joined in. A female voice, rather shrill. 'Doan't be in such a hurry gettin' in it, Ruby, it won't run away. Reckon you got summat else to do first, my gel.'

Ruby was still holding her bouquet, she knew what was expected of her. They stood there in a semi-circle, all the unmarried ladies with Elsie in their midst, and Miss Cousins on the step behind. Who had invited her to the wedding, Ruby wondered, taking umbrage. She disliked Miss Cousins whom she thought, erroneously, looked down on her. Didn't even say good morning when they passed in the street and everybody said good morning to everybody else in Thornmere. Mr Harker had sent out the invitations, and knowing he didn't do anything by halves she guessed he had invited everyone in the village. Some hadn't come of course; all the newcomers in the better-off houses, they hadn't come and neither had Mrs Roseberry. But the vicar was there, all smiles as usual. He was liked a lot better than the old parson who, it was said of him, was too frightened to smile in case he cracked his face.

She lobbed her bouquet straight at Elsie. Poor little Elsie, she didn't get much fun out of life since their mother died, doing all the housework and cooking as well as looking after their father – she deserved a treat. She took careful aim, but either Elsie was too slow or Miss Cousins too nifty, for one minute she was leaping forward and the next minute standing there with her arms full of flowers. Ruby clamped her lips together and climbed into the car and didn't recover her powers of speech until several miles were behind them.

'What d'you think of that! Nearly knocked our Elsie over, she did, so anxious she was to get that bouquet. An' the wedding was nothing to do with her either. I wouldn't have asked her if I had had any say in the matter.'

Reuben had grumbles of his own. 'Trust that Bill Giles

to put in his spoke. Did you hear him? That dig about garridge bills. A little bit of green eye, if you ask me.'

'More than a little bit, I'd say.' They exchanged furious looks which very quickly melted into laughter. Their resentment registered, their grievances aired, they could now begin to enjoy themselves.

'She do purr bootifully, this ole bus,' said Reuben fondly.

When he was in Sir Roger's employ he always referred to the Daimler as the motor car. When Mr Harker took over it became the Daimler, to distinguish it from the Chevrolet. Now it was the ole bus. Ruby smiled indulgently, knowing it wouldn't be long before it was 'my ole bus', but that was how it should be.

They had booked a room with a sea view in a boarding house at South Denes, and as well as the sea they found they also had a good view of Nelson's Column. There was no parking space for the Daimler but Reuben was directed to a garage not far away. He carried their cases up to their bedroom first, then went to the window to check that nothing untoward had happened to the car in the last five minutes. 'Won't be long,' he said, and Ruby heard his footsteps clatter down the stairs and out of the door as if the house was on fire and didn't flatter herself that his haste was due to his desire to get back to her as quickly as possible.

She knew she would have plenty of time to unpack her case. Reuben wouldn't be back until he had returned the car to its usual pristine condition, removing any trace of the journey. Her few things took up very little space in the double wardrobe. She hesitated whether to unpack for Reuben but decided against it. Reuben had been looking after himself for so long he might resent what he saw as her interference. But she couldn't resist having a quick look to see if he had bought a pair of pyjamas. He had. Her heart beat with pride. Her brothers and her father slept in their underwear as did most of the men they knew of. That Reuben had taken the trouble to buy a pair of pyjamas she took as a compliment.

She herself had spent more than she could afford on a nightgown, making up for the lack of a wedding dress. Mrs Webster praised her for her commonsense. 'Much more sensible getting married in a good suit – something you can wear afterwards. What's the good of a wedding dress? All that money on something you can only wear once. What could you do with it afterwards? Couldn't even wear it as a nightgown, not these days when wedding dresses barely cover the knees.'

The sight of the bed caused her another flutter. She wondered which side of the bed Reuben preferred to sleep on. When she had shared a bed with Lottie she had slept on the left. She placed her nightgown on the left-hand pillow.

The toilet set on the washstand was decorated with large fat red roses, a pattern that was repeated on soap dish and tooth mug. Her eyes roving round the room fastened on the object under the bed. That too was decorated with the same pattern. The sight of the chamber-pot filled Ruby with misgivings. She had used one all her life, though never one with roses on it. But decorated or just plain white it was there for a certain purpose and she went cold as the full impact of the intimacy of married life hit her.

In no way would she be able to use a chamber-pot in front of Reuben. Even if it were too dark to see her, he'd hear her. Nobody could go about that sort of thing quietly. The landlady had mentioned an indoor water closet at the end of the passage; she'd seek that out, just in case. But though she walked on tiptoe every floorboard along the way creaked, and she could imagine how that would sound in the dead of the night – like the crack of rifle fire. She decided not to drink anything more that evening.

They went for a stroll after supper, her hand resting in the crook of Reuben's arm. She had imagined moonlight on a darkening sea and walking along the promenade to the sound of water lapping on the sands. In the event, sight and sound was muffled by a thick sea mist. Somewhere out at sea a buoy bell was tolling, and every time the distant and melancholy warning sounded it was answered by a long drawn-out howl from some unseen dog. Ruby shivered.

'You're cold,' said Reuben instantly.

'No, it's not that. It's that dog; it do sound so eerie. D'you think it's a real dog? That noise it makes crazes me.'

'Then time we be getting back. You're shivering in that thin jacket. Besides, this damp is bad for the brasswork, an' that worries me.'

For one alarming moment she thought he was referring to her wedding ring. Brass! Then realised he was thinking of the car. All evening he had been worrying about the car, wondering if where he had left it was safe. It was her first inkling that she was going to share her honeymoon with the Daimler. They walked back to the boarding house in some haste, no longer arm in arm but with Reuben hurrying ahead. He left her at the door. 'Just going to see if the ole bus is all right. I'd like to get her under cover – perhaps arrange something with the garridge.'

She didn't mind. As a matter of fact she welcomed this opportunity of getting undressed in private. She was shy of Reuben seeing her bare feet. She washed in the rose-patterned toilet bowl and cleaned her teeth in the rose-patterned tooth mug, but before this she made a trip

275

along the passage, wincing at every creak of the floorboards. Her toilet complete, she undressed and got into bed and waited for Reuben. She waited so long she fell asleep, and woke up suddenly when she heard the door being stealthily closed.

'Is tha' you, Reuben?'

'Sorry. Didn't mean to wake you.'

'What time is it?'

'Just gone midnight.'

Two hours! She'd been asleep two hours. 'What you bin doing all this time?'

'Talkin' with Mr Barker, the man who keeps the garridge. We got mardling about the war. He was with the Royal Norfolks right from the beginning – went through the war without a scratch.'

It was always the same when two men of that age got together. She forgave him. 'D'you want the light on?'

'No, I can manage in the dark.'

She heard him splashing at the washstand, the rustle as he undressed, then the creak of springs as he climbed into bed. She moved over to make room, but he lay with his back to her. She could tell that by the outline of his shape in the dim light from the street lamp. She waited. He didn't move and she wondered if he had gone off to sleep. Timidly, she touched his shoulder.

'Reuben.' No answer. She said it louder. 'Reuben.' Then, 'Are you all righ'?'

He didn't exactly shrug her hand off, just moved his shoulder out of reach.

'Can't you let a fellow say his prayers in peace,' he muttered gruffly.

TEN | 1929

The world remembered October 1929 for the Wall Street crash. For the rest of her life Helena would remember that same October as the month when a robin first sang from the branches of the mulberry tree in the Doughty Street garden.

They had settled down, she sometimes thought, like Darby and Joan, leading their quiet and uneventful lives. Uneventful that is since the traumatic occasion of Paul's haemorrhage. She had learnt the hard way that Paul's condition could not be taken for granted. It could spring, like an untamed animal, taking them unawares at any moment. For that reason they rarely went out now, and did little entertaining – just an occasional dinner party for Midge and Dr Percy, or former colleagues from the *Encounter*.

Helena was content. Paul was in remission at present and as well as he could be under the circumstances, and that was all she needed to make her happy. She did most of her work at home now, sitting with Paul on the balcony, looking down into the garden which was just a small space round the mulberry tree and rejoicing when the robin sang to them. Often in the spring she heard a blackbird in Bedford Square, but never before a robin. Were there other robins in London, she asked of acquaintances, and they looked at her as if she were mad. Here was a woman enquiring about robins when the world was toppling about their ears!

She never quite tamed the robin sufficiently to get him to come and eat out of their hands. She put grated cheese on the outer sill of the balcony windows and when he had got used to coming for that, she coaxed him inside with a scattering of titbits on the window seat, for except in very cold weather, the windows were always kept open.

Paul, too, took an interest in the robin. Nothing would have given him greater pleasure than to have the robin come at his call. He had infinite patience, sitting for ages with hand outstretched, bait in palm, but the robin would never oblige. But if Paul sat absolutely still the bird would alight on the ledge, snatch at something from the sill and fly off again.

'These city robins are a canny lot,' Helena said.

'Perhaps they have reason to be with all these stray cats around.'

The idea of a sanatorium was shelved for the time being. Paul had stayed in hospital until fit enough to be discharged. He did look fit, too, Helena thought, for he had put on weight and had more colour in his face. But something was missing. It took her some time to fathom out what it was, and then it came to her one day when they were listening to a report on the wireless concerning the growing support for the Nazi party in Germany.

'The crowd's chant of "Heil Hitler" is now common

in Germany,' the announcer intoned, very much as if he were giving out the latest fat stock prices.

Paul's eyes had a far away and rather despairing look in them. Helena looked for the spark that once made them flash and found it lacking.

'Doesn't it make you furious, the way that wretched little man is being turned into some crack-pot hero? It would have done once. I remember you saying that his ranting was enough to set off another World War. Doesn't the very thought frighten you?' she said.

'Frighten is too strong a word.'

'Then does he anger you? He angers me. Why can't people preach peace instead of war? That man is full of hate, and he calls himself a Christian. Hasn't he ever heard of the gospel of love? Why are people hated just because they are different? Because their skin is the wrong colour or their noses the wrong shape. I find it sick. Oh Paul, my darling, here am I ranting on the way you used to. Why aren't you joining in? I fell in love with you partly because of your crusading spirit. It was like a fire burning inside you. What has happened to that fire, Paul?'

He smiled thinly. 'The bloody flux put it out.'

Her eyes saddened. 'Not out, Paul, never out. It's damped down a little but it isn't out.'

'If you say so.' He looked tired and she left him to go and nurse her grief in private, giving way to a crying jag that left her feeling drained in heart and spirit. Only when she had disguised all trace of her recent tears did she return to Paul to find him making notes on a pad.

'What about a little run out somewhere on the next fine day?' he suggested. 'It's a long time since we've been out together and a change of scene would do us both good.'

It was a peace-offering, a consolation prize, she knew, for the loss of her Don Quixote.

'But I thought you wanted to get on with your book? Every time I've suggested an outing, you've said you couldn't spare the time. You've said you wanted to keep going until you've written the two most glorious words in the English language – The End.'

He laughed. 'I thought you knew me well enough by now to know that what I say and what I do are two different things.'

'Sometimes I doubt whether I shall ever know you well enough.'

Later that week he said, 'What about having that trip tomorrow if this weather holds good? It's not often we get a touch of spring in November, so let's make the most of it.'

It was a tonic to hear him so cheerful. Like his sense of outrage, his enthusiasm had been on the wane. 'I'll phone the car-hirers right this minute before you change your mind.' Her eyes reflected her joy and delight. 'Self-drive or chauffeur-driven?'

'Actually,' said Paul, with a hint of the old mischief in his smile. 'I prefer a chauffeuse.'

It was many weeks since Paul had been in such a light-hearted mood, and she promised herself that wherever he wanted to go, even if it stretched her to the limits, she would indulge him. That evening they sat together as usual, the wireless playing softly in the background. Neither so completely absorbed in their own occupation as not to be aware of the other. If Paul coughed or even shifted his position, Helena was immediately on the alert.

She worked with crayon on cartridge paper, and at present she was engrossed with ideas for a spring collection.

Midge had suggested hiring a room at an hotel, and having professional mannequins to model their latest creations. It was an idea that excited them with its possibilities. Helena was determined to give of her best. Her best so far among the rough sketches was a little number made of black chenille with a green silk lining that followed on the contours of the narrow upturned brim. The unfortunate part of working so far ahead, she thought, was that by the spring of 1930 cloche hats might no longer be all the rage. Fashion, she had learnt, was a very fickle mistress.

The concert ended. Then came an announcement about the next item – a discussion on fashion. Helena put down her pencil to listen:

'Is the modern woman with her cropped hair and short skirts in danger of losing her femininity? Is she, by aping men, becoming more masculine in personality as well as appearance? To put it in a nutshell: are women dictating fashion, or fashion dictating women . . .?'

'Switch off that pontificating ass,' said Paul. 'And come and sit near me. We haven't discussed tomorrow yet.'

'Why do I suddenly feel alarmed? Is it something in your tone of voice?'

'Nothing whatever to be alarmed about. This run out tomorrow. You said you'd take me anywhere I want to go, within reason. Then I'd like to visit Southend, and on the way look in at that place the girl Amy told you about. What was the name – Raneleigh – that's it. I want to satisfy my curiosity. I have never been within a hundred yards of a sanatorium. I'd like to look it over.'

A clammy feeling of disquiet took hold of her. 'Why, Paul? Why now? We've been over this before and you dismissed the idea. You were adamant when Dr Percy first suggested it. Is it that you feel you need more nursing? More than I can give you?'

'No, of course it's not that.' He almost snapped the words at her. Then his tone changed. 'I feel as if I'm taking advantage of you. Day after day you give up your time to minister to me, doing things for me that by right should be done by a trained nurse. You're too young to be a prisoner like this. You have a life of your own. You should be out with your friends, having a good time, going to all the places you long to go to, doing all the things that you enjoy doing. Night after night, sitting here with me, sketching away at those blasted hats. That's no life – that's only half a life.' And as she made no answer, only stared expressionlessly at her hands, he added on a note of defeat, 'If you must know, Helena, you make me feel damned guilty. Knowing that because of me, you are making a martyr of yourself.'

'Have you quite finished?'

'No. But if you want to speak, the floor's all yours.'

'Then first of all, you poor, self-deluded, sorry-for-yourself, beloved nit-wit, how the dickens do you know what's going on inside my head? What makes you think I'm pining to do all those things you mentioned, and see all those things you think I want to see? What things? I've never been one for exhibitions or art galleries. I like going to concerts or the opera, but we can get all the music we want on the gramophone or the wireless. And there's some good plays on the wireless, too, if only you had the patience to listen. I'll tell you what I prefer more than anything else – that's being with the ones I love. And I've got the best of that right here, in this house.'

Paul's eyes were wet but he managed one of his quirky smiles. 'Does that include Jake down below, or Mr Pickford above or the Spicers on the top two floors?'

'No, it includes only one rather spoilt, but very precious and talented ex-army officer who excites me every time he smiles at me which he doesn't do often enough.'

Paul obliged by grinning fiendishly. 'Does that excite you enough to come to bed with me?'

'No it does not, it turns me off. Besides, I want you to keep all your strength for tomorrow. Think, Paul. Get your grey cells working. Think up something really different for us tomorrow.'

He gave her a part-earnest, part-teasing look. 'Please, ma'am, permission to visit Raneleigh Sanatorium.'

Fog descended on London. One of the typical, impenetrable, pea-soupers that often in November blotted out towns and cities and brought all transport to a stop.

So much for the outing into Essex. So much for visiting Raneleigh. Helena was not too disappointed at first hoping that by the time the fog lifted, Paul would have got over his mad idea. I mean, she thought, Southend! But when she saw how dejected he became, and realised how much he had set his heart on this trip, her disappointment equalled his.

Sunday, and the fog was as thick as ever. She stared moodily out of the windows at a soundless and obscured street, and recalled a verse from her schooldays.

> No warmth, no cheerfulness, no healthful
> ease,
> No comfortable feel in any member,
> No shade, no shine, no butterflies, no bees,
> No fruits, no flowers, no leaves, no birds,
> No-vember!

But Thomas Hood was wrong, she thought, her mood changing. Her memories of November were not so jaundiced. It was often a month rich in colour. What about chrysanthemums, she thought, and asters, and Michaelmas daisies – they were all November flowers. Even roses, she recalled, often went on blooming at that time of year. They certainly did at Rodings, and thinking of Rodings brought a sudden, intense yearning for the crisp and invigorating air of Norfolk.

Now, there was a place they should be visiting, not Southend. Paul might stand a better chance of recovery in Norfolk. If only her mother . . . She turned from the window with a sigh. If wishes were horses, etc., etc. She was full of old saws this morning. Oh, if only the beastly fog would disappear. They had had three days of it already. What they needed to wash it away was a steady downpour of rain.

She got her wish. It rained the following day, and then went on raining for three more days unceasingly. Paul spent most of that time staring morosely out at the sodden garden and longing, Helena could tell, for a cigarette. She nearly succumbed to the temptation to give him one, for she had a packet hidden away against an emergency. She too began to feel the need for something to ease her nerves for she could feel tension building up between them.

In the old days, when they had first set up home together, she would often, in quiet companionship with Paul, enjoy an after-dinner cigarette. But since his haemorrhage she had not touched them or, on Dr Percy's instructions, allowed him one either. She was aware that he resented this, resented her authority, and on that afternoon, unable to bear his restless and testy mood any longer, and frightened how she herself might react, saying something she would bitterly regret later, she put on her mackintosh, fetched her umbrella, and escaped.

She walked along Guilford Street and into Southampton Row, and then New Oxford Street until she came to Lyons Corner House at the junction of Tottenham Court Road. She walked as in a dream hardly aware of the rain, for her desolation gave her the feeling of isolation. When Paul was bogged down by despair as he was now she felt she had lost her anchor. For even though he was so debilitated she still looked upon him as her mainstay, her prop, her safe harbour. Without him, she felt, she would fall to pieces, and yet she knew, little by little, he was going from her and it was that dreaded thought she was trying to run away from.

She sat at a table in a ground-floor restaurant at the Corner House and ordered tea. A waiter brought it. The orchestra began playing a selection from 'The Merry Widow'. Ah, the old melodies, what nostalgic memories they evoked. She had danced with Rupert to the Merry Widow waltz on his last leave. Round and round the ballroom she had floated, in the arms of her golden-haired prince, wearing a gown of primrose silk with a nosegay of Parma violets pinned to the bodice.

Tears slowly filled her eyes, overspilled and plopped into her saucer, and she could not be sure whether they were for Rupert or for Paul or for herself. All three perhaps she thought as, unselfconsciously, she wiped them away. She collected her belongings from the cloakroom and went out prepared to face the rain once more only to find that it had stopped at last and a pale and watery sun was putting out peace feelers.

Paul was by the window watching out for her, and when she opened the front door he was there in the hall waiting for her. He said, with a touching look of contrition, 'I love you so. I know that must be hard to believe after the way I shouted at you, but in my way, my darling, I worship you.'

She outlined his mouth with her forefinger and then kissed him full on the lips. 'The day you stop shouting at me,' she said, laughing into his face, 'is the day I start worrying whether you still care enough.'

The next morning the sun was up before they were, for they both slept late. Helena had needed no coaxing to go to Paul's bed and stay all night. She loved to lie drowsily when all passion was spent with her legs still entwined with his, and to feel the warmth and closeness of his body, and even when he began to twitch in his sleep, which he did quite violently, she had no wish to leave him. When she awakened the next morning, he was propped up on his elbow studying her.

'I've been feasting my eyes on you,' he said. 'I never wake in the morning without fearing that you may have left me. I live in a state of terror in case I find you gone, yet I never make it any easier for you to stay. Why do you put up with me? You are independent as far as money goes. You are not tied to me legally, you gain nothing by staying, yet you do. It can't be easy for someone like you nursing someone like me, especially as we both know the outcome.'

'Has this morbid introspection got any bearing on your wish to visit the Raneleigh Sanatorium?' she said after a moment's silence, hiding from him how such talk frightened her.

He smiled reluctantly. 'I see. It's "Miss Bright and Breezy, and never mind the weather" in bed with me this morning, is it?'

'It is if you want me to drive you to Southend. No time for philosophical conversation this morning, my love. Breakfast will be ready in ten minutes.' Only when she was safely outside the room did she let her feelings get the better of her. Please, God, don't let it be another day like yesterday, she prayed. Today, particularly today, please give me back the old Paul.

The car that drew up outside the house in an hour's time was an open tourer. The driver got out and touched his cap.

'Sorry about this, sir, but the one we intended for you blew a gasket. If this won't do we'll have a nice little saloon available tomorrow.'

'Don't apologise to me, I wouldn't know a gasket from a starting handle. Apologise to the lady, she's the boss.'

Was there just a hint of sarcasm in his voice? Was that a dig? Her eyes searching his saw no malice there. She smiled, and teasingly he returned her smile. You're getting too touchy, she chided herself. It's staying in too much.

She said, 'I think we'll risk it. I'm well wrapped-up. But what about you, Paul? Will it be too cold for you, in an open car? Would you rather put the trip off until tomorrow?'

'And risk another wet day, not likely. Besides, plenty of fresh air is part of the treatment, isn't it?' He was full of bravado and *bonhomie*, like a small boy looking forward to a treat, she thought fondly. She tipped the driver. 'Take a taxi back to the garage.'

'Thank you, madam. I'll collect the car about ten tonight. Will you be back by then?'

'Gracious, I hope so.'

Jake appeared with an army blanket and tucked it around Paul's legs. 'Drive carefully,' he said to Helena. 'Mind how you go.' He was genuinely apprehensive. He always was where they were concerned.

Yet, was this kindly man with the bloodshot eyes the same raving monster who had kept them awake until the early hours of the morning? He had been in good form then, reeling home after closing hours, letting forth a stream of fruity expletives when he tripped and fell down the area steps. Then the singing started. In the room below them came a clear and tearful rendering of 'Just a Song at Twilight', which was bearable, though not at that time of night, for he had a fine bass voice. It was when he started on a repertoire of old army songs that they held their breath, for they knew what was coming next: the silence, the sobbing, and then the violence; china smashing and wood splintering. Jake's hangovers were his *mea culpa*; his penance was mending the furniture and walking down to Leather Lane to replace the china. By the sound of things last night, thought Helena, he had a busy day ahead of him.

The road to Southend began its course in East London. It was a dreary journey: factories, shops, houses, ribbon development. Once clear of the suburbs and deep into the Essex flatland, there was nothing about the landscape to inspire them. On one occasion they passed a small community of old trams and buses and railway coaches, each with a stack pipe sticking through the roof and net curtains at the windows.

'Slow down,' said Paul. 'This I must see. Homes fit for heroes to live in. Poor devils, look what they've come down to.'

'Paul you can be so bitter sometimes. And wrong. People buy these old vehicles to use as weekend retreats and holiday homes.'

'Another one of Jake's tall stories?'

'It's not a tall story. It's the truth, and I got it from Midge's cleaning woman at the shop. She and her husband bought a plot of land somewhere in this area for next to nothing, and then got hold of a bus dirt cheap. They set it up on their land, made a few adjustments, dug a little garden to go with it and she can't wait for her husband to retire so that they can move down here permanently. She says after London she can't believe the peace and quiet.'

'You can get peace and quiet in a cemetery. I think I would prefer a cemetery than living in a bus on an arterial road.'

'Try to imagine what it's like living in a tenement in Poplar, darling. This must seem like heaven by comparison.'

'What's this place called?'

'Basildon, I think.'

'Not my idea of heaven.'

Raneleigh, when they came to it was basking in sunshine, and the approach road through the village was like driving along a country lane with trees on either side the colour of burnt sienna. Unlike other villages they had passed, Raneleigh was surprisingly prosperous-looking, with well-tended gardens and attractive old timber cottages. Both church and churchyard were in apple-pie order, a further sign of prosperity. A sixteenth-century inn, a small estate of new houses, and a row of shops made up the community. A finger-post pointed along a footpath to the station.

'I must admit this all looks much more encouraging than Amy gave me to believe,' said Helena. She had hoped Raneleigh to be so off-putting that Paul would decide there was no point in looking further. As it was his interest was kindled.

'That must be the sanatorium up ahead, that large building,' he said. 'Either a sanatorium or a prison or a boarding school. What do you think?'

'Far too cosy-looking to be a school. At least the one I went to.'

The gates to the drive were open. There was no one in sight.

'Drive on.'

'Paul, you wouldn't have made an appointment to see the matron or superintendent or whoever's in charge without telling me, would you?'

'No, my love. I just want to see what's on offer, that's all.'

They sat in the car in the curve of the drive and took stock of their surroundings, and both, though they didn't say so, were pleasantly surprised.

Was this the place Amy had run away from, Helena pondered, remembering the grim, Victorian structure Amy's words had conjured up. Perhaps the fog had had a lot to do with it in her case, for it had been foggy most of the time she had been there. Now, on this clear, crystal-like day, it looked really splendid. Flowerbeds had been newly dug over and planted out with wallflowers. In the spring they would be a mass of colour, filling the air around with their warm and lingering fragrance. She knew from what Amy had said that the wards were invisible from the drive, built as they were deep among the trees. If they wished to have a closer look there was nothing to stop them getting out of the car and taking one of the many paths that radiated away from the main walk. When she put this idea to Paul he said it smacked too much of trespass. They were both surprised that nobody had as yet appeared to enquire of them their business.

If the patients were looked after as well as the grounds

were, she thought, then she had nothing to fear. It was just the idea of Paul burying himself away so far from her. She was relieved when he said he had seen enough and as time was running short they should be getting on. As they drove back past the administrative buildings, a face appeared briefly at a lower window and stared after them. Helena had an impression of a white cap, but on the other hand it could have been white hair. She heard Paul give a deep and long-drawn-out sigh as she drove back through the gates.

He was silent for the rest of the journey, his chin sunk into the collar of his overcoat, his cap pulled well down over his eyes. All she could see was the set of his mouth and the lower part of his face, and wondered what was going through that ever-active mind of his. Presently, as the environs of Southend slowly came to meet them, he sat up and sniffed.

'Is that the famous ozone I smell?' he said. 'Are we nearing the end of our journey?' The wind was fresh. It reddened the tip of his nose and drew tears to his eyes. 'Christ, I'm frozen.'

She had been driving at a steady forty miles an hour, now she increased her speed, and the wind bit deeper. 'Just three miles to go.'

'Have you visited Southend before?'

'No, but I've heard about it.'

'What have you heard?'

'That it has the longest pier in the world and a large amusement park called the Kursaal. It is famous for its cockles and "Kiss me Quick" hats, and it is so crowded on Bank holidays that when one more tripper steps out of the train, another falls off the end of the pier.'

Paul chuckled. 'Who was your informant, Jake?'

'No. Mrs Hooper, Midge's cleaning woman.'

'I spent a week there with my nanny when I was quite small. I was recovering from whooping cough and she took me to convalesce with her sister who kept a boarding house. Southend's ozone was believed to have great healing powers. It was Easter at the time and I remember the cliff gardens were yellow with daffodils. Nanny Rowland liked to sit in the pavilion in the afternoon and often she fell asleep, and then I would go off and explore. I never got far. She had a sixth sense where I was concerned. As soon as I was missing, she would wake up and come looking for me. I desperately wanted to ride a train on the pier, or stow away on one of the trip boats, or eat a saucer of cockles at one of the stalls. I was never allowed to do any of those glorious and forbidden things and I've felt cheated ever since.'

'I never know when to take you seriously, Paul, but if that story is true I think it's rather sweet. So that is the reason you wanted to visit Southend? A journey of nostalgia?'

'Not completely. At the bottom of the High Street here turn right onto the esplanade and continue towards Westcliff. I'll tell you when to stop.'

'Oh dear, I do hate having to concentrate on my driving when there is so much to see. There were some very attractive hats in the window of a store we passed back there . . .'

'This is our day off, Helena, so stop thinking shop and concentrate on enjoying yourself instead. Take a whiff of that ozone. If it could be bottled it would make some pharmaceutical company a fortune.'

'Is that what you call ozone, that awful smell! I thought it was gases coming off the mud. And where is the sea? I can't see any sea.'

'The tide is out, my love, far out, but I assure you it will return. Hopefully after lunch, when we take a stroll along the promenade.'

'I know just the place for lunch,' she said, turning to him with a bright smile. 'I heard Mrs Hooper describing it to Midge. A fish restaurant somewhere under some arches. She says the fish is delicious, straight from the sea and freshly cooked for each customer.'

'Sounds fine, but I've already booked a table for two in an hotel just along here.' Paul looked at his watch. 'And we'll have just ten minutes to freshen up beforehand. I must say I'm ready for my grub. That drive has sharpened my appetite.'

'You had all this planned, you wretch. You should have warned me. I'm wearing my old sweater with the darn on the elbow.'

'Nobody is going to notice your darn. Draw in here, yes here. This is the place.'

It looked like the one-time home of some prosperous merchant which it could well have been a hundred years before. Inside were the thick carpets, discreet hangings and an air of unhurried efficiency taken for granted in such places.

'Not the sort of place I'd expect to find in Southend,' Helena said. 'A far cry from fish and chips, I must say.' She cast surreptitious looks beneath her lashes at the other diners as they followed the waiter to their table. War-profiteers with their wives or lady friends, she decided, noting somewhat scornfully their well-fed and over-dressed appearances. Even after all these years she could not rid herself of the feeling of distaste the word aroused in her.

'I'm the only one here not wearing a hat,' she said when seated. Her headscarf, folded, was in the pocket of her motoring coat. 'Not a very good advertisement for my trade.'

'Your hair is far prettier than any hat – even one of yours.'

Helena, after much speculation had finally succumbed to being shingled. The style suited her for it emphasised her well-shaped head and drew attention to her shapely neck. Her hair, in the hands of an expert, had ceased to exasperate her. It had been tamed, as far as it could be tamed, to stay in place. Only now, rather windswept, was it unruly, and to Paul far more becoming.

Oysters were brought and a bottle of Chablis.

'Paul, what extravagance! But please don't make me eat an oyster.'

'Try one. You'll love it.'

It slipped down tasting only of the lemon juice she had drowned it in. Paul was obliged to eat the rest.

Whiting followed, boned, and stuffed with eggs and herbs.

'Who told you about this place?'

'D'you remember my chum on the *Encounter*, the one who used to write about the best eating-places in London? He followed that up with the best eating-places within an hour's drive of London, and this place was on his list. He stayed here. He told me that if ever I required a quiet hotel where I would be well fed and well looked after, and with a good train service from town, I couldn't better Murray's. Mind you, he's an Essex man, so I expect he's biased in its favour. He warned me not to come in the summer because of the trippers.'

'He sounds a bit of a snob.'

'Only when it comes to food.'

The tide was creeping back over the oozing black mud, bringing with it flocks of hungry gulls searching for pickings among the flotsam. The line of sea that separated

Kent from Essex was a broad blue band that scintillated with a million flecks of light, and above the sun floated like an enormous orange balloon in an opaque sky. She was glad they had come. Even the thought of the homeward journey in the dark with nothing to protect them from the cold but Jacob's old blanket could not dim the gloss of her enjoyment.

The fish was removed and guinea fowl, garnished with watercress and served with Espagnole sauce, was placed before them.

'This is all very delicious,' said Helena. 'But are we the only ones having *table-d'hôte*? I didn't see you with a menu.'

'When I booked a table I asked them to prepare a meal for an invalid.'

She giggled. 'There is nothing invalidish about your appetite at present. But oh, how glad I am to see you enjoying your food again.'

Cigarettes were offered with the coffee. Paul refused. 'I won't break my word to you,' he said when the waiter had gone. 'Not even when I'm staying here on my own.'

She stared. '*Staying here on your own*! Paul, is this some kind of game?'

He told her simply and in words that sounded well rehearsed. When he had phoned the hotel to book for lunch he had also enquired about booking a room – or a suite, preferably – from January until Easter. A provisional booking was made at the time and that was to be confirmed today after he had seen what they had to offer.

'I didn't tell you about it beforehand because I knew you would try to talk me out of it,' he said.

'Three months without you! Of course I would try to talk you out of it!'

He reached across the table and took her hand, stroking the back of it with his thumb. 'It's a twin-bedded room; there'll be room for you to come and visit whenever you like.'

'Every weekend,' she said.

'I want to finish my book, Helena, and this would be a grand opportunity for me. Three months here without interruptions will give me all the time I need.'

His eyes pleaded and she lowered hers to hide her fear. Uncertainty was always with her nowadays. 'Was I so much of a hindrance to you? Do I really fuss around you too much?'

'Far too much, but by Jove, wouldn't I miss it if you stopped.'

'Yet you accuse me of interrupting your work.'

'Not exactly.' He withdrew his hand as the waiter hovered with fresh coffee and left with orders for liqueurs. 'You misunderstood me. I wasn't accusing you of preventing me from working. It is rather that — and this is going to sound very foolish to you — your very presence is an interruption because when you are around I'm unable to think of anything but you. I lose all inclination to work — I just want to watch you.'

Her eyes sparkled through ready tears. She didn't believe a word he said, but she loved him for saying it. 'That is the nicest compliment you have ever paid me,' she said.

The manager showed them over the suite on the first floor. Two large rooms and a bathroom. The sitting room overlooked the sea and had a glazed door leading on to a balcony. The suite at present was unoccupied, nevertheless someone had filled a vase with long-stemmed yellow roses. They looked as if they were made of silk, but they were real as Helena discovered when she felt one.

Paul came in from the balcony full of enthusiasm. 'There are unrestricted views from here. Up river and down river and clear across to the coast of Kent. I'll have to buy a pair of binoculars or a small telescope. I'd get a lot of pleasure just sitting here looking out to sea.'

'And what about your writing?'

'And that, too, of course. But you know what they say about all work and no play.' He gave her one of his lopsided grins, then shivered. 'It's turning cold. And it will seem a bally lot colder once the sun sets. How about a walk to the pier and back to get our circulation working before we make tracks for home?'

They left the car parked outside the hotel and crossed over to the promenade. They turned up their coat collars and Helena put on her headscarf for the wind off the sea was biting her ears. There were very few people about, and when they arrived at the pier the fishermen were packing up for the day. One man showed them his catch. Four minuscule dabs, each one less than the size of his palm. 'Not much for a day's patience,' he said. 'But enough to keep the missus quiet. Very nice fried and put between two slices of bread. Very tasty.'

Helena was thoughtful as they retraced their steps. 'Are you really moving into the hotel expressly to get on with your book?' she said. 'Or like the man said, "Just to keep the missus quiet?" I mean, I can't help fussing about you, and that for a man like you must be a constant source of irritation.'

He walked with his arm around her, and even through their joint clothing she could feel the heat from his body. Yet, he felt the cold so. She couldn't understand that. His arm now tightened its hold, giving her a squeeze.

'Dr Percy has been on at me to go to a sanatorium,

just for a few months, just for the worst of the winter, he suggested. I believe he thinks another winter in London – the soot and fog – could kill me. According to him I need all the fresh air I can get. He's still on about this place in Bournemouth, but that would be too far from you. There's a place at High Beech near Epping, and I did consider that. Then I remembered what you told me about Raneleigh – and Raneleigh is near Southend. Southend wouldn't be such a bad place to winter in I decided. Plenty of ozone, plenty of fresh air, plenty to see on the river. There's nothing more boring than staring out at an empty sea, and the sea around here is never empty: Thames barges, cockle bawlies, coasters making for the London ports, fishing boats, private yachts, pleasure boats – you name it, they've got it.'

'And the beauty of this place,' he added, as they arrived back at the car, 'is that Murray's is willing to take a chance on me. Should my condition worsen, the manager said there is a hospital nearby and Raneleigh Sanatorium, if needed, only five miles away. You see, everything has been taken care of.'

'Yes, I can see you have got it all very nicely buttoned up, and not a word to me about it. But I suppose you discussed it with Jake?'

'I had to tell Jake. I want him to arrange to have my trunk and writing material sent to the hotel when the time comes. But my typewriter he insists on bringing to me personally. He thinks it too valuable to entrust to carriers. You didn't know I had been practising on it, did you? I can type expertly now with one finger.'

'I know little of what you get up to behind my back,' she said. 'But it seems I am not so indispensable as I thought.'

'There are some things, my love, that only you can do.'

Later, Jake was to tell her: 'He really did it for your sake, Miss Roseberry. He was getting himself so worked up because he thought you were sacrificing yourself for him. All your free time, all your energy, any life of your own, he told me one day, was in hock to him. Of course, he will feel the benefit too – convalescing by the sea, I mean – but it was all planned with you in mind. That's why he swore me to secrecy. He thought you might try stop him. Don't take it to heart, Miss Roseberry, it's all for the best.'

But that conversation was to take place in the future, at present they were homeward-bound. The lights of Southend were far behind them. Other dwellings they passed *en route* shed a little light from curtained windows. Only in built-up areas did they have the benefit of street lighting. Her thoughts reverted to Paul and his plans for spending the winter away from her. She could not help but feel anxious for him. Also a little hurt that he had gone ahead without consulting her. Was it a gesture to reassert his independence? Was she making him feel more dependent on her than he needed to be? Was she – and this thought made her stomach churn – milking him of his manhood? It is I who is dependent on him, she thought. Without him I shall only be half a woman. How am I going to get through those lonely winter months on my own?

Rediscover yourself, a small voice of reason intruded. Do all those things he suggested and which you told white lies about, like going out and enjoying yourself. Make new friendships, renew old ones. Go and see your mother more often. Yes, I must do that, she thought. She had always put Paul first for he was her number one priority, and perhaps, for all she knew, was the reason for her mother's antipathy towards him.

It was up to her to put that right. When Paul came home again in the spring she would take him to Thornmere to meet her mother. It would be a goal to work towards, she told herself, and thinking that her feelings took a turn for the better.

The nearer she got to London, the more she had to concentrate on her driving. There was only a wavering small, red, rear light to warn her when another vehicle came in front. She slowed down then, for she had not the confidence to overtake in the dark.

She was cold, but not conscious of it. Paul was sleeping. Once she reached out and pulled the rug higher around his shoulders, and in so doing her hand brushed his cheek. It felt like ice. She experienced a moment's panic, then she touched him again. He was only cold – just cold, thank God. All the same she threw caution to the winds and pressed down on the accelerator. What a mad stupid risk to take him on a journey in an open car at this time of year. What crass folly. If he got a chill now, and the coughing started again, it could trigger off another haemorrhage.

In her anxious haste she began to take risks. She lost patience with a tram and overtook on the nearside, and only just in time saw the shadowy figure of a passenger running for the kerb. The sudden jolt as she braked threw Paul forward and he hit his head against the windscreen.

He woke instantly. 'My God, Helena, what were you trying to do, kill me!'

She was shaking. 'No, just anxious to get you home. I'll never forgive myself if you catch a chill.'

'Catch a chill! I'm more at risk of getting killed in an accident. Slow down woman or you'll kill us both.'

In the dark she smiled to herself. There was nothing wrong with Paul that a whisky and soda wouldn't put right.

Warmth and light greeted them at Doughty Street. Jake took charge. He phoned the garage for somebody to fetch the car, added fuel to the already banked-up fires, made a jugful of hot toddy, and while they sipped it, exulting as warmth seeped into their extremities, he scrambled eggs and finally put hot water bottles in the bed.

'I almost expected him to wipe our noses when he said good night,' Paul remarked.

'Shush, darling, he might hear. He's just in the hall.'

He was back with a letter. He had overheard; they could tell that by his fixed expression. 'This came by the afternoon post and I left it on the hall table, then forgot it. Sorry about that.' He withdrew once more.

'It's from Thornmere, from Mother. Ticking me off for not answering her last letter, most likely.'

'When you said it was from Thornmere I thought it might be another epistle from your war-profiteer.'

She pulled a face at him. 'You know he gave that up for want of encouragement.' She opened her letter and began to read and almost at once her expression changed. A look of incredulity crossed her face. 'This is impossible!' she cried. 'I just can't believe it!'

'Let me guess. Your mother has invited us for Christmas?'

'*Amy Cousins has run away*! But why, for heaven's sake? She and Mother were getting on like a house on fire.'

'Perhaps she's eloped with your war-profiteer.'

'Oh shut up, Paul, remarks like that don't help.'

'Sorry. Tell me what your mother says.'

'Not a lot, actually, and what there is doesn't make sense. Poor Mother, she's taken to her bed. This happened on Sunday – that's four days ago. She must have been too upset to write before. Though I would have thought Mrs Taylor could have phoned.' Helena referred to the letter again. 'Apparently Amy went off to church as usual on Sunday morning but didn't return and they have heard nothing from her since. I can't believe Amy just walked out like that. It doesn't make sense. I'll phone Mrs Taylor. She may have more news by now.'

Helena returned looking even more baffled. 'I don't know what's going on at Thornmere. The whole place is in turmoil. Now it appears that a body has been found in the lake at Thornmere Park. No, Paul, don't say it. This is not the time for one of your jokes. It is *not* Amy. It is not even a body, according to Mrs Taylor. It's a skeleton of a man. The general opinion is that it's some tramp or poacher lost his way in the dark and stumbled into the mere. I know it sounds far-fetched, but all sorts of rumours are flying about. By comparison Amy's disappearance is of no consequence – except to Mother, of course. I must go to her, first thing tomorrow. You won't mind, Paul?'

'Anything to take that anxious look from your face, my sweet. Any of that hot toddy left?'

They discussed the events at Thornmere for the rest of the evening, but without certainty there was nothing left but speculation. When tired of talking they sat by the fire in a close and cosy silence, both a little tipsy, but whether from the effects of the outing and an overdose of fresh air or Jake's hot toddy, neither cared. Helena lifted her head from Paul's shoulder.

'I know exactly what Midge will say when she hears about this: "Once a bolter, always a bolter." Poor Amy.'

ELEVEN

If October 1929 was, to the world at large, the month of the Wall Street crash, and to Helena Roseberry in particular the month of the Doughty Street robin, to Amy Cousins it was the time she had her one and only permanent wave.

Though permanent waves had been around for some time, only in the spring of that year had they reached Coiffeurs, the hairdressers at Beckton Market where Amy went once a fortnight to have her hair marcelled.

As soon as she saw the advertisement in the local paper – 'First time demonstration of the permanent wave in Beckton Market. Prices range from thirty shillings to three guineas. Tests free. Make an appointment now and look your best for Christmas' – she could think of nothing else.

Christmas was two months away, but the harvest supper only two weeks. She wanted to look her best for the Harvest supper even more than for Christmas, for the supper was a social occasion where if she made herself attractive enough she might catch the attention of the Reverend Francis Thomas.

Having a perm would mean of course going without

a new dress, but she thought that a fair exchange. And even that wasn't a great loss for Miss Roseberry, on her last visit to Thornmere, had passed on to Amy three of her old dresses.

Yesterday's length was just right for Amy, for skirts were now being worn slightly longer. One of the dresses in particular could have been made for her. Though very plain, just like a chemise really, it felt rich to the touch, but it had a drawback – it was sleeveless. Would a sleeveless dress be considered too fast for a church social? She took her problem to Mrs Taylor rather than to Mrs Roseberry who, if she was in one of her tetchy moods, would be likely to squash her by asking whom did she think would notice her, anyway?

She hoped very much that Mr Thomas might notice her. She had given him plenty of opportunity to do that already. Since she had put her name on the rota for doing the church flowers and for cleaning the brass on Saturday mornings, and had joined the Bible-class which met at the Vicarage once a week, he could not help but notice her. But did he see her as a woman in her own right or just as a member of the congregation, she wondered.

When she had her hair tested for a permanent wave she was told that as it was so fine it would be best if she went for the steam wave which was more gentle on the hair, and it was only after she had agreed to this that she discovered that it was also the most expensive. Bang went the idea of a new winter coat.

She sat in a cubicle curtained off for privacy while her hair was shampooed and then wound in strands around long pencil-slim metal curlers. These were in turn strung up and hooked to small square iron cups attached to a machine that looked like something from another planet – she had recently worked her way through the *War of the Worlds* which, much to her surprise, she enjoyed.

She became apprehensive when the metal curlers began to heat up, and when they became so hot that they began to burn her scalp she took her mind off her fears by reminding herself it was all in the cause of beauty, like having one's eyebrows plucked. When the condensation in the cups began to boil and steam drifted about her head she yelled for help.

Mrs Roseberry's customary remark on seeing Amy after a marcel wave had always been: 'I see you've been having your hair fried, again.'

Today, Amy thought, she would answer if she had the nerve, 'Not this time, Mrs Roseberry. I've had it boiled instead.'

But disappointingly Mrs Roseberry didn't notice her hair, or if she did made no comment. She had something else on her mind. 'What's all this nonsense Mrs Taylor has been telling me about you having nothing to wear for the Harvest supper? What about those dresses my daughter gave you? Surely one of those is suitable.'

'They are all sleeveless. It doesn't seem right somehow, to have bare arms at a church social, it would be like having a bare head in church.'

'Good gracious, child, can't something be done about sleeves? I'm sure Mrs Taylor could make you a pair, she's very handy with her needle.' Mrs Roseberry paused, giving Amy a keener look. 'There's something different about you. Oh, I see you've been having your hair fried again. They're getting better at it, aren't they?'

The dress, when Mrs Taylor had finished with it, was in Amy's eyes a Cinderella-like transformation. What had once been plain was now endowed with floating sleeves that narrowed into neat little cuffs and a rose of the same material pinned to the left-hand shoulder. 'You'll be the belle of the ball,' said Mrs Taylor, standing back to admire her own handiwork. 'Go and show yourself to Mrs Roseberry.'

Mrs Roseberry for once was quite complimentary. 'I preferred it without sleeves,' she said. 'But it looks well on you. What are you wearing over it? Your tweed?'

An unnecessary question, Amy thought, for she only had her tweed to wear. It had been a present from Mrs Roseberry the Christmas before. 'I must get you something to replace that awful velour,' Mrs Roseberry had said, and for days after Amy had gone about dreaming of a coat with a fur collar. Not a white fox fur like Mrs Harding's, she knew that was out of the question, but perhaps astrakhan or a narrow strip of mole skin, either would have been acceptable. What she got was a sensible, good quality tweed with wide lapels and a belt round her hips.

Mrs Taylor approved. 'Feel the quality,' she said. 'That coat will last you a lifetime.'

A lifetime of going around looking like a school-girl! She would have given her eyes for fur fabric.

'This Christmas,' said Mrs Roseberry, 'I shall give you a handbag. Your present one is a disgrace.'

She arrived early at the Memorial Hall having promised to help set out the Bring and Buy stall, but others had got there before her. She could hear laughter and talking coming from the inner room as she hung up her coat in the lobby. Bearing in mind Mrs Roseberry's remark about her handbag, she had put all the things she needed for the evening into one of the coat's deep patch pockets. Her purse, a comb, a spare handkerchief, and a tiny box of face powder which she bought at Woolworth's for two-pence.

She checked that her petticoat wasn't showing and that her handkerchief was safely tucked in the leg of her knickers. Yes, everything was as it should be but still she hung back, frightened in case she didn't see in Mr Thomas's eyes the admiration she yearned for. She thought she would shrivel up if he didn't notice her.

Her entrance, though quiet, still attracted attention. Everyone stopped what they were doing and heads turned to see who the latest arrival was. The good ladies of the committee, the members of the Ladies' Church Group and those on the church's electoral roll were all, without exception, wearing their Sunday best. On the most part plain and serviceable dresses, which when no longer good enough for high days and holidays were relegated to everyday wear. Therefore, suddenly confronted by a silk dress with exclusive written all over it, they naturally showed their disapproval.

On one of them it would have been galling enough, but that this young upstart from some foreign part of the country should be the one to put their noses out of joint was just too much. With one accord they returned to their tasks as if there had been no interruption and Amy, who went through life trying to ingratiate herself with everybody, almost convinced herself that she wished she had come in a jumper and skirt instead.

A wish that soon vanished when she saw Mr Thomas approaching, wearing one of his warm and friendly smiles. 'The Bring and Buy stall is over there. Come along . . . Miss Davies has been keeping an eye open for you.'

Miss Davies came to meet them, jerky and quick in her movements, like a bird. 'Ah, there you are.

I was beginning to wonder what had happened to you.'

'Don't you think our Miss Cousins is looking particularly charming this evening?' Mr Thomas said, and Amy blushed, not becomingly, she felt herself go hot all over, but what did it matter? Mr Thomas thought her charming!

Miss Davies looked at her over the top of her spectacles. 'Too overdressed for a small affair like this,' she said, but Amy wasn't listening. He had called her *our* Miss Cousins. Surely that was only one step away from *my* Miss Cousins. She basked in his approval.

'Well, I must away . . .' He seemed reluctant to leave, she thought, and wondered if she should take that as a compliment. 'I seem to be in great demand at present, helping to blow up balloons, wrapping gifts for the bran tub, that sort of thing. I bet you I get waylaid before I'm halfway across the room.'

'That young man has no sense of propriety,' Miss Davies tut-tutted at his retreating back. 'Blowing up balloons! Surely he could have got some of the Sunday school children to do that.'

Amy didn't answer, her eyes were fixed on Mr Thomas, now marooned in the centre of the room surrounded by some half-dozen ladies. They were all talking at once, asking his advice, seeking his approval, anything to get his attention. Amy hated them one and all. Every female in that room was her rival.

Miss Davies said, 'Well, make yourself useful, Miss Cousins. No time to spare.' She had never quite lost her schoolmarmish manner. Two generations of Thornmere villagers had much to thank Miss Davies for. Those who merited it, she encouraged to better themselves, and there was many an ex-pupil now in a managerial position or one or two rungs up on the social ladder who had cause to remember her with gratitude. If in her old age she had become, well, a little eccentric, still thinking she ran the village school and acting accordingly, or taking it upon herself to lecture those, irrespective of their age, she felt fell short of the standards she had established, they forgave her. 'Stands to reason,' they said. 'A teacher can't help being bossy. It goes with the job, doan't it.'

She was now rummaging in a box of oddments, sorting them out ready for pricing.

'What shall we ask for this tasteless object?' she said, holding aloft a china jug in the shape of a cow. 'A shilling, no, that's too much. Sixpence? Let's split the difference and say ninepence.'

Amy was quite taken with it. 'Could I buy it?'

'But what do you want with a milk jug? Are you starting a bottom drawer?'

Amy sighed. Such a question, such a stirring of hope. 'I thought it would do for my aunt for Christmas.'

Miss Davies looked askance. 'A piece of junk from a Bring and Buy stall as a Christmas present! Is that all your aunt is worth to you?'

Last year, Amy remembered, she had sent Aunt Flora a bed-jacket trimmed with swansdown. She had had no reply, no acknowledgement. It was Dr Hamilton who wrote and told her later that her aunt had been wearing the bed-jacket when he paid her a recent call . . . Nothing serious, just a touch of flu, he went on to assure her. 'Your aunt is as tough as old boots. She'll survive the lot of us.'

'It's the thought that counts,' she rebuked Miss Davies, primly.

The hall was filling up. The village fiddler arrived. It promised to be a lively evening and got off to a good start with a rowdy game where the rules seemed to be made up as they went along. It was called Farmyard Noises and Amy found herself dragooned into taking part without any idea of what was going on. She had never been good at group games, or games of any kind except Solitaire. She hated making a fool of herself, and who could look a bigger fool than she in her silk dress and floating sleeves, flapping her elbows and cock-a-doodling. She wished the floor would open and swallow her up.

'Hi you, miss — yes, you with the dress halfway up to your backside. What're you doing over there crowing with that lot? You should be over here gobbling with us.' Mr Pye the verger had a powerful voice but not powerful enough to drown Mr Thomas who, at the further end of the room, was braying whole-heartedly with the rest of his group.

Why couldn't she be like him, she mourned, as reluctantly she left the cockerels and crossed over to join the turkeys. He threw himself into whatever he was doing, whether preaching a sermon, leading the choir, playing silly games, or blowing up balloons with no self-consciousness whatsoever. A vicar's wife would be expected to support her husband; to make herself agreeable to the parishioners, and to put on a smile on occasions like this no matter how much she was shrinking inwardly. How did the wedding service go? For better for worse, for richer for poorer, playing childish games or reading good books together, till death us do part. Oh dear God, please just give me the chance. I'd do whatever he wanted.

From the far end of the room came one last, drawn-out, melodious bray, and then applause. The game was over. The donkeys had won. When Come and sit on my lap was suggested next, Amy pushed Miss Davies forward. 'I'll keep an eye on the stall,' she said.

After the refreshment interval the evening began to improve. A more mellow, more gentle mood prevailed. There had been enough noise and excitement; people wanted to rest now and gossip, or listen to the old and familiar tunes being played on the fiddle. Some of the younger ones got up and danced. Amy shrank in upon herself, dreading being made to look a wallflower, and on the other hand dreading also being asked to dance, for hadn't she already made an exhibition of herself once that evening?

When she saw Mr Thomas bearing down on her with a certain purposeful look in his eye her first emotion was one of alarm, quickly followed by a wave of joy.

'Will you dance this veleta with me?'

'I have never danced a veleta' – she had never danced, full stop – 'I don't even know the steps.'

'Neither do I. We will just have to do the best we can. I don't think,' he added on a lower note, 'we'll be up against much competition.'

He was surefooted and light on his feet. She was floating on air – she was in heaven. Her hand was in his, a good strong hand that guided her, led her, and held her back when she would have made a false move. When the playing stopped he escorted her back to her chair and then went off to seek another partner from among the unescorted ladies. She watched jealously as other partners in turn were whirled around, but his arm did not seem, to her, to be so tight round other waists as when round hers.

It came to an end all too quickly. Mr Thomas approached her again. 'It's raining pretty heavily. Could I give you a lift home?'

Rodings was at the far end of the village. All that time alone with him in his car, *in the dark*. Anything could happen!

'Would you wait for me in the lobby? I must thank the ladies of the committee,' he said.

Three other ladies were also waiting in the lobby. The most voluble of the three, the buxom Mrs Lister the butcher's wife, approached Amy. 'You waiting for the vicar, dear? Isn't he a lovely man, offering to see us home. One of nature's gentlemen.'

'Yes,' said Amy, tight-lipped.

The vicar came. 'Ready, ladies. Mrs Lister, would you like to sit in the front with me?' Only because she's too fat to fit in the back, thought Amy sourly. She cheered up a little when she remembered she lived the furthest away. She wasn't to be entirely cheated after all, she'd have about three minutes alone with Mr Thomas.

He made a dash with her to the door of Rodings, sheltering her with his umbrella. There were no street lamps in the village and the house was in darkness. One of her precious minutes was spent fumbling with the lock.

'I should have thought to bring a torch,' he said. 'Can you manage?' Rain was dripping from the umbrella down both their necks.

'I've got it!' She opened the door, reached for the light and switched it on. Bringing electricity to Thornmere was one of the last of Sir Roger Massingham's neighbourhood benefits. Mrs Roseberry, through necessity or preference, nobody knew for sure not even her daughter, had had it installed on the ground floor only. Every house in Thornmere, except for the poorest cottages and the farms well off the beaten track, now had light at the flick of a switch.

'Could I make you a hot drink? Coffee or cocoa?' said Amy, desperate to keep him a little longer.

'Thank you, but I must get back to the hall to help put the things away.'

She racked her brains for some other reason to delay him. She couldn't let him go like this. She had imagined a long and romantic good night, culminating in a deep and meaningful kiss. But he was very wet and dripping on the rug, and there was the width of the hall between them.

'Good night then, Miss Cousins. See you as usual on Sunday?'

'Oh, yes, I wouldn't miss that for anything.'

'I wish I could say the same for others in my flock. You are the most faithful of my parishioners.'

Could she count that as a compliment she wondered as she lighted her way up the stairs. The hungry must be satisfied with crumbs, she thought, having read that somewhere. She set her candle down on the dressing-table, and lighted the two over the looking-glass. She stared at her reflection which, in the flickering candlelight, looked shadowy and insubstantial. Her eyes seemed to have sunk even deeper into her head, but perhaps that was because she was tired, and her hair, damp from the rain, had begun to frizz.

She was reluctant to get undressed and to take off the dress that for one night at least had turned her into an enchantress. She got into bed and snuggled down feeling with her feet for the heated brick she knew Mrs Taylor would have put in for her. Though physically tired, she was too keyed up to sleep. Besides, sleep would deprive her of wakeful dreams of Mr Thomas. She would often lie at this time of night conjuring up images of him: his arms around her, his mouth on hers. She had never been kissed so she had to work her imagination really hard to visualise what it was like, for nothing she had read or seen enacted on the screen had enlightened her.

She took great care with her appearance for the coming

Sunday. She washed her hair and squeezed lemon juice into the rinsing water to make it shine, then set it into waves with her fingers and rolled the ends into pin-curls. She had knitted herself a blue and white jumper to go with a navy-blue skirt she had bought in the market at Beckton, and she felt far more comfortable in this than she had in the silk dress with its chiffon sleeves. Though she couldn't put her thoughts into words she had felt she was something like a domestic chicken trying to pass itself off as a bird of paradise.

Mr Thomas took as the subject for his sermon the story of Martha and Mary. Amy had always thought when reading this passage in the New Testament that poor Martha was rather hard done by. It was Mary who earned the approval of her Lord, when all she did was to sit at his feet and listen, whereas poor Martha, busy with the housework and cooking, making life easier for the others, got little thanks. That's the story of my life, she thought. But not this morning. Mr Thomas made her see the story in a different light. What it was really about was love. Putting love for the Father and love for his Son before everything else. Finding time for love.

Amy, hanging on to his every word, became convinced when the word love kept cropping up that it was no coincidence. Was Mr Thomas trying to tell her something? Was there a coded message in his sermon? She sat in a state of feverish expectation. Surely, he must have something to say to her now?

He did, but to the whole congregation. He came down from the pulpit and into the aisle to address them.

'Good people,' he said, and because he sounded a trifle nervous, the lilt in his voice became more marked. 'I am taking this unusual step of making an announcement before the end of the service because I want us all to sing the last hymn together as in a spirit of celebration. I have reason to be a very happy man and I want you to share in my happiness.' Amy clasped her hands together and her mouth went dry. 'When I went back to Wales this summer for my annual holiday, I asked a young lady I have been courting for many years if she could name the day for our union. She has now done so and we are to be wed in the New Year.' A ripple ran through the congregation. Mr Thomas's smile was all embracing. 'You have made me very welcome here,' he said. 'You took me, an outsider, to your hearts, and made me feel I belonged. I ask you please to extend that same warmth and friendliness to my wife. Thank you, everyone.'

There was almost a round of applause at that. Mr Thomas held up his hand for silence. In the dim light of the smoking lamps his eyes looked larger and more lustrous than ever as well as suspiciously moist. 'We will now sing hymn number 195, "O Love Divine, how sweet thou art!"'

Amy did not wait for the end of the hymn; she slipped out while they were still singing. She looked about her when she reached the lych-gate as if she were in some unfamiliar place and didn't know which way to turn. Then she began to run, heedlessly and often stumbling, and blinded by tears.

The shock and despair and insufferable pain that she was running away from were still with her when she stopped for breath. She found herself among trees and she leant against the nearest of them, lowering herself until she was on the ground, her back propped up against the trunk. She no longer had the strength in her legs to stand. She sat hunched up, her face in her hands, crying like a child.

Crying for something she could not have. Crying because her heart was breaking.

How could he have deceived her, a Christian, and a good man? How could he have been so treacherous? He had raised her hopes with his winning smiles and tender looks. He had danced with her, he had held her in his arms. He had called her 'our Miss Cousins', which was only one step away from 'my Miss Cousins'.

Was it all in her imagination then? Had *she* been the deceiver and he the victim? Was she really such a fool as all that? Oh, Francis, Francis. I love you so, I can't help it. She felt in her pocket for her handkerchief, and within minutes it was just a wet rag. The cold was coming through the ground, through her coat and her skirt and her underwear. She pulled herself to her feet and looked blindly at her surroundings. She was deep in Thornmere Park and she was surprised in a dull and indifferent way that she had come so far without realising it.

So where would she go now? All she had on her was the sixpence she had intended for the collection, and that would only get her as far as Beckton. But it wasn't a case of going anywhere so much as getting away from Thornmere. She couldn't stay in Thornmere. She couldn't risk the smirks and titters behind her back, for she was sure many had guessed her secret. More than that, she couldn't risk ever coming face to face with Mr Thomas again, for she knew she couldn't trust herself not to break down when confronted with him. And even if she was able to control her feelings, which she doubted, what about when he brought his bride home? What about when a family started? She moaned as a fresh agony gripped her.

Death would be preferable to this. Death, in fact,

seemed inviting – for what had she got to live for now? The thought of the empty years stretching ahead of her – the despair and shame of rejection – oh yes, death was certainly more preferable.

She looked about her out of stupefied and swollen eyes. It wasn't easy to do away with oneself when out in the open and without the means. There was always the railway, of course. She could throw herself in front of a train, but they ran so infrequently on Sundays she might lose her nerve while waiting for one to come along. Or worse still, make a mess of it like she did everything else, lose one of her legs instead of her head.

Please, God, won't you just let me die – here – now. Please answer my prayer, just for once.

She had never been kissed and now she would never know what it was to be kissed. A sudden rush of pity for herself and for all those other unloved spinsters, a legacy from the war, swept over her, and she began to cry out loud, great racking sobs that were forced out of her like the cries of a wounded animal.

The light was draining out of the day. She had no idea how long she had been aimlessly wandering about, it seemed like hours. A mist was rolling up, creeping through the trees like a wraith, obscuring the beautiful colours of autumn and turning everything grey. She shivered, but not from cold – she was too numb to feel the cold any longer.

Everywhere was so quiet. The mist muffled sound, but this silence was eerie. Perhaps she was dead already? She felt dead. Her pain had stopped; now all she wanted to do was to lie down and sleep.

She came upon the mere by chance. She missed the path and suddenly there it was, lying dark and menacing under the drifting fog. She stared at it trying to place it in her mind. It was half empty, dank and uninviting. She remembered now. After talking about it for several years Daniel Harker was at last having it cleaned out. Tools and appliances belonging to the men working on it were stacked neatly to one side.

There was still enough water left to drown in came an idle thought. Dare I, she thought. Have I the courage? It would solve all her problems. No more waking up to empty days with nothing left to look forward to. No more thought of the years ahead in the service of others. No more living in other people's houses and never one of her own. No more going through life unloved. It would be a relief to put all that behind her.

The border of thick rushes that had choked the edges of the mere had been removed and where the men had been working the ground was churned up like liquid mud. She slipped as she inched her way forward and instinctively made a grab at the nearest support. It was a branch from a dead tree, white and spectre-like, poking out of the water. It broke free at her grasp, and then she saw it wasn't a branch. It was the arm and hand of a human skeleton.

Daniel Harker, out on the cricket field inspecting the damage caused by moles and wondering if it was worth doing anything about it before the spring, heard a scream coming from the direction of the mere. He thought at first it was a fox until he recollected that foxes were nocturnal animals and then went off to investigate with Bass skittering about his heels.

TWELVE

Amy, slowing coming back to consciousness, gave a little moan as light stung her eyes. It came from a lamp hanging above a large deal table scrubbed white with a neat arrangement of cooking utensils on a linen cloth at one end. She saw all this without actually taking it in. Her head ached abominably and she couldn't think why because normally she didn't suffer headaches.

She was sitting in a wooden armchair beside a cooking range with a blanket draped around her shoulders. She wondered vaguely how she had got where she was and where was she anyway? She was stiff with cold, and even though the stove gave out a lot of heat, she was unable to stop shivering.

The kitchen she noted, with the detachment of an onlooker, was extremely large and well-stocked with modern appliances. It struck her that there was only one house in Thornmere – assuming she was still in Thornmere – large enough for a kitchen this size, and that was the Hall. So that's where she was, Thornmere Hall. She had hoped to wake up in a different world, but none of her hopes ever materialised. Under the blanket her clothes still felt damp; her coat she noted was hanging to dry from the airing rack above her head. Her shoes were on the hearth and on her feet were a pair of men's carpet slippers. She stared unseeing at the opposite wall, trying desperately not to remember the events of earlier.

The door opened and Daniel Harker came in and she instinctively recoiled. Good grief, Dan wondered with alarm, did she think he was going to rape her! Good thing he had changed his mind about removing all her wet things. That wouldn't have looked good, would it?

He said, 'How are you feeling now?'

She tried to rise to her feet but was hampered by the heavy folds of the blanket. 'Don't you come anywhere near me,' she cried.

'I'll remember that the next time I rescue someone from drowning,' he retorted. He saw her flinch and immediately regretted his harshness. The poor kid was scared stiff, and no wonder considering what she had been through. 'You have nothing to fear from me,' he said reassuringly.

She began to cry, and as always when he saw a woman crying he felt completely at a loss. She looked at him in a piteous manner and uttered, between her sobs, what sounded like a plea to let her stay. First she wouldn't let him come near her, now she wanted him to let her stay. Had he heard aright, he wondered? She was distraught, too distraught to know what she was saying. He was beginning to feel somewhat distraught himself. He shifted his position uneasily.

He had been sitting, half perched on the table, now he moved to the comfort of a chair. He was dying for a smoke, but his cigars were in his office and he was reluctant to leave her in this condition in order to fetch them. In this state of near hysteria there was no saying what she might do. To his relief her sobbing gradually subsided, tears flowed less freely. She groped for her handkerchief but couldn't find it. He took his from his breast pocket and passed it over. She blew her nose.

'Thank you,' she said in a whisper. The calm after the storm, he hoped.

'Feeling better now?'

'Yes, except for a headache.'

'That is no headache, my dear,' he said in a jokey fashion. 'That's a hangover. You swallowed a whacking large glass of brandy before you passed out.'

She looked at him in bewilderment. 'I don't know what you're talking about. I don't drink!'

He was hard put to it not to laugh. 'Then you did a jolly good imitation. I've never seen a drink disappear so quickly.'

'But I never drink. I signed the pledge – years ago. I don't like drink, I don't like the smell of it, even.'

He released a great burst of belly laughter that relieved the tension and even coaxed from her a glimmer of a smile. Her indignation had not been faked, it was real. A healthy sign, he thought, for unlike crying indignation was a positive emotion. He leaned forward and took her hand – a childlike hand it looked in his, small and limp.

'You honestly don't remember, do you? I don't believe you remember anything. Fainting? Or falling in the mere? Not even what you found?'

He saw the panic in her face, felt her hand flutter in his and realised that her defence against a horror too strong to face was loss of memory. Faked or real, it didn't matter, the end result was the same.

'Please don't ask me any more questions,' she whimpered.

'Just leave me alone. That's all I want - to be left alone.'

That's rich, he thought. It would have been better for him too if he had left her alone, but who, unless completely inhuman, could have done so, for even if she had not been in danger of drowning she was certainly in danger of exposure.

He had had his day nicely planned. With Mrs Webster out of the way he would have lunched in the kitchen, sitting with his feet up on the fender and a plate of bread and cheese and pickles on his lap. And afterwards, forty winks in his office before getting down to some outstanding correspondence. Then spending the evening listening to a selection of records on the gramophone.

He had recently bought some recordings of the songs from *Show Boat*, the show starring Paul Robeson that had taken London by storm the previous year. He had, by a stroke of luck, got four seats for the opening night and had asked George and Mollie Gilbert and young Joey to come along as his guests. He had thought the story would have been lost on George and Mollie but, with the help of the programme, they had followed easily, picking up vibrations from the performers, enjoying the colours and movement, the acting and the dancing; showing their enthusiasm with thunderous applause. Joey had been bowled over by the entire performance and later, back at Ivy House, he had played as much as he could remember from the score. Daniel, listening with enthusiasm, had his determination to set young Joey's feet on the path to a musical career strengthened.

Yet, here he was instead, landed in a situation which would have been beyond his imagination earlier that day. He had come upon Amy half in and half out of the water, clutching part of a human corpse in which Bass instantly took a frenetic interest. He had bawled at him to clear off and Bass, not used to being shouted at, had retreated reluctantly, barking defiance from a safe distance.

When he attempted to lift the girl she had come round and struggled, screaming at him, 'Leave me alone . . . Let me go . . . I want to die . . . Just leave me to die . . . Let me go!'

That had angered him. Why did a young girl with all her life before her want to die? For the usual reason? He clenched his jaw. God, what a society we live in, he thought, when a woman would rather die than face the consequences of an illegitimate baby. And the gruesome object she was clutching in her hand, which though he was not normally squeamish made his gorge rise. How had she come by it? Had she found it? He had an impulse to fling it into the water and forget it, for he felt that no good would come of this discovery. But then he realised he had a duty to the dead as well as to the living.

He had lifted her, a dead weight in her sodden clothes, and carried her to the house. Bass lagged behind, stopping every few yards to look behind him and bark afresh until shouted at to come to heel.

It was almost dark then and getting colder; the mist was thickening into fog. Dan's first impulse was to take the girl to his office where there was a comfortable sofa to lay her on, but remembering the fire there had been left to die down he took her to the kitchen instead and sat her by the Aga. He then poured them both a stiff brandy for he was as much in need of something to steady his nerves as she.

He watched with alarm, and to some extent amusement, as the girl swallowed her dose in one gulp, and wasn't at all surprised when almost immediately she passed out.

Rivulets of liquid mud ran down her face. He wiped them away with a drying-up cloth and then began to mop at her clothes until, seeing that he wasn't so much removing the stains as spreading them further, he took off her overcoat and hung it on the airer to dry. She was pitifully thin. Beneath her woollen jumper, her collar bones stood out like ridges. She had the form of a child and looked not unlike one with her dirty face and tousled hair. Even asleep – if it was sleep that had overcome her and not a drunken stupor – a childlike sigh escaped her, and it was then that sympathy for her plight overcame his commonsense.

He made no mention of her when he phoned the police, which he did as soon as he had changed out of his own wet clothes. He parried awkward questions by making out it was Bass who had discovered the bones.

'There's more where that come from, I'spect,' said Tom Barley, the village bobby. He had been the first to arrive and Dan had taken him down to the mere where by the light of torches, they had poked around in the black water, stirring up nothing but mud. With what they already had they went back to the house just as a sergeant and inspector from Beckton Market arrived by car.

Dan took them into his office, made up the fire, and used the bellows to bring it quickly into life. Bass, who was making a nuisance of himself, was shut in the stables from whence at regular intervals a high-pitched howl of protest could be heard.

'Reckon 'e got a taste of that bone,' said the constable, ignoring the looks from his superiors. As sole upholder of the law in Thornmere he knew how far he could go.

'It's too dark to do anything about it now,' said

Inspector Harris. 'First light tomorrow we'll start draining the lake.'

Dan broke in. 'That's already in hand. My men will be here tomorrow morning to finish the job.'

'Tell them to hold off until we've made a thorough search for the rest of the corpse.' The inspector was another who was not too pleased at having his Sunday plans interrupted. 'I expect it'll turn out to be some tramp or poacher, or somebody the worse for drink wandering off the path. Anybody reported missing in the past few years, Constable?'

'Not from Thornmere, sur.'

'And you, sir, would you know of anyone?' The inspector looked at Dan.

He would be the last to be told if there was, he thought, but didn't say as much. Seven years master of Thornmere Hall and he was still an outsider. The police went their way taking the evidence with them, refusing his offers of refreshment, though Dan felt sure if P.C. Barley had been on his own there would have been no such misgiving.

They had hardly gone before he regretted not telling them about the girl. Should it ever come out it would place him in a very awkward position. Yet he could not forget her tone of voice when she had begged him to let her die. Goodness knows what would happen to the poor kid if he had informed the police of that. She could be arrested for attempted suicide – or worse still clapped into a mental home. Young girls had been institutionalised for less.

He was glad he had honoured her plea, he thought, looking across at her now. She looked so . . . he groped in his mind for a suitable word. Helpless? Uncared for? Whatever, she looked as if she needed help.

He caught her eye. 'I suspect you've had nothing to eat since breakfast? I haven't and I'm hollow. Come and join me at the table, Miss Cousins. I would enjoy my food twice as much if I saw you eating, too.'

'You knew who I was all the time,' she said.

'Everybody knows everybody else in Thornmere. Isn't that a well-known saying in the village? I didn't know you at first, not until I brought you into the light. D'you know who I am?'

'Yes. You're Mr Harker.'

'So you know where you are, too. Your name is Amy, isn't it? Would you mind if I called you Amy?' She gave no answer either way. He smiled. 'Well, Amy, I'll take that as a yes. Is it also yes to something to eat?'

'I suppose so', she said, grudgingly.

She watched him as he filled the kettle, took cups and saucers and a tea-pot from the dresser, buttered bread and sliced ham from the bone. For such a heavy man his actions were deft and quick and she guessed he was well practised in looking after himself. She wondered if they were alone in the house as there was no other sound of movement.

As if in answer to her thoughts he said, 'I'm on my own today. My housekeeper is down at the lodge looking after Reuben. She should be looking after Ruby, for Ruby is the one who's been doing all the work, spending all last night and this morning, giving birth. But it's Reuben who's getting all the sympathy because he's in such a bad way, poor chap. It's his first baby.' Dan chuckled. 'Of course I'm forgetting, you know the Stonehams, don't you, you came to their wedding. Well, now they have a little daughter and they are going to call her Jessie. Mrs Webster sent word that mother and baby are doing fine, but that she would be staying at the lodge overnight in case she's needed.'

'Does Mrs Webster know I'm here?'

'Nobody knows you're here, Amy. Isn't that what you want?'

'Yes,' she said, and added after a pause, 'thank you.'

She joined him at the table, sitting at the end nearest the fire. He put out mustard and pickles and fetched a bowl of fruit from the pantry, and gave her tea in a cup the size of a soup bowl. She wasn't hungry but she pretended to eat to please him, picking at the ham, crumbling the bread and sipping the hot sweet tea which was too strong and too sweet, for normally she did not take sugar. She came to the table not to eat but to be near him. She felt safer with him close by.

'That dreadful man with the plebeian features,' Mrs Roseberry once said of him. Amy didn't know what plebeian meant but she rather suspected that she and Mr Harker had that in common.

Replenished, he sat back in his chair and picked his teeth with a matchstick. Quietly he contemplated her, then, as if the moment was ripe said, 'I found you face down in six inches of water. I know you must have fainted, but why were you so near the water? Was it intentional? Did you mean that about wanting to die?'

Her face crumpled. 'Don't ask me, please, I c-can't bear to talk about it. I'm not ready to yet.'

'You can confide in me, Amy, I promise you it won't go any further.'

A mulish look settled on her narrow face. 'There is nothing to confide,' she said.

'If you say so.'

He hid his disappointment. For a moment there he felt she was ready to tell him everything, but the moment had passed, and her face was closed against him. He felt helpless in the face of such obduracy. Let her sleep on it, he thought. She's too tired to think straight at the moment. He went off to his office to fetch a cigar with which he normally finished a meal, and when he returned he saw that she had fallen asleep at the table. He roused her gently.

'Come along, girlie, bedtime,' he said.

She had never seen a bathroom like it. To call it luxurious didn't do it justice. It was magnificent — large and warm which surprised her, for she had always equated bathrooms with freezing conditions. The one at Chancel Terrace had just the basic necessities, a bath and a WC and a cold-water tap. The one at Rodings included a pedestal basin and hot water was supplied by the copper in the scullery, carried up to the bathroom in brass cans. But this one had everything. Hot water on tap; a boxed-in bath; patterned tiles from ceiling to floor, except for one wall which was mirrored — and a shower.

She looked askance at the shower. It was a large brass hood that arched over the narrow end of the bath and when a lever was pulled, water sprayed out of dozens of little holes pierced in its underside. Mr Harker demonstrated and soaked himself, the walls and the floor in the process; she decided it was safer to have a bath.

He left her a warm, fleecy towel the size of a sheet, some bath crystals, an unused toothbrush, one of his pyjama tops in lieu of a nightgown, and a loofah. As she had never come across one of these before, and Mr Harker did not demonstrate how to use it, perhaps thinking that one demonstration was more than enough, she took it to be a new-fangled type of lavatory brush, and wedged it in its rightful place behind the pan.

She was beginning to take an interest in her surroundings. The mist in her mind was clearing, though some events were still curtained off, for she had found the facility to close her mind against anything that disturbed her. She had no idea of the time. The day had passed without her knowing it. She stepped out of the bath onto a white fur rug, and when she turned she gasped, for at first sight she thought she was being watched by a naked woman.

She was even more embarrassed when she realised it was her own reflection. She couldn't bear to see herself with nothing on. She didn't see anything beautiful in the human body, not her own anyway, which was all the wrong shape – sticking out where it should go in, and too flat where it should stick out. What man would ever desire her?

The curtain in her mind trembled a little, was in danger of lifting. She felt sick and began to quake. Quickly, with her back to the mirror, she towelled herself dry and put on the pyjama top, which came to just above her knees and over that, Mr Harker's paisley dressing-gown. Only then could she face the mirror again. She was safely back in her curtained-off world.

The bedroom was huge. The main guestroom Mr Harker called it. Never yet christened, he said and laughed; she didn't know why. The four-poster bed was swallowed up in so much space and the newly-lit fire that flickered uneasily in the grate did no more than warm the chimney.

Mr Harker knocked on the door, but made no attempt to enter, just to ask her if she had everything she wanted. 'If there's anything you need in the night, I'm just down the corridor,' he said. 'Good night, and sleep well.'

He was so thoughtful. He had left milk and biscuits on the bedside table, a hot-water bottle in the bed – a stone one. The curtain fluttered again but she quickly drew it back against memories of Raneleigh Sanatorium, and once in bed between icy linen sheets hugged the bottle until it began to scald her through the thinness of the pyjama top. She pushed it down then to warm her feet and hugged herself instead, and slowly and thankfully surrendered herself to sleep.

It was half-past midnight and the first time that day that Daniel had had the chance to look at the Sunday paper. He was propped up in bed with a whisky at his elbow and the *Sunday Dispatch* spread out before him, reading the reports on yesterday's sport, when a slight sound made him look at the door. The handle was turning.

He reached for his dressing-gown, but before he could put a foot out of bed the door opened and Amy stood on the threshold. She hesitated for a second or two as if not sure of herself or her whereabouts, then literally flung herself across the room and into the bed beside him, where she pulled the bedclothes up to her chin and gave him a mixed look of defiance and apprehension.

'Nothing on earth will make me go back to that room,' she said.

He recovered his power of speech. 'What's wrong with it?'

'It's not the room, it's just that I don't want to be on my own. Every time I fall asleep I have a bad dream. I don't know now what is real and what I've dreamt, and I'm so scared. Please, please, let me stay here with you. I feel safe with you.'

Obviously she didn't realise what she was asking of him, and dare he take the risk? She only wanted his company. His comfort too, perhaps. He had never denied that, even to Bass, who often shared his bed. There was a difference, however, between a girl and a dog, and it was no good thinking of her as a child anymore – in that revealing pyjama top she looked all woman. She trusts you, he thought, and as long as he kept that thought in mind he would be safe, and she would be safe.

Her closeness, the warmth of her body, the spicy fragrance of the pine bath-salts she had used, the memory of the child-like voice when she pleaded with him to let her stay, all that soon transpired to bring him out in a cold sweat. As soon as she had gone to sleep and she was nearly there, he vowed he'd slip away and spend the rest of the night either in the bed she had discarded or on the sofa in his study.

He tried to compose himself for sleep but was prevented by a tiny, indefinable sound which he put down to mice behind the wainscoting – the place was riddled with them – then realised the sound was much nearer at hand. It was Amy sobbing quietly beneath the bedclothes. He said her name, and it seemed the most natural thing in the world to him that as he turned to comfort her, she at the same time, turned to him for comfort.

It all came out then, what he had wanted to know earlier and a lot more besides. Her early life with Aunt Flora; the short sharp lesson at the Raneleigh Sanatorium; the first, few difficult days at Rodings, and finally – though now she was speaking in little more than a whisper and he had to put his head close to hear her – her hopeless and painful love for Mr Thomas. Nothing surprised him less than that. On the few occasions when he had put in an appearance at church as befitted the largest landowner in the district, he had noticed, as had others he guessed, the way she gazed adoringly at the vicar. He hadn't taken it seriously. Amy was only one of many who felt the same way about the romantic-looking Mr Thomas.

'And you wanted to kill yourself because of him!' And yet he really wasn't surprised. She was young enough and unstable enough to believe that death was preferable to a broken heart.

'I was too miserable to care what happened to me. Yes, I did want to die, I suppose. I knew I couldn't stay in Thornmere . . . and there didn't seem any other way out but dying.'

'And how do you feel about dying, now?'

'I don't know. I don't know what I want anymore, except one thing is certain. I can't stay in Thornmere, I can't take the risk of ever facing Mr – him again.' She stifled another sob.

'Look, you're tired, overwrought. Let's talk about this in the morning, after I've had a word with the police about . . .'

She went rigid. 'Don't . . . don't say anything about that . . . that's the part I don't want to remember, the part I kept seeing in my dreams . . .'

He comforted her as he would a frightened child, holding her in his arms and stroking her hair. He felt her tension ease away, her body grow limp and flaccid against his. When he kissed her she kissed him back in a way that showed a hunger he could only guess at. 'That's the first time I've ever been kissed,' she said, and gave a breathless, self-conscious little sigh.

Never been kissed! And he had thought . . . Oh my God, did that mean?

'Amy, hold on a minute. Have you ever slept with a man before?'

'Of course not! Who do you think I am!'

He didn't know whether to laugh or cry. She was such a funny and unpredictable little thing, but she was also a virgin and he had enough decency to feel reluctant about taking advantage of her innocence. On the other hand . . . The alternative was too tempting to dismiss so lightly, and she so sweet and available. A pool of winsome compliance in which a man could drown and ignore the consequences.

So he drowned and she drowned with him, and when they surfaced, floating drowsily in the afterglow of passion, they lay clasping hands, smiling at each other.

'I'd better go back to my own bed,' she said at last. 'Don't worry, I'm all right now, I won't have any more nightmares.'

'No, stay with me. The other room will be freezing cold, anyway. I would like you to stay . . . please.'

Her only answer was to squeeze his hand and presently he heard the even breathing that told of sleep. He was nearly asleep himself, and his last conscious thought was the pleasure of looking forward to finding her in bed with him in the morning.

But when he awakened, later than he intended, daylight already edging round the curtains, he discovered she was gone. No longer in his bed, no longer in his house, for he checked and found that her clothes were missing. His immediate disappointment was soon replaced by a rueful acknowledgement that nothing could have come of that brief and memorable encounter, anyway. There was nothing about their feelings for each other to keep them together. They had both taken advantage of the opportunity to snatch at something each desired. He flattered himself with the thought that perhaps he had done her a favour, for she had certainly done one for him. He felt a new man this morning. Ready to face the chain of events caused by yesterday's discovery.

He whistled as he shaved and showered. He dressed in haste, for his men had already arrived, and the police would soon follow. He had left his watch on the dresser; he distinctly remembered taking it off and placing it on the brass ashtray as he always did – but it wasn't there. He went through the pockets of his dressing-gown, of the sports jacket he had worn yesterday, of the blazer he had changed into. Even the pockets of his pyjamas which he found mixed up with the bedclothes. He stripped the bed, then quartered the floor on his hands and knees, but without success. He rose to his feet reluctant to face the only possibility. Amy had taken it.

For God's sake, why? If she needed money he would have given it to her. His wallet was in his jacket pocket, and he remembered he had hung his jacket up before undressing for bed. So not finding money available she had taken his watch instead? Why – to remember him by? Not very likely, she knew what she was doing. The watch-case was solid silver, the works jewelled. Oh yes, she knew what she was doing, the sweet and innocent Miss Amy Cousins. And what was more she'd be miles away from Thornmere by now, so there was no point in chasing after her. There was a sour taste in his mouth as he went downstairs to meet the law.

'Oh, Miss Helena, I can't tell you how glad I am to see you. I've been counting the hours . . .' Mrs Taylor's fervent welcome told its own story. Mother was giving her a bad time.

'How is Mother?' Helena asked.

Mrs Taylor sighed. 'I can't do anything right. It's, "Amy would know where I put my embroidery scissors", "Amy knows just the right temperature for my malted milk", "Amy knows how I like my toast". It's "Amy knows" from morning to night.'

Mrs Taylor picked up Helena's suitcase and led the way upstairs. 'I've been sleeping in since Amy went off, and to tell you the truth, Miss Helena, my Stan is getting a bit narked about it. Having to get his own meals, I mean. I wondered . . .' She hesitated.

Helena was prepared for this. 'Of course. That is why I've come, and I intend to stay until we hear from Amy. Any further news?'

'Only something we heard this morning and that hasn't been confirmed. Somebody answering her description got on the workmen's train at Thornmere Halt, on Monday morning. The porter remembered her particularly because of her condition. He said she was bare-headed and looked as if she had slept in a ditch all night. She had a ticket to Beckton Market, but as she wasn't seen to alight there it's presumed she went on to Norwich. The porter didn't give her another thought until he heard that a young woman from Thornmere was missing.'

'What did my mother say to that?'

'She didn't believe a word of it. She said the porter was mistaken or jumping in to get a bit of the limelight for himself. She has convinced herself that Amy has been abducted.'

'And the police?'

'A fat lot of help they've been, Miss Helena. They say that as Amy is over twenty-one she is quite at liberty to go off anytime she likes and only if foul play is suspected can they take any action. They said they'd list her as a missing person, but of course at the present they have their hands full with this other business.'

'Yes, what about that, Mrs Taylor? Any fresh developments?'

Mrs Taylor's gloom lifted a little. She had had it up to her eyebrows with Amy. She was glad of a change of subject. 'There are all sorts of rumours flying around the village. The latest is that the body is that of Mr Crossley. You remember, Miss Helena,' as Helena at first looked puzzled. 'Sir Roger Massingham's land agent. He left the village when the estate was sold off and told everyone he was going to Australia. Now they say he committed suicide by drowning.'

This news shook Helena. An unknown body – a vague someone – could arouse pity. But a person with a name, a one-time familiar figure in the daily life of Thornmere, that was a different matter. She shuddered as if someone had walked over her grave.

'What makes them think it is – was – Mr Crossley?'

'There's talk – and it's only talk mind you – that some clothing found on the skeleton has been identified as belonging to him. Tom Barley's looking very full of himself these days.' Tom Barley? Helena racked her brains. Oh yes, of course, the village policeman. 'I wouldn't be at all surprised if some of the rumours didn't start with him. After hours, off duty, down at the Ferry Inn, he's let more than one cat out of the bag.'

'But why suicide? It seems incredible, a man like Mr Crossley. Isn't it possible he lost his way in the dark and stumbled into the lake?'

But was it so incredible Helena wondered as a sudden image of a solitary figure standing by the mere came back to mind. She had gone there to refresh her memory of Rupert that March day in 1923 when the effects of Thornmere Hall were being disposed of, and had felt strangely disturbed by the despairing look on the face of the man she had met by the side of the lake. His eyes, she remembered, were the eyes of someone who had lost all hope, and again she shivered involuntarily.

Mrs Taylor said, 'And now Mr Harker has gone off to some place in Hampshire to make further enquiries.'

'Why Hampshire?' asked Helena, more out of politeness to Mrs Taylor than interest in Mr Harker's movements.

'Because they say that's where Mrs Crossley, the agent's wife, came from originally. Mr Crossley was supposed to join her there when everything was settled this end.'

'Then don't you think, if the body is that of Arthur Crossley, his wife would have made enquiries about him before this, especially if they had planned to emigrate to Australia?'

'I suppose you're right.' Mrs Taylor was reluctant to accept such an easy explanation. The excitement of the gruesome discovery, the speculation of its identity – would keep tongues wagging for many more weeks, then would fizzle out for want of further stimulation. She wasn't Norfolk born; she came from a small village in North Essex where gossip was often the only form of entertainment. She suspected it was the same in small villages the world over.

'Your room is ready for you,' Mrs Taylor had said on her arrival, but now gazing around her, Helena felt with a surprising and unexpected twinge of regret that the word 'your' no longer applied. The term now related to another room that looked out onto a London street; a man's room, for Paul had obliterated any trace of femininity by the mere strength of his personality.

This room was just on loan to her, a visitor, and such a pretty room it was too with its colour scheme of white and yellow; a refreshing combination that gave one a sense of spring freshness, and a view from the window of a glorious silver maple still hanging on to the last of its yellowy coppery leaves. A vase of winter jasmine on the dressing-table caught her eye. Her face lit up.

'Oh, you are a darling, Mrs Taylor. You remembered that I love flowers in my bedroom. And from the garden, too. That makes them extra special.'

'I can't take all the credit. It was Amy who reminded me the last time you came.'

'But Amy is not here and you remembered. That's the one thing I miss about living in London – not having a garden to pick flowers from. But I mustn't stand here chatting, I must go and see Mother.'

'She's sleeping, Miss Helena. It's her first time out of bed since Sunday and she tires very quickly. She insisted on getting up because you were coming. She's had her lunch and is now having a little nap in her sitting room. What about you? Can I get you something?'

'I had a snack in Norwich, thank you, but I wouldn't say no to a cup of tea.'

'Something to go with it? A piece of my dark fruit cake?'

'How can I refuse a piece of your dark fruit cake! Then what about you getting off home?'

'I'll set the tea-trolley first. And I'll be back here at my usual time in the morning.' Mrs Taylor hesitated as if reluctant to leave a job unfinished. 'If anything crops up that you can't cope with don't hesitate to send for me. The butcher's boy is good at running errands.'

Helena smiled. 'What could possibly happen in the next few hours that I couldn't manage, Mrs Taylor, but thank you for the offer.'

But how would she manage if Paul should phone her and demand her instant return which she would not put past him considering the mood she had left him in that morning. He had been so cooperative the evening before.

After their enjoyable day at Southend he had been in a happy mood all evening and had agreed on hearing the news about Amy's disappearance with her decision to go up to Norfolk to be with her mother.

This morning, however, it was a different story, for he had one of those swift changes of mood which his declining health had induced – begging almost tearfully for her not to leave him. She had talked him round in the end, though at a cost to her nerves and, getting from her a promise to phone him every day, he had given her a grudging goodbye kiss. Then fired his parting shot as she was about to leave the room. 'Deserter!' he shouted after her.

She changed out of her travelling clothes and into a jumper suit she had left behind from her last visit. It was a pale coffee colour which she rather liked but which Midge said reminded her of sludge, so she had livened it up with some narrow fur trimming round the neck and sleeves. That, with a long necklace of amber beads, transformed it. She brushed out her hair and set it back with her fingers, a final dab of powder, but no lipstick, not in her mother's house, and she was ready.

The sitting room door was open wide enough for her to catch a glimpse of her mother asleep in a straight-backed, winged armchair. Even in sleep she looked autocratic. She didn't loll or let her jaw drop or allow her head to fall forward. She sat so upright there was daylight between her back and that of the chair. Helena had thought the time would never come when she would feel a sentimental attachment to her mother, but it had come now and with it a rush of tears. Carefully she drew the door to, then went off to telephone Paul, and as is sometimes the case, the phone rang just as she reached out to it.

'Just to say I'm sorry.' It was Paul of course, full of

contrition. She could imagine his look of penitence – she had seen it so often; his vivid blue eyes begging forgiveness. 'Just to tell you I didn't mean a word I said, and of course I understand that you must be with your mother at a time like this.'

'Have you missed me?'

'Of course I haven't, I've been able to get on with some work for a change, and later on this evening Jake is coming up for a game of chess.' His voice changed. 'Of course I'm missing you, you tease, and if you're not home soon I'll jolly well come there and get you.'

'Oh, darling, if only you could.'

'That's entirely up to you. You've only got to face up to your mother.'

She had a sudden feeling she was not alone. She looked round and sure enough, there was her mother standing in the doorway of her sitting room catching her as she had on another occasion, years ago, speaking on the telephone to Paul. That very first time her mother had been querulous and frowning. Now she came forward smiling a welcome.

She said, 'I was asleep and heard you speaking and thought I was dreaming. Helena, my dear, I can't tell you how happy I am that you are home.'

Helena said a hasty goodbye to Paul, promising to ring back shortly, then went across to greet her mother. Kissing her mother's cheek was like kissing scented tissue paper. Because of her frailty she looked as if the slightest touch could bruise her if Helena didn't know otherwise.

They had their tea by the fire and sat on talking about any subject other than that uppermost in their minds, as if Amy's disappearance was too serious to be the subject of idle chat over muffins and dark fruit cake. It was now dusk and the curtains remained undrawn, for they both felt disinclined to move. They were cosy where they were, with their feet up on the fender and the tea-trolley between them; a cosiness that was undermined by the thought of the question mark hanging over Amy's disappearance. It was Mrs Roseberry who broached the subject at last.

'What do you make of this pretty kettle of fish? A fine thing when it is no longer safe for a gel to walk home from church on a Sunday morning!'

Helena sighed inwardly. Mussolini's fascist regime in Italy was causing widespread concern. The Wall Street crash of the previous month was sending tremors throughout the Western world. Nearer to home the skeleton of a man had been found in the mere; the vicar had announced his intention of getting married; Ruby Stoneham had given birth to a healthy daughter, and the landlord of the Ferry Inn was dying: but to her mother all that counted as nought compared to Amy's disappearance.

'What makes you so certain that Amy has been abducted?' she said.

'What other explanation is there? She wouldn't run away – she was happy here.' Unusually for Mrs Roseberry, her voice shook a little, and Helena glancing at her saw that her mouth was trembling.

'I didn't realise how fond of her you were,' she said.

'Not fond of her in the same way that I am fond of you, my dear. After all, she is not family. But there's something rather appealing about her, and she could be amusing, too.'

'Amy – amusing!'

'Not intentionally. She had no sense of humour, poor girl, she took everything so seriously. It was the way she acted, the things she sometimes said . . . She made me laugh. Half the time she seemed to have her head in the clouds.

She became a lot worse after she got religious mania, and I blame her chapel upbringing for that.' A little of her old imperiousness returned to Mrs Roseberry's manner. 'All that church going. It didn't make her any happier – quite the opposite, in fact. If it hadn't been for that church I'm sure she would be here now.'

Mrs Roseberry's imperiousness did not last long, her concern for Amy was greater. She took her handkerchief from her bag and wiped her eyes. 'Last Sunday she went to church without her handbag. My fault. I had passed some derogatory remark about its shabbiness and Amy was sensitive about things like that. But that proves she had no intention of running away, because can you imagine any woman running away without her handbag or a change of clothing! She must have been abducted! There is no other explanation.'

'She could have eloped,' said Helena, repeating what Paul had said, but it sounded such a lame solution she wasn't surprised at her mother ignoring it.

Mrs Roseberry went on; 'She was a natural victim. Somebody only had to speak kindly to her and she was all over them. And all these cars that are about now. They are the cause of the increase in crime in my opinion. Never in one place long enough to be identified. A crime committed and the perpetrator safely away in the next county before the police are even alerted. Your father always did say we would live to rue the day the internal combustion engine was invented, and events have proved the Admiral right!'

'Mother, you are not suggesting that Amy was bundled into a car and driven away against her will?'

'What other answer is there! She's disappeared. She had no money or extra clothing. If you think that is far-fetched, give me another reason for her disappearance.'

'I just don't know, but Mrs Taylor did say that the porter at Thornmere Halt . . .'

Her mother interrupted impatiently. 'Spare me village tittle-tattle, I beg of you, Helena. I don't know who the young woman is who supposedly boarded the early morning train to Beckton, but I do know she couldn't be Amy. Where would Amy have hidden herself all Sunday afternoon and evening, to say nothing of the night?' Again, Mrs Roseberry's voice faltered. 'I sometimes fear she may no longer be alive,' she said morbidly.

Helena squeezed her mother's hand, giving comfort in the only way she knew. 'You mustn't think like that. There are so many possibilities. She could have made up her mind to visit someone on the spur of the moment.'

'Without money? Without baggage?'

Helena persisted. 'She may have made friends in Beckton. Someone could have picked her up from church and taken her back for lunch. As I said, the possibilities are endless.'

'Yes, I do see that, but it would be so unlike Amy not to have told me first. And if that is the case, where has she been hiding herself since Sunday?' Mrs Roseberry seemed reluctant to look on the bright side. She had, thought Helena, convinced herself that Amy was dead. Helena herself, and Midge, thought the likelihood was that Amy had run away again. But why? She had seemed so settled in Thornmere, had joined the church, made herself indispensable at Rodings. In Helena's opinion there were only two reasons for a woman, or anyone else for that matter, to run away: one was to escape a situation that had become untenable; and the other to find fulfilment. But Amy, was she the type ever to find fulfilment? An idea suddenly came to her.

'Has Amy been in touch with her aunt recently?'

Mrs Roseberry shrugged indifferently. 'I can't recall. She rarely mentions her. However, she did show me something she had picked up at a church social that she intended to send to her aunt as a Christmas present.'

'It just crossed my mind that she may have had bad news from home. Perhaps her aunt has been taken ill and Amy dashed off to see her.'

'Without telling me! Without money – without a change of clothes?' This lack of money or clothes was an important issue with her mother, Helena thought. Because she herself would never dream of going anywhere without a sufficiency of both?'

She said, 'I think I'll have a look through her things. You never know, I might find something that will provide a clue.'

Mrs Roseberry looked unimpressed. 'I'm afraid you'll just be wasting your time.'

It wasn't a waste of time entirely for the search revealed a little more about Amy's character. An obsessional tidiness for one thing, which made Helena recall ruefully the jumble of her own drawers and cupboards. Her search was made easier by the fact that Amy's possessions were so few. She was confronted by a dress in an almost empty wardrobe which she recognised after a second glance as once belonging to herself. She stared at it appalled. Full diaphanous sleeves and a chiffon rose on a dress that was, or had been – and that was what gave it its distinction – simple and elegant. What a travesty, what a waste of a good dress was her first reaction, quickly followed by a feeling of self-reproach. It was Amy's dress to do with as she liked and if Amy preferred it prettied up that was her affair. Perhaps there was a clue in that dress if she knew what it was she was looking for.

Perhaps there was someone Amy had wanted to impress and it hadn't worked. Perhaps then it was a case of running away from unhappiness rather than running off to find it. Poor Amy.

She returned to her mother.

'Well?' Mrs Roseberry looked up. 'Any clues?'

'Nothing, except this delightful little Staffordshire cow-jug I found in the top drawer of her dressing-table. Where did Amy pick up anything as valuable as this?'

Mrs Roseberry took it, turning it over in her hands to inspect it more closely. 'I had no idea it was genuine. This is the object she showed me that she got from the church social.' Their glances met and the same thought occurred to them both. 'She couldn't have gone running back to Aunt Flora then, or she would have taken this with her. I was praying that I was wrong, but now it seems . . . Oh, Helena, my dear, what are we going to do?'

Paul wasn't mentioned until late that night. Helena helped her mother to bed and took her up a cup of malted milk, 'Just the way I like it. Thank you, my dear.' Afterwards, she sat on the edge of her mother's bed to talk, something that once Mrs Roseberry would not have tolerated, but now turned a blind eye to. The subject of Amy had, for the time being, been laid to rest. There was nothing they could do about her today. Helena had promised to go to the police tomorrow taking with her the Staffordshire cow-jug which her mother considered a vital piece of evidence. She was considering how best to bring Paul into the conversation when, without any preamble, her mother did it for her.

'Isn't it about time I met this friend of yours,' she said, and Helena's quick retort died on her lips when she saw a hint of a twinkle in her mother's pale-blue eyes. She repaid her in kind.

'Mother, are you referring to Midge?'

'Stupid girl, of course I'm not, and I am in no mood to waste words at this time of night, either!'

Helena wasn't sure what delighted her more. Her mother still seeing her as a girl or wishing to meet Paul.

'You really do want to see him?'

'Do you not think it is time that I did?'

'Oh, Mother . . .'

'There is no need to cry all over me. I thought you'd be pleased.'

'I am pleased. I'm delighted. I thought . . . Oh, it doesn't matter what I thought. But Mother, you do realise that if you invite him up here to stay, he'll expect to share my bed?'

There was a longer than necessary pause. 'Yes, I do realise that,' Mrs Roseberry said, and now she was in earnest. 'These past few days have given me much to think about. You have been a good daughter to me, Helena. I haven't always been a good mother. I know that if it weren't for you strong sense of duty my intolerance would have driven a rift between us years ago. I hope you will forgive me, and I hope your friend will forgive me also.'

'His name is Paul, Mother.'

'Yes, I know. Paul, such a very civilised name. I may not have been won over so quickly by someone called, shall we say . . . Oscar?' They joined in laughter, but Helena's laughter was tinged with regret. It was a pity, she thought, that her mother's humour had been so well hidden all these years. It took someone like Amy, self-effacing and so anxious to please, to bring it out. Helena sent up a silent prayer for Amy's safety. She rose and eased her aching back for she had been sitting awkwardly. It had been a long day and had had more than its share of tension but now, she thought, everything was going to be all right.

'I'm staying, Mother. I'm staying until we hear from Amy, or if she doesn't return, until we find someone to take her place. You won't object if Paul joins me here?'

There was sadness in the look her mother gave her. 'I just want you to be happy, my child. Things that were so important to me once no longer seem to matter. I can't help wishing though that you could have married and had children. I would so much have loved being a grandmother.'

Oh Mother, thought Helena, weeping inwardly, you could have spared me that.

It had been a long and arduous day and Daniel felt he had been put through some sort of emotional wringer. He was drained of all feeling except that of profound satisfaction at being back at Thornmere, sitting before a roaring fire in his office, with a glass of whisky in his hand and some unopened letters on the table beside him.

He had left Norfolk that morning in drizzling rain but by the time his train reached Brocklehurst the sun was shining through a thin haze of drifting cloud. It was his first visit to Hampshire and he thoroughly enjoyed the car ride through the New Forest and wished it were longer, for he wasn't looking forward to arriving at his destination. On either side of the road ponies grazed. A scruffy-looking lot, he thought them, thin, scrawny and ungroomed, but tough little blighters nevertheless. They had to be, living wild.

'Is it far?' he asked the driver of the hired car. 'To Woodside, I mean?'

'About a coupla miles further on, sir.'

He settled back against the plush upholstery mulling over the events of the past few days. The identity of the body in the mere had been confirmed as that of Arthur Crossley. The police were pretty certain after bits of clothing found on the skeleton were identified by a Norwich tailor as part of a jacket made by him for Arthur Crossley, but the matter was finally settled by a dentist in Beckton Market who recognised the gold filling in one of the corpse's molars as his own work. He kept records of all the gold he purchased, when it was used and for whom. It was then that the police got in touch with Dan again.

Out of courtesy, for there was no need for them to impart what information they had gathered, they told him that the only living relative of Arthur Crossley they had been able to trace was his mother-in-law, a widow, living in a village on the outskirts of the New Forest who, unfortunately, was extremely uncooperative. They suggested that as the body had been found on his land, he should pay her a courtesy visit. Off duty and over a glass of port the inspector went further.

'The old girl's holding something back. She's frightened. Perhaps of being accosted by police. Perhaps because of the thought of a suicide in the family – her husband was a colonel in the Royal Horse Artillery. Whatsoever, she wasn't very forthcoming. Now to you, especially if you use your charm on her, she might open up.'

'I am not on familiar terms with charm, Inspector. As a matter of fact charm cuts me dead.'

'Oh, I wouldn't say that.' The Inspector stared reflectively at his empty glass. 'I think some ladies might find you extremely charming.'

Mrs Fellowes obviously did not. Face to face she was even more aloof than she had sounded over the phone when he made the appointment to see her. He was shown into a room of such perfect proportions and so tastefully furnished that it struck him as a display in a showroom rather than somewhere to live. He half expected the figure in black standing with her back to the window to be a model, until she moved forward with hand extended. 'Mr Harker I believe,' she said imperiously.

He refused to be intimidated. He had more than enough cheek to match her pride. He apologised for being late for his appointment, but she brushed his apology aside.

'Shall I ring for refreshment?' she said.

'No, thank you, I had something on the train.'

She was older than her voice had suggested, rising seventy or even older, he thought. She was a handsome woman with white hair in a style that took him back to the years before short hair became fashionable. Her dress was an unrelieved black. She's left it a bit late for mourning, he thought harshly, but his feelings softened when he noticed a nerve ticking in her cheek. She was not so sure of herself as he thought.

'You are absolutely certain that the body found in the lake at Thornmere is that of my son-in-law, Arthur Crossley?' she said in a way that convinced Daniel that she had been rehearsing the words very carefully.

'Why? Have you any doubts?' he countered.

She drew herself up. She tried to outstare him; then to his amazement and no little consternation she went to pieces. Before his eyes he saw her turn from an overbearing woman to someone so racked by emotion that it took all her strength to stumble to a nearby sofa. There, she gave way to tears.

He found the sound of her crying heart-rending. His first impulse was to ring for the maid but something told him that Mrs Fellowes wouldn't thank him for doing that. He stood there feeling utterly useless as he always did in the presence of a weeping woman. She looked so pitiful, this crying figure, that any animosity that still remained turned quickly to compassion. He drew up a chair and waited.

With a self-control that he could only admire she pulled herself together. She wiped away the last trace of tears then delicately blew her nose. 'I apologise for my weakness,' she said, not looking at him.

'It was the shock.'

She looked at him then with an expression he couldn't fathom. 'No, it was not shock. It was relief.' She stared down at her hands, restlessly twisting and untwisting the handkerchief around her fingers. 'I've been waiting – how long is it now? – seven years. Seven, long, nerve-racking years for this to come out. Thank God, at last, it has.'

'You knew that Arthur Crossley drowned himself!'

She shook her head. 'I only knew he intended to take his life, I didn't know how. He wrote to me soon after Louise left him. He said he had no job, no home, no future, so all he could give Louise was her freedom. It wasn't a happy marriage and it had been getting worse. Divorce wasn't possible. There were no grounds, and anyway neither could face the thought of going through the divorce court. They really thought at first that they could start a new life in Australia, but then everything went wrong when the Massingham estate was split up and Arthur just gave up hope. That's when Louise came home to me.'

She grew still, even her hands were now at rest. She turned on him a rather forced smile.

'Mr Harker,' she said. 'I don't normally take a drink in the afternoon, but now I feel in need of one. In that corner cabinet you will find drinks and glasses. Will you please pour me a dry sherry, and help yourself to whatever you wish.'

At that moment, what he needed more than anything else was a cup of strong sweet tea, for he felt as if he had suffered something in the way of a minor shock. He poured himself a small brandy instead.

'And your daughter. How did she take her husband's death?'

Mrs Fellowes stared dully into space. 'I didn't tell her,' she said. 'Do you think I could put her through that torment? All her life blaming herself for her husband's suicide. Oh no, Mr Harker, I would do anything but that .. and I did. I lied and I cheated.' Her voice broke and she took a quick sip of the sherry. 'I let her think Arthur had gone on to Australia as they planned. I told her he had called here to say goodbye. She was working in London then, sharing a flat with a friend. Later, much later, I said he had died of a recurrence of his malaria. I said friends in Australia had written to tell me. I even got someone to write a letter purporting to come from them and sent that to Louise. She was living in America by then, and letters took a week or more to reach us. She guessed I was concealing something, but she didn't know what. She wrote and told me that she suspected Arthur was dead because he had made no attempt to get in touch with her since she left Thornmere. Before she went to America she got in touch with Australia House to try and trace his whereabouts, but of course they had never heard of him. She's married now, living in Boston, and has two lovely children. I wouldn't want anything to spoil her happiness. But now, of course, it will all come out. All the ugly publicity. I tried to spare her that, I thought I had succeeded, but I have only postponed it.' Her tears welled up again and spilled over onto her cheeks. 'It will all have to come out now, won't it?'

He didn't know how to answer that. 'I think if the police are tactful, it might not be as bad as you fear.'

'No. The worst part for me has been living a lie all these years. I'm glad that's over.' She rose to her feet and Daniel did the same, steadying her as she swayed.

'Are you all right? Would you like me to ring for your maid?'

'No, no. I shall go to my room and rest. I shall need my strength before I face the police again.' She wasn't quite so imperious as before, but getting that way, Daniel felt.

She paused at the door, looking back at him. 'What will happen to him, now? Arthur, I mean, when the police have finished with – with his body?'

'He will be buried in the usual way. I don't think they bar suicides from consecrated ground in this day and age.' He saw her wince and realised he had been less than tactful. He quickly added: 'Have you any wishes on the matter? I would be happy to act for you.'

'Thank you. Yes, I would like my son-in-law to be buried here, in the village churchyard.' She managed a thin smile at his look of surprise. 'I didn't do much for him while he was alive, so perhaps I can make up for that now that he is dead. Good afternoon, Mr Harker. Molly will see you out.'

The fire had died down to glowing embers, the miniature whisky carafe was nearly empty. He drained what was left into his glass and then turned to the letters, two or three that had come by a later post.

One was written on cheap paper in an unformed, unfamiliar hand and with an East London postmark.

When he opened it a pawn ticket fell out and fluttered to the floor. He picked it up, frowned, then turned to the letter.

Dear Mr Harker,

You will find your watch at the pawnbrokers in Butler's Loke at Beckton Market. The ticket is enclosed. I only had enough money to get as far as Beckton that Monday morning, otherwise I wouldn't have taken such a liberty as to borrow your watch. The money I got for it has helped me get some cheap lodgings here in London, and I have also found a job as a waitress. I start next week. As soon as I get enough money together I will start paying off what it will cost you to redeem your watch. I'm not a thief and I wouldn't have borrowed your watch in the first place if I wasn't desperate to get away from Thornmere, and I don't have to tell you the reason why.

I've had time to think things over and I realise I wouldn't have killed myself, though I felt like it at the time. I shall always be grateful to you, Mr Harker. I shall never forget your kindness. You could so easily have turned me away, but you didn't. And about that other thing . . . I don't want you to think that I regret it or feel ashamed, I don't, just the opposite. Please don't worry about me, I shall be all right.

Yours very truly,
Amy.

There was no address. The handwriting on the letter swam a little before his eyes as he read it through a second time. He knew that with the right agency he could trace her without difficulty but she obviously wished to keep her anonymity. He would honour that.

Funny little thing. The letter had left a warm glow in his heart where before there had been a bitter core of disappointment. He thought of that other woman for whom he had yearned without let-up since the first day he saw her, and then of Amy, warm and compliant in his arms. Someone he might have grown to love, he thought, if it hadn't been for Helena.

THIRTEEN | 1936

Paul's book was published in March 1936. In June that year the following item appeared in Tom Tiddler's column in the *Daily Encounter*:

Paul Berkeley, one-time foreign correspondent on this paper, after a six-year-long and arduous gestation, gave birth to the first of his, hopefully, many progenies, on 15 March this year. *Travelling Unquietly*, we are pleased to inform our readers, though giving cause for concern at first, is now thriving very satisfactorily.'

'Ruddy cheek,' said Jacob Church when it was shown to him. 'Who does this Tom Tiddler think he is?'

'An old buddy,' said Helena, laughing. 'And Paul is highly amused.'

'Is there any truth in it, about causing concern at first?' asked Dr Percy when he was shown the same piece later in the day. It was a beautiful June evening even for central London, with an arc of blue sky softly speckled with cotton-wool clouds.

They sat on the balcony sipping cocktails. Paul was resting in the bedroom. His periods of rest, thought Helena sighing inwardly, were becoming longer and more frequent. It hadn't worked out, Paul's plan of taking periodic respite visits to Murray's of Southend. He had overtaxed himself that time in 1929, immersing himself too much in his book, cutting down on sleep and food and fresh air. Writing feverishly while he felt fit to do so, resenting interruptions, even her visits Helena had sometimes felt. It had all come to an abrupt end one day when he had had another haemorrhage; not as bad as the first one but serious enough for him to be admitted to the general hospital.

When he was well enough to travel she had arranged for a private ambulance to fetch him home, scotching any idea of his being taken to a sanatorium. All these years later Amy's description of Raneleigh still lingered in her mind, and even allowing for Amy's bias, she felt she could never let Paul out of her sight again. He had finished his book – an exhausting task which he could only undertake a little at a time – but which gave him immense satisfaction. She felt so proud of him, not so much for writing a book but sticking at it. Six years' arduous gestation. Tom Tiddler had hit the nail on the head.

'Is it true that Paul's book gave cause for concern at first?' Dr Percy repeated, breaking in on her thoughts.

'Not concern so much as disappointment. If you remember it was rather overshadowed by other, far more momentous events at the time. Hitler hogged all the headlines by marching his troops into the Rhineland. Not that we expected Paul's book to make headlines, but he didn't even get a mention.'

Paul, hearing the news from Germany on the wireless,

had slammed his hand against the wall. 'The bastard has put paid to my book,' he said, and stamped off to the bedroom.

Helena gave him ten minutes to recover, then went off to calm him down with a packet of cigarettes in the pocket of her slacks. He was sitting on the edge of the bed, his head in his hand. She knelt beside him. 'Oh, Paul, darling, it isn't really your book, is it?'

He lifted his head. A brooding, worried look deepened the lines on his wasted face. 'It's starting again, the tramp of jackboots across Europe.'

She put her cheek on his knee and caressed his hand. There was nothing she could say.

'I don't care a bloody damn about my book, but I do care about what's happening in Germany,' he said. 'I care about what's going to happen in the future, and there's damn all I can do about it. Seven, eight years ago I would have been out on the streets with other anti-fascists. I would have been fighting Mosley's mob any way I could. I would have rammed their filthy propaganda down their throats. But look at me now, I'm weaker than a six-day-old-kitten. What good am I to anyone?'

She got up from her knees and sat on the bed beside him. 'You are good for me, Paul. You are my life. I couldn't live without you, you know that.'

His expression changed to one of remorse behind which lurked a heart-aching sadness. 'And look what I've done to you over the years. I've sucked you dry of all that vitality that made you what you were. Your eyes used to shine as if they had a lamp behind them. That lamp has now gone out.'

'If your intention is to make me feel depressed, you are succeeding beyond your wildest dreams,' she said, sniffing back her tears. 'I now feel old, withered, and undesirable ... Paul, I need a cigarette, will you join me?'

'No, I don't need a cigarette, and neither do you, but thank you for the thought. I'm passed the stage of finding comfort in nicotine. You are all the comfort I need now.'

'In spite of the fact that my lamp has gone out?'

He laughed, and when she got up to go he pulled her down beside him and pinned her to the bed. Once, such nearness would have led to a brief and exhausting passion, but no longer. Hers was not the only lamp that had burnt out, and at the thought that would once have made her laugh, her eyes grew wet.

'What's the matter?'

'I was just thinking that after all that time you spent on your book, you now say you don't care a damn.'

'Of course I care. Six years' gestation is a hell of a time, and there were times when I thought I wasn't going to make it. But I did – so bugger Hitler. Helena, what do you say to a launch party, here in the flat, just our friends?'

'Do you think there will be room?'

'We'll make room.'

It was a fine spring evening for the party and the guests overflowed into the bedroom, onto the balcony, out into the garden. Jake, though invited as a guest, felt more at home playing the butler, circulating among them as silent as a shadow, his drinks tray never empty.

Midge arrived wearing a white fur jacket, a present from her latest admirer – a furrier, a little fat man who adored her and whom she exploited relentlessly.

'I feel like a bally polar bear in this thing,' she said in such a way that both she and Helena collapsed with laughter. 'Not that I know what a polar bear feels like,' she added.

She was irrepressible, she was fun, and a dozen Hitlers couldn't quench her optimism or her conviction that the world had never been a better place. Toppers was doing so well she was thinking of opening a branch in Paris.

'That would do my erstwhile husband one in the eye,' she gloated. 'I'll open a shop in the boulevard where he lives. He will have to pass me every morning when he goes to buy his bread, and the ringing of my cash registers will fill his ears. My spies tell me that things are not too good with him at present – either marriage-wise or financially. He lost a packet in the Wall Street crash. Ha ha.'

She flung her coat on top of others on the bed and looked at Helena from beneath her long sandy-coloured lashes with an enigmatic smile. 'I see you've invited the lesbians,' she said.

Midge's joke about the Spicers, the top-floor tenants, was wearing thin, as was Helena's patience. Also she was tired, having spent the previous week preparing for this party, and was now worrying herself silly in case there wasn't enough food to go round. 'I've invited the two Spicer sisters,' she said. 'So we'll leave it at that, shall we?'

When she returned to her guests with another plate of canapés she noticed the younger Miss Spicer – the pretty one, the domesticated one – deep in conversation with Mr Pickford from the first floor, and hoped that Midge would take note, but Midge had stayed behind to renew her make-up, and by the time she came into the room the twosome had become a threesome. The elder Miss Spicer – the Eton-cropped, suited, manly-looking one – had joined them.

Mr Pickford was a bachelor of quiet habits who worked as the chief clerk to a firm of solicitors in Lincoln Inn Fields. In the ten years Helena had lived in Doughty

Street she had only exchanged words with him on four or five occasions, yet he had accepted as eagerly as had the Spicers when she had issued her tentative invitations. She wondered sometimes if the other tenants of the house thought her unsociable, for they seemed more at ease with Paul.

He, being at home all day, had got to know them better. He surprised her once by telling her that when she was away visiting her mother, Mr Pickford would often call in to see how he was and sometimes stay to play a game of chess. The younger Miss Spicer too, if she had been baking, would bring him down a taster. This weighed on Helena's conscience, for Paul and her job had become her life to such an extent that she had shut out the rest of the world and in so doing had also isolated Paul. The party, she hoped, would change all that.

We must do this more often, she decided, looking across the crowded room to where Paul was standing talking to a group of old cronies from the *Encounter*. His colour was heightened, his eyes feverishly bright, but that wasn't always a good sign. He was over-excited. No good would come of it, she thought.

Her eyes met those of Dr Percy who obviously shared her misgivings, for he gave a slight shake of his head which Jake, always on the alert, noticed. Shortly after that the party broke up.

'I don't know how Jake does it,' said Helena, as she helped Paul undress for bed. 'No fuss. Just courteous and smilingly persuasive, and suddenly the guests are leaving, saying how much they enjoyed the evening. I wish I could be as natural.'

'Did you notice any suspicious bulges about his person when he left?'

'Bulges! What bulges?'

'Bulges like a bottle of whisky, two bottles of plonk and one of port.'

'Don't tell me you counted the bottles?'

'They just happened to be on the table one minute and gone the next. I've looked everywhere – even among the empties. No luck.'

They exchanged rueful looks, then laughed.

'He's worked hard all evening. I suppose he looked upon them as perks. You don't begrudge him them, do you, Paul?'

'No, but if he gives us a rendering of "Just a Song at Twilight" tonight, I'll go down and crown him.'

'And now the book is selling well?' said Dr Percy, looking over the rim of his glass at her.

'Far better than we expected. The publishers are anxious for another book as soon as possible. Not another non-fiction book necessarily. They said there was more fiction in *Travelling Unquietly* than fact, and that's what makes it such a good read.'

'How does Paul feel about tackling another book?'

She shook her head and for a moment seemed unable to speak, or perhaps to find the right words. 'I doubt whether he'll ever write another book. He hasn't got the stamina for one thing.' She kept her eyes lowered, but hopelessness came through in her voice. 'You know how long it took him to write his present one. You know what it cost him. He was battling against ill-health the whole time, and it left him drained.' She swallowed back a deep sigh. 'It all started so well, too, that winter he spent at Southend. He got the first draft finished so quickly but I don't think he is well enough to go off on his own anymore. It would mean a nurse and a wheelchair, and you know how he would hate that.' She gave Dr Percy a steady look. 'Please be honest with me . . . how long has he got?'

He was unable to meet her eyes, dreading to see them dull over. 'You know I cannot answer that. Tonight, for instance, he was on top form.'

'And tomorrow,' she interrupted flatly, 'he'll hardly be able to catch his breath. That's how he lives – from day to day. I've found specks of blood on the sheet, on his handkerchiefs. I dread another of those awful haemorrhages.' Her voice was thick with tears. For a moment or two she was unable to speak.

The doctor, filled with pity, watched her silent struggle without attempting to help her. There was nothing he could say. He knew she valued honesty above anything. How could he fob her off with the usual hackneyed words of comfort? He respected her too much for that.

Over the years she had grown more attractive, he thought. Her remarkable bone structure was more defined, though alas, that could be through loss of weight. He felt that her love for Paul, plus his need of her, had given her an inner strength that sustained her courage. He knew he was a little in love with her – what man wouldn't be! Her colouring was still eye-catching. The combination of green eyes, red-gold hair, and porcelain-like complexion had the same impact on him every time he saw her afresh.

There had been a time, two years ago, when her outstanding good looks had been illuminated by a deeper happiness than she had ever known before. That was when, for a few weeks, she had thought herself pregnant.

She ached for a child, had almost given up hope that she would ever have a child because Paul would not even discuss the matter. She had come to him on a spring-like day in late February. She had virtually danced into his surgery. 'I am late,' she cried. 'I am late. Oh joyful day, oh, heavenly bliss. I am late . . .'

He was puzzled. As far as he knew she didn't even have a timed appointment. Then the penny dropped.

'My dear, I'm delighted for you. How late? Two months?'

'Oh no, only three weeks.' Then seeing how quickly his smile faded, she said, 'But I am always so regular.'

'And I am a cautious old bachelor. I should give yourself another month before being too hopeful, and a further month before being certain. An examination should confirm it, then. All fingers crossed in the meantime.'

A week later she came to see him again. The glow had gone from her cheeks, the light from her eyes. 'Forget about that examination,' she said curtly. 'It won't be necessary. I've only popped in to ask you if you would keep an eye on Paul. I'm going up to Norfolk for a few days.'

In the past few years she had regularly used Norfolk as her bolt-hole – a place of solace, somewhere to run to when her nerves were on edge. Every time Paul had another relapse and was sent to the clinic for observation, she invariably fled to Thornmere. 'My own private Lourdes,' she told Dr Percy. 'Norfolk always works a small miracle on me.'

And certainly it did on that occasion, though when she returned to London he noticed a few faint lines about her eyes and mouth that hadn't been there before.

Her eyes, those remarkable expressive eyes, were fixed on him now with an intensity that should have warned him what to expect.

'Will Paul still be with us for Christmas?'

'You are making it extremely hard for me, Helena. Do you want the truth?'

'I wouldn't have asked you otherwise. You have never lied to me before.'

'I wish you wouldn't pin me down. It is so difficult to give you a cut and dried answer. He could celebrate Christmas with us, or even the Christmas after, come to that. On the other hand . . .' His voice petered out.

'On the other hand what, Doctor?'

'He could slip away from us one day without any warning. How would you prefer him to die, Helena, in peace or fighting for every painful breath he took?'

She turned her head. 'Now you are making it hard for me,' she said.

She didn't tell him that she had asked specifically about Christmas because she had Hugo Frame in mind. Hugo had written to say that he was coming back to England to stay for a while before going on to America. He was disillusioned with Berlin. It was no longer the carefree happy place he remembered from the Twenties. Everything had changed since the rise of Hitler. There were sinister undertones which he would tell them about when they met. He had a close friend, a brilliant violinist who had lost his job in one of the premier orchestras because he was a Jew. He had been offered another job in Hollywood, of all places. Musicians, writers, playwrights, poets were all flocking there, escaping from something he only hinted at. Hollywood would become the centre of culture of the New World he wrote – with his tongue in his cheek, she firmly suspected. He intended to follow Leon there, but first he would come back to London to see all his old friends, and especially to spend one more Christmas in the old house in Doughty Street.

She told Dr Percy all this now as they sipped their second cocktail. A breeze had arisen and gently stirred the leaves of the mulberry tree and somewhere nearby a pigeon was cooing. If she closed her eyes she could almost imagine herself back in Norfolk. Almost.

She said: 'Remember that time I thought I was pregnant? Life was hell for a few days. Now I thank God that my wish didn't come true. Just imagine if I had a toddler now. How would I be able to care for Paul and a small child too? One or other would suffer. No, I gave up that dream long ago. Paul is my child, I wouldn't have it any other way. The thought of losing him is killing me.'

He felt impotent against such hopelessness. He searched his mind for some words of comfort that wouldn't sound like time-worn clichés, and sat silent.

Helena jumped to her feet. 'Enough of gloom and doom,' she said. 'I asked you round here for the evening because I wanted someone to cheer me up and all I've done is moan at you. You must be wishing you hadn't come.'

She was making a tremendous effort to overcome her leaden spirits. She smiled and though her smile lacked the old sparkle, the mere sight of it warmed his heart. She's a fighter, he thought, nothing can keep her down for long. If anybody could give Paul the will to live, she could.

'You invited me, I recall, to sample some Italian cooking. I think those were your words. A spaghetti something or other.'

'A spaghetti Bolognaise – from a recipe my Italian hairdresser gave me. Have you tried it?'

'I've never even heard of it. I'm not very adventurous when it comes to foreign food.'

'Then, Doctor, you're in for a treat.'

On this warm August day in 1936 nobody from Thornmere, looking at the down-at-heel woman at the bookstall on London Bridge station would have recognized in her the Amy Cousins who disappeared from the village seven years ago. The intervening years had not dealt kindly with her.

She was thirty-one but looked ten years older. Her slender girlishness had given way to an angular gauntness, and her face was drawn into a mixture of fatigue and worry.

The man in front of her had just selected a book to read. *Travelling Unquietly* by Paul Berkeley, she read over his shoulder. Paul Berkeley? A door on the past suddenly opened. Surely that was the name of Miss Roseberry's gentleman friend? Hadn't he been a writer of sorts? She picked up another copy and turned to the title page on which a dedication was printed: 'For Helena with very deep gratitude for her patience and encouragement during the writing of this book'.

The words cut deep into Amy's heart and her eyes grew misty, for though she had convinced herself years ago that she had finished with any form of sentiment like that it still had the power to reduce her to tears.

She replaced the book, picked up a copy of *Tiger Tim's Weekly*; twopence, twopence ill-spared. She looked down at the small boy beside her and he looked back at her out of a pair of wondering eyes. Usually when comic papers came his way they came in the form of *Comic Cuts* or *Chips*. Penny comics, black and white or dun-coloured. Coloured picture papers were a rarity in his life. He held his breath and watched as his mother took two pennies from her purse and gave it to the attendant. She took the paper and handed it down to her son with a smile.

'Something to keep you amused on the journey,' she said.

Only when Amy smiled, which she did whenever she looked at her little boy, did the lines in her face soften. When serious, she looked sour, which was unfair on her for inwardly she was not so very different from the girl who had always been seeking love. She had someone to love now which she did with a passion that burned inside her like a steady flame. The rejection and humiliation she had suffered because of that object of love had given her an extra skin which, like her stand-offishness, was a form of protection.

Danny thanked her with his usual gravity. Like his mother he rarely smiled, but when he did his whole face lit up. Now, she saw the surprised delight which sprang instantly into his sloe-black eyes. He knew as well as she did that twopence made a sizeable dent in their meagre budget. What he did not know was that his mother was trying to make up to him for his previous disappointment. She had told him they were going on a train. A train to Danny meant a steaming, shrieking iron monster, a locomotive, an object of veneration to all small boys.

Instead, when they got to London Bridge they found that the trains ran by electricity: no engine, no firebox, no rhythmic pistons – all the things that made up the magic of a steam train. His mother gauged the extent of his disappointment by the depth of his silence. It was then she turned back to the bookstall and saw the book with Paul Berkeley's name on the jacket, and bitter-sweet memories which for years she had suppressed instantly triggered into life.

Sweet memories to begin with, thinking back to happy days at Thornmere. Turning bitter when inevitably they began to slide towards a forbidden zone. She took Danny's hand and hurried with him onto the platform and they boarded their train just as the whistle blew. They were the only occupants of the compartment, a *Ladies Only*.

The train rattled smoothly over the lines. The telegraph wires dipped and rose in mesmerising motion. Amy had been up since dawn packing a lifetime's possessions into one not-very-large suitcase, and now she felt sleep coming over her. Sleep was a form of escape, but she wasn't running away today – she was running to. She was on a pilgrimage to discover her roots.

Danny was already engrossed in his comic, staring at the captions until they made sense. He could read simple words: he was a willing learner and she a dedicated teacher. She was determined to give him the best start in life she could. She was trying to model him on his father who had dragged himself up by his boot-straps out of a poverty greater than theirs. She had never known what it was to sleep on the streets, though she had come dangerously near to it in the past few years.

She had lost count of the number and variety of jobs she had had since she left Rodings. None had lasted long. As soon as it was discovered she had a child to support she was out. It wasn't so much prejudice, though that came into it too, it was a matter of expediency on the part of the employers.

'It is not our custom to employ married women,' she was once told by the weasel-faced little man who was interviewing her.

'But I'm not married,' she said, something that wild horses would not have dragged from her at one time. At the beginning she wore a Woolworth's wedding-ring, but gave that up when she found that that pretence became a millstone round her neck.

The interviewer shrugged. 'It's all the same in the long run. You're tied to a kid, that means days off when he's sick of there's no one to mind him. Sorry. Next please.'

Sometimes, there was a kinder refusal. 'Sorry, love, times are hard. We're cutting down on staff.' That was to become a regular refrain during the years of the Depression.

The longest period of employment had not been without

its good points. She was taken on as a housekeeper to a middle-aged widower who didn't mind taking a child as long as she kept him quiet. There was no difficulty there. Danny did not know how to be other than quiet.

Mr Smith was a man of few words which suited her, too. Though not sociable he was easy to please, and as long as there was a meal waiting for him every evening when he came home from work there were no complaints.

He was a carpenter by trade and lived in a small terraced cottage in Barking. She saw little of him for he left the house early and didn't arrive back until after Danny was in bed. As soon as he had eaten he took himself off to his local where he stayed until closing-time.

For the first time since leaving Thornmere Amy began to feel a sense of security. She enjoyed housework when it was she and Danny who benefited by the end result. After years of scrubbing other people's floors and steps, washing their clothes, polishing their brass and cleaning windows for a shilling an hour, it was a joy to know now that she could do them in her own time and at her own pace. She might have known, going by the pattern of her life so far, that it wouldn't last for ever.

Whenever she thought back to that Saturday night when things more or less came to a head, a little ripple of laughter shook her. Not that there was anything to laugh about at the time. She had been frightened then, and angry, but now, looking back, she could see the funny side of it.

It was one Saturday night and she was standing at the tallboy putting curlers in her hair. Danny was asleep in the bed they shared. She heard Mr Smith's key in the lock of the front door and then she heard him come stumbling up the stairs. She pulled a face. The only time Mr Smith came home with a skinful, as he called it, was on Saturday night because then he could sleep it off the next morning.

He had had more than a skinful tonight by the sound of it. She hoped he wouldn't wake Danny. Danny had been off colour for days and now, thick with catarrh and sleeping with his mouth open, was snoring a little. The noise in the passage ceased. Amy breathed more easily and put another curler in her hair.

Suddenly the door burst open and Mr Smith reeled into the room with his flys unbuttoned. He proudly showed her what he had to offer. 'Got any use for this?' he said with a broad and foolish grin.

She went cold. She went hot. She felt faint. She felt sick. When her supper rose into her throat and she began to gag Mr Smith fled.

The next morning when she took him in his bacon and eggs she gave in her notice. He only grunted. When he was ready to leave for work, wearing his rolled-up apron and bowler hat, he called to her: 'No need to do anything hasty,' he said. 'It won't happen again.'

'Not to me, it won't. I shan't be here.'

'I'll give you an extra five bob a week to stay,' then seeing the refusal in her face he added quickly, 'Ten bob, then, an' you can have your bedroom redecorated.'

She hesitated, but not for long. 'All right, but promise me there'll be no more funny business.'

'I don't understand you,' he grumbled. 'A slice off a cut loaf is never missed. None of the other housekeepers I had before you made any fuss about doing me a little favour.'

'Then why don't you look for someone like them to replace me?'

'Because you can cook and none of that lot could,' he replied gloomily.

She had no more trouble with Mr Smith, for now on Saturdays he stayed out all night and she guessed that someone less squeamish than herself was doing him a little favour. Then, just before Danny was due to start at the infants' school round the corner, he announced that he was getting married again.

She felt as if a trap-door had opened beneath her feet. Homeless and jobless in one sweep! A wave of nausea swept over her. She thought of the pretty little back bedroom with its rose-patterned wallpaper and cretonne curtains and furniture that she polished weekly. She thought of the new jersey and shoes she had bought Danny to start school in, and she thought of the neat little garden behind the house which she had just planted out with wallflowers and Brompton stocks and would not now see flower. Her eyes watered and Mr Smith looked away, clearly embarrassed.

'I'm sorry, girl,' he said in a rough but kindly manner. 'I would have let you stay on for a bit until you found yourself another crib but the lady in question wants you out of here before she moves in.'

Amy knew by then who 'the lady in question' was. The woman in the purple hat who recently Mr Smith was seen escorting to the Three Tuns. A drinking companion, happy-go-lucky and loud with laughter, blatantly free with her little favours, flaunting her dyed hair and rouged cheeks and untrammelled breasts. One of the hearts of gold type, a merry widow, the antithesis to all that Amy aspired to be. When occasionally they passed each other in the street they cut each other dead. Born adversaries.

Mr Smith looked anything but the happy bridegroom when he gave her her last week's wages, though it was hard to judge by his manner which never varied. She had a certain satisfaction in knowing that his diet would soon revert to fish and chips and cooked meats from the pork butchers. The windows of the house would go uncleaned, the brasswork unpolished, the garden run to seed. But Mr Smith would have someone to drink with and someone to go to bed with. Man cannot live by bread alone, the Bible said, but could he if he had a little jam to go with it? With someone like Bessie Beckham it would be all jam and she hoped viciously that an excess of it would make Mr Smith sick.

So it was back to charring. Cleaning private houses in the day and offices at night and paying Mrs Broom, her landlady, a few shillings a week to give Danny his supper and put him to bed.

He was asleep now, his head against her shoulder. His comic paper had fallen from his hands onto the floor. She picked it up and smoothed it out and tucked it between the two of them. The train stopped. She looked up; Dartford. Only two more stops to Gravesend. Her inside tightened with nerves. All she knew of Gravesend was that her mother had been born there and her grandparents had owned a substantial house in Acacia Avenue.

When Mrs Broom had told her, unable to meet her eye, that she had let her room to someone else, Amy was not surprised. She knew the room that she and Danny were occupying was worth twice what she was paying for it.

'I wouldn't do it if I didn't 'ave to, you know that, dearie,' Mrs Broom whined. 'But such a nice gent 'as offered me ten bob a week – extra if I cook 'im an evening meal. I can't afford to turn 'im down.'

'I was thinking of moving on, anyway.' She hadn't, the idea had just occurred to her in a sudden surge of hopefulness. 'I used to have family at Gravesend. I'd like to see if anyone belonging to me still lives there. It's worth a try, isn't it?'

She was desperate for reassurance. She was torn between hope of finding a welcome and fear of rejection. She looked down at Danny and saw there in his childish eyes an adult fear of insecurity. That settled it.

Acacia Avenue was past its prime. The acacias which gave the avenue its name had been lopped unmercifully. Little more than stumps now, perhaps to meet the demands of modern traffic for the avenue, no doubt a quiet byway in days gone by, was now a busy thoroughfare.

Many of the houses, Amy could see, had been converted into tenements, though one or two such as number twenty-nine, still had matching curtains on all three floors.

Number twenty-nine was definitely a cut above its neighbours. For one thing roses bloomed in its narrow front garden and jasmine, starred with white scented flowers, grew thickly around the bay window. With her heart knocking against her ribs Amy walked up the tiled path with Danny clutching her hand as if she were some kind of lifebelt.

After a short wait her knock was answered by a woman wearing a pinafore over a neat, cotton dress.

'You've caught me at an awkward moment,' the woman complained. A delicious smell of roast pork wafted out to them from somewhere at the back of the house. Amy was suddenly aware of a vast emptiness in her stomach. She heard little Danny swallow.

She blurted out the reason for her call, giving the names of her grandparents. The woman frowned.

'I'm afraid you must have come to the wrong house.

We've lived here twenty years and the previous owner was called Waring. Sorry I can't be of more help to you.'

She was, Amy could see, impatient to close the door on them. She made one more attempt to break through that veneer of indifference.

'I'm sure this is the house where my grandparents lived. I remember seeing the address stamped on the back of their photograph. That was before the war, of course.' She corrected herself. 'I mean, the photo was taken before the war.'

The woman said, 'I'm afraid the name Cousins doesn't mean anything to me at all. I'm sorry.' Sick in her stomach, Amy turned to go. A wasted journey, blasted hopes. The story of her life. The woman called after her.

'Just one moment, it's suddenly occurred to me. Two houses down, number thirty-three. It's been converted into flats and Miss Stacy, she's the owner, she lives on the ground floor. She's lived in this road longer than anyone else so she may remember your grandparents. I think you might find it worth your while calling.' Her eyes rested on Danny and her manner softened. 'Take care of your little boy. He doesn't look all that well.'

Nothing that a good meal wouldn't put right, thought Amy. She thanked the woman for this information, though she thought nothing would come of it. Still, there was no harm in trying.

The two houses were identical, semi-detached, solid, well-built; where thirty-three differed from twenty-nine was in its general air of seediness and neglect. An enormous ginger cat with one ear badly torn was sitting on the step. It arched its back and spat at them. Danny cowered against his mother.

The door was opened by an elderly lady with thin

white hair falling out of its pins. She peered at Amy short-sightedly. 'If you are a Jehovah's Witness,' she said, 'I must warn you that you will be wasting your time on me. I'm staunch C of E.'

'I'm not a Jehovah's Witness. I'm . . .'

'I thought you were one because of the child. They always seem to have a child, the ones that come to me, anyway. We get a lot of religious callers in these parts. Last week it was the Mormons.'

Amy took a deep breath. 'Actually,' she said, 'I was sent here by your next-door-but-one neighbour. I'm trying to trace my grandparents, Emily and William Cousins . . . They lived at number twenty-nine – Oh, I don't know how long ago exactly – but my mother was born there in 1875 or '76, I'm not quite sure. She was one of twin sisters and her name was Flossie and her twin sister was Flora –' She stopped, breathless, determined to get in as much as she could before the door was shut on her.

A look of bewilderment settled on the other's face, which in turn gave way to mild suspicion. Danny gave one of his nervous coughs. Any doubt Miss Stacy may have had faded. She invited them in.

The smell of cats in Miss Stacy's front parlour was overpowering. Amy suspected that the room hadn't changed since the days of Miss Stacy's childhood. It stayed, encapsulated in the past, as a memorial to her parents. Everything – furniture, ornaments, knick-knacks, whatnots, piano, cabinet, bookcase, pictures, photographs, and even the aspidistra in the window – was covered with a thick layer of dust. And over all the devastating feline smell that caught at her throat.

Miss Stacy brought Danny a glass of milk, but Amy refused an offer of tea. 'About my mother, Miss Stacy,' she said, hardly able to curb her impatience. 'Can you tell me anything about my mother?'

'I remember her so well. Such a neat little thing Flora was, never got untidy like other children.' With nervous fingers Miss Stacy plucked ginger hairs from the front of her skirt.

'And Flossie,' Amy said. 'Was she neat and tidy, too?'

Miss Stacy's faded eyes glazed over. She said ruefully, 'Usually, things that happened years ago I can remember as if they happened yesterday. But things that happened yesterday, I can't remember at all. Flossie – I had forgotten that name. Yes, that was what her mother called her, that was her pet name for her. What were you saying about twins, dear? I don't remember any twins. Flora was their lammas lamb, you might say.'

Amy felt as if her bowels had turned to water. She had never quite understood that phrase before, but she did now. She began to shiver, numbed by an unnatural chill that was spreading throughout her body.

'I remember your grandparents very well, of course I do,' Miss Stacy droned on. 'Not intimately, but well. They were very strict chapel people. Very strict with their little daughter, too. She was such a quiet, modest little thing. My mother used to worry about her. When Flora was born – I was, let me see, about fifteen then – I was out shopping with my mother and we met Mr Cousins and he stopped and told us he had a daughter. "We are so delighted it's a girl," he said. "Because we now have someone to look after us in our old age." My mother repeated that remark to my father, later. "Poor little mite", she said. "Hardly born, and her life mapped out for her, already." '

Miss Stacy's eyes rested wistfully on Danny. 'Is your

little boy comfortable on that slippery sofa? Would he like a book to look at?'

'He has his comic,' Amy said. 'We're both all right, thank you.' She wondered why her voice, if it was her voice, sounded so unfamiliar.

And so it went on, the torment of listening to the slow unravelling of the story of Flora Cousins: her life of service to her chapel and to her parents; her role as her father's unpaid housekeeper; and finally, when she had given up hope of ever doing so, falling in love.

Miss Stacy smiled, reliving some fond memory. 'But of course, I'm forgetting. You must have heard all this before.'

'No, I haven't. I know very little about my family, but I'm learning fast.'

'I don't know how she met her young man, she was a bit secretive about that. We thought he must have picked her up, but she would never admit to it. She wasn't young, you know. In her middle thirties then – getting on a bit for a first sweetheart. But better that than no sweetheart at all, like me,' Miss Stacy added, stating the fact without any trace of envy.

'That was a happy summer for Flora,' she went on. 'Her father, being a senior custom's officer, was away a lot, seconded to other ports, I believe. How Flora changed. She blossomed out. You could see she was in love. My mother tried to persuade her to bring her lover home to meet us, but she wouldn't.' Here Miss Stacy interrupted herself to explain; 'When I say lover, my dear, I use it in the meaning that it had in my young days. A young woman's suitor was always referred to as her lover. These days, alas, it has quite a different meaning.'

'I don't think there was any difference in this case,' said Amy in a brittle voice.

Miss Stacy gave her a doubtful look. 'Do you want me to continue?'

'Please do, I'm finding it fascinating.'

'Well, as I said, dear Flora was like a different person that summer. She had a little money her mother had left her and now she bought herself some new clothes and she shed years. She was never what you might call pretty but she certainly looked handsome when she dressed up. And then – oh, I shall never forget the day – she told us she was going to get married. Her father was away and they were getting married by special licence. She wanted Mother and me to be her witnesses.

'She wore her best navy-blue costume to be married in, and on the way to the registry office we stopped at a florist's and she bought a tiny posy of moss roses which she pinned to her lapel. She loved moss roses.'

Miss Stacy paused to clear her throat. 'You are not getting bored with me rambling on like this, are you, dear?'

'I'm riveted,' said Amy.

'We arrived early at the registry office. There was a wooden bench in the waiting room and we sat there and we ... erm ... waited ...' Miss Stacy paused once more.

'Don't stop,' said Amy. 'I don't want to miss a word of this.'

'Oh dear, I find this so very distressing, even after all this time. We waited all that afternoon. We tried to persuade Flora to come away, but she wouldn't. Every time the door opened, she started up, but it was always somebody coming to ask us whether we thought it worth-while waiting any longer. Finally the registrar himself came and told us there would be no more weddings that day as it was nearly six o'clock. I won't dwell too much on what happened next, dear. Suffice it to say that poor Flora became rather unmanageable. Eventually we calmed her down and got her home – to our house, I mean . . . Are you sure you want to hear any more of this, dear?'

'I've never been so sure of anything in my life,' said Amy with a ghastly smile.

Miss Stacy's shoulders sagged. Her voice now sounded strained. 'Well, as I said, your – I mean Flora – was inconsolable. She told us then about her lover. He was a commercial traveller, a temporary job, he told her, until something better turned up. When she told him that she was – to put it politely, dear, in the family way – he promised to stand by her. Leave everything to him, he said. He'd take her to London and they would find lodgings, and as soon as he was settled in a new job, they would look around for a little place of their own.

'It was all planned very hastily, but haste was essential as Mr Cousins was due back from Dover any day . . .' Miss Stacy's voice trailed off into a sigh. 'Would you like a cup of tea, Miss Cousins? No? Well, it doesn't matter. I'm nearly finished.

'Mr Cousins returned from Dover,' she said. 'And Flora resumed her duties as if nothing had changed. But it had, oh indeed it had. Mr Cousins may not have noticed the change in his daughter but we did. She had been a gentle person before but now, I suppose bitter would be the only way to describe her.

'Of course, we were both worried about what would happen when her condition showed – how her father would react, I mean. My mother was certain he wouldn't turn Flora out because it would cost too much to replace her.

We never knew if that was true or not because he had a stroke and became bedridden and Flora couldn't have left him anyway. It was a hard time for poor Flora then. She was up on her feet a few days after you were born, seeing after her father.'

It was the first time Miss Stacy had acknowledged Amy's part in the drama. She waited for some response but when none came she carried on, her words dragging a little.

'I looked after you almost entirely for the first three months. Poor Flora couldn't even feed you as her milk dried up. To me it seemed as if she was too frightened to let herself become fond of you, in case she had to give you up. She became very hard, I thought . . .' Another pause fraught with repressed memories. Miss Stacy roused herself.

'When your grandfather died he left all his money to the chapel. That was his way of punishing your mother, I think. She had the house, of course, but nothing much to live on, so she sold up and moved away from Gravesend. We kept up a correspondence for a time, but when my mother fell ill I didn't have so much time and . . . well, you know how it is. I still have Flora's address, somewhere, if that is what you came for.'

'No it isn't. But I have got what I came for.' Amy rose to her feet and at once Danny scrambled up and took her hand, staring up with speculative eyes.

Miss Stacy seemed to be having some inner struggle with herself. 'Speaking from experience, my dear, the events that seem so tragic when you are young lose their sting as one grows older. What I am trying to say is, as all this happened so long ago, would it not be better to forget it?'

Amy's smile lacked warmth. 'Unfortunately,' she said, 'I have an extremely good memory.'

Miss Stacy went ahead to open the door for them. 'For old times' sake,' she said, and kissed Amy's cheek. 'I was always doing that when you were a baby. You were so adorable. You had a lot of fluffy fair hair, just like your mother at the same age.' Tears welled up in her eyes. 'I am sorry if my news has been a shock to you, but please don't let it make you bitter. Bitterness is like a canker, it eats away inside you. Your mother turned into a very bitter woman and it didn't do her any good.'

'Shall I give her your love?'

A surprised but happy look spread across Miss Stacy's face. 'You are going to see her! Oh, how splendid. I am so pleased. I didn't like to ask, but I gather that there has been – how can I put it – a rift between you?'

'You could say that.'

'What a lovely surprise for her when you turn up! Yes, please do remember me to her. And you, dear, when you have the time, perhaps you will write and tell me how you got on.'

'I promise,' Amy said, knowing it was a promise she was not likely to keep.

Danny was hot and tired and hungry. He had not eaten since breakfast and that was so long ago it seemed like yesterday. He couldn't keep his mind off the sandwiches Mrs Broom had cut for them. He had seen his mother pack them in the case that morning, and now the case was being looked after at the station. And the station was such a long way off.

He didn't complain or beg his mother not to walk so fast, for he had caught a glimpse of her face as they left Acacia Avenue and it frightened him. He had seen his mother look angry before but never like this. Plucking up courage he said, 'Are we going to have our sandwiches soon?'

'No, we are not.' His mother, when he had least expected it, broke into one of her rare smiles. 'We are going to throw those dry and tasteless sandwiches to the gulls. Then you and I, Danny, are going to have a plate of fish and chips, and if you like you can have a glass of sarsaparilla. What do you say to that!'

There was nothing he could say. He was bereft of speech. He adored his mother with his eyes.

'And when we have had our dinner,' she said, 'we'll make enquiries about a bus to Sunsfield. That's the place where I grew up — where I lived with my Aunt Flora. I don't think I have ever told you about Aunt Flora, but I have told you lots of things about Sunsfield. About the oast-houses and the orchards and the sea only two miles away. You'll love Sunsfield.'

'Are we going to live there?'

'That all depends,' she said, but she didn't say what it depended on. Danny didn't mind. All he could think of now was a dinner of fish and chips and a glass of sarsaparilla. His mouth watered.

For no reason he could think of his mother was suddenly in very good spirits. 'Keep your eyes peeled for a fish and chip shop, Danny,' she said. 'And I'll keep mine open for a florist's. I want to buy some moss roses for Aunt Flora. I want to give her a surprise — and won't she be surprised!'

Chancel Terrace when they reached it late that afternoon, looked meaner than Amy remembered. The houses looked smaller, too; narrow slices of houses in a tight little terrace. The roses had begun to wilt, her case was getting heavier with every step, and Danny was so tired he leaned against her as he walked. Poor little Danny, bewildered and overwhelmed by all that had happened that day. The journey in the rattletrap of a country bus had taken nearly two hours, and on top of that an endless walk from the bus stop.

'Bear up, son,' she said, 'We're nearly there.'

And they were now right outside Aunt Flora's gate.

'She hasn't got a cat, has she?' Danny asked warily.

'She hasn't got a pet of any kind. Don't cling on to me, dear. Hold yourself straight, be a little man, that's the way.'

Amy put the case down just inside the gate and eased her hand. Is this what it feels like to face a firing squad, she wondered. Yet, whether from weariness or tension, she was incapable of feeling any strong emotion; just a kind of hollowness and an irrational fear of what was yet to come.

She rang the bell and almost immediately it was answered. At the sight of the frail and stooping figure, the ageing face from which a pair of watering eyes stared anxiously at her, she recoiled. Could this be Aunt Flora? Worse than that, could it be her *mother*? She remembered the photograph of the smiling woman perched on a branch of a tree in Greenwich Park, and her throat thickened with tears.

'I've been watching out for you,' said Flora eagerly. 'I've been sitting in the window ever since Alice Stacy's telegram came. And so this is little Danny?' Tentatively, she touched his cheek. 'What a dear little boy, what lovely eyes. Oh, do come in, you both look so tired.'

No questions, no strictures, no door slammed in her face. Miss Stacy's telegram must have been extremely explicit.

'Mummy bought you some roses. For a surprise,' said Danny.

Amy felt the humiliation, not her mother, for except

for some quivering of the lips Flora showed no emotion whatsoever. 'It was a very nice thought,' she said, and only her voice betrayed her inner feelings.

So this is what a hollow victory means, Amy thought. No triumph, but a sinking feeling in the pit of the stomach.

'It wasn't a nice thought,' she cried. 'It was a mean and spiteful thought. And the roses have wilted anyway. That's a sure sign.'

Flora attempted a smile. 'You always were one for signs and omens – you haven't changed.' She took the roses from Amy's unresisting hand and sniffed them. 'Yes, how well I remember that scent. I'll never forget it.' Her eyes met Amy's then slid away. 'All they need is a drink of water to revive.'

Danny wriggling, said plaintively, 'I want to wee wee.'

'Oh, you poor lamb, why didn't you say before? Come along with me.' The speed with which Flora led Danny away made Amy wonder if her mother welcomed this diversion as much as she did. Flora looked back at her. 'The table is set for tea – I did that before I did anything else. There's nothing to do except put the kettle on. You'll find everything in its usual place. Nothing's changed.'

Amy called after her. 'But we can't leave it just like that! We've got to talk things over. We can't just sit down to tea as if nothing has happened.'

'Don't forget to warm the pot, dear. Come along, Danny.'

They had their talk, much later on, after Danny had been put to bed in the slip of a room that had once belonged to his mother. Even for August the day had been hot but now that the sun had gone down there was a decided nip in the air. Flora lit a fire in the front room and they sat in the light of that, for neither felt disposed to expose themselves or each other to the brighter light of the gas mantle.

Finally Flora spoke, breaking a deafening silence. 'How much do you know?'

'Only what Miss Stacy told me.'

'Then there's not much more to add. It is just a repeat of the old old story.' Flora gave a short and mirthless laugh. 'I deluded myself. I believed every word your father said – about loving me, marrying me and taking me away to London. I believed because I wanted to believe. When I told you, years ago, the day you found that old photograph, that I hated him I meant it. But I hated myself more because I was such a willing victim. Nobody likes to admit that they've been made fools of – they have to have a scapegoat.'

'Like me. I was your scapegoat.'

Flora caught her breath. 'Oh, no. You mustn't say that. It wasn't true.'

'You let me believe my mother was dead. You showed no affection for me. You took out your revenge on me.'

'I could never make you understand,' said Flora despairingly.

'You could try.'

'I suppose I could say I was frightened of ever loving anyone again, but it wasn't as simple as that. A lot of other complicated reasons came into it. When we moved here, away from everybody who knew my story, I thought we'd start a new life. I passed you off as my niece for your own sake. In my clumsy way I wanted to spare you some of the stigma of being illegitimate. I didn't want you to be ostracised, but once one starts on a course of deception it – it kind of steamrolls. I found that out. I thought if I made out you were my dead sister's child – nobody likes to speak ill of the dead – you'd more likely be accepted. An orphan arouses pity, but a – a . . .'

'Bastard? Is that the word you want?'

'You have every reason to be bitter,' said Flora tonelessly.

'I'm not bitter. Miss Stacy said that bitterness is like a canker eating away inside of us. Wouldn't you say that referred to you rather than me?'

'Oh, child, if you only knew what you're saying.'

Amy felt suddenly extremely tired. More than anything she wanted her bed, to sleep, to forget that today ever happened. All the pent-up grudges she had fostered for years no longer seemed to matter. The questions not yet asked could go unanswered, at least for the time being. She was tired of the cut and thrust of accusations and excuses that were getting them nowhere. The sound of muffled crying from the pitiful figure in the chair opposite was almost more than she could bear, but she hardened her heart.

'Why couldn't you have shown me some love – even the love of an aunt would have been sufficient,' she said. 'I so wanted to be loved.'

Flora leaned forward, offering her hand which Amy ignored. 'I was too frightened to trust my feelings. I believed I wasn't capable of loving anybody again. It wasn't until you left me that I realised how much I had been deceiving myself. I wanted you back, Amy. I told myself I would make it up to you if I had you back again, but I also realised it was better for you if I let you go. I thought you couldn't make more of a mess of your life than I already had. When your letters came from Norfolk telling me about the good life you were having I was pleased for you. When you stopped writing I imagined all sorts of things for you: a good home, a husband, children. I convinced myself that by letting you go I had given you the chance to better yourself.'

Amy's smile was cuttingly scornful. 'Look at my clothes, look at my hands. That shows you how much I've bettered myself.'

'You've got Danny.'

'Yes, I've got Danny. And he's made up for everything, and never once have I been ashamed of acknowledging him as my son.'

'Amy, have pity, child. I don't think I can take any more. Please say you forgive me.'

What's in a word, thought Amy. 'I forgive you,' she said.

The robin returned to Doughty Street early that year. They first heard it at the beginning of September.

'I wonder if it's related to the one we heard that very first time,' Helena said, putting on the table within Paul's reach his morning glass of milk and two digestive biscuits.

Paul's gaze was fixed on the robin who was making short work of some grated cheese left on the outer sill of the balcony window.

'I don't know the life span of a robin,' he said, 'I can't believe it's anything like six years, but if this is not our original caller it must be a sprig off the same shoot. I always thought robins were friendly little creatures but ours seem very aloof. Look, if I put out my hand, he flies away. Frightened of catching TB I shouldn't wonder.' Though his voice was little more than a whisper these days, he could still crack a joke, the kind of joke that stabbed Helena to the heart.

She put a hand on his shoulder and gave him a little squeeze. 'He'll be eating out of your hand one day,' she said, in the flippant way she had perfected as a smoke screen. 'Everybody else does, so why should the robin be exempt?'

Paul brought her hand round to his mouth and kissed it, something he used to do quite often, though not recently.

His lips were hot but dry. Caresses were rare between them now. The slightest exertion left him breathless or even worse, triggering off a painful spasm of coughing. But his old needs and longings lingered. She saw it in his eyes as they followed her every movement. All the time, these days, he watched her.

The telephone bell rang.

'Always some interruption. Why can't we be left alone?' said Paul, but without his old irritability.

'Some problem up at the shop, I expect.'

It was not the shop.

'Hugo! What a lovely surprise. Where are you?'

'Dover. Just got off the jolly ole ferry. Have you got a cold?'

'No, I haven't got a cold.' The trouble was tears came so readily these days, even if Paul just smiled at her. She groped for her handkerchief.

'You sound as if you have a cold. I hope you are being honest with me. You know I won't come within fifty miles of a germ.'

'I'm just feeling a little bit blue this morning, feeling a little bit sorry for myself. Just hearing your voice has bucked me up.'

'More than that, darling, I'm on my way. I do so want to see you two old dears.'

'Come now, Hugo, please come for lunch. Paul will be so delighted to see you. It will cheer him up tremendously.'

'How is the dear boy?'

'Patient, long-suffering, uncomplaining, lovable . . . What more can I say?'

There was a pause at the other end, then Hugo again, slightly sceptical, 'You're being ironic, of course.'

'Oh God, I wish I were.' Helena reached for her

handkerchief again. 'He's changed, Hugo. Even in the past two months, he's changed. In appearance, too. He's much thinner – very frail. I think it's best to warn you. To prepare you for something of a shock.'

'I'll be there as quickly as I can. I'd fly if I had wings. That's an idea, I wonder if I can hire a plane? Where's the nearest airfield to Bloomsbury?'

'Just catch a train, Hugo. I'll have lunch ready for you.'

'Oh, I forgot to tell you. I'm a vegetarian, now. Nuts and things, you know.'

'Very well, Hugo.' Helena replaced the receiver. Her tearful state had turned to one of fragile laughter. Hiring a plane! She was still laughing to herself when she went back to tell Paul that Hugo was coming to lunch and that she was just popping out to the shops.

She wasn't away more than fifty minutes. She got all she wanted at Gamage's food hall, plus a bottle of hock which she thought appropriate for the occasion. It was the season for nuts, fortunately, and there was a wide selection on display. In Leather Lane market she bought salads and fruit and then went on to the fish stall for fresh salmon for Paul. He ate so little now, and she was always thinking of ways to tempt his appetite.

The house seemed inordinately quiet as she fitted her key in the lock, leaving the door on the latch for Hugo. She left her shopping in the kitchen and took a quick peek at Paul. He was asleep. Good. He was always better for a sleep.

It was nearly one o'clock before she finished. The salad was made and chilling in the refrigerator. The salmon cooked and also being chilled. Now there were only the grapes to wash, the pineapple to prepare and the mayonnaise to make – all last-minute jobs. The table was set, gleaming with Hugo's best glassware and silver, and the nuts displayed in one of his Art Deco dishes: french bread, butter, cheeseboard – she checked and double-checked the place settings. She was as excited as a child and confident that much would come of this visit. They hadn't entertained a guest for so long, not since their launch party, back in June. Hugo's visit would make for a happy ripple in the placid waters of their life. More than that it would be a shot in the arm for Paul.

She had not exaggerated to Hugo the change in Paul. He was all those things she said he was: patient, long-suffering, uncomplaining, lovable. It was almost impossible to remember how difficult he had once been: moody, at odds with her in all she said or did. Sometimes it had exasperated her beyond reason. Sometimes it had driven her to tears, though she could understand and sympathise why he acted so. For one with such an independent and rebellious spirit it must have been impossible to be so dependent on others. But for all his moods, he was still the Paul she had fallen in love with – and though his unintentional demands were almost too much of a burden at times, there were other times when the old Paul flashed through at her and made it all worthwhile. Making audacious suggestions, reducing her to helpless laughter with his quips, and sometimes as tender and as lover-like as in the first halcyon years of their relationship.

Now a mere shadow of his former self, his radical spirit quelled, he could have made a pitiful figure, except that he wouldn't suffer pity, not even from himself, and any sign of it from her or others brought the old angry spark to his eyes.

He was dying, they both knew that, though neither spoke about it. It was a pact between them as if unmentioned it might not happen. Once, her conscience nagging at her, Helena brought up the question of a priest.

Paul stared at her with a wistful and somewhat condescending expression. 'Why should I want a priest?'

She felt awkward, gauche, as self-conscious as a schoolgirl. She wished she hadn't started this. 'It's just that I thought ... you being a Catholic, I mean ...' Her voice faded.

'I have not practised my religion for a very long time,' he said. 'I am not now running back to my church because I've got myself into a bit of a hole. I deserted my God a long time ago. Don't you think it would be a bit hypocritical of me now to try to strike a bargain with him?'

'But repentance ... absolution. Doesn't that mean anything to you any more?'

He gave a weak smile. 'Yes, oddly, it does. But you know me, Helena. I'm an awkward cuss. I'd rather make peace with my God in my own time and in my own way, and without the help of a priest.'

Helena looked at the clock. Time to change, then wake Paul. She imagined the way his eyes would light up at the sight of his old chum. She was glad she had had the opportunity to warn Hugo about the change in him. She could rely on Hugo not to say or do anything to mar their reunion.

She put on a dress that Paul particularly liked: olive green with wide sleeves and a cowl neckline. A locket that Paul had given her one birthday fitted snugly into the hollow in her throat. Her hair had grown again, much to Paul's delight, who had never got used to her shingled, bare-necked look. Figures were in again, emphasised by the way materials were cut on the cross, and waists were back in their rightful place. The fashions of the Twenties now seemed comic.

She returned to the sitting room. Paul was still asleep. She poured out a sherry. Wafting that under his nose might wake him. She approached the balcony carrying the glass carefully for she had rather overfilled it, and stood stock still in the doorway with surprised delight. The robin was back and perched boldly on Paul's chest, pecking at a few scattered biscuit crumbs.

She wanted to wake Paul up, she wanted to say, 'You see, you only needed to be absolutely still and he came to you. Next, you will have him eating out of your hand.'

You only need to be still, she repeated parrot-fashion to herself. Paul was still, very still. The robin fed on, reaching up to take a crumb from Paul's chin, and still Paul did not move. The sherry glass slipped through her fingers and fell on the floor. The plop it made as it hit the carpet startled the robin, and it flew, straight as a dart through the open window. Helena saw the sherry spread out into a dark stain on the pale grey carpet. What a waste of good sherry, she thought inanely. How Paul would have begrudged that.

'Paul.' She said his name aloud. Going nearer, sinking on her knees beside him, taking his cold hand in both of hers, chafing it to make it warm. 'Paul, wake up, darling, Hugo will be here shortly.'

Hugo was there, helping her to her feet. It wasn't until she saw his tears that her feelings began to come to life. Then the agony started.

'I shouldn't have gone out,' she said when later they were sitting together in quiet but remorseless despair. 'I shall never forgive myself for leaving him. I didn't have the chance to say goodbye. I wasn't able to tell him how much I loved him.'

Hugo slowly raised his head and gave her a long and questioning look.

'Do you really think he had to be told?' he said.

FOURTEEN | 1938

Dan's favourite walk was still through the woods to the mere, with Bass lagging behind. Bass was an old dog, now; he had long outlived his canine equivalent of six score years and ten. He carried too much weight and was stiff in the back legs.

Looking down into the clear waters of the lake Dan found it hard to believe that it was eight or more years since he had had it drained, cleaned, and restocked. Cost him a pretty penny that had, too. Now it was a pleasure to see the fish lying motionless on the bottom, and weeds swaying as if stirred by some underwater draught. There had been a wonderful show of water-lilies that summer, and even now when the flowers had finished, the pads themselves made an ornamental pattern on the surface of the water: useful islands where baby frogs in danger of drowning could climb to safety.

The news from Czechoslovakia that morning made disturbing reading. The headline in his paper said, 'Sudeten Germans hold mass rallies to call for union with Germany.'

War was looming. Anyone with half an eye could see

that. Good grief, it was only twenty years since the last one finished. He was thirty-three then and felt younger. He was fifty-three now and felt much older than his years warranted. There was a lot more white in his hair than even a year ago. And what did his years amount to, he asked himself, feeling an attack of indigestion coming on. Mrs Webster had died the previous year and had been replaced by Ruby's younger sister, Elsie, a bright and willing girl but unfortunately lacking in Mrs Webster's culinary skill. She fed him mostly out of tins, which put him at a disadvantage for he was in no position to complain.

He had amassed a fortune. He owned a beautiful house set amid the Norfolk countryside, and after nearly twenty years had been accepted by the villagers as 'one of us'. But he hadn't got a son, and he hadn't got a wife, and the only woman he had ever wanted for a wife was now nearly past child-bearing age and with no guarantee she would marry him anyway, though he never gave up hoping. A fondness on her part and a deeper love on his had blossomed between them during that time two years ago when she had returned to Thornmere following the death of Paul Berkeley.

He had not seen her for several days, which in part accounted for his moodiness. This was the time of year when she made her annual pilgrimage to the place where Paul was buried. September – a time of mellow thoughts, of harvesting memories of summer to put in store for the winter – was, for Helena, a time of sorrow and introspective reflections.

She had never forgiven herself for not being with Paul at the moment of his passing. The thought of him dying there alone, no one with him, stabbed at her heart every time she remembered it. She had let him down – she felt she had betrayed him she had confided to Daniel on one occasion. He was convinced that until she had purged herself of this self-imposed guilt, she would never be free to come to him.

They had met that September day two years ago on the last Norwich-bound train out of Liverpool Street. He wasn't aware she was on the train, let alone in the same coach.

He had just filled in the last word in the crossword puzzle in his evening paper as the train steamed slowly into Thorpe Station. 'All change here for Cromer, Yarmouth, Lowestoft, Beckton Market and stations beyond.' Everybody rose, collecting bags and luggage from the racks. He was travelling light – he'd only been to London for the day – and was the last to trail along the corridor. In the very last compartment of the coach he saw the figure of a woman dressed in black, slumped in the corner by the window.

She had her back to him, but he could see, reflected in the glass, the pale oval of her face. Was she so engrossed with the view – another set of rails; an empty platform – that she couldn't tear herself away? Or had she fallen asleep? He couldn't tell from where he was standing. The cleaners were already boarding the train – it could quite soon be shunted off to a siding. He stepped into the compartment and gently touched her shoulder.

'Madam . . .'

Slowly she turned her head and the shock of coming face to face with such naked grief struck him dumb. He felt he had stumbled into a private hell; he felt he had besmirched her by his intrusion. He found his voice and murmured a clumsy apology. As he was backing away she said expressionlessly; 'Have we arrived?'

'At Norwich, yes.' He pulled himself together. 'Do you need any help?'

'If you wouldn't mind lifting my case down for me.'

He wasn't sure whether she knew him or not. Certainly there was no recognition in her eyes. But then there was nothing in her eyes. She stumbled as she alighted from the train and he took her arm, and kept it tucked in his until they were clear of the station precincts.

He said: 'I have my car parked round the corner. Could I drive you back to Thornmere?'

'That is most kind of you.' And they were the only words she uttered on the whole of that seemingly endless journey.

She was expected. All the lights were on at Rodings, and the woman he knew as Mrs Taylor came hurrying out of the house as he drew up alongside the gate. It was she who helped Helena out of the car, helped her along the path murmuring words inaudible to him. He was forgotten. He had played his part.

He had read Paul Berkeley's obituary in *The Times*. He learnt all the salient facts from that: his past career and his success as an author. His war record was rather glossed over, Dan thought, for there was no mention of a recommendation for the Military Cross, much more about his wife and her work for war orphans. An announcement about the funeral arrangements, but nothing about Helena. No tribute to the woman who had devoted more than ten years of her life to him and without whose devotion Paul might not have lived as long. Might not have had the time or stamina to write his book, even.

God damn them all, he thought, and tore the offending article into pieces, then painstakingly fitted them all together again. He wrote Miss Roseberry a letter of condolence, and

398

two days after he had met her on the train she called to thank him.

'I should have done so before this,' she said, as he ushered her into his office. 'I should have done so the other evening when I had the chance. But I really wasn't myself then.'

'The funeral?' he said, remembering her black garments.

'Yes. I had been to Paul's funeral that morning.' She was pale but composed. The puffiness and tear-stains had gone. And she was no longer in black, and he was glad of that because black didn't suit her. It acted like a snuffer to a candle, he felt. It extinguished all that was warm and bright.

She looked about her with a mild interest. 'This was the billiard room, and you have turned it into a lady's boudoir! Half of it, anyway.' She smiled faintly.'I don't think Sir Roger or Lady Massingham would have approved, but I like it.' She recognised many of the pieces that had been in the Massingham sale: the escritoire, the Chippendale chairs and beaded footstools particularly. They were all grouped around a Chinese rug at one end of the room. The other end, the end by the fireplace, was a different century altogether. Heavy mahogany and burr walnut furniture, including a massive roll-top desk and several chairs covered in dark red leather. Very much his and hers, she thought. It was a room, she imagined, designed with the idea of the master of the house dealing with his correspondence at his desk, while his wife, on the Regency sofa, busied herself with her needlework. She wondered without interest whom he had had in mind.

She refused refreshments. She mustn't stay, she said, her mother was expecting her back before it got dark. He was grieved to see how quickly she had slipped back into her old subservient role to her mother. Where now was the determined lift of the chin, the steady assured gaze, the upright stance? She sagged as if it were too much of an effort to square her shoulders. He mourned to think of that once proud spirit humbled by grief.

A sudden bright flash of colour, a jewelled dart, brought him abruptly back to the present. A kingfisher had taken a fish from under his nose! He chuckled, delighted at its audacity. Reuben had warned him that something was taking the fish from the mere and blame had been put on the stable cat until Ruby, out for a walk with Jessie, had seen a kingfisher dive into the water. Since then Dan had hoped for a sighting too, and if he hadn't been so wrapped in thought, he would have seen it more clearly now.

He hadn't lost his chance. Nearby was a cedarwood seat he had had erected on the spot where Amy had nearly drowned. Nobody guessed he had had the seat erected in that precise spot from sentimental reasons. They just saw it as another example of a townsman's lack of country lore. The seat was on the northern shore of the lake and when the trees were in full leaf it would be entirely in the shade. Once the villagers would have tittered maliciously among themselves. Now they made excuses for him. ''E knows how too much sun can pickle a man's brains. If 'e prefers to sit in the shade, good luck to 'im.'

He didn't prefer the shade, he loved to feel the sun warm on his face, but it was too late to do anything about it now. He settled himself on the seat, prepared for a long wait before the kingfisher struck again, then looking up he saw Helena coming across the grass towards him. Too stiff to move, Bass gave a welcoming woof as Dan prepared to rise.

'Don't get up,' Helena said. 'I've come to join you. I

arrived home earlier this afternoon, and Rodings seemed so lonely. I wanted company – yours because you don't badger me with questions.' She gave a faint sigh. 'It doesn't work anymore you know, visiting Paul's grave, trying to conjure him back to life. It isn't Paul lying there. It stopped being Paul the moment his spirit left his body.' Her voice came to a stop, and Dan waited, feeling as he always did when she unburdened herself to him a mixture of pain and pleasure.

'There comes a time,' she said, 'when you have to let the dead go. And my time has come . . .' Again, her voice faded.

'But you will still remember him?'

She looked at Dan reproachfully. 'I don't have to visit Paul's grave to be reminded of him. I think of him every moment of every day.'

And she's thinking of him now, Dan thought, seeing from her expression that she had retreated into that other place that was barred to him – her memory. He folded his arms and settled down to wait for her to come back. In the meantime, there was the kingfisher . . .

It was Hugo who took her to Paul's funeral. It was he who had broken the news of Paul's death to his parents. 'Why not his wife too?' Helena had asked.

'Because I find her saintliness brings out the worst in me,' Hugo admitted. 'I say naughty things to her on purpose and she smiles and forgives me. And that makes me naughtier still.'

It all seemed like some deadly and unreal dream to Helena. The drive to the charming little village in Gloucestershire; the introduction to Paul's family who were courteous and hospitable, assuming her to be a friend of Hugo, and Hugo, as Paul's oldest and closest friend, was made much of. Paul had rarely spoken of his family. He kept his past life and his present life in two separate compartments and made no attempt to mix the contents.

Helena felt the odd one out amid this depleted and ancient Catholic gathering. Their lineage was centuries older than her own. She wondered if they looked askance at her as she had once looked askance at Daniel Harker, but there was nothing in their manner to suggest it. The first surprise had been Haverill Hall, Paul's home, a moated Tudor manor house built not of Tudor brick but honey-coloured Cotswold stone. So unlike Ardleigh House, she thought, her own ancestral pile, a mock horror sham of turreted nineteenth-century brick.

Berkeleys had lived at Haverill Hall since the fourteenth century; an unbroken line that survived the turbulent years of the Reformation and the bloody ones of the Civil War. Stripped of their former wealth and importance, they had nothing left but their pride, and there was no lack of that, she felt.

Paul's remains were placed in the family tomb in the small private chapel in the grounds. She was surprised to see Hugo genuflect and then cross himself as they entered the chapel, for until then she had had no idea he was a Catholic. Lapsed like Paul, she thought. Sinners both. It all seemed so unreal to her, as if she were someone detached, watching players in a ritual that had no part in it for her, but at the same time grateful for that feeling of unreality for it sustained her throughout that day. After the service she followed the other mourners across the moat by way of a humped stone bridge, then through oak-studded doors into an immense hall where whole branches hewn from ancient trees burned brightly in the open hearth. Refreshments were being partaken of in an atmosphere of sombre reflection, and looking around at those sad and mostly elderly faces, it dawned on her that whereas Paul's death had been for her a personal tragedy, for his family it was a dynastic disaster.

They had just buried the last of the Berkeleys. There was no one left to carry on the family name. Now, if she had had a son – but there her thoughts broke off, for a bastard, she knew, could not under the present law inherit a title or family estate.

She turned away, sick at heart, longing to go home. But which home? The little flat in Doughty Street was no longer a home. Without Paul it was just a shell.

Norfolk? Yes, there she would find solace. There, in the silence and comfort of the countryside she would remember Paul. She looked round for Hugo and instead she found herself looking into the quiet grey eyes of a woman she knew instinctively to be Paul's wife. Her heart beat rapidly, her palms felt wet. Please Hugo, she prayed, rescue me *now*.

'I'm Sylvia Berkeley,' the woman said. She was good-looking in a classical way with premature silver hair. She held out a slender gloved hand, which had an astonishing grip. 'And you must be Helena Roseberry. It was so good of you to come.'

Helena ran her tongue over dry lips. 'Hugo told you?'

'No. I heard about you from your business partner. I've known about you for many years. I've been wanting a chance to thank you for all you did for Paul. You made him very happy.'

Helena tried to control her quivering lips, but without success. 'I feel an intruder here,' she said. 'And please don't be nice to me, I shall only make a fool of myself.'

The other leaned towards her. 'My dear,' she said in a lowered voice. 'You mustn't think of yourself as an intruder. You are among Paul's people – his family. You don't know what a relief it has been to us all to know someone as loyal as you was taking care of him.'

Helena stood back. 'It was not loyalty that kept me with him,' she said. 'It was love.' She no longer felt under obligation to this saintly-looking woman. She no longer felt at fault. She was pleased for Paul that after all these years his family had forgiven him. This she thought, her eyes roving around the gathering, was the outward form of his absolution. But absolution for her? Never.

'To me,' she continued, 'Paul *was* my husband. I shall always think of him as such. If things had worked out differently . . .' Only then was her voice not quite as steady. 'If I had been his wife in the eyes of the law perhaps then I would have been accepted, become part of the clan.' She stopped. A near-quarrel at Paul's funeral? She burned with shame. 'Forgive me for that,' she said contritely. 'I'm afraid it just slipped out.'

Sylvia's smile was tender and sympathetic. 'I know just how you feel' – You can't, you can't, how can you? thought Helena, despairingly. 'You must not think I did not grieve about the situation but, my dear, there was nothing I could do about it, you must understand that. Now come and meet Paul's parents. No, don't hold back, they are very charming people.'

Charm didn't hold much attraction for Helena at that moment. Sylvia oozed charm, and Helena despised herself for submitting so easily to its spell. What she wanted was Paul's ability to come out with some pithy remark. What she wanted, dear God, was Paul.

Hugo rescued her. Across the width of the hall he saw her beginning to wilt. He made his apologies to the Berkeleys, extracted Helena from Sylvia's overwhelming kindness, and led her out of the token fortress and across the moat to where the cars were parked.

'What we both need is a drink,' he said. 'Several, in fact.'

The following year, she had made the pilgrimage on her own. It was a dull grey day, more like November than September, and she had driven there in her newly-acquired Morris Oxford, bought from the proceeds of her mother's legacy.

Contrary to Dan's fears, she had had three good months with her mother, that otherwise heart-breaking autumn of 1936. She fled to Rodings on the day of Paul's funeral, catching the late train to Norwich and had been at Thornmere ever since, except for short sojourns with Midge when her presence was needed at the shop. In December that year, the country was riven by the news that Edward VIII was prepared to give up his throne for the love of a twice-divorced American. Helena, who had already received rumours of this via Hugo and the American press, hoped he would. She didn't consider him a great loss to England or the Empire, but her mother was devastated.

'It's unheard of,' she moaned, holding a handkerchief soaked in eau-de-Cologne to her forehead. 'Giving up his throne for a *commoner* – and an American at that. Not something his grandfather would have done. Why couldn't he be content with having her as his mistress? Doesn't duty mean anything to him?'

'Not as much as Mrs Simpson, seemingly.'

'Don't mention that woman's name in this house!'

Helena, ever loyal to the ideas Paul had instilled in

her, thought a change of sovereign was of less significance than the plight of the hungry and jobless. Though at last the country was shaking free from the miasma of the Depression there were still nearly three million unemployed, and still long queues at the Labour Exchanges and pawn shops, and still that heinous obscenity of the Means Test. Helena, steeped in apathy since she first took refuge at Rodings, discovered that as her numbness began to fade, so her feelings were coming back to life. And though it was good to be able to experience some good healthy emotions again, the pain of her loss was sometimes unbearable. She tried not to grieve, for she felt that the grief was more for herself than it was for Paul. She yearned for the time when she would be able to remember him with joy rather than sadness.

But in spite of coming back to life, she found she was unable to get worked up over Edward VIII's abdication. She said, hoping to make her mother laugh, 'I bet Edward VII would have thought twice before giving up his throne for a woman. After all, he waited long enough to get possession of it.' But her mother, instead of being amused, took umbrage.

'You young ones,' she said irritably. 'You have no sense of decorum. You show no respect whatsoever for the Royal Family. Please fetch me my smelling-salts.'

'Mother, I am hardly young. I will be forty-one on my next birthday.'

This unfortunate remark reminded Cecilia that she had outlived her allotted span by nearly thirteen years. She turned her face to the wall. 'Tell Mrs Taylor I don't wish to be disturbed,' she said.

This was hardly the moment, Helena thought, to remind her mother that Mrs Taylor was no longer with them. Mrs Taylor had, just a month before, left them.

'I hope you won't take offence,' she had said tearfully to Helena when she gave in her notice. 'It isn't that I want to leave, and just when you need me too, but my Stan has retired now, and honestly, Miss Helena, he needs me more than your mother does.'

When Mrs Taylor's last day at Rodings came it was overlaid with a feeling of an impending catastrophe. Everybody went about metaphorically on tiptoe, including the window-cleaner who had to come indoors to do one upstairs window which he couldn't reach from outside. Voices were subdued. Mrs Taylor was to be seen at odd moments, wiping her eyes. Though the cleaning woman had been in the previous day and cleaned the cooker and polished the grates, Mrs Taylor felt the need to do them all over again. She was reluctant to leave. Helena practically had to push her out of the door when the time came.

Her basket was stocked with produce from the store-cupboard. There was a generous cheque from Mrs Rose-berry in her purse, and her arms were filled with chysanthemums and dahlias from the garden. Helena's gift of a gold-plated wrist watch rendered Mrs Taylor speechless and Helena suspected it would never leave its velvet-lined case. But her other gift, a hat she had made herself with a Toppers' label stitched in the lining, was met with loudly expressed words of gratification.

'Oh, Miss Helena, maroon, my favourite colour. And plush, and lined with real silk – I can tell by the feel. Is this the latest fashion then, tilted over one eye? Oh, Miss Helena, it seems much too good for Thornmere, even for Sundays.'

'If you don't wear it, Mrs Taylor, I shall think you don't like it.'

'Oh, I like it all right, don't you fret yourself about that. Just wait 'til my Stan sees me in it.' Another and more rewarding thought struck Mrs Taylor. Her eyes lit up. 'Just wait 'til my next-door neighbour, the one who's always rubbing it in about her husband working in an office, just wait 'til *she* sees me in it!'

It was, she told Helena days later, her moment of greatest triumph. Even now, though officially retired, she couldn't keep away from Rodings.

'Wouldn't you consider trying another companion for your mother?' she said on one occasion, while sipping coffee with Helena in the kitchen. It was a crisp and sunny December morning. Christmas was just around the corner; Christmasses at Rodings were always low-key occasions. 'It worries me to think of you managing here without any help.'

'I do have help. More help than I need sometimes. There always seems to be someone here, cleaning and polishing, or washing and ironing.'

'But it's your mother. She's one person's work alone, and you mustn't neglect your hats. Like I said, don't you feel like having another try for a companion?'

'Have you forgotten all those respectable middle-aged ladies who tried to take Amy's place? Mother would have none of them. Don't worry, Mrs Taylor, I can manage very well as things are.' Helena stared vacantly into space. 'She's no bother at all these days, I wish she were. She seems to have lost the will to live. Sometimes, I feel she's willing herself to die.'

Mrs Taylor looked startled. It was so unlike Miss Helena to have ideas of that kind. 'You can't mean that, Miss Helena? Not your mother – she's not the type to give up.'

Helena shrugged. 'I used to think that too. But lately

my mind keeps going back to the king's Abdication speech. When it was over my mother switched off the wireless and said: "That's final then. He's given up the throne. I didn't think he would go that far. Such a thing would never have happened before the war. Kings or commoners, they all knew their duty. They knew their place. I don't like this world anymore, and the sooner I leave it the better." '

'Is that what she said!'

'More or less. I may have got some of the wording wrong.'

'And you take that as wanting to die?' Mrs Taylor, sitting stiff-backed on her chair, looked at Helena thoughtfully.

'I didn't at first. I just thought she was upset, but then so were a lot of others at the time. The Abdication took different people different ways. In days gone by it could have led to civil war. Mother, as usual, took it personally. Her monarch had let her down. It was a sign of the times, she said, and she had nothing left to live for.'

Mrs Taylor tched-tched. 'Have you had the doctor to see her?'

'I did suggest it when Mother first took to her bed, but she made such a fuss, and I didn't want to upset her, so I dropped the idea. But yes, I must get the doctor. She's hardly eating and showing no interest in anything. I can't let it go on.'

Dr Morley, a new young doctor who had replaced, on his retirement, the elderly practitioner who had seen to the births, deaths and illnesses of two generations of Thornmere folk, arrived within minutes of Helena's phone call.

'A weak heart!' repeated Helena in disbelief when Dr Morley, after seeing her mother, sought her out to tell her his diagnosis. 'How can you be so sure? Did she allow you to examine her?'

'I didn't have to. I felt her pulse . . . and a job I had

finding it, too. Her lips are blue and and she's breathless. Do you really want to submit her to a more harassing examination? Harassing to one so frail and old?'

Helena realised then how much she would miss her mother. That indomitable figure who had overshadowed so much of her younger life and whom she thought would live for ever. She didn't want her mother to die. It came to her with a sudden lurch of her heart that it would be another link with the past severed. A death, in a way, of her own childhood.

'How long has she got?'

He spread his hands. 'I'm sorry, I'm only a doctor – not a clairvoyant.'

'I'll tell you something, Doctor,' said Helena, fighting a losing battle with her tears. 'My mother is not dying of a weak heart. She's dying out of sheer cussedness.'

Cecilia Roseberry died in January on a grey day with fog looming around the edges. It was the kind of day that would plunge the sunniest of natures into depression, and Helena had some sympathy with her mother for wanting to escape to what she knew her mother believed would be a sunnier clime. However, a week later the sun did put in an appearance for the funeral, and standing in the quiet churchyard with the other mourners – very few, Cecilia had outlived most of her friends – above a noisy chorus from the colony of rooks in the churchyard elms, Helena heard in the distance a drone of an aircraft. To her it seemed a symbol of this modern age, an age her mother had turned her back upon. 'Sleep well, Mother,' she whispered below her breath. 'Peace be with you.'

She was walking back to Rodings alone when Daniel overtook her in his latest car, a Lanchester. He had switched to British cars as a gesture of loyalty in these troubled times. It was British cars for him in future he declared. Reuben's Daimler was the exception. It was now a museum piece and given all the honour due to a veteran. Reuben still polished it once a week.

Dan opened the passenger door for Helena. 'Hop in,' he said.

'It's hardly worth it for such a short distance.'

'Please don't do me out of a cup of your excellent coffee.'

She had a soft spot for Daniel. In the two months since she had returned to Norfolk she had got to know him a lot better. She knew, for instance that he shared a lot of Paul's views and she felt that the two, if they had ever met, would have become firm friends.

But he was also a man who, offered an inch would take a yard, so as much as possible she kept him at arm's length. Today, however, wasn't one of those occasions. When she had seen him at the graveside standing with head bowed, a gush of warm feelings had swept over her for her mind had gone back then to the time in 1929 when Amy Cousins had disappeared.

It was about a week after Amy's disappearance, and she had just arrived at Rodings the day before. Early that morning Daniel Harker had called and she had led him into the morning room, puzzled by his sudden appearance, for she had hardly exchanged two words with him.

He apologised for calling so early but said he didn't think his news could wait, and then proceeded to tell her a story which at the time she could hardly believe. It was about Amy on that fateful Sunday, finding the remains of what was now thought to be the skeleton of Arthur Crossley. Of giving the poor girl shelter for the night as she was in such a state of shock, and the next morning lending her some money to take her to London as, for reasons of her own, she had wanted to get well away from Thornmere. Late the night before, after returning home from a journey, he found a letter from her telling him she was well and had found not only a job but some lodgings, too. He had called to tell Mrs Roseberry as soon as he could, he said, to put her mind at rest. He had heard she had made herself ill with worry.

Helena was grateful for his thoughtfulness and told him so. She was also vastly intrigued. 'I didn't know you knew Amy that well,' she said.

'I didn't know her. What I mean to say is, I knew of her, but hadn't spoken to her before then. But since last Sunday, I feel I know her very well.' Helena thought then that he looked rather pleased about something. An agreeable expression flickered across his roughcast features. 'I was jolly relieved to hear she was safe myself.'

'And why should she run away? What prompted her? Did she say?'

'Unrequited love,' said Daniel Harker, cryptically. 'It turns one's head.'

Helena was in no mood for a remark like that. She was beginning to wonder if she was not the victim of some practical joke, and was not amused.

'Well, the least she could have done was to write to my mother. It strikes me as extremely odd.'

'Oh, she'll write,' said Daniel Harker with maddening assurance. 'Give her time.'

Amy's letter arrived a week later but left them no wiser as to her whereabouts or reason for running away. It was fulsome with apologies and lavish with gratitude for the happy years she had spent at Rodings. She ended by saying that she had left a little china jug in the top drawer in her room and would Mrs Roseberry like it to remember her by.

'She doesn't intend us to know where she's living. This letter is full of words, not explanations,' said Helena crossly. She felt that this was the end of the companionship era for it was unlikely her mother would entertain such an idea again. But her mother, as always, was unpredictable.

'If you are going upstairs, Helena,' she said, 'fetch me that little cow-jug from Amy's room. I think I can find room for it on this mantelshelf.'

'Penny for them?' Dan's voice, deep like Paul's but booming and unmelodious, broke her hold on the past. She smiled. He said that on every occasion she was lost to him, and must have had a pile of unused pennies stored up somewhere for she never gave him the chance to pay.

'Actually,' she said, 'I was thinking of Amy.'

She wondered if he had ever regretted the day when, in a burst of confidence, he had told her the full story of that night with Amy. After she had got her second wind she felt quite amused. This clever and successful man, she thought, who had hauled himself out of the gutter by sheer hard graft showed a human fallibility she found rather touching.

'And what were you thinking about her?' He was a bit sensitive on the subject now.

'Just wondering how she was. What happened to her. I often think of her.'

'Me, too,' he admitted. 'I expect she is a happily-married suburban housewife, with a neat little house and a neat little garden and two neat little children . . .' His words trailed off for he wasn't too sure about that. Somehow, he thought, the Amys of this world never had neat endings to their lives. 'Anyway,' he said, 'Let's not talk about Amy. Let's talk about us.'

She put a restraining hand on his arm. 'Please, Dan, not today.'

In the course of the past eighteen months or so Daniel had proposed to Helena quite regularly, and not taking him seriously she usually met each proposal with a good-natured quip. Only once did she lose her patience, and that was back in June, on a lovely silvery blue day when they were strolling along a lane between hedgerows fragrant with the musky scent of elderflower blossom. He had made his plea on the spur of the moment, for it wasn't quite three weeks since the previous one. The soporific sound of the bees in the cow parsley made him feel drowsy, and drowsiness made him think of bed, and bed naturally turned his thoughts to Helena. So he proposed.

He came back to earth when she rounded on him.

'Look,' she said. 'If I could guarantee that having sex with you, just the once, understand – because I don't intend to make a habit of it – but if that would cure you of this obsession you have for me, I would agree to it. But marry you! That's out of the question.'

Daniel, shaken to the core, hadn't proposed since. On that occasion he had stamped off home, angry with himself and angry with her, and devastatingly disappointed, for he knew no lady in love would ever have suggested such a thing. He rephrased that sentence in his mind: no lady would have even *thought* like that.

He felt let down. His cherished dream of sixteen years was about to wither. He had nursed it, kept it alive by repeated doses of hope, and now with one cold blast of reason it was frosted. Helena had laughed when she made her suggestion but she had meant it. He knew that. As if he could take her on those terms. The thought alone was enough to make any man impotent, and he felt she had emasculated him. He swore to himself he wouldn't demean himself by proposing to her ever again, yet here he was, only three months later, bewitched by her smile and heady with her nearness, thinking up ways of putting his case in a different form.

He stole a look at her. She was staring dreamily into the lake, and he knew she was thinking of Paul. She was always thinking of Paul. She was hatless and a lock of her hair had fallen across her forehead. It made him sad to note that her blazing red-gold curls had darkened to auburn. Since Paul's death she had changed – not aged as such – but matured. Grief had stamped her face with a few more lines. But her eyes were still undimmed, those brilliant green eyes that mocked him in his dreams shone as steadfastly as ever.

Dan stretched out his legs and squared his shoulders. The wooden seat was only meant for short pauses and he was beginning to ache with sitting still so long.

'Any news of Midge?' he asked. He was fond of Midge. It was Midge who had first egged him on to propose to Helena, telling him on the quiet that he was just the kind of man she needed. Midge, after more than a year debating it, had gone ahead and opened another salon in Paris, leaving a manageress in charge of the London shop. She had come to Daniel for business and financial advice which he had gladly given, knowing that he was doing himself no favour, for if Midge made a success of the Paris venture he knew he would see less of Helena. As it was she had been making regular trips to Toppers in the two years since leaving London, staying with Midge at Hanover Mansions. She had never returned to Doughty Street.

Helena, Daniel knew, was not too happy about Midge's move to Paris. She said so now.

'Why, oh why, when the world is in such a state of flux does Midge have to take such a risk? Not as far as business is concerned, that's sound enough. But for her own safety. One never knows what that madman is going to do next. Is there any fresh news? I've been travelling all day and haven't had a chance to see a paper.'

He shook his head. 'Things look pretty grim over this Sudeten affair. The appeasers go on appeasing and the warmongers go on warmongering. And what do we do? We kit out our children with gas masks.'

He sounded so like Paul that in spite of herself Helena had to laugh. A few days before millions of gas masks had been distributed to regional centres throughout the country. Thornmere folk had had to go to Beckton Market and many went with the idea of a good laugh, which they had in plenty when they caught sight of each other. A lot of hooting and mocking followed the trying for size. Only when they saw the masks on children and babies did horror strike them. It was a sober bunch that made their way home afterwards. And now the threat of war over Czechoslovakia was growing daily.

Nobody was under any delusion that war could be averted or that when it came they would not all be in it. Gone were the days when the armed forces alone waged war. Now civilians were just as likely to be in the front line as the soldiers. Nobody who had sat through cinema newsreels in the past few years and watched bombs raining down on villages and towns in China and in Spain had any doubts about that. If war was declared London, it was rumoured, would be flattened in a matter of weeks. Plans were already afoot for the evacuation of children.

'If you're thinking of going up to London soon, you'd better make it before the 1 October,' Daniel said.

'Why the 1 October?'

'Hitler said he would not do anything about Czechoslovakia before that date, and you know he's a man of his word.'

'I don't know how you can joke at a time like this.'

'Because joking at a time like this is the only thing that keeps me sane. Weren't you due to go to a wedding sometime in October?'

Helena had received an invitation from the Doughty Street house. The younger Miss Spicer from the top floor and Mr Pickford from the first were getting married, very quietly, at the Holborn Registry Office. There was to be no reception as such, just a few friends to drink their health.

Helena, out of mischief, had intended taking Midge with her, gleeful to have this opportunity of proving her wrong about the Spicer sisters, but Midge was in Paris. She decided now, on the spur of the moment, to ask Daniel instead.

She needed somebody by her side when she took that first step over the threshold of Doughty Street. She couldn't think of anybody among her circle of friends as reliable as Daniel Harker. He had seen her through the first few difficult months after her mother's death, untangling the tangled web of Cecilia's financial affairs. Helena's suspicions that her mother had a long stocking secreted away somewhere proved false. Nearly all her capital was tied up in shares in Russian oilfields, bought by the Admiral during the days of the Czars and then considered a good investment. Now they were not worth the paper they were printed on.

'The freehold of this house is yours,' Daniel told

Helena, following a session with the family solicitor. 'But the capital from the trust your grandfather set up reverts to the Ardleigh estate. How are you off for . . .?' He hesitated. 'What I am trying to say in my delicate fashion is are you skint? If so, I can negotiate a loan to tide you over, interest free, of course.'

'No, I am not skint. Paul's book is still making money and we're doing very nicely at Toppers, thank you.'

'That means you won't be selling Rodings.'

'Sell my link with Norfolk! I'd rather sell my share of the business.'

The kingfisher had alighted on a branch of an overhanging willow. Dan gave Helena a gentle nudge, and with his eyes indicated the place where it was perching. They were just in time to see the quick flash of electric blue as it hit the water, and then it was away again, drops falling from its brilliant plumage, a fish skewered in its beak.

Helena said, 'Would you do me a favour, Dan? Would you come to Miss Spicer's wedding with me?'

Dan's rugged features lit up. 'That's the sort of favour I like. Not too difficult to carry out. Don't want to go on your own, eh?'

He was dismayed to see her eyes slowly fill with tears. 'It's on the 21 October. That's the anniversary of Paul's birthday. I wish it had been any other day but that.' She put her hand on his. 'I might need your pair of broad shoulders to cry on.'

'Always at your disposal,' he said, hiding his dashed hopes behind a steady smile.

Eight days later, Neville Chamberlain flew to Munich and arrived back at Heston Airport to tell the country, 'Peace in our time'.

'How long is time,' growled Daniel. 'The length of a piece of string?'

'Oh, Dan, don't spoil it. I'm tremendously relieved. I'm ashamed of feeling so relieved but it doesn't make me feel less like cheering. I know that we've betrayed Czechoslovakia. I know that war is inevitable – but at least we've put off, for the time being, killing one another.'

Sunsfield lay basking in a spell of Indian summer. Flora with Danny as her helpmate was weeding the small vegetable bed at the end of the long narrow garden. Amy at the window of her bedroom stood idly watching.

Danny followed Flora like a little shadow. He called her Nan. He thought that the sun shone out of her eyes. She had time for him, she never said no. When he went to bed she read to him or told him stories from the vast font of her memory. Mostly fairy tales from the Brothers Grimm, though she altered the endings so that everyone lived happily ever after.

Flora had changed. The process had already started before Amy's return to Sunsfield, now it accelerated under Danny's softening influence. She learnt to laugh. More importantly she learnt to love. She worshipped Danny and, given the chance, Amy knew she would have lavished the same deep feelings on Danny's mother, except that Danny's mother had no intention of letting her.

Amy had forgiven her mother long ago for the simple reason that she had become weary of bearing a grudge. Though she could never forget or understand Flora's rejection of her, she no longer wanted to talk about it or think about it even. It was something best hidden away as she had herself, in a sense, been hidden away for many years. She thought it easier on the emotions if she and her mother went on as it were living with a neutral zone between them which Danny filled completely.

They were good friends, though not intimate friends, for she had never been able to tell her mother who Danny's father was or give a hint about that other man she had loved, because sometimes she got quite confused herself, mixing the two together. Often, looking into Danny's coal-black eyes, she would think how like his father, and always an image of Francis Thomas came into her mind. She didn't think of the Reverend Mr Thomas as often as she once did, and she didn't think of Daniel Harker at all. She had learnt to bury the past and live each day as it came, and give no thought to the future. That way, she discovered, she could avoid getting hurt.

She put on her hat and coat and gloves, took her handbag and a shopping basket, and went down into the garden to tell her mother that she was going into town and was there anything she could bring back with her?

Danny looked up and grinned. He had been away from school with a heavy cold which he had passed on to his mother, but he didn't look any the worse for it. He was still undersized for his age but two years of country air had put a healthy colour in his cheeks. At present his face was crimson from all the effort he had used in filling the wheelbarrow with weeds.

'Why don't you look in on the doctor?' suggested Flora. 'Ask him for a tonic. You can't seem to throw off that cold.'

Her mother had an uncanny habit of voicing what was already in her daughter's mind. Amy's main reason for going out now was to call on Dr Hamilton, but not on her own behalf. She and the doctor had quickly renewed their acquaintanceship, mainly through Danny, who went down with one childish ailment after another as soon as he started at the local school.

It was only a short walk to the High Street which, on this fine day, was thronging with shoppers. Was it her imagination, Amy wondered, that everybody seemed to be walking with a lighter step than a week ago? Then they had been under the threat of war, now it was 'Peace in our time', and yet, she thought, looking around her, there were just as many sailors in uniform about. The naval dockyard was only a few miles further on, and during the Munich crisis the traffic going that way had considerably increased. And showed no sign of lessening, she thought, as a convoy of trucks went by.

'So you think you need a tonic?' said Dr Hamilton.

'My mother thinks I need a tonic.'

'How is your mother?'

'That's what I've really come about.' She couldn't quite look him in the eye.

'Go on,' he said.

'Sometimes she's in considerable pain. She makes light of it, and says it's nothing but indigestion, but I don't remember her having indigestion when I was here before. At other times you wouldn't think she had anything the matter with her. Danny has made such a great difference to her life. Sometimes I think she looks better than when we first came, but at other times she looks so frail it's a marvel to me how she manages to keep going.'

He rested his elbow on his desk with his chin in the palm of his hand. 'What is it you want to know?' he said kindly.

'Has my mother got a stomach ulcer?'

'No, I can guarantee that.'

'What is the matter with her then? There must be something the matter with her – she's losing weight. Can't you tell me?'

He got up from his seat and began to pace the surgery,

his hands in his pockets, a habit she remembered from the past when faced with making a decision. He stopped in front of her.

'You should know, you have every right to know. Flora is ill – seriously ill. She asked me not to tell you and I promised I wouldn't, but the time has come when you must be told.' He paused. Amy held her breath.

'Your – your mother was operated on for breast cancer about .. it must be seven or eight years ago, now. You had left Norfolk by then so I couldn't even get in touch with you.' It was not an indictment on his part, just a statement of fact, but enough to give Amy such a pang of conscience that she felt shrivelled. He sat down beside her and gripped her hand.

'At first it looked as if the operation had been a success, I saw a change in your . . .' He couldn't rid himself of the habit of saying aunt. He nearly said it then. 'A change in your mother. She became more sociable, started to go out a bit, as if she realised she had been given a second chance. Then, just before you returned to Sunsfield, I had to tell her the old enemy had flared up again. She asked me how long she had and I said two years if she was lucky. She's living on borrowed time, Amy.'

Tears were falling unchecked down Amy's cheeks. 'Why didn't she tell me? Why has she kept this to herself?'

'She didn't want to spoil the time you have left together. She's a very determined woman, Amy, but also a very unhappy one, in spite of the front she puts up. Can't you bring yourself to forgive her?'

'I have forgiven her,' said Amy, her voice muffled through her handkerchief.

'Not completely you haven't and she can tell. She acted monstrously towards you, but don't you think she's been punished enough?' He was an unsentimental man but he felt the need just then to blow his nose. 'If you let it, Amy, the past can become a prison. Try to escape from that.'

'Tell me what I can do,' Amy begged.

'Just what your heart tells you. But remember – no pity. That won't help at all.'

He walked her to the door of his surgery. He took her by her shoulders. 'Can I rely on you, Amy Cousins?'

She managed a watery smile. As fast as she wiped the tears away, they spurted again. 'Have you ever been able to rely on me?' she said.

'Unfortunately not. But now I think you have had a change of heart. Try and forgive your mother. Really, I mean.'

'I have.'

'Tell her that.'

'I won't tell her, I'll show her.'

She bought flowers for Flora. Not moss roses, that was something she would never forgive herself for. But tall-stemmed dark red carnations, which in spite of being hot-house plants were heavily fragrant.

Flora buried her face in them, hiding her tears.

'Dr Hamilton has told you?'

'Yes.' Amy's voice was nearly as inaudible. 'But let's not say anything about it now. There's something else first.' She saw dread come to Flora's face and added quickly: 'I didn't mean about that. No more talk about the past, that's all finished with. No more keeping anything from each other – that's why I want to tell you about Danny's father. When we're alone. When Danny's in bed.'

They went about their individual duties as if nothing of significance had changed the course of what little future was left to them. It was as if they had moved to another zone where life was freer and neither had anymore fear of putting a foot wrong. Amy began to set the kitchen table for tea. Flora, at the sink, arranging the carnations in her tallest vase, was humming softly under her breath. Suddenly, she said:

'Did you remember to ask Dr Hamilton for a tonic?'

'Oh, my goodness . . . first I remembered, then I forgot!'

They began to laugh, laughter that was diluted by ready tears. But it didn't matter. Tears or laughter, they were doing it together.

It took Amy some time to get to sleep that night. Her breathing was difficult because her nasal passages were blocked with catarrh. Her mother had rubbed her chest with camphorated oil and a piece of flannel soaked in the oil was tied round her throat. A remedy from childhood that had always worked. But she couldn't get warm. Her feet were like ice. She had opened her window to get rid of the smell of the camphorated oil and now a cold blast of air was blowing over her. She felt too lazy to get up and do anything about it. She'd soon get warm she assured herself. She felt happier than at any time she could remember.

Flora found her in the morning. At first she thought Amy was sleeping, she looked so peaceful, even smiling a little, though that could have been a trick of the imagination.

'One of the nicest ways of going,' said Dr Hamilton gruffly.

'But why – why?' Flora was inconsolable in her grief and he had had to sedate her. Now she moved and spoke like a sleep-walker.

'There'll be a post-mortem of course. It could be her heart – she was never very robust. I may be putting my neck out but I think it was a very virulent form of pneumonia. It can strike very quickly. I had a patient once, a hefty young chap, a rugger player. He had a bit of a cold one Saturday but not enough to prevent him playing in a match that afternoon. He didn't stay for the usual drinks afterwards. He said he was feeling a bit off colour and wanted to get home. He died the following day. Virus pheumonia. Rotten shame.'

'Isn't there anything that can be done?'

'Not when it strikes suddenly. A person can be alive one minute and dead the next. How was Amy last night?'

'Tired – but happy.' Flora was dry-eyed but tormented looking. 'She so wanted to talk about Danny's father. She has never mentioned him to me before, but last night she couldn't stop talking about him. Do you think she had a premonition?'

Dr Hamilton shook his head. 'I don't believe in premonitions, but I do sometimes think that when your number comes up, there's not much you can do about it. Well, I'll have to go and notify the right people, I suppose. A nurse is on her way – will you be all right until then?'

'Yes, I'll be all right,' said Flora drearily.

At the door he looked back. She was kneeling by the bed her cheek resting on Amy's arm. Carefully he closed the door behind him. In the passage stood a small boy in pyjamas, his hair tousled, his eyes still filmed by sleep.

'Where's everybody?' he said, yawning.

Dr Hamilton took his hand. 'Busy. Come along old chap, I'd better get you some breakfast.'

FIFTEEN | 1939

That year Empire Day, 24 May, fell on a Wednesday. It also happened to be Derby Day. Nobody among those paying homage to the Union Flag in different parts of the country – indeed, in different parts of the world – could foresee that very soon this old custom would disappear, as also would Armistice Day. Two early casualties of the coming war. Derby Day, however, would survive, an ongoing proof of the English love of sport, and on this particular Derby Day Daniel felt the urge to break a lifelong rule and have a flutter on Blue Peter. He didn't study form, he knew nothing about the merits of the different horses, but Blue Peter happened to be the name of a pub he used to frequent in the balmy days before the Great War.

On his way now to the Ferry Inn to place his bet, he passed the school just as the pupils came streaming out to take part in the Empire Day ceremony. He stopped to watch, for the sight of young children always gave him pleasure. They were assembled around the flagpole according to age, and to one of the older boys was given the honour of hoisting the flag. The children watched as it rose rather jerkily to the head of the pole, where it was caught by the breeze and fluttered proudly above their heads. It was a solemn moment as their expressions testified. At a word from their teacher they all saluted. Among them Daniel caught sight of the short plump figure of Jessie Stoneham standing stiffly to attention. Emotionally his blew he nose and walked on.

Daniel had become very fond of Jessie and as often as her parents could spare her he would have her up at the Hall, listening to her prattling away in the soft Norfolk burr that was a constant source of pleasure to him. He had picked up quite a few Norfolk expressions himself over the years but had never mastered the accent. His voice was still heavily underlined by Cockney vowels as was young Joey Gilbert's for all his years at a grammar school.

Dan sighed, more in sorrow than exasperation. He was having problems with Joey. He had disappointed Dan by giving up his place at the academy where he had been studying music for the past two years. He told Daniel he wanted to join the RAF and train as a Spitfire pilot. He had been mad on planes ever since his first visit to Sir Alan Cobham's flying circus when a lad of twelve.

Dan tried to talk him out of such a drastic step, but Joey's mind was made up, and for one whom Dan had always thought of as an amiable young chap, he could be extremely stubborn.

'I'm going to be called up, anyway,' he reasoned. 'You know conscription for all those over twenty is on the cards. I'd rather enlist and choose which service I want. If I'm conscripted I won't have any choice.'

'All that talent going to waste.'

'Not wasted, Uncle Dan. It will be my second string,

my let-out when things get tough. And I shall always be invited to parties and much sought after in the mess.'

Dan scoffed at that. 'Playing jazz!'

'Swing these days. Popular songs – good for the morale.'

'And I had such hopes for you. I saw you as a concert pianist – what do they call them? A virtuoso? I expected so much of you.'

'Too much, Uncle Dan. That was the trouble. I couldn't live up to your expectations. You looked upon me as a child prodigy. I was no such thing. I just had the talent for knocking out a tune. I soon found my level when I went to the academy, and if I hadn't found it for myself my teacher would soon have pointed it out to me. He said I would never become a musician of note. That my playing was too pedestrian, that it lacked emotion, and my only course if I wanted to stay with music was to teach it.'

'Blithering idiot,' said Dan indignantly. 'Talking through the back of his neck!'

'Talking sense. And it was a relief to have my suspicions confirmed.'

That conversation had taken place a month ago, and with the speed in which events were overtaking one another during this time of anxious foreboding, Joey was already in training as a fighter pilot.

'Peace in our time,' muttered Daniel to himself, kicking a stone out of his path. He felt suddenly very disgruntled. Peace in our time had turned out to be a frantic preparation for war. Everywhere he went he saw evidence of this. Sandbags piling up against public buildings; air raid shelters appearing in every main street; and already the Government was distributing Anderson shelters to those living in districts likely to be bombed, free if their income was less than two hundred and fifty pounds a year. And the most ominous sight of all, air raid sirens being erected at nominated places. The nearest one to Thornmere was on the roof of the Corn Exchange at Beckton Market.

The locals considered that they had been short-changed. 'We won't even 'ear the botty thing if the wind's in the wrong direction,' they grumbled.

'Doan't you fear you'll miss anything,' came the comforting response. 'The warden'll come round on his bike and knock you up if anything starts.'

Daniel was overtaken by a green and black Morris Oxford. Helena wound down the window. 'Where are you off to at this time of morning?' she asked.

Just the sight of her raised Daniel's spirits. 'For a snifter at the Ferry and a flutter on the Derby on the side.'

That made her smile. 'You, placing a bet! You always told me gambling was a mug's game.'

'Just a fancy on my part, that's all. I don't suppose it will come to anything.'

'You could have a snifter at my place, or a coffee if you prefer it. There's something I've been wanting to talk over with you.'

Gladly Daniel got in beside her. She was hatless and her hair, drawn back behind her ears and secured by two matching combs, was the colour of old copper where the sun caught it. He hadn't seen her for many weeks, for she had been too tied up with the shop. He had no idea she was back in Thornmere. The thought that she hadn't immediately phoned him depressed him.

'You might have let me know you were back in circulation,' he said.

'What's up, Dan? You sound very down in the dumps.'

'Just generally fed up. I heard today that the Germans will be on the march as soon as the harvest is gathered in.'

She heaved a troubled sigh. 'Let's just have one day without any talk of war, please,' she begged.

'That won't stop us thinking about it.'

'Then let's keep our thoughts to ourselves.'

The morning coffee extended to lunch time. During the winter Helena had had a corner of the house where two walls met glassed over, telling the men who came to do the job that a lovely old-fashioned and sweetly-smelling rose growing against one wall was not to be uprooted. They would just have to glass over it as best they could, she said. They accepted this ultimatum with their usual Norfolk phlegm for as far as they were concerned the piper played the tune, and Helena's music was much appreciated, for she kept them generously supplied with beer and sandwiches.

As for Helena, her reward was a sunny spot to sit out in and roses that bloomed two months earlier than usual. Never before had she picked such an abundance of roses in May. The hall was fragrant with them.

'What do you think of my Maiden's Blush,' she said.

'Your what!' Daniel looked startled.

'My roses, you idiot.'

'Oh.' He grinned for the first time that day. 'I thought you meant something else.'

'I know you did. And I may as well tell you right now that I'm too old to blush.'

'But I'm not too old to try and make you.'

'Forget it, Dan. I'm not in that sort of mood today. Actually, I want to pick your brains, but first we eat. There's a bottle of plonk in the fridge. Could you deal with it, please?'

They ate in the shade of the roses, for the sun shining through the glass was too hot to sit in. Bumble bees, tumbling among some wallflowers kept up a constant hum against a background of birdsong. Far off from the direction of the river a cuckoo called repeatedly. Helena set a low garden table with slices of ham and tongue, rolls and butter, cheese and fruit. Daniel rubbed his hands in anticipation. 'Better than tinned soup,' he said.

He ate well. Afterwards he sat back in his chair with his hands folded across his stomach. Never had he felt less like talking business. He studied Helena from under his brows, wanting her so much it gave him an ache in his groin. He thought the old passion had died out long ago but at times like this he was made uncomfortably aware that it was as strong as ever. To his concern he saw a solitary tear slide down her cheek. He sat up.

'You're thinking of Paul,' he said ruefully.

She brushed the tear away. 'I know. I can't help it. We used to do this so often – eating out of doors, I mean, on the balcony. I haven't done so since – not until today.'

'It's nearly three years, Helena. Let him go.'

'I don't want to let him go,' she said miserably. 'Memories are all I've got left, and I'm clinging on to them as hard as I can. I've forgotten the sound of his voice, that's what hurts me most. I try so hard to conjure it up, but I can't. Not satisfactorily. I have photos of him, I have his letters which bring him to life for me in a different way. But his voice – that's gone. Oh, Dan, I miss him so.'

She had no idea that every word she uttered touched Dan on the raw. He took a minor comfort from the thought that she valued his friendship enough to confide in him. Not knowing how to comfort her in return he thought he might try chivvying her out of her despondent mood instead.

'I suppose this wouldn't be a convenient moment to propose to you?' he said.

In spite of herself, laughter bubbled up through her tears. 'Oh, Dan, you blighter, you know just how to make me laugh.' She reached for her handkerchief and dried her eyes. 'You're good for me, but you know that already. You never allow me to feel sorry for myself. Whatever am I going to do when you hive off to America?'

'Come with me, of course.'

At the end of 1938 Dan had had an extremely tempting offer from a food production company with a household name, for the rights and goodwill of Thurgood's Tinplate and Cannery Company. The offer was too good to turn down but he was still reluctant to cut the final cord.

He knew the old canning works as such were doomed anyway. It was now fenced in by a sprawling conurbation of shops and offices and domestic dwellings which left no room for expansion, and without expansion or modernisation profits would shrink. It wasn't profits the company was after. It was the valuable site and even more valuable trade mark which was known throughout East Anglia. With capital he received from selling the works Daniel could indulge in a long-held dream: to go to America and study the technique of the frozen food industry. He had discussed all this with Helena during the Christmas holiday as they sat one evening in his office, roasting chestnuts over the fire and drinking Napoleon brandy.

He told her about Dr Birdseye, the American biologist, who in the Twenties had developed a method for freezing food, and had later sold the rights to a large food corporation who, under the trade name Birds Eye, now sold their products throughout the world. He was anxious to learn more about this method of preserving food he said. America was the place to obtain that knowledge. Others before him had thought the same. Already small amounts of frozen fruits were available in Britain.

He had grandiose ideas of widening the field. Why not complete meals that could be thawed and heated up within minutes? Something geared to busy mothers or working girls or bachelors like himself. An alternative to tinned food. There was a market out there waiting to be tapped.

So far he had done nothing more than think about it. War hung like a shadow over his mind, that and the conviction that he could never uproot Helena from her homeland. Where Helena was, there he would stay.

'That was a rather wistful sigh,' she said.

He wasn't going to give her the satisfaction of explaining why. He parried with, 'You said you had something you wanted to talk over with me?'

'It's about Toppers. Now that Midge has established herself in Paris she wants to stay permanently, unfortunately.' Helena hesitated, then added rather petulantly, 'She's in love with Paris. She's like a lovesick adolescent and there's no talking sense into her anymore.'

It was more than that. Midge had fallen in love with her ex-husband all over again. She now confessed that she had never completely fallen out of love with him, a secret she had kept well-hidden thought Helena, a trifle cynically. Helena, who thought she could read Midge like a book, didn't like to think she had been deceived. She could accept the fact that Midge had taken Douglas back after his second wife left him, knowing Midge had a soft spot for a loser. What she found harder to accept was the resurgence of a love Midge had always declared to be dead. Midge had known Douglas since she was a girl of seventeen, she had married young, she had been hurt more than she ever showed when he left her for another woman. She had lived a pretence ever since which she enlarged upon in a letter to Helena.

He has lost everything. His money, his wife and his home. He looks terrible – he looks ill – he is completely lost without someone to look after him. And here am I with this huge apartment all to myself. It would be so inhuman to turn him away. Besides, Helena, I want him back. There, now you know the truth. I didn't really know how much myself until I saw him again. I came to Paris to flaunt my success in his face, at least, that's what I told myself. What a fool I've been, pretending for the sake of my pride all these years. I'm not saying I didn't hate Douglas when he first left me, though perhaps hate is too strong a word. I certainly smouldered with resentment and went on stoking that particular fire for years. But that's all over now. Douglas needs someone to care for him and I need someone to care for. We've both got over our giddy years and want to settle down and live in peace. Old age can be lonely without a partner, Helena. I saw that with my mother. Dougie will never go back to England and I have fallen in love with Paris and the Parisians. Such practical people – no nonsense with them, very little sentiment, either. There's only one teeny-weeny little thing, darling, lack of funds. After paying off Dougie's debts, there's not much left in the kitty. Could we come to some business arrangement? Could I sell you my half of Toppers? Cable your reply.

Helena did so. 'Will help as much as I can, but have you overlooked Hitler?'

To which Midge responded with another cable. 'Thanks for the promise of help, and have you overlooked the Maginot Line?'

When Helena told Dan of this he grunted: 'Wish I had as much faith in the Maginot Line.' Then remembering their pledge of no war talk turned to the other matter. 'Could you afford to buy out Midge if you wanted to?'

Helena pondered. 'I suppose I could,' she said thoughtfully. 'I could raise the capital if I were to cash all my assets and take out a mortgage on Rodings, but I don't want to do that. I'd rather sell the business outright and go fifty-fifty with Midge.'

'You'd give up Toppers!'

She regarded him solemnly. 'I've told you many times that I'm no business woman. I couldn't deal with customers. I couldn't deal with reps and suppliers either, and I'd be lost with all that paperwork. All I ever wanted to do was to design hats and I can do that anywhere. If I were to take Toppers over we'd be bankrupt within a year. And there's another thing. The war. If it does come the first casualties are sure to be the luxury trades like milliners and couturiers. And then I'd be out of a job.'

'If you're right about that you're not likely to find any takers for the shop.'

She shrugged. 'There's always somebody willing to take a risk.'

'I wonder,' said Daniel frowning. He rose and stretched. 'Talking about risks, let's find out how Blue Peter makes out. The Derby's being broadcast this afternoon.'

They listened in to the race in what was once Mrs Roseberry's sitting room. The sun was creeping round to that side of the house, shining through the window and highlighting the signs of delapidation on the worn but still beautiful pieces of furniture. Blue Peter won.

'I'm so very sorry,' said Helena, trying to look contrite but failing dismally. 'Have I lost you a fortune?'

'I don't know about a fortune. I don't even know what the odds are, but I intended to put on half-crown each way.'

She laughed at that. 'Surely it wasn't worth the shoe leather, walking all that way to the Ferry Inn to put on a measly half-crown each way. You and your risks.'

'Lady, I never take risks where money's concerned. But affairs of the heart . . . now, that is a different matter.'

She gave him a warning look. 'Not today, Dan, don't spoil the lovely time we've had together.'

'Have I helped you make up your mind about the shop?'

'No–o,' she admitted. 'But that's not to say it hasn't been a most enjoyable occasion.'

He didn't push his luck by asking how.

She walked to the garden gate with him. The walnut tree, reputed to be as old as the house, was filmed over with fresh green shoots. The lilac hedge that marked their boundary on the south side was heavy with blossom. 'I love this time of the year,' she said, inhaling the lilac's fragrance as if it were some life-giving drug. 'Birds singing . . . flowers blooming. I couldn't part with Rodings – I couldn't give up my lovely garden.'

'But you could part with the shop?'

'Much more easily.'

'Well, let me know when you've made up your mind if you do wish to sell and I'll arrange for you to meet my accountants. They'll advise you. When will you be in London again?'

'Soon, I think.'

Dan kissed her. Aiming for her mouth and as usual getting her cheek instead. Helena was always too quick for him. She leant on the gate, watching him as he walked away, a clumsy man but surprisingly light on his feet, and his back as straight as a die. A handsome man, too, in a rugged sort of way, for the years had softened the coarse outlines of his features and the heavy white swathes in his hair gave him a look of distinction.

Her friends thought she was mad to refuse his advances. It was not only wealth and security on offer – it was he himself. Candida at the shop was most outspoken. 'He's got more sex in his little finger than any Deb's Delight in his whole body. You don't know what you're missing.'

But Helena did. She missed that side of life very much, but while memories of Paul were still so powerful no substitute was possible.

She visited London again in the second week of June without telling Daniel. She wanted a few days on her own at the flat finishing off some unfinished business, or rather schooling herself for tasks she had been putting off for nearly three years.

It was a day in accord with her mood, grey and overcast, and as she opened the front door an unwelcome rush of cold air met her. She shivered. It was always like this when she returned to Doughty Street. The soundless and empty sense of a deserted home. The loss. Paul was gone, the one who, by an inflection of his voice, a word even, could make her laugh or cry, feel happy or sad. In Norfolk, away from Doughty Street, she could conjure him back. But here, in this place of memories, she had to face the heart-breaking truth that Paul was no more.

That first time on returning to Doughty Street, nearly a year ago for the Pickfords' wedding, had been a painful ordeal. Without Dan's strong arm to support her she doubted whether she could have made it. Memories of Paul were everywhere. But not his presence. She had never believed in ghosts, but she would gladly have suspended her disbelief to see Paul again, just to sense his nearness, but even that solace was denied her. Here in Doughty Street Paul was irrevocably dead.

Until today she had not been able to stay overnight. She had flitted in and out of the flat like an intruder, leaving notes for Jake if he wasn't about. It was Jake who had disposed of Paul's clothes for her, who had accepted, with a masterly control of his feelings, a few personal possessions for himself.

'Not his watch! It's gold, Miss Roseberry. I can't accept anything as valuable as that.'

'He would have wanted you to have it, Jake. You were a good friend to him – to both of us.'

He was terribly moved. She caught sight of the give-away quiver of his lips as he turned away. He too had aged. What little hair still remained was pure white. Even so he was still very much the old soldier with a straight back and brisk walk. During the Munich crisis he had been one of the first in the area to volunteer as an air raid warden.

And the Pickfords, she thought, as she unpacked her case, what a success that marriage had turned out to be. A *ménage à trois* that actually worked – especially for Mr Pickford. A wife to see to his bodily comforts, which she did most excellently, and a sister-in-law he could sharpen his wits on. They argued about everything from politics to ballet. There wasn't a single subject they agreed upon but oh, how they enjoyed the disagreeing.

This Jake confided in Helena, plus the added information that if war did break out, the firm Miss Spicer worked for, an advertising agency, was planning to evacuate the business to a safe area.

'You mark my words,' he said. 'If Miss Spicer goes, I bet the Pickfords go too. I can't see those sisters being separated, and I can't see old man Pickford giving up his verbal bouts with his sister-in-law. He'd rather take early retirement.'

'And you, Jake. What will you do in the event of war?'

'I'm staying put, Miss Roseberry. You won't catch me taking any run out powders.'

The house was unnaturally quiet. No sound from above. Mrs Pickford was possibly out shopping, or gone to a matinee. The other two at work. Helena went through to the sitting room and switched on the electric fire. She drew the curtains and unlatched the French windows that opened onto the balcony. That struck her as chilly, too, but if the sun came out which it showed signs of doing it would quickly warm up.

For the first time it seemed to her that the garden looked rather dingy. Coming from a garden bright with living colour this small patch looked very dull. The roots of the mulberry tree spread wide, sucking all the nourishment from the soil, preventing anything else from growing. But with such a magnificent specimen of a tree to admire who needed flowers when they could be bought from a flower-seller at any street corner.

She turned away. The silence mocked her. No one in that long cane chair to talk to. No one to laugh with. No one to cry with as she was crying now. In one swift blow she had lost a lover, and a friend, and a child. It would have been so easy then to give up and just weep until she had no energy or desire to do anything else but feel sorry for herself. But that wouldn't have been Paul's way. He was a fighter. Many the time he had struggled to his typewriter to tap away at a page of his manuscript when he could hardly find the strength to sit. It had been agony to stand by and do nothing, but she had no alternative, for offers of help Paul regarded as an onslaught on his manhood. So how could she not now live up to his example? She marched across the room and switched on the wireless. At least that would put paid to the silence.

The task she most dreaded was going through the many letters she had received following Paul's death. She had read them hastily at the time then bundled them into a battered old attaché case belonging to Paul before escaping to Norfolk. The case was under the bed. That was the worst part, going into the bedroom. She had avoided doing so on her other hasty visits to the flat. Today there was no option.

She steeled herself against a rising tide of panic as she opened the door to the bedroom. She expected a darkened room, musty-smelling and oppressive, for it hadn't been aired in years. She expected memories so overwhelming that her resolve would crack. Instead she was greeted with sound and light. The steady, homely sound of ticking from the Parliament clock on the wall, and light from the windows that had been freshly cleaned. The room was dust-free, cared for, the bed made up, the furniture smelling pleasantly of wax polish. This hadn't been done in preparation of her visit, for no one knew she was coming. Somebody was keeping this room in prime condition and she knew it could be none other than Jake, for his hallmark was everywhere, even to the fire built ready for lighting in the grate. It was his way of keeping memories of Paul alive.

And her way? Burying Paul deep in her heart. Mourning him in secret. Avoiding places where they had once been happy. Through her tears she looked sadly at the bed. She would have denied him that, too, planning to escape to the ottoman tonight, as she had done sometimes when he was alive. Was that the way to bring him back? Was that why a sense of his presence eluded her here in Doughty Street where it should have been at its strongest?

She flung herself face down on the bed and buried her head in the pillows. And gradually, it seemed, a whiff of cigarette smoke teased her nostrils. She lifted her head and sniffed. Everything on the bed had been laundered. Everything in the room had been cleaned and polished, and yet the smell of cigarette smoke lingered. Whether it was in her fancy or not it didn't matter. She felt that Paul was very near. Smiling to herself she drifted gently into sleep.

She awakened about an hour later feeling greatly refreshed. The house was no longer silent. There were now definite sounds of movement from above. She rose, and going to the bathroom rinsed her face with cold water. When later she went into the kitchen she found a half-pint bottle of milk and some fresh bread rolls and a message from Jake. 'Saw you arrive and thought these might come in useful.' Dear Jake. She owed him far more than milk and rolls. The debt was insurmountable.

Tea refreshed her. Now she was ready to tackle the first of her tasks. She sat on the bed with her legs tucked under her and the attaché case by her side. Most of its contents had been redirected from the offices of the *Daily Encounter*. Personal friends had sent their condolences direct to the flat, but the tributes from those who had known Paul most of his life – school friends and college friends and old army pals – had been sent to the office. His colleagues had not forgotten him either, nor those on foreign newspapers with whom he had worked during his roving days. From all over the world the letters had come. From friends and fans and complete strangers, writing of admiration for him in spite of, or perhaps because of, his radical views.

And finally, the pale mauve envelope which contained a short letter from Lottie. Just a few simple words of comfort, sincere and heartfelt. Helena had intended to call and thank her but she never had. One day, she thought.

Re-reading these letters after all this time, often reduced to tears by their poignancy, nevertheless Helena felt she had reached a cornerstone in the tide of her emotions. The time had come to remember Paul with joy rather than with sadness. She felt she was coming alive again.

The phone rang. Who knew she was here? It was Dan, speaking from Thornmere, and sounding extremely put out. 'Why didn't you tell me you were going to London?' he said. 'Why did I have to find out from your domestic help?'

'Because I knew if you knew you'd insist on coming with me and I wanted a few days here on my own.'

A few rumbling words of discontent came over the phone. 'What is so important that you have to keep it a secret?'

'Nothing secret at all. I just wanted to sort out some of Paul's private papers.'

'Have you finished, because if you have, I want to see you.'

'I've only scratched the surface. There's all his notebooks to go through yet. Cuttings, old manuscripts, things like that. There's a desk and umpteen drawers to turn out – it will take me days.'

'I have something rather important to tell you.'

'Can't you tell me over the phone? I am really short of time, Daniel.'

'I would rather tell you face to face. But all right, if that's

how you want it. It's a surprise – a pleasant surprise I hope.
I know someone who is interested in buying Toppers.'

She took so long to answer Dan thought she had hung
up. 'Helena! Are you still there?'

'I – I'm speechless. I just don't know what to say.'

'It's a genuine offer. One you should consider very
carefully. I don't think you'll get another like it, not as
things are at present.'

'Do you know who it is? Can you vouch for him . . . her?'

'Willingly. It's a far-sighted chap with a sharp nose for
a bargain. You can trust him, Helena.'

Still she hesitated. Now that disposing of Toppers
could be a possibility she felt an irresistible urge to hang
on. That smart little shop in which she and Midge had
staked everything they had. Watched as their hopes and
dreams turned into reality. The happy hours, for her, in the
workshop. Midge's enthusiasm and encouragement which
for the most part had got the business off the ground in
the first place. All that to go! But Midge had left already
and the future hovered menacingly.

'This friend of yours?'

'Business acquaintance.'

'Is he willing to take a risk at a time like this?'

'He looks beyond a time like this. Even if war comes
it will be followed eventually by peace. Then trade will
boom. That's what he's investing in.'

'He must be an optimist,' she said sceptically.

'Optimism is the hallmark of a successful entrepreneur.'
He answered with the confidence of one who knows what
he's talking about.

She sighed, not wanting to be rushed.

'Give me time to think it over, Dan. And I must get in
touch with Midge. I can't make this decision on my own.'

'Don't take too long, Helena. The sands are running out.'

The sands seemed to have run out completely when on the 23 August the Nazi-Soviet pact was signed. War before had been predictable, now it was inevitable. Hitler could march westwards with confidence, no longer worried about what was going on behind his back. But during the intervening period, during the unsettled weather of June and July, both Helena and Daniel had, for them, more personal things on their minds.

The sale of Toppers had gone through without a hitch. Helena was amazed by the ease and swiftness in which the whole transaction was finalised. She owed this to Daniel, who carefully scrutinised the small print of every contract before passing it on to her solicitors. She owed it to the solicitors of the buyer who, in the absence of their client on another business deal abroad, smoothed the way for her. And finally she owed it to Dan's accountants who painstakingly advised her on the way to compartmentalise each separate deal: the shop, the stock, the lease, the goodwill and the trademark. They all, she felt, combined to help her find her way through the complexities of company law, making sure she got the best possible figure for her business, leaving her with a sum of money, even after Midge's share had been dispatched to her and all fees and expenses settled, beyond her wildest expectations.

'I don't understand it,' she said to Daniel. 'I really don't understand how one small shop could could be so valuable.'

'What you don't understand, my dear, is that it isn't the shop as such, it's the name. A Toppers' hat will sell anywhere, the label guarantees that.'

This statement, meant to reassure her, filled her with

doubt. 'I hope I haven't made a mistake,' she said fearfully.

'What mistake?'

'Selling off the name. Does that mean I can't make any more hats?'

'You can't sell any more hats under the trademark Toppers, but there is nothing to stop you making hats and selling them. Though I should think what you need right now is a good, long holiday.' His manner, she thought, was rather tetchy.

'Designing hats *is* my idea of a holiday,' she said. 'It is what I like doing best. And I'm still making hats for Midge, that's not against the rules, is it?'

'Not if she changes to a new trademark.' But already Helena could tell by his furrowed brow and far-away look that she had lost his whole-hearted attention. He had business matters of his own to think about. She was grateful for all the time he had spent on hers and did not press him further.

In July Dan received an official notification from the war office informing him that in the event of hostilities Thornmere Hall was likely to be requisitioned. It was the sign he had been waiting for. He had dithered long enough over his answer to the Amalgamated Food Production Company. This was the prod much needed to galvanise him into action. He hoped he hadn't left it too late. He hadn't. Within weeks his solicitors and accountants and business managers were sitting around another boardroom table negotiating with their counterparts from the other side. Dan, once the preliminaries were over and his attendance at the meetings no longer necessary, escaped to Cornwall to lick his wounds, but not before he had drafted a memo to the

War Office saying he was willing to part with Thornmere Hall in exchange for suitable compensation.

That he had wounds to nurse was not unsurprising. One just could not sever a whole part of one's life without bleeding. He felt drained, empty, and for a few days, restless. Commitments brought responsibilities and for the first time in his life he was without either. His last responsibility had been to find an alternative home for the Gilberts, for Ivy House along with the oldest part of the cannery was due for demolition. He wanted to buy them a bungalow on a new housing estate in Chingford, but they would have none of that. They preferred a small, clapboard cottage on the village green under the shadow of the church. They had always dreamed of a cottage in the country, they said. Dan thought that compared to Leytonstone yes, it was feasible that Chingford might be thought of as country, situated as it was on the fringe of Epping Forest and with the wide expanse of the Plains restful to the eyes, though it was far from his idea of a rural retreat. Still, the Gilberts were content and that was all that mattered.

Helena was back in London tidying up a few strands left over from the sale of Toppers, but it wouldn't be long before she began to put two and two together and he wished to be well out of the way when the balloon went up. He spent most of his time at St Mawes lazing in the lounge of his hotel looking across the estuary at Falmouth, and trying to imagine what it was like in the old days before steam replaced the tall ships that once forested the harbour with their masts. Sometimes he would take the ferry and explore Falmouth at first hand, but he was always glad to get back to St Mawes. Norfolk had taught him to appreciate peace and tranquillity.

He left St Mawes on the 22 August, broke his journey

at Taunton, and arrived back at Thornmere in the early evening of the following day. Reuben was waiting for him in the stableyard and helped him to unload the car. He had grave news, he said. Poor old Bass was dead.

Daniel stared at him morosely. 'He was all right when I left. What happened – an accident?' His tone was an accusation.

'Just old age. He was getting on. He went peaceful like, yesterday evening. I suddenly missed him and went looking for him, and there he was curled up under the hedge by my vegetable garden. Some animals are like that, they just want to go off and die in private.'

Bass was dead. His friend, his loyal companion. And for the last two or three weeks he hadn't given the dog a thought, he had had other things on his mind. He could have wept. 'So you found him dead?' It was a statement rather than a question.

'Not quite. He died in my arms as I lifted him up. His eyes glazed over and then he went limp. I haven't buried him yet. I left him in case you wanted to see him.'

'Bury him,' said Dan harshly. 'Bury him where you found him. I prefer to remember him as he was.' He turned away.

'Another thing, sir. Mrs Fraser . . .'

'What about Mrs Fraser?' Dan panicked. Someone else he hadn't given a thought to lately. 'Has she –' He couldn't finish.

'She had a stroke last Thursday and was taken to the East Norwich. Ruby visited her yesterday, and she said she looks a poor thing. She doesn't know anybody, she can't move or speak.'

Reuben's voice trailed off. The two men stood silent. Dan was thinking of the many times he had tried to persuade Mrs Fraser to give up her damp old cottage in the Street and come and live with him at the Hall. Or if she preferred a place of her own, to move to somewhere with modern conveniences and one of the village girls to look after her. He'd arrange it, he said, but she only laughed and reminded him that you can't transplant old trees. She was always saying that when he tried to persuade her to move. And now, without any say in the matter, she had been moved to a hospital bed, but not for long he vowed to himself. He'd transfer her to a nursing home where she'd have every comfort that money could buy. Nothing was too good for someone who was the nearest he'd ever had to a mother.

His first impulse was to dash off at once to see her. But no good would come of that. He was tired and she wouldn't know him. Best to leave it until tomorrow when he was fresh. He ached all over from the long hours spent behind the wheel. He ached, too, for the big-hearted little woman and a loyal little dog.

'I suppose you haven't heard the news,' said Reuben, as he checked that nothing had been left in the car. 'Hitler and Stalin have signed a non-aggression pact. After all this time at each other's throats, now they're suddenly bosom pals. I s'pose that means they're going to gang up on us.'

Daniel lost his temper. 'Bloody hell, man!' he shouted. 'If you can't find something cheerful to say, say nothing!'

Reuben, unmoved, carrying a suitcase in either hand, followed his master into the house. The guv'nor looked tired, he thought. His eyes red-rimmed from staring fixedly at the road ahead. Reuben knew the feeling. He followed Dan up the stairs and into his bedroom.

'Come and have a bite of supper with us,' he suggested.

'Ruby's made some pork brawn to make your mouth water, and she could fry up some bubble and squeak to go with it. You're partial to bubble and squeak. Come down to the lodge with us. It's lonely for you in this girt ole house.'

Daniel was nearly tempted. He felt calmer now and ashamed of his outburst. He squeezed Reuben's arm. 'Thank you for the offer, but no, I think I'll have an early night, and hope I wake up in a better mood tomorrow.' He looked remorseful. 'You know what they say about shooting the messenger. Sorry, Reuben.'

Reuben, embarrassed, stared at his boots. He didn't mind when Dan blasted off at him, but he did mind when Dan apologised which he always did because he never knew what to say in return. 'There's a whole stack of post come for you while you was away,' he mumbled. 'I left it in your office.'

'That can wait till tomorrow. Any news from Rodings?'

'I hear Miss Roseberry will be back tomorrow.'

'Ah. Well, good night Reuben.'

'Good night, sir. Sleep well.'

'I could sleep on a clothes-line tonight.'

And he did sleep well in spite of his heavy heart and did not wake until daylight was several hours old. Finally, the smell of bacon frying lured him out of bed.

Elsie was back. She had slept at the lodge during his absence because she was nervous of sleeping in a house alone, especially a house the size of Thornmere Hall. Now she was frying bacon and egg and mushrooms and fried bread. An English breakfast, he sniffed appreciatively. Something that hadn't as yet been canned. But frozen — could it be frozen? Already his mind was back in gear, questing, probing, planning. He was free now. He had no encumbrances. Time to make plans.

He breakfasted in his dressing-gown then shaved and showered and dressed informally, for he meant to spend the morning in his office attending to his correspondence. First he phoned the hospital and an anodyne voice informed him that Mrs Fraser was as well as could be expected. He'd go along and see her later and make arrangements when possible about a private nursing home. He knew of one with a good reputation near Cromer, and Mrs Fraser loved Cromer. She and Mr Fraser had once spent a holiday there, she had told him. That was in June 1914. 'That last bootiful summer before the war,' she said as if there had been no beautiful summers since. Perhaps for some there had not.

He didn't get down to reading his correspondence until well into the middle of the morning. He had left it on one occasion to go along to see if Reuben had done anything about Bass, and found that job completed and a fresh little mound had appeared under the sweetbriar hedge.

'He couldn't have chosen a pleasanter spot,' he said, and though he had well prepared himself he couldn't avoid his voice from thickening.

'D'you want me to put up a stone or summat to his memory?'

Dan's first impulse was a vigorous refusal, for nothing depressed him more than the thought of some Victorian cemeteries he knew in London dotted about with crumbling headstones like rows of rotten teeth. What a way to be remembered he thought every time he saw them. To his regret, Timothy Thurgood was buried in such a cemetery. When his own time came he would leave instructions to be cremated and no nonsense about having his ashes scattered, either. Death for him was very final.

All the same, his thoughts reverted to Reuben's suggestion. He didn't want Bass's grave inadvertently desecrated should the army take over, which now seemed a possibility. 'Not a stone,' he said. 'Just a marker with his name on it and the date. A nice piece of oak. Could I leave it to you?'

Elsie called from the stableyard. 'You're wanted on the phone, Mr 'Arker.'

It was Helena. No sound of wrath or resentment in her voice, just her normal clear and friendly tone. 'I've just got back and the house smells stuffy. The larder's empty and I've loads to talk about. Could you take me out to lunch?'

He wanted her to himself. He didn't want to share her with a crowded restaurant, and being August there were very few restaurants to be found uncrowded. 'Come and take pot luck with me,' he suggested.

He hung up and went off to consult Elsie and together they looked in the pantry and then the fridge. Neither gave Dan cause for rejoicing. At the back of the larder was a neat stack of tins with familiar green and white labels. 'I see Thurgood's is well represented,' he said dryly. 'What have we got besides soup and vegetables?'

'There's a tin of tongue an' a tin of 'am an' a tall tin of red salmon.' This latter suggestion in a tone of deference, for to Elsie tinned salmon, like chicken, was a luxury which came to the table only on special occasions.

'Open the salmon. Can you make mayonnaise?'

An anxious expression clouded her face. He might just as well have asked her to fly to the moon. She knew nothing about mayonnaise, she said.

452

'Then find out from a cookery book.'

She looked self-righteous. 'Oh, I never use a cookery book. That's cheating.'

'Forget it. I'll make the mayonnaise. You pop down to Ruby and see what she's got in the way of salads.'

Elsie returned with lettuces and radishes and spring onions, so fresh that garden soil still clung to their roots. Dan went off to see what he could conjure up in the form of liquid refreshment. A bottle of hock would do nicely, he thought. Better still, two bottles. He wanted Helena in a mellow mood.

She arrived looking as if she had just stepped out of a bandbox and not a dusty train. She had changed obviously, for she was now dressed in a green linen suit, her favourite colour, piped with white. And hatless, with her hair hanging loose. She looked incredibly young and her eyes seemed greener than ever, he thought, searching them anxiously for any signs of anger. There were none. Reassured he led her into the morning room where the table was set for lunch.

'It's good to be back,' she said, running her fingers through her hair. 'It's good to breathe Norfolk air again.'

'Things not too good in the capital, eh?'

'Nobody says much – very casual on the surface actually, but you can feel the tension building up underneath. And the sky is dotted with barrage balloons. They looked rather pretty, actually, and at night-time the searchlights look fantastic.' Her smile faded, her eyes slowly turned wet. 'They've started to evacuate the children. Oh, Dan, it's heart-breaking to see them lining up at the station with their little cases and their gas masks. So small, some of them – so bewildered.'

He went across to the side table and poured out a drink. He needed a drink. His worries seemed duplicated by the intensity of her emotions. He said, 'Can I pour you a gin and bitters to cheer you up?'

'Just a small sherry please.'

They sat with the width of the room between them. She looked across at him and laughed. 'You seem a long way away over there. You're not frightened of me, are you?' She said it as a joke but there was something about her voice that put him on his guard.

'Haven't you something to tell me?' she prompted when he didn't immediately answer. 'Such as . . . I'm sorry I underestimated your intelligence. I didn't mean to deceive you. I did it with the best of intentions. I knew you wanted to sell, but I didn't think you would sell to me so I made up all that rigmarole about a – what was it you called him – a far-seeing entrepreneur who offered me a very good price for my business. Who agreed to all the terms my lawyers laid down and was as anxious as I was that the staff wouldn't lose their jobs and had a clause to that effect written into the contract. In short, an entrepreneur with a heart. Dan, don't make me laugh!'

This wasn't how he had imagined it at all. He had expected fireworks. Instead he was faced with this surprising and gentle mockery. The way she was making him feel now, he would have preferred her anger.

'When did you begin to suspect?' he said gloomily.

'About three hours into the transaction.'

He glowered. 'And you let me go on making a fool of myself.'

'I enjoyed it. I admit I was very angry at first. I felt as if I could strangle you with my bare hands.' Her eyes flashed, then melted with laughter. 'I would have had a job wouldn't I, with that bull-sized neck of yours. But oh Dan, I was so furious. I thought very evil things of you. I thought you were doing it because you thought that once I was free of the shop you'd be in a better position to persuade me to go to America with you.'

Dan groaned.

'I apologise for thinking so little of you. I hope I was wrong. You did it to help me out, didn't you? You knew I wanted to sell. You knew that was unlikely under present circumstances. What I can't fathom out is why you had to be so devious about it.'

'Would you have done business with me?'

She pondered for a bit. 'No.'

'Why not?'

'Because I would have suspected that you only wanted to winkle me away from my shop so that I'd be free to go to America with you.'

'Actually,' he said, speaking slowly. 'That was the reason. That's why I had to be so devious.'

She gave him a long searching look, then laughed. 'You make a rotten liar. I know why you did it, and I do appreciate it, really, but I just wish you had been more open with me. Never mind, it all seems rather foolish and childish doesn't it, bearing grudges I mean, when you think of what is going on in Europe. All is forgiven, Dan, so now let's have lunch. I'm starving – and that salmon looks delicious.'

'I made the mayonnaise,' he said modestly.

By the time they reached the coffee stage they were once again talking business, but this time openly. 'Where did you find the money to buy the shop?' she said. 'It wasn't so very long ago you were bemoaning the fact that you were hard up. I hope you didn't have to borrow. Not at the present rate of interest.'

'A short-term loan, that's all. I'll be able to pay it back when the agreement with the Amalgamated Food Company is signed, sealed, and delivered. It shouldn't be long now. Now that *was* a genuine offer from a firm far-sighted enough to see into the future, Hitler or no Hitler. And I'm off to America, Hitler or no Hitler. And I'm asking you, Helena, for the umpteenth time – come with me.'

He thought he had won her over then. There was a look of such longing in her eyes he thought of all the years she had been denied doing anything to please herself: caring for her mother, caring for Paul, sacrificing herself for others. He could free her of all that. He could smooth out life's wrinkles for her. They could start afresh in another country, a new life for them both – but the moment passed. He watched with disappointment as she literally pulled herself together. She gazed at him from under her lashes.

'If the future were more settled, yes, I would come with you,' she said. 'But as things are now, it's impossible.'

'You mean you couldn't leave your country in its hour of need,' he said, easing his disappointment with sarcasm.

'You could say that,' she answered, unperturbed.

He didn't get down to finishing dealing with his correspondence until late that evening, when because of a decided nip in the air Elsie had lit a fire in his office, and he sat there in the comfort of his favourite chair smoking a cigar with a tot of whisky close at hand.

In spite of some disappointing moments he had spent a pleasant afternoon in Helena's company. She had accompanied him to the hospital but had waited in the car while he went in to visit Mrs Fraser. She said she only knew her as the baker's wife who had delivered the bread for a time during the war. She remembered her as a smiling cottage-loaf figure, and wanted to retain that memory, not spoiling it by seeing Mrs Fraser as she was now. Dan rejoined her after an hour looking very down in the mouth.

'She didn't know me,' he said. 'But at least she's not in pain. I had a word with the consultant. He's quite happy for her to be transferred to a nursing home. He says they have instructions to clear the wards anyway. They want the beds free in case of air raid casualties.'

No matter what subject they took up it invariably led back to war.

Later they took a run-out as far as Horning. They parked near the village staithe and walked alongside the river. Boats of all descriptions ploughed up and down the water-way: yachts, cruisers, launches, rowing-boats – even a wherry. They were delighted to see a wherry – a working boat amid all this holiday craft – beating upriver to Norwich with its load of timber. War just then seemed very remote.

Helena, seated before her mirror in her dressing-gown, cold-creaming her face, heard the telephone bell below. She glanced at the clock. Five minutes to eleven! Who could it be at this hour? It was Dan, barely coherent. 'Have you been drinking?' she asked sharply.

'One small whisky, and I haven't even finished that. Helena, I must see you.'

'At this hour!'

'I must. I've got to speak to someone or I shall burst. Helena, I've got something momentous to tell you, but I can't tell you over the phone – not with half the village listening'.

'Dan, talk sense. Nobody's listening.'

'I can't talk sense – I feel too light-headed. Helena, take pity on me.'

'Oh, come round then. But don't make a noise. I don't want rumours to get around that I entertain midnight callers.' She still thought he was drunk and went off to the kitchen to grind some coffee.

He made so little noise she didn't know he had arrived until she recognised the familiar whine of the Lanchester's fluid flywheel. He didn't appear drunk, but he certainly looked feverish with a high colour and staring eyes. He grabbed her by her shoulders.

'Helena,' he said, 'I've got a son.' Then he bent his head and began to weep.

He had fallen asleep in the chair where her mother used to sit. The coffee pot on the table between them had grown cold. The young house-martins in the nest under the eaves were twittering a welcome to the new day. Sunrise was beginning to streak the sky. They had talked the night away.

Helena's emotions had run the gamut from disbelief to delight, but now an empty, sinking, debilitating feeling of envy gripped her. She stared at Dan's lumpish, unconscious figure, not with resentment for she really rejoiced for him, but with a feeling that life was beastly unfair. She wanted a child. God, how she wanted a child, and now it was too late. It was never too late for a man, she thought bitterly. A son, handed to him on a plate one might say, and he didn't even have to go through the agony of giving birth. A son whom she could share. Dan had tried so hard to persuade her.

'He'll need a mother. I know nothing about children. But you're a woman, mothering comes naturally to a woman. Helena, don't say no, think it over first.' His voice changed, dropped its wheedling tone. 'But don't take long because I've finally decided about America. I've been thinking about the Great War as a lot of us have lately, particularly the shortage of food. There'll be food rationing again if there's another war, but on a fairer basis this time, I hope. Either way, I could be helping my country out there, learning different and newer methods of preserving food. Knowledge I could bring back here when things settle down again. Then I got to thinking about you. How I might not see you again for years, and I didn't think I could face it. I was in half a mind to chuck the whole idea about America, until I opened Dr Hamilton's letter, and then everything seemed to fall into place.'

He leaned forward, watching her earnestly. 'Suddenly America loomed large again. A place of safety, somewhere to take my son away from the bombs and threat of invasion. I've got to get him away from here, you see that, don't you? Starting afresh in another country, making a new life together. It seems to me it was meant to be, finding out about him just at this point in my life when I didn't know which way to turn. If I let slip this opportunity, another might never come, and God knows what will happen in the years ahead. I want to get him to a place of safety. I don't want to lose him now that I've found him. You do understand?'

It was the longest speech she had ever heard him make. It left him slightly out of breath as if he had been running, which emotionally he had. 'Complete my happiness,' he begged. 'Come with us. Make a team. Please, Helena.

She very nearly gave way, for the attraction of a husband and a child was almost too great. A family, one of a family. She would never get a chance like this again, but even as that thought came an image of Paul rose up before her. Would he turn his back on his country? Would he take the easier option? No. Whatever people thought of his views they never doubted his deep-rooted patriotism. He hated war. He hated what he saw as the unnecessary slaughter on the western front, but he hated Hitler and his evil doctrines even more. Running away from England now would be like reneging on all that Paul had stood for, and that was unthinkable.

She stretched out her hand to Daniel in a token of peace. 'I'll compromise with you,' she said. 'I'll make you a promise. When all this trouble is over, when Hitler and his mob are defeated and I have no doubts that they will be, I'll come to you. Yes, and I'll marry you. No, let me finish . . .' for he had started towards her. 'It may be years, you realise that, and you may by that time have settled permanently in America. I wouldn't be a bit surprised if you didn't buy yourself into another business for I can't see you sitting by idle. If that is the case, then I'll come out to you. But if you do come home when all this is over, and if I come through, then you'll find me waiting for you. I give you my word.'

She pretended not to notice that he was very near tears. When he finally spoke his voice was gruff, almost ungracious.

'And what will you do to help your country? Find work at the war office like all the other nice young ladies?'

'I am not always nice and I'm not young,' she retorted. 'And I would be bored doing an office job. I hope the Civil Defence will find a niche for me, driving an ambulance perhaps, I would like that. And another thing,' she added in a lighter tone. 'I don't see why I should not also carry on with my millinery work. I can foresee that in a time of hardship and shortages a pretty hat could be a powerful morale booster.'

He gave her a grudging but admiring look. 'It will take more than Hitler to get you down,' he said.

He had gone to sleep on her then, lolling back in her mother's chair with his mouth open and breathing loudly. But she couldn't sleep. Her thoughts leapt from subject to subject churning away any hope of following his example. The letter from Dr Hamilton was still in his hand. She extracted it without disturbing him.

She had read it once and they had both discussed it endlessly: the terse explanatory note from the doctor, and the letter it enclosed, addressed quaintly to 'Danny's Father' and signed, 'Danny's Grandmother', which surprisingly had turned out to be Amy's Aunt Flora. It had taken some little while to work that one out. It had taken a while longer for the whole fantastic story to sink in, but there it was written out extensively in the barely-decipherable handwriting of a dying woman. The heartbreak she had experienced at the death of her daughter, knowing her own end was near and that her beloved grandchild would have to go to strangers was not touched upon. That had been left to Dr Hamilton.

'I should have got this bloody letter a week ago,' Dan had said when he first showed it to her. 'And I would have done if I hadn't shoved off to Cornwall. My first bloody holiday in years – and this has to happen.'

He was all for phoning Dr Hamilton then and there, until Helena pointed out the lateness of the hour. 'Leave it until the morning,' she said.

Well, it was nearly morning now. She rose and stretched. She had kept her vigil over Daniel, not liking to leave him for he had been in a strange and volatile mood, but now he looked more peaceful. Sleep had erased the lines of pain and worry in his face. She went upstairs and bathed and dressed and when she came down again he was up and speaking on the phone. She tiptoed past him and went into the kitchen.

It was only six o'clock. She hoped Dan found Dr Hamilton in a good mood.

He must have done. He appeared in the kitchen doorway looking unkempt and villainous with a twenty-four hour's growth of thick black stubble but, she thought, looking more joyful than she had ever seen him.

'Well?'

'Everything is going to be all right. He was a bit shirty with me at first until I explained I had only just got his letter, now he's pulling out all the stops to help me. A junior school from Sunsfield is being evacuated to Norfolk today and Dr Hamilton is putting Danny in the charge of one of the teachers. Today, Helena, did you hear that? Danny will be here, today. I would have gone down and fetched him anyway, but it will be quicker if I let him come by train. I can hardly wait. Bloody half-past twelve before the train gets in.'

'Dan, a word of warning. You'd better moderate your language if you're going to be a father.'

'I never swear, I just get a bit excited, that's all.' He suddenly caught sight of himself in the overmantel and rubbed his chin. 'I'd better go and get rid of this. I'd better sneak off before anyone sees the car.'

'The milkman has already seen it. He comes very early.'

'Really!' He grinned delightedly. 'Now I *will* have to make an honest woman of you.'

'Just go please, Dan.'

He lingered. 'Isn't there time for a cup of your excellent coffee first? I never feel fully awake until I've had my early morning tea or coffee. There's so much still I want to talk over with you.' He watched as she ground coffee, put out cups. 'I want you to meet my son, Helena. It might be weeks before I get a passage to America – there's sure to be an exodus. I'd like to think there'll be time for you two to get to know one another.'

She gave him a willing smile. 'I shall look forward to that,' she said.

Helena arrived at the station early, but Daniel had got there before her. She stood behind the bookstall where he couldn't see her and watched him. He prowled up and down like a caged lion unaware of the attention he was creating. He was on an emotional treadmill and her heart went out to him. She knew he was fearing rejection by the little boy who wasn't aware until recently that he had a father and who in the past year had lost his mother and grandmother. He might think a stranger a poor exchange for the loss of those he loved. All this was going through Dan's mind, she suspected. Poor Dan. She amended that. No, lucky Dan. He had everything to fight for.

A train was approaching. A murmur ran round those waiting – officials, prospective foster parents and billeting officers – all made an involuntary movement towards the barrier. Dan, she noticed, was well to the fore. At the sight of the straggling line of evacuees coming towards them along the platform, pale-faced and anxious, staring about them with wary eyes, the crowd fell silent. But not for long. Soon the hum of voices broke out afresh. The billeting officer began to call out names.

Dan saw him at the tail-end of the queue hanging on to the hand of a motherly-looking woman. He recognised him because he could have been looking at himself at that same age. History had turned full circle. What was it Mr Fraser had called him then? A scrawny little ole barrow pig. Well, here was another scrawny little ole barrow pig with the same blue-black eyes, but instead of a shaven head, a mop of thick dark hair on which a grey school cap sat insecurely. Dan came to a halt as soon as he was near enough to read the name on the label pinned to Danny's jacket, Daniel Cousins. His eyes filled. That's the first thing I must put right, he thought as he blew his nose.

Out of sight behind the bookstall Helena, through misted eyes, witnessed their meeting. She saw Dan squat down beside his son. She saw him speaking and the small boy listening and nodding. When Dan stood up the boy let go of his escort's hand and took Dan's instead. Dan spoke to the woman, then raised his hat. They passed within a foot or two of where Helena was standing, but neither saw her. Helena doubted whether they saw anything. They both wore the strained look of someone making their way through quicksand. She had a sudden anguished impulse to run across and put her arms round both of them, but stopped in time. This was something they would have to work out on their own – father and son together. She walked, deep in thought, out of the station making for the place where she had left her car.

Dan, deeply asleep, surfaced reluctantly as he felt someone shaking him. He switched on the light and saw a small figure in pyjamas standing by his bed with his eyes screwed up against the glare.

Dan struggled to a sitting position. 'What's the matter, son? Couldn't you sleep?'

'I'm frightened all on my own in that great big room. And I heard a lot of noises . . . they woke me up. I think we're being burgled.'

'You do?' Dan bit back a smile. 'Shall we go and investigate or would you rather get into bed with me?'

'I'd rather get into bed with you.'

This is how it all started thought Daniel happily as the small figure snuggled down beside him. Within minutes they were both asleep again.

Dan awoke a second time to see the sun shining through a chink in the curtains. Danny was still curled up asleep by his side, his bushy hair falling loosely across his forehead. Dan longed to touch him, to brush the hair out of the way so that he could feast his eyes on him – even dare to drop a kiss on the boy's flushed cheek except that it would be a pity to disturb him. Danny, too, had a great deal of tension to sleep away.

Somewhere out there in the grounds could be heard the sound of voices, shouting. A bunch of workmen taking a short cut through the park? He dragged himself out of bed, felt around for his slippers, then yawning went across to the windows and pulled back the curtains.

His eyes nearly popped out of his head. 'Strewth!' he uttered aloud. The barrels of four anti-aircraft guns pointed in his direction. Men in khaki were everywhere; shouting orders, directing vehicles, erecting tents. The army had taken over. When the devil had they arrived, he wondered. He hadn't heard them. Then he remembered, Danny's burglars!

Danny was stirring now, rubbing his eyes. Dan went across and sat on the bed beside him. 'D'you like playing with soldiers, lad?'

Danny eyed him expectantly. 'Yes.'

Dan, grinning, tousled his son's hair. 'You'd better get up and dress then. There's some life-size soldiers waiting to play games out there in the garden.'

At five a.m. on the 1 September Helena was awakened by the sound of the telephone ringing. She was on the alert immediately, thinking that war had started.

She expected Dan with some inside knowledge, though why Dan she didn't stop to ponder. It wasn't Dan, it was Hugo speaking from Los Angeles. She lost her temper. 'You idiot. Do you know what time it is over here?'

'Sorry, dear, I can never stop to work out whether the time goes backwards or forwards. Helena, I'm coming home.'

'You're safer over there,' she retorted.

'Don't be like that. I'm bored with over here. I want to come home. Helena, don't laugh, but I've come over all patriotic. I want to do my little bit. You wrote and told me you were going to do your little bit and it made me feel left out of things. I want to be in there with all the dear people I know.'

She bit her lip so that he wouldn't hear her laugh, though she didn't feel like laughing so much as crying. Hugo could put on that silly manner but it didn't deceive her. His motives were the same as hers.

'If you do come, Hugo, you'll find plenty of room at Doughty Street. The others have moved to Buckinghamshire. No – not Jake. He's joined the ARP. Yes, I'm moving back to London this afternoon. No, I'm not giving up Rodings. I might need it as a funk-hole occasionally. This call must be costing you a fortune, Hugo. Cable me when to expect you.'

Later that morning she learnt that guns had appeared in Thornmere Park. Nearly the entire village turned out to go and stare at them. Later still she heard the more ominous news that Hitler had marched into Poland. She was sitting on a seat on Thorpe Station waiting for the London train when a man in workman's clothes came along and sat beside her.

He opened his newspaper. 'Looks like war again,' he said. 'I was in the last lot.'

'And my brother.' She could have said father and sweetheart, too, but that would have seemed like overdoing it.

He looked at her and then at her case. 'You going up to Lunnon?'

'Yes.'

'You'd be safer staying here.'

'I know. But I've got work to do.'

'Then take care, lady.'

She was all alone in the Doughty Street flat. Jake was on duty at the warden's post. It was a beautiful sunny Sunday morning, that 3 September, and difficult to believe that the nation was now at war. It was official. She had just heard the tired and disappointed voice of the Prime Minister announcing that fact on her wireless set and moments later, as if to ram the message home, came the warbling alert of an air raid siren.

Air raid rehearsals had been a way of life for the past few weeks, but this was no rehearsal. She looked out of the window and saw people hurrying to the nearest public air raid shelter, others standing staring up at the cloudless sky. There was some shouting from over-zealous wardens, Jake among them? and blowing of whistles.

Helena was still undecided where best to shelter from the raid when the All Clear sounded. A false alarm. She could breathe again. But they wouldn't all be false alarms, she told herself, and went out on to the balcony. Here she did not feel so much on her own, for here Paul seemed very close.

She wouldn't be on her own for long. With luck, Hugo could be joining her in the course of the following week. Four days it took to cross the Atlantic in peacetime.

Would it take longer in war? Yes, if ships had to take avoiding action to escape the U-boats. It wasn't only Hugo – she thought of Dan and his little son soon to make the same hazardous journey though in the reverse direction; of Midge, the wrong side of the Channel; and of that good friend Dr Percy, living in retirement in Jersey. Dear God, keep safe all those I love, I beg you. She hadn't prayed in years. She had forgotten the words of long unsaid prayers. But if she were to start attending church again, the familiar words of the service would soon come back to her. Praying had helped in the past and it would again.

'If your knees knock kneel on them.' She spun round, thinking the words had been spoken aloud, half expecting to see Paul behind her, smiling teasingly. There was nobody there of course, but only Paul could have put such a thought into her head. Or Dan. It was the sort of thing Dan would have said. She smiled. Two men so dissimilar in many ways and so alike in others – what good friends they would have made if circumstances had been different.

Her smile vanished as it came home to her with a sudden painful jab of the heart that she wouldn't have Dan to depend upon for much longer. For all her glib promises of joining him when the war was over she knew such promises were meaningless, words she had uttered as a palliative, for how did any of them know where they would be or even if they would still *be* when the war was over?

And Danny. Danny had hardly been out of her mind since their one brief meeting. He had looked like some long lost waif with his tangled hair and wary eyes: outstanding eyes, dark and lustrous like his father's, but unlike his father's shy and downcast. He had gentle, quiet ways like a girl, and his hair was long like a girl's, too, the consequences she guessed of being reared by two women. Now he had a father, a father who would have him at the barber's and then on the cricket field – or baseball field if they were in America – before he knew what had hit him, and her heart ached for the lonely boy suddenly thrust into a masculine world. She wanted to pet him, to love him, to help cushion the blows that life had dealt him one after the other in the past two years. In other words she wanted to do what Dan had once suggested, mother him – but she had lost the chance.

From somewhere nearby in the mulberry tree perhaps, a robin began to sing. She had forgotten all about the robin. She had stopped putting out scraps after Paul died. She had lost heart then, now her heart quickened. Possibly it wasn't the same bird who had sung to Paul, but that didn't matter. The robin had returned, and she took that as a happy omen and even as such a thought came into her mind, the doorbell rang, and her thoughts immediately flew to Hugo. Only a month ago BOAC had inaugurated a weekly service by flying-boat between New York and Southampton. She wouldn't put it past Hugo to wheedle a passage and now be standing on the doorstep waiting to give her the surprise of her life. She'd fake the surprise, she thought, so as not to disappoint him, but in the event she didn't have to pretend for it wasn't Hugo standing there, but Dan and her surprise was genuine. She made no attempt to disguise her pleasure at seeing him.

'A friendly face,' she exclaimed. 'And just when I was feeling so much alone. Where's Danny?' For since his arrival, the boy and his father had been inseparable.

'I didn't think he would enjoy traipsing around London with me, so I left him in the care of the Stonehams. We're staying at the lodge for the time being as the army now has taken over the Hall. I could have stayed on if I'd liked until I'd decided what to do about the furniture, the CO's a very obliging kind of chap, but I thought it best if I made a clean break. In any case . . .' His words trailed off and he stood there with some hesitancy as if waiting to be invited in. 'I hope I haven't caught you at an awkward moment,' he said.

She was amused by his excessive politeness. He was like a small boy, she thought, on his best behaviour, frightened to put a foot wrong. She said, 'If you had got here a bit earlier you could have shared my moment of panic when the siren sounded. Where were you when that happened?'

'On the train. I knew nothing about it until we got to Liverpool Street. Somebody with the jitters sounding a false alarm, wasn't it?'

'I think we're all a bit jittery at the moment, but I suppose we'll get used to it. It's hard to believe, isn't it, at war on a beautiful day like this?' She led him through the flat and out on to the balcony where Paul and she had entertained their guests when the weather was fine. He seated himself on Paul's old chair which up to now had been sacrosanct, and her instinctive urge to protest died for he looked so right for it. He gazed about him with approval.

'So this is your London hideaway – and very nice too. Quiet, not overlooked. Is that Paul's robin I can hear singing?'

It pleased her that he could say 'Paul's robin' in such a natural way as if Paul were still alive, which in a way he was and would remain so as long as memory lasted.

'He's tuning up for the winter,' she said, then sighed. 'A long cold winter has been predicted. Because of the amount of berries about, I suppose.'

'Winters are always long and cold in wartime,' he warned her.

Something was nagging at him, she thought. He was frowning and chewing on his bottom lip. She leaned forward. 'You're not worried, about taking Danny to America? I think you're doing the right thing getting him away from danger.'

He scowled. 'Well, actually I'm having second thoughts about it. The whole thing has blown up in my face. Red tape, Helena. God knows in normal times there's enough red tape to go round the British Isles a dozen times. In wartime red tape comes in triplicate. We'll all be strangled with the stuff before it's over.'

He was blustering, she thought for the sake of it. An act to hide some deeper or more genuine feeling. There was no real indignation or anger in his voice or in the look he flashed at her from beneath his brows. 'The latest communication I've received, and it came yesterday afternoon, is that I have to show proof that I am Danny's father before taking him out of the country. This could mean weeks of delay – blood tests, that sort of thing. Then there's the question of adoption. I have to adopt my own son before I can declare our relationship legal! More delay. I might as well chuck the whole idea up.' He sounded, she thought, not in the least put out. As for herself, she felt suddenly very light-hearted.

'What you are really telling me, Dan, is that you don't want to go to America after all?'

'Not without you,' he said.

'*Dan!*'

He gave a rueful shrug and his face fell into lines of laughter. 'I'll come clean . . . you're right, as you always are. I can't . . .' he shrugged his shoulders again, 'run away, if you like. Not even for Danny's sake. Like you, I feel I owe something to this old country, and whatever's going to happen to it, I want to be part of it. And one never knows,' he said, his voice lightening. 'It might just be a question of postponing the idea. I might go yet, when the war is over.'

He had other plans which he wanted to discuss with her. That is why he had called, he said, to take her out to lunch. Somewhere discreet where they could talk.

'Nowhere could be more discreet than this balcony,' she suggested. 'And I could give you ham and eggs and a passable claret. Afterwards you could help me hang my blackout curtains and later, perhaps, take me out to dinner.'

'I'll go along with that.'

Over coffee he enlarged on his alternative plan, as he called it, this idea that had simmered under the surface of his mind even when he had been fully occupied with dreams of America. 'A farmhouse in the Cotswolds, just outside Stow-on-the-Wold where I stayed once on a walking tour. A beautiful spot – so peaceful; just the place to hole up in wartime. Somewhere safe for Danny. And it's for sale – I've checked.'

'You, a farmer!' she scoffed, highly amused.

'The land's not for sale. Just the house and the outbuildings, and it's the outbuildings I'm after. I'm going to do some experimenting in freezing food. I've been reading up on the technique for years, having papers sent over from America. I've got the capital and I could employ some bright young bacteriologist who'll fill me in on the scientific side. I can spend years – as long as it takes, as long as the war lasts – improving my skills, making tests, making it all come together. And after the war I'll start afresh: Harker and Son. Frozen Food Specialists. How does that sound? I'll do it, Helena I promise you.'

She had no doubt about that. Watching him, as with glittering and eager eyes he expanded on his idea, thumping his fist on the table to emphasise a point, she felt this must have been the way he looked when he sold his idea of canning their own produce all those years ago to old Timothy Thurgood. She saw in his well-used face an image of that younger man whose zest and energy had driven all obstacles out of the path on the way to his goal. And so it would again, she thought, for Daniel Harker was the type of man who didn't know the meaning of failure. And if enthusiasm measured success, then he had it all before him, and she envied him this single-mindedness of purpose.

'I wish you all the luck in the world,' she said sincerely.

He went quiet. His eyes, thoughtful now, rested upon her. 'And you. You are still determined to stay here in London and join the Civil Defence?'

'I have joined. I report for duty tomorrow.'

He sighed. 'Well then, when the bombing starts, and it will start, if ever you want a day or two of peace . . .' She looked as if to interrupt, but he forestalled her. 'I know you have Rodings, but for a change of scene there's this charming old sandstone farmhouse near Stow-on-the-Wold I could recommend.'

'I might take you up on that.'

A warm and companionable silence fell, for Dan had talked himself to a standstill. He leaned back in his chair, his hands clasped behind his head. His heavy brows obscured his eyes so that she couldn't see whether they were closed or not. Faintly in the distance she could hear the traffic, and in her imagination it all seemed to be streaming west. Westwards to safety. Dan was going west, but not so far west as she had feared. The relief she felt was a revelation to her and kept her wrapped in thought for several minutes.

'I suppose,' Dan said, stretching lazily, 'I'd better retrieve my case from the cabbie's rest where I left it. Tomorrow, early, I'll have to start on my round of official visits. First on the list Danny's adoption papers. I haven't phoned through to my club yet about a bed for the night. Can I do it from here? If you can put up with plain but extremely good cooking, you could join me there for dinner.'

'There's a bed here,' she said, surprising herself as much as Dan by saying it.

'Paul's bed!' The expression he put in his voice made her laugh, though with a wobble in her voice.

'Paul would be the last one to quibble about that, but if the thought upsets you there's always the ottoman. I warn you, though, it's not very comfortable.'

He rose, came across to her and, gently pulling her to her feet, gave her a long and searching look. Then: 'Helena, this is the very last time of asking. Please, marry me. I love you so.'

Tears started to her eyes. It was the first time he had admitted to loving her. Perhaps, if she had known that sooner . . .?

'There will be plenty of time to discuss marriage, later,' she said, smiling back at him. 'First, there comes the honeymoon.'